MITFORD
I0761105
Winnie and Thomas
First Baptist
Stone Wall
Orchards
Fernbank
LITTLE MITFORD CREEK
Mitford School
Church Hill Road
Hope House Road
Hope House
Wash House
The Yellow House
Apple Barn
Baxter Park
To Hospital
To Holding
Mitford Hospital
Bolick House

Praise for the Mitford Novels

"Jan Karon reflects contemporary culture more fully than almost any other living novelist."

—*Los Angeles Times*

"The faster and more impersonal the world becomes, the more we need . . . Mitford."

—Cleveland *Plain Dealer*

"Karon knits Mitford's small-town characters and multiple storylines into a cozy sweater of a book. . . . Hits the sweet spot at the intersection of your heart and your funny bone."

—*USA Today*

"Jan Karon offers her readers another chance to escape their own world, if just for a while. . . . Her readers say they wish Mitford existed so they could move there."

—*Richmond Times-Dispatch*

"Karon holds varying aspects of humanity up to the light, from staggering cruelty . . . to the awesome power of love and forgiveness."

—*The Atlanta Journal-Constitution*

"Karon has a gift for breathing life into small moments that make readers both laugh and cry."

—*BookPage*

"It's hard for a review to capture the magic of Jan Karon's writing and of the characters readers have taken for their own since the first Mitford book was published. But the magic is there. . . . The delightful reconnections you'll experience will both gladden your heart and satisfy your soul."

—Bookreporter.com

"Delightful . . . Familiar characters, lots of love, some humor, and a few surprises make this essential for all Mitford fans."

—*Library Journal* (starred review)

"Karon's Mitford series continues with all the beloved characters, down-home charm, and deep faith in God that are the hallmarks so beloved of fans."

—*Kirkus Reviews*

"Loyal fans of Karon's Mitford novels and Father Tim will be delighted once again to spend time in this quintessential American village with its leading citizen and his colorful coterie of friends, family, and dependent souls."

—*Booklist*

MY BELOVED

MITFORD BOOKS BY JAN KARON

At Home in Mitford

A Light in the Window

These High, Green Hills

Out to Canaan

A New Song

A Common Life

In This Mountain

Shepherds Abiding

Light from Heaven

Home to Holly Springs

In the Company of Others

Somewhere Safe with Somebody Good

Come Rain or Come Shine

To Be Where You Are

Esther's Gift: A Mitford Christmas Story

The Mitford Snowmen: A Christmas Story

Jan Karon's Mitford Cookbook & Kitchen Reader: Recipes from Mitford Cooks, Favorite Tales from Mitford Books

The Mitford Bedside Companion: New Essays, Family Photographs, Favorite Mitford Scenes, and Much More

FATHER TIM'S COLLECTED QUOTES

Patches of Godlight:
Father Tim's Favorite Quotes

A Continual Feast:
Words of Comfort and Celebration, Collected by Father Tim

Bathed in Prayer:
Father Tim's Prayers, Sermons, and Reflections from the Mitford Series

CHILDREN'S BOOKS BY JAN KARON

Jeremy:
The Tale of an Honest Bunny

Miss Fannie's Hat

The Trellis and the Seed:
A Book of Encouragement for All Ages

JAN KARON

G. P. PUTNAM'S SONS
NEW YORK

My Beloved

A Mitford Novel

PUTNAM
—EST. 1838—
G. P. Putnam's Sons
Publishers Since 1838
An imprint of Penguin Random House LLC
1745 Broadway, New York, NY 10019
penguinrandomhouse.com

Town map by David Caine

Library of Congress Cataloging-in-Publication Data

Names: Karon, Jan, 1937– author
Title: My beloved : a Mitford novel / Jan Karon.
Description: New York : G. P. Putnam's Sons, 2025.
Identifiers: LCCN 2025028572 | ISBN 9798217047178 hardcover |
ISBN 9798217047185 ebook
Subjects: LCGFT: Christmas fiction | Novels | Fiction
Classification: LCC PS3561.A678 M92 2025
LC record available at https://lccn.loc.gov/2025028572

Printed in the United States of America
5th Printing

The authorized representative in the EU for product safety and compliance is Penguin Random House Ireland, Morrison Chambers, 32 Nassau Street, Dublin D02 YH68, Ireland, https://eu-contact.penguin.ie.

For Candace

Beloved Child of Light

1952–2021

Beloved,

let us love one another,

for love is from God.

1st John 4:7

MY BELOVED

FATHER TIM KAVANAGH

Pen in hand and his notebook open before him, he was ready to do what he did every November:

Get started on his Christmas list.

He had vacated the French desk in the study and adopted the kitchen island as a command center. At the east end of the island, he wrote letters, paid bills, stashed his laptop, and kept a handy trove of books. The west end was reserved for culinary pursuits.

When Cynthia cooked, he often read aloud to her from Mary Oliver, Billy Collins, Wendell Berry, or, out of long affection, George Herbert and Wordsworth. Early on, they agreed that poetry paired well with food prep, fiction worked best after dinner, and nonfiction was for reading alone, silent as a monk.

By seven-thirty a.m., he had prayed with his wife, checked his sugar, had his shot, and polished off his stone-ground oatmeal with raw honey and multigrain toast. This upbeat start on the morning had made him overconfident—his pen was poised but nothing was happening. The grand expectation of churning through the list was morphing into a muse.

He considered the books spilling out of their allotted space and encroaching on the laptop. Back in the day, which seemed a cool hundred years ago, he'd been a bachelor priest in his slip-covered wingchair, avidly reading through a pile of books. Books were his friends, his family, his mode of travel, his relief from the woes of the vestry.

Somehow, and certainly not by his own effort, he'd gone from a bachelor with blood kin consisting of one lone cousin, Walter, to a family his cousin called 'humongous.' While such a family delivered equally humongous dividends of pleasure, his reading time had taken a hit.

Before Cynthia, he'd been unmoored by the prospect of sharing his *time* with a wife. How much of his time could a wife possibly need? Now he knew and he did not regret even a minute with his cheerful, artistic, and beautiful wife. He was unmoored no more, but settled in. In a groove, you might say, though definitely not in a rut.

And there was Dooley—not of his blood, but of his heart. At the age of eleven, Dooley had landed on his doorstep, a thrown-away boy—barefoot in shredded overalls, with a mouth that a mother of yore would have washed out with soap. Call it a miracle that today his adopted son—now a successful veterinarian with his own practice—had a beautiful, artistic wife himself. And two kids that Cynthia and he were over the moon about.

A phenomenal string of events had cast him in roles he'd never dreamed of fulfilling—father, husband, father-in-law, brother, brother-in-law, great-uncle, grandfather.

There was Jack, a lovable seven-year-old mash-up of cowboy boots and imagination, and Sadie, a going-on-three-year-old who had taken down every defense in her grandpa's arsenal. He'd never given his heart so freely.

With Cynthia, he'd fought giving his heart. There was the inarguable fact that he'd already given it to God—though only to a certain degree, as he later realized. That had seen him through a decades-long passage until he had a revelation: God's love for his children wasn't just for them to have and to hold, it was to freely, spontaneously give away—and to gratefully receive from others. Why hadn't he understood this before?

That awakening had opened both his heart and his intellect to a sober realization—while he'd spent years being afraid to love, he'd been far more terrified of receiving it. He had begun at once to work these truths into daily practice. Not easy. And not overnight. But the process had performed its share of miracles—had, in fact, at the tender age of sixty-two, gotten him married.

His abandoned French desk, given to him recently by a former parishioner, now displayed an archive of framed family photos. There was Dooley and Lace's Sadie, miraculously born to a mother long pronounced unable to conceive.

A few years ago, he learned he had a half brother. Out of time and despair, hope and prayer, Henry—a *brother.* They both resolved to drop the 'half' business. He and Cynthia had attended Henry's Holly Springs wedding—an event that gave him a witty and agreeable sister-in-law. He studied the wedding photograph, searching Henry's face for any resemblance to his own. Zero. But they both loved poetry and starched handkerchiefs and letters written in cursive. He had a laugh at the memory of taking Henry by the shoulders, looking him in the eye, and saying, 'Brother, I forgive you for being taller and better-looking.'

To go from a family consisting of a cousin to the present-day slew was a sea change, calling for a new way of dealing with Christmas giving. In years past, he had made a list. Now he must make A List.

Cynthia breezed into the kitchen in a vague cloud of her signature wisteria scent.

'You wear perfume for the grans?'

'Jack says he loves the way his Granny smells—it makes him sneeze. He also loves making his own picture book. You'll see it soon; it's about bugs. When he turns all that talent loose in the world . . . wow! How about your Poetry with Grandpa syllabus?'

'I need one more run through the town library. Poetry for three-year-olds is scarce.' As Lace's mural-painting commissions increased, she needed help with the kids. He and Cynthia were giving a hand when Lily Flower was otherwise employed.

His wife was applying lipstick without the aid of a mirror. It was his job to give a thumbs-up if she hit the mark. She hit the mark while eyeing the kitchen island.

'Could you clean some of the stuff off the counter?' she said. 'It runneth over.'

'I was just thinking that.'

'I'm making pasta for the weekend and . . . ' She gestured. ' . . . all those Billy Collins books.'

'But you love Billy Collins.'

'I'm crazy about Billy Collins, but not when I'm making pasta, which takes up gobs of room.'

'Consider it done.'

She gave him a smooch on the cheek. 'Love you, sweetheart.'

'Love you back.'

'Are you off to the hospital?'

'Tomorrow,' he said.

'See you at five, then. Could you pick up a lemon for tonight?'

'Will do. Anything else, give me a shout. Love to the kids. Tell them I'll be out soon.'

'Ooops, I got lipstick on your cheek.'

'Leave it. I'm branded.'

And away she flew, eager for what life had to offer.

He had always started his Christmas list with the nurses. Who could make it without nurses? Not the doctors, not the patients. How many years had he spent plowing up the hill to visit the ever-changing stable of patients, assisted by nurses in his labors of consolation? Even the sour ones had their place in the scheme of things.

And didn't nurses love chocolate? Wasn't that their favorite thing to go home to even if they had a husband who was good-looking and would carry out the garbage? But the rules had shifted when he wasn't looking. He'd been told that what nurses want now is gift certificates. Nurses want to choose their chocolate themselves.

Good for nurses for speaking out and taking charge!

Five gift certificates for chocolate. It felt good just getting that on paper. Unlike his free-ranging wife, he enjoyed the boundaries imposed by a list.

He would save his wife 'til last on the list because she required more than a bit of head-scratching. 'Don't buy me anything,' she said just yesterday. 'I have everything I could possibly want or need. Just write me a love letter. Please, honey.'

He loved it when she called him honey.

He remembered the Year of the Bathrobe—he had searched for one-hundred-percent cotton with pockets—she favored pockets—and matching slippers. Though he was convinced he had a home run, she had seemed . . . what? Dismayed wouldn't cover it.

A more recent Christmas gift had its own downside. According to rule, they agreed to give each other one gift only—no cheating by giving more. It had to be *utilitarian*, and they had to keep mum so it would be a *surprise*. She liked surprises.

They had ended up giving each other the same thing—a smoothie blender. The same make and model. Surprise all around! Hers, however, had been on sale and she had saved thirty bucks. Which meant that he'd be returning the one he bought. All he had to do was hike to the recycle bin in a freezing rain and retrieve the box and dig through the foam peanuts that went berserk all over the place and locate the shipping label and the form that asked why the item was being returned, to which he replied *It's a long story*, and then rewrap the blasted thing and schlep it to the UPS drop-off.

Looking back, his own biggest want had once been for a world globe, and she had been thrilled to give him one. Years later—six or seven, maybe—he was still perfectly satisfied with his globe. Lighted. In a mahogany stand. How could he want more?

'I'd love to give you something you'd really, deeply enjoy,' she said yesterday. 'Something that would make you feel, I don't know, seventeen again?'

'I have her,' he said.

She seemed to like that argument, but still . . .

Since they married, he'd written a love letter or two. The one in which he plagiarized a passage from Duff Cooper had been a hit. Cooper had enjoyed a career of writing torrid love letters to his wife, Diana, before dying at sea in '54. But the letter currently under consideration would have to come entirely from his own striving.

Gus was awake and panting at his feet.

The red leash that his hundred-and-ten-pound Bouvier had worn was of course too large for a rescue of thirty-three pounds soaking wet. He had punched a few holes and used his leather cutter to nip the excess.

Out they went into the mountain fog.

So far, November was an unseasonably warm month, not cold enough for a fire in the hearth. This weekend would be different; the temperature was predicted to drop by several degrees, and they had a half cord of hardwood he was itching to burn.

This was ground fog; those headed down the mountain would be driving the first few miles in a cloud. He was a fog fan. And no wonder—he was Irish. Gus also had a touch of the Irish. His dog was fond of music, had once lapped up a spilled Guinness at a Meadowgate party, and was inclined to good humor often resulting in a grin.

He had believed grinning dogs merely a staple of YouTube, but now he had one of his own—who, by the way, could also bark with a ball in his mouth. He absolutely did not deserve such a talented dog.

He spied Emma Newland barreling around the corner with Snickers, a twelve-year-old rescue. At this distance, he could not run nor could he hide from his former church secretary and personal Genghis Kahn. He zipped his jacket, turned up the collar, armored himself. He could tell by Gus's bark that his dog was not into this encounter; Gus had met Snickers on other occasions and was unimpressed.

'Why don't you get another leash?' she yelled over the barking.

'This leash is *fine*,' he yelled back.

'Seems like it would remind you of *you know who*.'

She had seldom called his former companion by name.

'I *like* being reminded of *Barnabas*!' he shouted into the din.

Snickers retreated behind his owner, growling, as Gus took leeway to sniff Emma's shoes. Black. Sturdy. Size ten. Triple A. She was proud of the triple A. As her former priest and so-called boss, he knew almost everything about this woman whose desk had sat less than three feet from his own. He had to hand it to her—Emma Newland could, in a heartbeat, make three feet feel like three inches.

She gave him the eye, as if she'd caught him being naughty in some inconceivable way. 'What brings you out so early?'

'Gus!' he said.

Up ahead, the first squirrel of the morning. And away they went at a trot.

He and Gus were blowing across the parking lot at Mitford School when he met Grace Murphy, speed-walking toward the school's front entrance. Blond hair in braids, bifocals firmly in place, a wide-open smile displaying a hatchwork of braces on wayward teeth. Grace was one of his favorite people.

'Good morning, Father! And good morning, Gusarino.' She stooped, girded by a backpack of considerable size, to give his happy dog a head scratch.

'We're glad to see you out brightening up the world,' he said.

'I'm reading to our English class this morning. I'm sort of nervous!'

'What are you reading?'

'*Willa Cather On Writing*.'

'Willa Cather? Remind me what grade you're in?'

'Fifth because I skipped third,' she said. 'Next week, we'll be reading from Eudora Welty's book on writing. I'm co-teaching a whole American Literature unit with Miss Phillips. Got to go, Father! Bye, Gussie! Have a great day!'

'The Lord be with you!' he called after her.

'And also with you!' she called back. Grace was an acolyte at Lord's Chapel, wise in the ways of liturgical response.

He felt the smile on his face, the way it softened his skin that was busy drinking clean mountain air.

Two squirrels later, he was back in the kitchen, staring at The List.

He was a dash fatigued from their walk. Supplying St. Mark's in Holding had been a mixed blessing. Full priestly duties June through October, combined with driving up and down the mountain, had been a stretch. In the five months of priesting a troubled parish, he had counted heavily on the prayer that never fails.

Back to business.

His mother had been the Christmas-list maker of all time—everything inscribed in a stenographer's notebook by July seventh, when she closed her gardens to the public. She set at once to the task of making pin cushions, pillowcases, embroidered dresser scarves, the occasional sweater or baby blanket, and stacks of tea towels and aprons from printed flour sacks.

'Th' woman is an *industry*,' said his grandfather.

She also used flour sacks to make boxers for her mortified son. He could depend on the sight of them under the tree—a starched four-pack wrapped in white tissue and adorned with a holly sprig.

He remembered hiding like a common thief when exchanging his britches for running shorts in the school locker room. He had nonetheless been spied in this covert maneuver, and the shamings were a memory he detested. He was fourteen when he finally wrangled store-bought from his mother, the family exchequer.

He rolled out the tea drawer with its tempting array of tins.

Tomorrow morning, up the hill to Hope House and a visit with Louella, then off to the Children's Hospital and a board meeting. Today's obligations—a lemon. And a town meeting that promised to be a whole other lemon.

He would have lunch at Feel Good, pick up his one item at the Local and a book at Happy Endings, then attend the meeting and get home to clear the counter. As for what to read to their in-house *pastaia* as she labored over the linguine this weekend, definitely Billy Collins from the book he'd buy today.

He put the kettle on the flame, ran hot water in his mug to heat it, and waited for the kettle to sing. Looking for a lunch partner, he rang Mule Skinner, now fully retired from local real estate. *Leave a message.*

'Tim here. Feel Good at noon!' he said.

He rang J. C. Hogan, still hanging in there as editor and publisher of the *Mitford Muse*, typo warts and all. *Leave a message.*

'Tim here. Feel Good at noon!'

He'd finally persuaded the Turkey Club to call him Tim, which was a milestone.

He foraged in the fridge for a carrot to tide him over, thinking again of the Christmas robe.

It had been a perfectly nice robe. *Lined!* With *pockets.* His wife had been pleased, he supposed, but by no means thrilled.

He could not afford another dud.

ESTHER CUNNINGHAM

Four of her fluffy, good-lookin' daughters were hot-wired this mornin'. She preferred one at a time, but they usually came in a drove. They had lined up like boxcars in front of her recliner; this was lookin' like trouble.

'Mama,' said Marcie— th' oldest of five—'we have a proclamation.'

'You know I like a good proclamation.' As the former mayor of Mitford for sixteen years, she'd made many a proclamation.

'Give us your Christmas list as soon as it's ready,' said Charlene.

'An' we'll shop for all th' presents you an' Daddy want to give,' said Winona. 'We'll go online, we'll do th' runnin' around.'

'You won't have to lift a finger,' said Tammy Leigh.

Marcie sneezed, a stress-related whatchamacallit that first appeared in fifth grade. 'We're here to help you spice it up, Mama. Daddy said it would be great with him if you spice it up!'

'Spice *what* up?'

'Your gifts. No more of the same old same old.'

'We'll wrap every single one!' said Tammy Leigh. 'Nice bows, pretty paper. Turnkey!'

'An' we'll deliver everything personally,' said Winona. 'As long as it's local.'

'Plus,' said Marcie, 'an' this is a real plus, Mama—we don't have to all pile in at your house for Christmas dinner, we can just come for pie an' ice cream! We know that big dinner last year half-killed you an' Daddy.'

'I didn't do a bloomin' thing but sit in this chair. Y'all brought everything but deviled eggs an' th' fruitcake. You know your daddy slaved over those sixty deviled eggs an' not one left on th' platter! He was proud of that an' he intends to do it again. As for my fruitcake, it had been soakin' in Wild Turkey since July, so there wadn't any work to it an' I was *not* half-killed.'

Marcie sneezed. 'But thirty-five people in this little bitty house . . . '

'An' some of 'em drinkin',' said Charlene.

'*Some?* It didn't sound like *some* to me an' your daddy.'

'I promise you, Mama, us girls did not participate, an' you know Dwayne never touches a drop. You said it was *all too much*, I personally heard you say it.'

'Yes, ma'am,' said Winona. 'I heard you say it was all *way* too much.'

'Drinkin' is for th' *back porch*. So is smokin' as y'all know. Carryin' on in th' kitchen with a window open does not count. Why're you so slow teachin' your men what porches are for?'

'We're not slow teachin',' said Marcie. 'They're slow learnin'.'

'But we'll do better, Mama,' said Tammy Leigh. 'That did get a little out of hand.'

'I was thankful to th' Lord th' neighbors were in Tallahassee.'

'Let's stay on message,' said Marcie. 'So, Mama, what do you think? We do th' shoppin', we do th' wrappin', Daddy makes th' pies—cherry an' pumpkin, he said, and we all agree—an' we bring th' ice cream. He said vanilla would pair well with th' pies 'cause it goes with anything.'

Th' *pies*? What about her fruitcake? Didn't they all love her fruitcake? Wadn't it a tradition to have only *one* dessert, which was her fruitcake made from their great-grandma's recipe?

Her breathin' was gettin' short. Every last one of her girls was a daddy's girl, an' all of 'em tickled to death with what they'd drummed up behind her back. If they had a brain in their heads, they knew she would be killin' Ray Cunnin'ham for gangin' up with her own flesh an' blood.

As for vanilla ice cream, she had no respect for anything vanilla. They all knew she loved Cherry Garcia, which would also pair well with whatever.

Their fifth daughter, Ramona, also loved Cherry Garcia and would back her up, but where was Mona when you needed her? At th' beach! For a year! To find herself, she said. No calls or texts or any contact allowed. She hated to say it of her own child, but Mona was always a little on th' mousey side, this had been a shock.

There went a couple of blotches breakin' out on her face like popcorn—her own stress-related whatchamacallit. She didn't need th' monitor to read her blood pressure; she could read it in her bones. A hundred an' eighty over one-ten, easy.

Four sets of eyes starin' at her, not even blinkin'. Tammy Leigh had a look reflectin' her many childhood disappointments. Winona had one eyebrow cocked, the usual.

'Mama,' said Marcie, 'we're offerin' you an' Daddy *a new kind* of Christmas. No stress, no tryin' to do everything on a walker an' a cane, an' a nice break for Daddy. This is an offer you can*not* turn down.'

Just for spite, she turned it down.

TIM

Hadn't she made him laugh more, feel more, rest more, love more? Hadn't she changed his life? Hadn't she supported him through the difficult months of his recent supply at St. Mark's? Why would he deny her this small pleasure?

Could he not spare an hour or two to say what he really felt but was generally too bashful, even too puritanical to say? In any case, she knew he loved her. She also knew she was consoling and smart as the dickens and fun to be with. Why hammer it with a pen?

Because she really wanted a love letter.

And what did he really want? Why had he dismissed her question as frivolous? Possibly because of her remark about him feeling seventeen again. Not going to happen. He got off the stool at the kitchen island, did a turn around the study, and stared out the aptly named picture window with its mountain view.

Pacing, pacing, pulling at his chin, her question demanding useful thinking . . .

Something was going on in him—something like carbonation rising in a moderately priced prosecco. Something with sunshine in it, the smell of nature, something *green*.

He was getting close.

And, *ha*!

There was the answer.

He stopped in the middle of the room. How amusing. Even amazing. No trip to an island. No sports coupe with a ragtop. He was easy. What he really wanted was to go out on a summer day, and lie in the grass with his wife.

On a hilltop, to catch the breeze.

He would like to share that vision with her as something only she could give him. No one else in the world could help him satisfy this heart's desire.

Obviously, it couldn't be satisfied at Christmas, only on a day in summer. With birdsong and dragonflies and the scent of crushed grass.

As a boy, he'd skipped endless opportunities to lie in the grass, scared off by crawling things. Boys were supposed to love spiders and snakes and bugs of every order, but not he. Time, of course, changes everything. What's a Granddaddy Longlegs or two when lying in the grass comes with a bonus of staring at clouds? Cumulus, cirrus, stratus, cumulonimbus—all morphing into illusions of everything from bear families to buttermilk and dinosaurs, a veritable slideshow of wonders.

He was amazed by how little effort it had taken to get to the core of what he really wanted. And what could possibly have driven such off-grid thinking?

This single sublime truth:

There was someone in his life who would *understand* what it means to lie in soft summer grass and look at clouds and love another soul with every fiber of their being. Right there was the content of his letter; a paean to a woman who matched him deep for deep.

As the kettle burst into its chosen key of C, he felt relief flow in.

'*Soli Deo gloria!*' he exclaimed to the four walls. Gus jumped off the sofa and ran to the kitchen to look him in the eye. The little guy was grinning.

He opened the desk drawer and took out the Montblanc pen she'd given him, and the bottle of blue-black India ink, and the featherweight crème-colored stationery from his cousin, Walter.

He would not sit at the kitchen island to write this; it needed the waxed walnut finish and refined French legs of his former work spot.

He sat at the desk, rolling the Montblanc between his fingers like a fine cigar.

Please, honey.

He loved it when she called him honey.

He had broken a sweat, as if digging a hole for a midsize tree. The result was two pages of what he'd hoped to say. How many sermons had he written without being able to express what he hoped to say? He was buzzed with relief. Wow, just wow. She would love it.

He folded the letter, slipped it into the envelope, and sealed it.

On the envelope, he inscribed the only word that might come even close to capturing the truest sentiment of his affections.

TIM

Wanda's Feel Good. Cold outside, warm inside. Their favorite table. Mule was sporting a fedora from a yard sale. More than a little wear on the hatband.

'How much?' he asked Mule.

'Two bucks. They had th' original sales receipt, said their grandaddy bought it in 1947.'

'A good year,' he said, pulling out his chair. 'I still had hair.'

'So what are you lookin' so smiley about?' said J.C.

'Cynthia's Christmas present. Done! Open road ahead!'

'What is it?' said Mule. 'I'm always after great ideas for Fancy.'

'Last year's great idea for Fancy was a twenty-dollar push mower from a flea market,' said J.C. 'I'm surprised Fancy's still speakin' to you.'

'She's not,' said Mule. 'But not because of th' mower. She sold it for sixty bucks and pocketed th' money. This year, she wants somethin' new, she said. New or nothin', she said.'

This was not the demographic for creative thinking, but why not? 'How about a letter?' he said.

'A what?'

'A letter.'

J.C. enjoyed an intense face mop with a paper napkin. 'That's th' trick you recommended to me a few years back.'

'And it worked as I recall.'

J.C. grinned. 'Did it ever.' And there was his morose look again. 'But it's too bloody soon to mess with Christmas. I've got issues.'

'Great,' said Mule. 'We've all got issues. They say men don't like to talk about issues, but I think talkin' about issues is . . . '

J.C. leaned in. 'So what a newspaper needs is news, right? But what does th' *Muse* get? Old news—siphoned offa th' street. Everybody already knows everything. Local, regional, worldwide—everybody knows everything all th' time. No wonder small-town newspapers are droppin' like flies. I'm ready to fold my tent.'

'You can't do that,' said Mule. 'Th' *Muse* is an institution. We depend on it.'

'What do you depend on it for? Linin' your shoes when your soles wear out?'

'I personally depend on it for th' Weekly Hint, which lets you know that newspapers are great for killin' your weeds, linin' your litter box, linin' your kitchen drawers, an' get this—stuff old newspapers in your smelly shoes an' whammo, odor gone. You wouldn't believe what I've learned from th' Hint. I'm still shinin' my shoes with a banana peel, thanks to one of your most popular Hints.'

J.C. let go with a word his Mississippi Baptist mother had once half-killed him for saying.

'So, Tim. Give me some intelligent feedback here. What I need is *breakin'* news. These days, all news is breakin'.'

He had waited too long to ask J.C. a single, burning question. 'If you don't answer your phone and don't check your calls or emails, how can you be the first to get news? Just sayin', buddyroe.'

'Excuse me,' said Wanda, 'for interrupting your brilliant conversation. I have breakin' news of today's special.'

Wanda had eavesdropped on their blather and was feeling good. Cowboy hat at a maverick angle, fringe on her shirt, sleigh bells on her boots. You could read Wanda like a thermometer.

'I thought this was your day off,' said J.C. 'Where'd you come from?'

'Dropped down from a tree where I was hangin' out with th' other crows. Today's special, listen up. We're slammed an' I don't have time to say it twice. Shrimp an' grits.'

'Shrimp an' grits!' said Mule. 'Hot dog! Can you believe shrimp an' grits? For *lunch*? In *Mitford*?'

J.C. could not let this pass. 'I thought you said Fancy has you offa shellfish.'

'Shrimp is *shellfish*?'

J.C. groaned. 'Throughout the ages, throughout the *ages*!'

He could see that Wanda was relying on the preacher to move this thing along. 'I'll have the grilled chicken sandwich. Whole wheat, low-fat mayo. The special sounds great, but grits are high carb.'

'Not these grits,' said Wanda. 'These grits are made from cauliflower. Totally diabetes friendly.'

'But this is the *South*!' said Mule. 'Grits outta cauliflower? Cancel my order!'

'You haven't ordered,' said Wanda.

Wanda was tapping her foot; he could hear the sleigh bells. Santa was on his way, albeit a few weeks out. 'I'll have the special,' he said. Shrimp an' grits without the carbs! Somewhere, a heavenly choir burst into song—alleluias, harps, the works.

'How big is th' servin'?' said J.C.

'Luncheon size.'

'Is this one of those little bitty lady's lunches you like to trick us men into orderin'? Bring me two. What I don't eat, you can put in a box for my afternoon snack.'

'I don't do boxes, Mr. Hogan. That's for pickup takeout.'

'That's what I'll be doin'. *Pickin' it up from this very table an' takin' it out.*'

'Don't mess with me, Mr. Hogan. I'll send Jenny to get your order. She's got th' shovel for this job.'

Wanda stalked away.

'Have you seen Jenny?' said Mule. 'She was a wrestler at th' college a couple decades ago when she was a student. Big woman. She could mop th' floor with all three of us.'

'Wanda,' J.C. growled. 'Dern woman acts like she owns th' place.'

'She does own th' place,' said Mule.

'Aren't you th' smart-ass?'

Year after year—why did he keep doing this? He could have had leftovers at home with Gus.

'Cool down, buddy. If they run us out of here, where will we go? Not the gas station.' They tried that after the new station owner rolled in. A warped plastic chair had tilted forward and dropped him on the concrete. A vending machine took their money and delivered yesterday's egg salad wraps. You could die in that place.

'Hey, boys, I'm Jenny.'

He noted that Jenny cast a large shadow over the table as if the sun had gone in. Maybe it was his forty years of priesting, but he could tell she had earned her wrinkles. He liked her at once.

'Today's special is . . . ta-da, you're gon' love this!'

'We already heard today's special,' J.C. snapped. 'I'll have it. Bring it on.'

'Too late. We're slammed. All gone. Today's special is now liver an' onions with coleslaw!' Jenny flashed a smile.

'I can't eat onions,' said Mule. 'Gas. An' th' cabbage in th' coleslaw wouldn't help, either.'

'Spare us th' details,' said J.C. 'You like a BLT; *order a BLT*.'

'Fancy has me offa bacon.'

J.C. sat back, rolled his eyes, mopped his face with the napkin. 'Year after year. *Why* do I keep *doin'* this?'

Jenny nodded, solemn. 'You know, that's th' question I often ask myself.'

He had on several occasions wondered why *he* kept doing this. His walk to Happy Endings allowed another occasion.

If by chance he could make it work without damaging two old friendships, Omer Cunningham would be a great lunch partner. Jovial, upbeat. But he hardly ever saw Omer since he married the frisky Scrabble Queen and owner of the tanning booth at A Cut Above.

Maybe the mayor? A great conversationalist. But Andrew went home for lunch to his beautiful Italian wife who, like Sophia Loren, probably owed everything to spaghetti.

Many of his old parishioners had died or moved away. And his good friend, Father Brad, did not indulge in lunch. No, he kept his boyish figure by having one meal a day—dinner—at home with his newish wife who was currently back and forth to Boston but soon coming to live full-time in Mitford.

The only way out of the Turkey Club was to croak.

ESTHER

She didn't want a new kind of Christmas, she liked th' old kind. Wrap a ten-dollar bill around a Hershey bar, tie it with a ribbon, an' sign th' tag *Love from Mamaw and Papaw.* What was wrong with that? Plus, this wadn't cheap hard candy, it was *chocolate.*

Twenty-one great-grans, or was it twenty-three, she had lost count. So thirty-one bars, which would cover th' girls, their husbands, th' grans, an' great-grans, which was two hundred bucks plus shippin', for regular seven-ounce, no nuts.

She an' Ray could not afford to live another minute in a family with the DNA of rabbits.

So what if the grans were all grown up, one already a senior citizen? Couldn't everybody use an extra ten these days, an' a nice bar of milk chocolate? She did not like to be reminded of what a few thankless blood relations had said over the years. '*Where's th' nuts?*'

Who was Esther an' Ray Cunnin'ham, anyway? Millionaires? They were livin' on Social Security, Ray's Army pension, an' the grace of God Almighty.

Did her daughters live on fixed incomes? No. An' except for Tammy, whose town house in Wesley had high-quality siding, they all had a *brick* house!

Her girls had done all right without movin' to Charlotte an' havin' a career. One husband owned self-storage buildin's an' a lawnmower franchise; one was a bigwig at a bank in Wesley; one was grindin' stumps an' takin' down trees all over th' place; an' who could remember what th' other one did, but he worked at home an' didn't touch alcohol.

When she was young, what was available for a husband? Maybe a doffer at th' cotton mill down th' mountain. An' then she met Ray at that picnic where she ate his fried chicken an' coleslaw an' Lord help, that did it. A real man who could not only cook like an angel but kiss like a bandit an' flatter the daylights out of Mitford School's 1945 Homecomin' Queen, which was her good-lookin' personal self, size eight.

Honey Babe, Sweetie Pie, Little Darlin', you name it, Ray Cunnin'ham was not afraid to show affection. They had sparked like two firecrackers in the back seat of his daddy's green Chevy.

Same old, same old? Spice it up? As if a ten wrapped around a Hershey wadn't a great present for anybody in their right mind.

She didn't cook Ray Cunnin'ham a bite of dinner after th' Proclamation, she made him pick up takeout from Wanda's Feel Good. She ordered barbecue, which she was not supposed to eat; he ordered fried chicken, which he was not supposed to eat; an' they forked it down at th' kitchen table without sayin' a word. After that little torment, she went down the hall, put on her nightgown, an' climbed in bed.

She heard Ray clatterin' around th' kitchen, then he came an' got undressed an' hung up his clothes an' sat on th' bed in his underwear.

'Let th' girls give you a hand, Dumplin'. It's a blessin' for them to give their mama a hand.'

'I know y'all. You're tryin' to take control of me; treatin' me like an invalid; tryin' to boss me around.'

Ray laughed 'til th' bed shook. 'That's a good one. Boy howdy! Boss *you* around?'

'Knock yourself out,' she said. 'An' where's my car keys?'

'That's for me to know and you to find out, Doll Face.'

'Don't Doll Face me, where are my keys?'

'Where they're at, you will never go,' he said, sober as a judge.

'The bottom of th' ironin' basket,' she said.

'You wish.'

'Do the girls know I don't know?'

'Th' girls know all they need to know to help keep you safe an' sound.'

'Do they know where you hid my keys?'

'That's for me to know and you . . . '

'Oh, hush up. Why are y'all in cahoots against me?'

'We're in cahoots *for* you, Honey Bun. That's what you got to get in your hard head. Th' doctor says you're a fall risk. We can't have you fallin' again. That bruise on your hip looks like Lake Michigan.'

'What if I need to go to the store when you're not home?'

'I'm always home. Once a week, I pick up groceries an' once every six weeks I get a haircut. Other than that, I'm right here, hung up to dry.'

'You went out for mayo th' other night.'

'Right. I went out for a jar of Duke's, an' you maybe needed the keys to go to th' bars in Wesley?'

'You old so an' so,' she said.

She was too give out, as her mama used to say, to kill Ray Cunnin'ham. She rolled over on her left side and Ray rolled in behind her.

Spoons.

That's the way it had always been with them.

TIM

When he was a kid, going to town was a big deal. You washed your face and maybe your feet, and you felt like something great was about to happen.

In 1940s Mississippi, the four-mile dirt track from their farm to Holly Springs had been a pathway to heaven. When he earned a quarter doing odd jobs at home, he asked to be paid with two dimes and a nickel so he could rub the coins together in his pocket. Going to town in the wagon with Louis and a packed lunch was usually a day trip. He had hours to decide how to spend twenty cents, keeping back a nickel for his savings account at the bank. That said, maybe going to town—even when it's just around the corner—would always feel like a big deal.

In Holly Springs, he headquartered at the library. In Mitford, all he had to do was open the door to Happy Endings Bookstore and wherever his eye roamed, voilà!—three hundred and sixty degrees of possibility.

In the far corner, Mitford School's third grade sat in a circle as their teacher read from a pop-up book. Near the sales counter, a dozen old people like himself had showed up for their weekly discussion of a Twain novel. Someone he recognized as a retired prof from Wesley sat by the window reading the store copy of *Our State* magazine. Full house. Happy Endings was Mitford's community center, disguised as a bookstore.

'In to blacken your bottom line if only by a smidgen,' he said to Hope Murphy.

'It's the smidgens that keep us going! So glad to see you, Father. It's been ages.'

'All of three or four days,' he said; they had a laugh. 'Wondering if you have the Billy Collins book with the cow on the cover. Published 2022, I believe. Somehow we missed that when it came out.'

'We have one copy left. I just reordered a lot of poetry.'

'It's a surprise for Cynthia.' A new book, his wife's superb pasta, their first fire—don't tell him Mitford is a one-stoplight town with no entertainment.

'You know it's what he calls his small poems?'

'Small poems?'

'Back in a flash,' she said, and disappeared into the Poetry section and returned with an open book. 'Page one hundred and ten. I read this to you as an insomniac since childhood.' She adjusted her glasses and read the poem aloud.

They had a big, rowdy laugh, which turned a few heads in the Twain group.

Father Tim was her favorite customer. He officiated when she and Scott were married. He sat by her bedside during a scary pregnancy and prayed her into well-being. He managed the bookshop for months while she could barely get to the bathroom, and through sheer native instinct he managed to make it the bookstore's best year yet. As if all that were not more than plenty, he never, ever, as far as she knew, ordered books from Amazon.

'I'm hoping to get Christmas in tow on the early side,' he said. 'Heads up, we'll soon be looking for books for Puny's twins and Jack and Sadie. And a book for Coot, as always. What's he reading these days?'

'Grace has convinced him to read the Boxcar Children.'

'I saw your remarkable daughter this morning. Teaching Eudora Welty!'

'And working on her novel. About a spinster who goes about looking for skullduggery. I think Miss Pringle may be the model for her lead character; Grace currently enjoys drawing from real life.'

'Us skullduggers must keep our heads down!'

'I'm so proud of her, Scott says she's smarter than both of us together. Anything else, Father?'

'Come to think of it, a signed Langston Hughes for my brother, Henry. He would cherish that.'

'I can definitely find the Langston Hughes for you. We'll give you a call before we buy it; there may be several on offer. As for all the rest, a big order is due in next week—let me go through and make recommendations. We also have fabulous jigsaws coming in. Puny's twins love jigsaws.'

'Keep that in mind,' he said. 'And I'll need a swell coffee table book on vintage cars. For my cousin, Walter, who despises driving and always takes the train.'

He made himself a decaf pour-over, strolled around the Poetry and Gardening sections, and had a sit in the DIY section, where he read how to repair the busted screen of their deck door. He viewed computer images of the book on vintage cars and enjoyed the Vivaldi, which, given the store's playlist to suit all comers, was followed by a Dolly number. A refreshing and productive hour. Hope could charge for this.

'How's business?' he asked as he swiped his card for the book.

'The college's big donor is expanding their bookstore and adding a café. With a French bakery.'

The college bookstore in Wesley was Hope's biggest competitor. Such an expansion could be good for the region, but could seriously impact Happy Endings.

'College students can't afford a French bakery,' he said, hoping to console. As for faculty, what did he know?

'They say they'll have a barista.'

'A barista.'

'Someone who makes coffee to order, like Starbucks.'

'Well, then. Sobering.' He noticed that she looked worn. Why had he not seen this before? But surely they were all a little on the worn side these days.

'Then there's the furnace,' she said. 'I wasn't going to tell you but . . . '

He didn't have to be told. He heard it laboring in the basement in its death throes—a thirty-year-old boiler from which they'd wrung every iota of utility. They'd all known it was coming. Hope had swung from periods of denial into stretches of sheer panic. She had diligently saved for it, but the balance thus far would hardly make a dent. Given the bookstore's current numbers, a bank loan was questionable, and would be more than taxing to Hope's bottom line.

'Mortgage payments and a new furnace,' she said, 'all at one time. We can't . . . I mean, I don't know how . . . '

He'd seen more than a few peaks and valleys for Happy Endings. Owning a bookstore in a mountain village of less than twelve hundred was a heroic endeavor. But what do you do with a big dream? Do you cast it out? Or go for it? He was no bona fide risk-taker but he knew this much—you go for it.

As he'd often done over the years, he took Hope's hand.

'Lord, you know where the money is. Thank you for helping us find it. Thank you for this bookstore that helps civilize us, and for Hope, whose given name reminds us how we must move ahead, expecting your provision . . . '

ON HIS WALK home, he had a better idea. He would not debut the new book this weekend—he would slip the envelope inside, wrap the book in his signature green paper, and that's what Cynthia would find under the tree. Something like a tortilla of wry poems with a hot sauce of romance.

He could hardly wait.

CYNTHIA KAVANAGH

She loved this yellow house where she and Timothy were making a life together.

It was the sort of house she might have built herself, except for the kitchen, which was clearly designed for a man, and one who didn't cook.

Her mother's bachelor younger brother, Joe, had it built in the 1950s, during his work as a civil engineer on the roadways of western North Carolina. He was the one who said which dynamite to use when cracking open a mountain.

She was grateful for the several amusing details in the house, like the broad windowsill in the kitchen that may have served as a table for one or a perch for a cat. When she and Timothy remodeled the house, it lost some of its eccentricity but gained a study and a mountain view.

Any memories of her uncle were vague. He had visited her parents in Massachusetts when she was seven or eight years old. She did remember that he smelled of tobacco and whisky and, according to her mother, nitrogen dioxide. He had given her a dollar bill folded in the shape of a bird. 'Origami,' he'd said. His teeth were almost black; she had no memory of his face.

Though her marriage to U.S. Senator Elliott Wainwright had lasted twenty-four years—a life that now seemed aboriginal—she couldn't recall his face, either. The good years with Timothy had obliterated the bad years; she was essentially left with scraps—a fleeting memory here, a blurred recall there.

A scrap that occasionally floated to the surface was the wallpaper in her Concord kitchen—watercolor images of safe country cottages, untamed gardens, winding lanes. The kitchen was where she went to beseech God in her desperate, agnostic way, and plan how to leave a man having children with other women.

The kitchen had been where she went to blame herself—for being what her husband cruelly, and often, labeled 'barren'; for not paying attention to red flags; for looking the other way.

It was also the only room in which she could conjure an image of leaving Elliott. In the image, she was standing at their open front door, not looking back. She had a cat carrier in one hand and a carry-on in the other.

There was nothing complicated in the carry-on—a change of underwear, a wrinkle-free travel outfit, pajamas, a tin of watercolors and a packet of brushes, a sketch book, a pair of walking shoes, a toothbrush, the Bible she never read but kept as a talisman, a nail file. She would take none of the jewelry given to her by Elliott's mother; she would leave her wedding and engagement rings on the kitchen counter and her seldom-worn Rolex in his bedroom. She sensed that he hadn't bought the watch for her, but for the statement it made in their circle of friends. He often reminded her that it was the Lady President model.

While Elliott was in Majorca, she had packed her paintings, canvases, oils, watercolors, easels, books, and a few clothes and shipped them into the void of an unknown future. The Stuff of Her Life as a writer and illustrator of children's books had gone to a storage unit in Mitford, North Carolina, where her declining Uncle Joe had a house that would one day be hers. She had never tried to find Mitford on the map, but knew it was her eventual destination.

She would go first to her friends on their farm in North Carolina and then to Uncle Joe's when the house was lawfully hers. His trust attorney had called yesterday to say that, according to the medical team, her uncle would almost certainly be deceased within the next few months, as if hurrying now to make room for his niece in her time of need.

If she'd been waiting for a sign, this was it.

The attorney reminded her that she would inherit Joseph McCarthy's mountain cottage 'of the Carpenter Gothic vernacular.' Two bedrooms, one bath. Her uncle had not made provisions for the contents; would she like them to remain?

Having no real contents of her own, she said yes. What the contents might be, she was afraid to ask, but she would take nothing from the house she had spent precious years trying to make suitable to Elliott's unpredictable taste.

She had written a note of thanks to her uncle and posted it to the trust attorney, who called to say Joe McCarthy would be unable to comprehend it. 'But he will have something to hold in his hand,' she said. 'Something with his name on it.'

She would leave Elliot not just as a woman humiliated, but as an artist too frightened to paint, a writer too numb to write, and a wife too angry to sit across the table ever again from the overpowering scent of Italian cologne.

These memories sometimes came as the holidays approached. Thanks be to God she was now safe in their study in Mitford, enjoying the simple act of making a Christmas list.

She looked up from the list, nearly finished now, and into the kitchen.

There was the essence of what she would have missed—the flesh-and-bone grace of her husband in his favorite flannel shirt, her onsite priest, the love of her life, creating cooking aromas with a language all their own.

She couldn't possibly deserve all this—it scared her a little.

He looked her way and grinned like a kid. 'So what are you giving me for Christmas, Kav'na?'

'My heart.'

'Who could ask for more?' he said.

SHE WOULD FINISH the list this evening—it was short and sweet but to the point of everyone's need.

Hatching a Christmas list in her old life had been agonizing. Elliott's mother and father had gobs of money and as owners of every possible gadget, actually craved more gadgets.

She looked upon gadgets as robots that vacuum the floor and terrify the dogs, turn on the porch light in Maine all the way from Florida, or mechanize a salad bowl to wash your socks.

She hadn't consulted Elliott, who did not enjoy conversation about his parents. She had been forced to come up with what she judged to be the most awesome gadget then known to the civilized world. Walkman. She hated it when something done out of absolute goodwill went ominously wrong.

That same Christmas, there was the turkey she had unwittingly undercooked, and Elliott and her in-laws throwing up all over the place. As she was vegan that year and had not eaten turkey, their looks were fiercely accusatory, to say the least.

She bent to her task.

Lace~ white shirt three-qtr sleeves, Rilke's Book of Hours

With the exception of what to give her husband, her list was a wrap. Though by no means a wealthy man, he somehow managed to have everything, including a Borsalino fedora she gave him years ago. Still, he needed something to keep his head warm, something casual. 'A hoodie!' she said just last night.

'No hoodie,' he said. 'I'll look like a burglar.' Children's Hospital, his hands-down favorite charity! Of course. A plan came instantly to mind. He would be thrilled.

She and Timothy were perfectly comfortable with the fact that she had money and he didn't. He didn't because he'd given it all to Children's Hospital. His aim now was to 'die broke.'

Though hard to buy for, he was an amazing gift-giver. Her favorite was of course the Nativity scene he restored for her in complete secrecy. It was his personal story of redemption, a theme on which he had preached for much of his life as a working priest. He found the twenty-something plaster figures—sheep, angels, wise men, Holy family—in Andrew Gregory's antiques shop.

He had examined every needed repair:

A lamb's ear or two gone missing, along with the occasional hand or finger, a couple of noses and an entire angel wing; a camel slathered with orange paint; the wise men looking every haggard mile of their two-year journey to the manger.

It would take skills beyond any he possessed to bring the tableau to life. He had walked away, and the next day surprised himself by returning to the shop and buying it.

Andrew agreed that the figures could be left temporarily in his storeroom. There her wonderful husband would spend all of Advent working undercover, disguising the truth of how he was spending serious blocks of time.

She knew something was up but was too occupied with her own work to follow the trail.

Timothy was a man who lived 'a life of the mind,' as a parishioner once said. And yet, by some miracle, he'd been able to manually re-cast the shambles of the Nativity figures into the sublime narrative of a world-changing event—the event that Christina Rossetti defined in the hymn 'Love Came Down at Christmas.'

The way he told it was, the many hours of reclamation in the storeroom of Oxford Antiques had been coming to an end.

The sole camel was at last looking like a camel. The wise men were looking sharp if not altogether wise. The two angels in robes of azure and scarlet—his greatest artistic challenge—had recovered their imperial beauty and each now had two wings.

He was carrying the newly winged angel to the shelf when he made a wrong move. He saw it happen in slow motion.

The angel plunging from his hands. Fragments scattering over the wood floor. Plaster dust lingering in the air.

He'd been devastated.

She was alarmed at how pale and distant he was that evening. 'Maybe I'm coming down with something,' he said.

Walking through the alley that afternoon on her way to Mitford Blossoms, she had seen the open box sitting outside Oxford Antiques for trash pickup.

She remembered catching her breath at the sight of the broken angel, and how she knew at once it was meant for her.

She had closed the box and taken it home. Unaware of what her husband was up to, she shut her studio door and began work on a secret of her own.

PUNY GUTHRIE

When she left th' house this mornin' with th' boys, she'd been in a hurry. She was always in a hurry. And because today was a teacher's work day, th' kids were all out of school. The girls begged her to take th' boys with her, which was a good idea, but th' boys hadn't wanted to go with their mama, they were only ten an' already actin' like teenagers. Lord knows it had been time-consumin' just to threaten them with their lives an' settle th' pushback by promisin' money for Sweet Stuff. As for right now, they were puttin' pieces in their jigsaw on a jigsaw board they could take anywhere.

Was her cell phone at home on th' kitchen table? Or in th' pocket of her jacket, which she forgot an' left in th' car? Mamaw Cunnin'ham said she was too young for dementia, so quit worryin.' She would go look in th' car but remembered she left it at th' Exxon this mornin' an' they walked to th' Kavanaghs, carryin' the box of toilet paper and her cleanin' stuff.

She wrung out th' mop. She was th' only person she knew usin' a rag mop and not a squeegee. She was still cleanin' house like she did in her twenties takin' care of her granpaw, who was a fire an' brimstone preacher.

Joe Joe said she could modernize and take a load off of herself, but she liked bein' th' only person on th' planet who cleaned a house th' right way. And unlike her in-laws, who didn't mind usin' household chemicals, she was proud to go green with her cleanin' supplies.

She had to drop her other cleanin' customers, but would keep Cynthia and Father Tim because she loved them like family. She even called him Father like he might sort of actually be her dad; he'd given her away at her weddin' and preached th' service into th' bargain. To tell th' truth, him an' Cynthia were way better than her biological family—what was left of it. Plus she was good with usin' Joe Joe's huge family as her own, even if some were kind of off th' rails.

But it was hard cleanin' even for th' Kavanaghs what with her kids goin' ever' whichaway. One to Wesley for ballet, one to Holding for therapy, one to piano lessons twice a week with Miss Pringle, one to band practice two days a week, plus one playin' soccer an' one playin' football.

Pickup an' delivery was totally her job as mom of two sets of twins and th' wife of a police chief who did not do grocery shoppin' or yardwork. Okay, he would take out th' garbage and break down boxes for recyclin', she would give 'im that.

But set Joe Joe Guthrie in th' yard with a rake an' th' whole town runs over to chew th' fat an' set on th' front steps like lizards an' generally waste his time 'til he hadn't raked a leaf. He was th' same as Mamaw Cunnin'ham with people—talk, talk, talk, laugh, slap his knee, be Most Popular like he was in high school.

Sassy was th' one takin' piano lessons from Miss Pringle. Did Sassy want piano lessons? No. Sassy th' Princess of Everything didn't want lessons of any kind whatsoever. When her an' Joe Joe told Sassy she had to take some kind of extra cultural lesson that wadn't taught in school, she said no an' you can't make me.

She could not believe her ears. Her an' Joe Joe both were jis' stunned.

I believe you know better, Joe Joe said, than to tell your mama she can't make you—because guess what.

'So guess what,' she said to the mop bucket. 'Miss Holier than Thou is takin' piano lessons—*as we speak*!'

She straightened up, took a deep breath. She could have been a nun, except Baptists did not have nuns.

Another reason she was still cleanin' for Father Tim an' Cynthia was because they couldn't do th' right kind of cleanin' by theirself. It was that simple.

This oak floor would go to th' dickens an' th' ironin' would pile up like Mount Mitchell. Thank God they could both cook; she'd be dead an' gone if she had to cook for somebody outside her immediate family.

Oh, no. Th' caller ID said this was Miss Pringle. Sassy's piano lesson was jis' over an' she'd been rushin' to pick up her car to get Sassy an' Sissy an' th' boys at Happy Endings, which they called their second home. There was no way Miss Pringle would be callin' her unless it was bad news. Sassy had been her pupil for three months and she had not called before.

She was in th' car an' was not supposed to answer, but she did.

'Hello?'

'Mrs. Guthrie?'

'Yes, ma'am?' She had practically begged Miss Pringle to please call her Puny.

Her heart was poundin'. What if Sassy had sassed Miss Pringle? Everybody said Sassy was livin' up to her name an' should've been named Gloria or Joy or even Heather. Though she had not invited their Sunday School teacher to weigh in, he came up with Dorcas. 'It's Biblical,' he said.

'I just wanted to report that Sassy is doing exceedingly well at her piano lessons. Her interpretive powers are undeveloped of course, but very promising. I know she practices on the school piano, Mrs. Guthrie, but I hope it may be feasible to have a piano in your home—at some point.'

A piano in their home? They did not have *money* for a piano in their home, much less *room* for a piano in their home. She saw a parkin' spot in front of Happy Endings but was too nervous to talk on th' phone an' park at th' same time, so she drove around th' block.

'It's fortunate,' said Miss Pringle, 'that you brought her to me at this impressionable age. I thought you and Chief Guthrie may like to know that Sassy has potential to become a star pupil.'

'Oh, thank you, Miss Pringle. Thank you thank you thank you, I jis' . . . *thank* you.'

Not knowin' whether to laugh or cry, she did both.

ESTHER

Marcie called two or three days after th' Proclamation.

Ever since fifth grade, Marcie had been th' official spokesperson for th' rest of th' girls. Tammy Leigh had tried to take over this role, but it hadn't worked. Only Marcie was official.

'Mama?'

'Of course it's Mama. Who else would it be?' This house was *not* little bitty, but she wouldn't bring that up right now. She may not win every battle, but she would not, under any circumstances, lose th' war.

'Please don't make me an' th' girls any crazier than we already are. We gave you the best offer you ever had, Mama. I know it and you know it.'

It was *not* the best offer she'd ever had. But she had thought about it. She said what Father Tim liked to say. 'Consider it done.'

She heard all four screamin'. She could just see 'em jumpin' up an' down, which they were too old to be doin', except for Tammy Leigh, who had a bladder tuck two years ago.

Yes, she had handed over a few battles to her daughters, but this was a big one. This was Ray's an' her *Christmas*, for crap's sake. Next time, they'd be after her credit card, which she had used a time or two for QVC. She'd never been loose with it, but th' cocktail ring with a four-carat fake diamond had scared th' daylights out of everybody.

They would be pawin' through her sock drawer one of these days, lookin' for that card, which she'd never tell them she'd cut up in little bitty pieces. As for the ironin' basket theory, that is not where th' keys were. Th' basket was prob'ly sittin' in th' basement empty as a gourd, because she an' Ray knew how to hang up their clothes so the wrinkles fall out.

TIM

He looked up from his computer.

On a freezing Saturday afternoon, his wife was the proverbial sight for sore eyes in her new pajamas. Parrots, toucans, orchids, banana trees, but no monkeys, thank goodness; he was not a fan.

'You wild creature,' he said.

'No, no, sweetheart, don't be using up the good stuff you'll be saying in my letter.'

'Your letter?'

'The one you're giving me for Christmas, remember?'

'Did I buy into that foolishness? Do we have some agreement I can't recall?'

'You were talking in your sleep and I rudely interrupted and asked if you were going to give me a love letter, and you said yes, of course, absolutely. Then you went back to saying something about a screen door.'

His guilt about not fixing the screen door had set up shop in his dreams? 'I'm not sure that talking in my sleep is a certifiable deal-maker.'

She curled up at the end of the sofa near the fire and gave him a smile. He couldn't forage around and find a smile of his own. He was feeling the impact of it all over again. It was like losing your cell phone and wallet at one go, except worse.

He had tucked the letter into the Billy Collins book and wrapped it in the green paper he always used, no ribbon. He thought he had shoved it in the desk drawer when he got the urgent call from Hope House about Louella's fall. Puny had shown up early and started her 'home improvements' by hoovering the kitchen and study while the boys watched football on their iPads. That was one distraction, then the call had sent him tearing out of the house and up the hill on foot, because Cynthia had their car and Puny's car was being serviced. Given his distress, he might have done any fool thing with the book he'd just wrapped.

He stayed with Louella 'til they knew nothing was broken; X-rays were ordered as a matter of course. He was totally done in from the uphill run; he would not do that again. Scott Murphy had driven him home, thanks be to God.

He was certain he put it in the desk drawer. But when he opened the drawer, nothing but the pen, the ink bottle, stationery, stamps, and a backup pair of reading glasses.

Maybe he'd left it on top of the desk, but it was nowhere in the study or kitchen. He'd made a hurried search of places in which he rarely set foot—the living room, the linen closet, the guest room, the guest bath—it was useless to look where he wouldn't have gone, but sometimes people did crazy things, and he was no exception. He later repeated the search, praying the prayer that never fails.

He could not rewrite the letter; he knew that instinctively. He could possibly write some version of it, but it would feel rehearsed. The spirit in which he'd written it was anything but rehearsed, and beyond anything he could summon again.

A kind of bereavement set in when he thought of it, so he was trying not to think of it. It would either turn up or it wouldn't. That simple.

'Are you okay?' she said. He could never hide his feelings from his mother or his wife. There was his face, hanging out like a billboard, revealing the good, the bad, and the ugly.

'Frankly, no. But I can't talk about it now. All will be well. And when it is, I'll spill the beans.'

They air-high-fived.

'What are you doing at your computer, may I ask?'

After a trying half-year of supplying down the mountain, he was supposed to be resting, idle, shiftless.

'Trying to help St. Thomas get its act together.'

'That's what you did this spring and summer.'

'I'm not sure that what I did actually worked.'

'If you couldn't make it work, then it probably won't work.'

'Thanks for your vote of confidence.'

'If St. Thomas's current condition were medical,' she said, 'how would you diagnose it?'

'Coma.'

'Loosely defined,' she said, 'as a period of unconsciousness brought on by injury or illness.'

'The injury being the damage done by the former priest. Many parishioners left, as you know, and the ones who stayed lapsed into a kind of unconsciousness. They quit paying attention and are doing any reckless thing to move ahead.'

'You fulfilled your commitment to them and gave them an extra month. You couldn't have stayed on, Timothy, it was messing with your health. Just a reminder. Let the bishop fix it if he can.'

He was a dog with a bone. Clergy never retires; that they let go is a falsehood.

She patted the adjoining sofa cushion. 'Come over here,' she said.

Gus saw this as a personal invitation, and up he leaped.

It felt good to laugh.

TIM

He'd lunched with the Turkeys again today—twice in one week, a record—then attended a town council meeting called to determine a zoning issue. He had declined running for council, but took a self-mortifying interest in municipal government in general.

On his way home, he spotted Avis Packard putting a poster in the window of the Local. He would always cherish—though that may be too strong a word—the months he spent managing Mitford's chief food source, the Local. Avis had been as close to death as you can get without the scythe, and asked him to step in and do the impossible. Clergy he may be, but his local side hustles as the town grocer and Happy Endings manager were among the favorite times of his life.

A mental note. Socks for Avis. What bachelor couldn't use another pair of socks? He threw up his hand, they gave each other a shout.

At Village Shoes, Abe was stocking his display window with hiking boots, work boots, fashion boots. A few pumpkins. He popped in.

He had a lot of favorite people in Mitford; Abe, bent over his task at the window, was one of them.

'How's it going, buddy?'

Abe straightened up, stretched, grinned. There was a joke coming on; he could tell.

'So, Father. Three Jewish mothers are arguing which one's son loves her the most. The first one says, "My son sends me flowers every Shabbos." The second one says, "You call that love? My son calls me every day."

'"That's nothing," says the third. "My son is in therapy five days a week and the whole time he talks about me."'

They had a laugh. He could depend on Abe.

'What's up with socks these days? Looking for warm and colorful.'

'Warm and colorful. Good line for a personals ad.' Abe gestured to a display on the counter. 'Merino wool blended with alpaca. Over the calf. Stripes, polka dots, checks, plaid. One size fits all. Highly recommended.'

Avis Packard in polka dots. Why not? 'Lime green and orange!' he said. This was fun. Maybe socks for his brother, Henry, and his cousin, Walter. Socks for Dooley and Harley and Willie for all that stomping around in muddy winter pastures.

'How about for yourself? You could stand a few polka dots in your life, Father. Or the plaid. You'd do well in plaid.'

'I don't know, Abe. I'm a pretty neutral guy.'

'To thine own self be true. I think you're kind of rogue down in there somewhere. The purple and green would suit you.' He'd never worn wild socks or even considered wild socks; this was exhilarating. As a plus, his wife, who was absolutely warm and colorful, would approve.

'Sold!' he said, grabbing the plaid.

He zoomed out of there, pumped. He had shopped for Christmas! And it was all gift-wrapped!

WHOA, THE KITCHEN was smelling good. The scent of beeswax from lighted candles, rosemary from the roasting chicken . . .

He hung his jacket and scarf on the peg. Kissed his wife. Put his pocket change in the Mason jar. Stowed his shopping bag under the French desk.

'You were shopping!' she said. 'A very rare occasion. Fur-lined slippers for your housemate?'

'Your time will come, Kav'na. Socks! For menfolk. Made a dent in my list before I hardly began writing it.'

'How was the town meeting?' she said.

'I can only quote Lincoln's contention that you can't please all the people all the time. Much less some of the people some of the time.'

She pulled on her oven mitts and brought forth the chicken, crackling in its herbed juices.

'What did you and the Turkeys talk about today?'

'Let's see. The woeful state of newspaper publishing, weight, wives, aches, pains. In that order.'

They washed up together at the double sink.

'What did you say about your wives? I'd love to be a fly on the wall.'

'J.C. says the MPD issued Adele a new Glock 22.'

'Why? As far as we know, she never used the old one.'

'One of the benefits of small-town living. So Mule says Fancy's having both knees done, though not at once. They say standing in spike heels for forty years is the culprit. Well ahead of the season, Wanda's decked out her cowgirl hat with colored lights. And the Hardware has snow shovels in the window. Oh, the Woolly Worm's prediction is in. You're rolling your eyes.'

'I'm hanging on every word.'

'Listen to me, woman, I've been out in the world and I'm bringing home the *news*. Show some respect.' He dried his hands.

'How many inches does the Worm predict?'

'Seven inches December twenty-fourth into the twenty-fifth.'

'If we lose power we'll burn the furniture. Where does he get this stuff?'

'Some say from the *Farmer's Almanac*, he says it's divine revelation.'

'So what did you say about me? Tell the truth.'

'Would I tell anything else?'

'Maybe in this particular case.'

'I said what everyone already knows. You're the dickens to live with, bossy, a spendthrift, you sleep 'til noon, and your ironing basket is out of control. The sort of thing people can get their teeth into.'

She laughed, which was one of his favorite things in this life.

What could be better on a winter afternoon than a wife who laughs and knows how to roast a chicken?

ESTHER

Comin' along th' hall this mornin' on her walker, she noticed somethin' was different.

They'd taken up her scatter rugs.

Now they were workin' their mischief at night! She could not believe her eyes. Ray an' th' girls had been sayin' it like she'd gone deaf. '*A. Scatter. Rug. Is. A. Fall. Risk!*'

She loved her scatter rugs. One with a pumpkin motif, one with a sunflower motif, one with a watermelon motif. She liked a motif on a scatter rug.

She'd heard this foolishness was comin' an' she'd been willin' to compromise. Okay, she said to Ray an' Marcie, but *wait 'til after Christmas*.

An' now this.

How could you stumble over a scatter rug with a watermelon motif as big as a Volkswagen? Th' size of th' motif itself would act as a warnin' not to fall. If she hadn't cut up her credit card, she would have new scatter rugs down in a heartbeat.

She stopped an' caught her breath. Meantime, nobody would hear a peep out of her. Nossir, she would save this little battle for another day.

RAY HANDED HER what looked like a gift without a bow.

'Must be for you, Love Bug. Just found it in th' box Puny brought over with our toilet paper th' other day. Eight mega rolls, thirty percent off. Can't beat that.'

Wrapped in green paper. Sort of Christmassy. Felt like a book. She read books on her Kindle to keep real books from pilin' up.

She looked at her husband, who was still tall but stooped like he was bowin' to th' Queen. As for herself, she had shrunk from five-seven to five-five. If she didn't get up from this recliner an' get some exercise, she would soon be five-five both ways.

She liked that his eyes were still blue an' still had that Cunnin'ham mischief. She said somethin' she rarely said, not bein' one to invite trouble.

'Give me some sugar.' She closed her eyes, puckered up, an' *blam*.

'How was that, Cupcake?' He looked proud, like he'd just pulled a rabbit out of a hat.

'I've had better,' she said.

'Is that so? An' when would that be when you had better?'

'Oh, about seventy years ago,' she said. She would not mention that their Big Seven-Oh was comin' up in four or five days.

Off he trotted with a list for Food Lion, whistlin'. Whistlin'! As if the world wadn't in the worst shape of everybody's entire life.

'Remember th' sausage!' she hollered as he went out the door. 'Jimmy Dean's mild, not hot!'

If it was a book, she could regift it in th' same paper. Th' trick was to open one end by pryin' up th' tape real easy an' pullin' out th' book like a popsicle from its wrapper.

It was a book, all right. With a cover showin' a cow on a sofa. Poems, it said.

She had not read a poem in a hundred years, not since she learned

'Th' Face on th' Barroom Floor' by heart. She had recited it at Mitford School in the ninth grade an' her teacher, Miss McCreary, had a taxi run her over to Wesley to recite it for th' college. It was her first taxi ride because her teacher's little boy, Bobby Joe, had to have his appendix out an' she couldn't drive her over there.

Without even listenin' to her recite th' poem, th' college sent her back to Mitford sayin' they would not allow a poem about a bar. Because they were too cheap to hire a taxi, they sent her home with somebody called a dean who tried to put his hand up her skirt but she smacked his hand so hard he nearly ran his Chevy off th' road.

Which is just one reason she never went to college. Over her dead body would she set foot in another college, much less in a taxi with th' windows rolled down messin' up her new Toni perm.

She opened the book. An envelope fell out. Somethin' written on it. She adjusted her glasses.

Beloved.

What in th' world?

There was no way this could be from Puny, her favorite granddaughter-in-law, married to her favorite grandson, who was Mitford's favorite police chief in th' history of th' department.

So maybe Ray remembered their anniversary comin' up on Monday an' this was an early present? But Ray Cunnin'ham would never in a hundred years give her a book of poems. He would never give a present early. An' sayin' he found it in th' toilet paper box would not be his style.

Plus, beloved was not his way of talkin'. You do not go from Baby Cakes to Beloved, no way.

She was a very curious person, which is one reason she'd gone far in life, but this whole thing was makin' her uneasy.

Beloved? Maybe because their seventieth anniversary was so special, he was tryin' somethin' new?

She took the letter opener off the table next to her chair an' pried up th' envelope flap. What if this was a joke an' somethin' jumped out like th' time Winona sent her that birthday card? It played music an' shot confetti all over th' floor an' Charlene's dog licked it up an' th' vet bill was two hundred an' eighty bucks.

A letter. On good stationery. She knew good stationery when she saw it. Hadn't she received a letter from th' governor for that beautification program in her third mayoral term?

This was not from Ray Cunnin'ham. This was handwritin' she'd never laid eyes on. *Dear Bookend . . .*

Bookend? This was from a total looneytoon, the likes of which Mitford had never seen before. An' wait a minute. *Good Lord!* Whoever it was wanted to . . .

She adjusted her glasses. . . . lie with her in soft summer grasses? She was ninety-three, gainin' on ninety-four! She felt swimmy-headed. She would read just one more line. But only one.

Whoa. What if Ray saw this? Or th' girls? She looked for the signature on th' second page. *Your Bookend,* it said. If that's what romance had come to in this modern age, she didn't want any part of it.

She folded th' letter, put it in th' envelope, licked the gluey part an' resealed th' flap, stuck it in th' book, an' stuffed th' whole mess back in th' green wrapper.

This was not somethin' Joe Joe would have written to Puny an' it got dropped in th' toilet paper box. No, her people did not talk in this manner. This was some kind of weird mistake, an' she would totally not be regiftin' it.

She speed-dialed Puny.

Please leave a message.

She did not leave a message.

SHE TURNED OFF th' coffee pot an' rinsed it out an' dumped th' filter in th' compost bucket, like Marcie was currently makin' them do. Then she rolled down th' hall with th' book in its green wrapper. In th' room where th' recyclin' was, she saw th' toilet paper box. She dropped th' book in there an' grabbed th' bag of Styrofoam peanuts they'd collected an' emptied th' whole bagful on top of th' book.

Out of sight, out of mind, an' off it would go on Thursday in th' recycle truck. Marcie said they wouldn't take Styrofoam peanuts, but that was a civic problem, not hers. For good measure, she unloaded a wad of plastic Food Lion bags on top.

Then she rolled up th' hall to her recliner, which was th' only place she could think straight. She needed a dose of Words with Friends; she was killin' it yesterday. Thank th' Lord for her iPad, which kept her up to date with this world.

Th' screen lit up an' there was a text from Marcie, buttin' in again to take over their Christmas.

Mama, we have all decided it would be fun for you and Daddy to give each other a surprise Christmas gift this year! Love, Marcie

She clicked Reply. To spice things up I suppose?

That wasn't exactly our intention Mama but what could it hurt?

We have all decided? They had decided *again* what was good for *her*? An' Lord knows what they might be hatchin' for her an' Ray's seventieth. She had plainly said don't do anything, just come by an' have a piece of OMC from Sweet Stuff an' bring th' kids. No presents. There's not a square inch left in this house to set down a present.

Th' whole family was goin' off th' rails, as usual. Every year, Christmas started at a trot in late September. Then it heated up in October to what Tammy Leigh, bein' a country songwriter, called a *fevered pitch*. By late November, all but th' kids were half-killed.

'Come December,' said Dwayne, 'we're goin' through th' motions.'

She would not waste her breath tryin' to tell these people how to live.

A text dinged in from Tammy Leigh.

Just surprise each other with one little surprise, Mama!

It does not have to be a big deal. I'll write a song about it.

Reply. A song about what?

About you an' Daddy giving each other a surprise gift. The look on your faces, the look in your eyes. Old love is gold love. It would sell, Mama!!!

Reply. Your Daddy and I have been married seventy years. We do not have anything left worth selling.

So now it was a surprise gift.

She was already surprised, thank you.

Surprised by bein' old as dirt; surprised by losin' her scatter rugs; an' surprised by goin' from a mayor everybody voted for to an old woman whose car battery died months ago from sittin' in th' garage with a mouse nest under th' hood.

'Who'd you see at Food Lion?'

She was starved for a little gossip. As mayor, she could get all th' gossip she wanted by steppin' down th' hall, walkin' to th' post office, or stayin' for coffee hour at church.

He set a bag on the counter.

'Ran into Willie from down at Meadowgate. Willie had a good bit of produce on th' truck—gourds, pumpkins, an' whatnot. Said Dooley told him go to town and give it away to whoever can use it. Gave us this nice bag of collards.'

She was raised on collards, but th' cookin' smell was like rotten eggs. 'I'll wash 'em,' she said, 'but you'll be doin' th' cookin'. With th' kitchen door open.'

'Sugar Babe, remember me? I'm always doin' th' cookin.' I can't think back to th' last time you dished up supper.'

'How about that roast chicken you raved over? I guess that didn't count?'

'What roast chicken?' he said.

'Two or three weeks ago, stuffed with rosemary an' rubbed with coarse salt an' a little butter. *That* roast chicken.'

'Marcie brought that over, Honey Bee.'

She would not pursue that, no way. Either her or Ray Cunnin'ham was gettin' dementia an' no need to speculate which one 'til after th' first of th' year.

'So I come in th' house an' grabbed a box,' he said. 'Went out an' told Willie to go in th' garden an' load up th' last of our winter squash. They didn't grow winter squash this year.'

'What box did you give 'im to load up?'

'That toilet paper box Puny brought over. Looks like you emptied th' Styrofoam peanuts in there, glad to see that mess go out th' door.'

'Let Willie deal with th' peanuts,' she said.

Ray had a laugh.

This was her lucky day.

PUNY

'Puny.'

She whirled around to see th' Father in his old maroon bathrobe.

'Oh, Lord, Father, you scared me to death! My nerves are right under my skin.'

'Where a good set of nerves should be,' he said. 'I thought I heard voices in here.'

'It's jis' me.' She knew he talked to himself sometimes, too, so she wadn't embarrassed.

'Has anything turned up?'

She knew what he meant, he had asked twice before. She felt personally responsible because she could not find what he was lookin' for an' her favorite thing was seein' him laugh, which he never did when askin' about th' book wrapped in green paper. Th' best thing to do was change th' subject.

'No, sir, not one thing. How is Miss Louella? I've been meanin' to ask.'

'She's fine, just fine. Only minor bruising left.'

She hated to see him look worried, it broke her heart. He didn't usually look worried.

She went through th' whole thing again to see if she could find a clue. When her an' th' boys got here th' day he ran up to Miss Louella, she'd taken out her cleanin' supplies and set everything on th' desk, which she was not supposed to do but just this once couldn't possibly hurt an' Father Tim had called to say he wouldn't be home 'til after her an' th' kids left.

She'd taken out their six rolls of toilet paper and put them in the powder room, their bedroom bath, and th' guestroom bath. Two rolls each. All that was left in th' box was Mamaw an' Papaw's TP.

Then she set th' box under the desk.

When she was about ready to go, she asked Tommy to put all her stuff back in th' box while she finished upstairs. When she got to Mamaw's, she took her own stuff out of th' box an' left it in th' car. She delivered th' rest of th' toilet paper to Papaw. Th' kids did not come in, they waited in th' car. Papaw would of unpacked th' box because he did most everything around th' house these days. But not one word had come from Mamaw or Papaw that a book wrapped in green paper had showed up in th' box.

Th' Father was still standin' there, lookin' around. 'No bow, no ribbon,' he said. 'Very important.' He had told her this twice before.

She thought he looked pitiful in that old robe. 'It'll turn up,' she said like she always said. 'My lost things always turn up. Have you prayed? Prayin' totally works for me. Jis' th' other day . . . '

'Right. It will turn up,' he said, walkin' away.

That maroon robe had been his blankie for a hundred years. One time she tried givin' it to a Bane an' Blessin' sale but he caught her in th' act and here it was, still up an' walkin' around.

She no longer tried to run his business like she did when he was single. He had Cynthia now to run his business.

PUNY

'Tommy says you took my stuff off th' desk at th' Father's house an' put it in th' toilet paper box.'

'Yes, ma'am. You asked Tommy to do it, but I ended up doin' it.'

'Why did you end up doin' what I asked Tommy to do?'

'I cain't tell or he'll kill me.'

'You're already killed if you don't tell me.'

'You jis' hollered, Mama.'

'I hollered? I beg your pardon, I do not holler.'

'You jis' did, I heard you with my own ears.'

'Would I be talkin' to you like this if it wadn't important? This is extremely important. Look at me, Timmy, extremely.'

'Did I do it wrong?'

'If you took all my things off th' desk, you did not do it wrong. But there might have been somethin' else on th' desk that shouldn't have gone in the box.'

'What?'

'A book wrapped in green paper. No ribbon. Did you see it? Book. Green paper. No ribbon.'

'Mama.'

'What?'

'Mama.'

'*What?*'

'I was blindfolded.'

'*Blindfolded?*'

'Please don't holler, Mama, it hurts my ears.'

'Why were you blindfolded?'

'I lost a bet to Tommy.'

'Oh, Lord, help us. A bet! Your daddy . . . '

'Are you gon' tell him?'

'Tell him you were gamblin' with your brother? No, it would break his heart. It would break your daddy's heart. He has seen pure tragedy come out of gamblin'. Pure tragedy. I'll tell you about it when you turn eighteen. Plus your great-granpaw was a preacher who preached that gamblin' is a sin; it was his lifelong mission to erase gamblin'. You know why it's a sin? Because it can become an addiction, it can ruin people's lives.'

'Will my life be ruined?'

'Oh, hush, don't cry. No, just repent and don't do it again, ever. Okay?'

'Okay. I promise. Would you like to feel th' bump on my head now?'

'What bump?'

'I hit my head really bad under th' desk but you said you were too busy to feel th' bump.'

'What desk are you talkin' about? We don't have a desk.'

'Granpaw Tim's desk.'

'Oh my God. *What were you doin' under his desk?*'

'Mama! Your face is turnin' red.'

'That's not all that'll be turnin' red if you can't give me a good answer!' Anytime she said Oh my God, she was truly, totally callin' on God.

'Tommy was movin' th' puzzle board to th' kitchen and some of th' pieces fell on th' floor. So we got down to look for th' pieces, an' I saw two under th' desk next to your box an' I went under there an' hit my head so hard it knocked some of th' pictures down on top. But I set everything back so good that you didn't even notice when you came down from upstairs. I wish you could have felt th' bump when it was really big, Mama, it's gone down now, but you could still feel it if you want to.'

He was her baby because he was last to come out. An' he looked so pitiful. She gave him a hug an' felt around on his sweaty little head for th' bump. It wadn't much but he was proud of it. 'It's like an *egg* under there, baby. I'm so sorry I was too busy to feel it when it was huge.'

'It's prob'ly a concussion,' he said. 'Like Tommy'll get if he keeps playin' football. I hope he gets one. Or even two.'

If she lived to see her kids graduate even from junior high without her havin' a fatal stroke, it would be a miracle.

MAYBE SHE DID see it and it didn't register because she was so addled that mornin' from bein' in such a hurry. But she could not worry about it another minute. Not even one. If it was meant to turn up, it would turn up. She would definitely pray for it to turn up.

She loved her kids, she really an' truly did. But havin' kids was th' most challengin' thing she'd ever done in her entire life. And here she was with two sets of *twins*. Two sets! She should have her tubes tied if they could do it by laser.

PUNY

'You blindfolded your brother at th' Father's house.'

'Yes, ma'am.'

'You made him rake my cleanin' stuff off into th' box, even though he couldn't see doodly squat.'

'Yes, ma'am.'

'He could have raked off a book wrapped in green paper. Did you see a book wrapped in green paper on that desk?'

'No, ma'am.'

'What did you see on that desk?'

'I saw a lot of pictures in frames, a bottle of Windex, two rags, folded, a spray can of furniture wax—Old English—a countertop cleaner, a brush for upholstery, a jar of Wright's silver polish, a spray for dog pee, an' a stick of Juicy Fruit, which I chewed because I didn't think you'd mind.'

'You saw all that and you remember everything that clear?'

'Yes, ma'am. My homeroom teacher says I have a photographic memory.'

She did not want to hear this. She would not know what to do with another genius in the family. A piano whiz and a tight end was all she could possibly deal with.

She hardly ever said this, but it's all she could think of to say.

'Jis' wait 'til your daddy gits home.'

HARLEY WELCH

Dooley an' Lace said him an' Willie could keep half th' winter squashes that come in on Saturday from th' ol' mayor.

So half th' squashes was left at th' big house. And he was unloadin' th' other half in th' basement of him an' Willie's little house out back.

He had moved to Meadowgate when Dooley bought it a few years ago. 'Til they could git th' weddin' settled, he had to move into th' big house, into th' bedroom with th' canopy bed. It was as frilled out as a show pony—pink ever'thing, includin' th' canopy. Ever' night he crawled in that bed he was embarrassed to be there. Right before th' weddin' an' all th' family comin' in, he was asked to move in with Willie an' here he'd been ever since.

Willie was th' one drivin' to Mitford these days while he stayed on th' farm messin' with two ol' houses—each one a flat hundred-an'-three years old. If it wadn't treads comin' loose from their stringers, it was mortar goin' bad in th' chimleys.

A man had to do whatever carpentry an' plumbin' he could plus help with th' cattle while he was at it. They had a Red Angus bull named Choo Choo who was famous in th' county, five Red Angus heifers, an' twelve head of steers with three new head comin' Monday, which was tomorrow. That would make fifteen steers to winter over and sell off in May.

Not that he didn't like cattle, he did. But he liked goin' to town an' seein' ever'body, too, since he used to live in Mitford. But he was not complainin', nossir, they wadn't nothin' to complain about. An' pretty soon he'd be switchin' off with Willie an' goin' to Mitford hisself.

Twelve, thirteen, fourteen . . . he was countin' squashes as he emptied th' box.

He had a good job with good wages an' a onsite house that him an' Willie lived in free an' kept clean like they was military. Ol' Willie he Swiffered th' floor ever' night. Some people go set on th' porch after supper an' drink sweet tea or whatever but not Willie. He'd be in th' house Swifferin'.

Livin' like this they wadn't much need to spend money so his savin's was growin'. His favorite thing to buy was whatnots for th' kids. A while back he got Jack a sheriff's badge an' Sadie a duck that talked when you pulled its string. Lace didn't much like th' duck 'cause Sadie had it talkin' twenty-four-seven.

Dooley was covered up with work an' th' animal clinic was doin' good. But it costed big money to maintain a animal clinic, a payroll, two ol' houses, a barn, a corncrib, a machine shed, a vegetable garden, a acre an' a half of pond, an' a hundred acres in pasture an' hardwoods. Plus tomorrow's load of steers would get Meadowgate up to twenty-one head of cattle, not to mention two donkeys, a pony, an' a unlimited number of barn cats.

You look at Meadowgate from th' road, it don't look nothin' but peaceful. But it was a handful ever' whichaway.

He'd thought a good bit about what to give Miss Pringle for Christmas. He didn't have to give her nothin'. But she always seemed grateful for his brownies an' th' produce he left on her doorstep. One time he give her a pot of collards already cooked as she said she'd like to taste th' food of his *native table* is what she said.

It was hard to think what to give a educated woman. Here was somebody born in th' country of France, schooled in th' town of Boston, an' teachin' piano. His family line runnin' liquor out of Wilkes County an' playin' the washtub bass was what Lace said you'd call 'a culture gap.'

Before movin' out to Meadowgate, he rented th' basement at Miss Pringle's house, which she rented from Father Tim.

She'd been awful good to him an' treated him kindly, listenin' to his stories an' whatnot, even laughin' at his jokes. She'd asked him upstairs for a meal now an' ag'in an' they'd got along fine. She didn't mind that he talked like a hillbilly—said she liked hearin' him talk. Three evenin's she played th' piano for him but he dozed off ever' time.

He was sorry for doin' that. He tried to explain why he couldn' keep 'is eyes open.

'It was what you call soothin',' he told her. 'Like water runnin' over stones in a bold creek.' If a man owned a piece of land he'd want a *bold* creek on it so that was a good thing to say.

'It's a compliment, Mr. Welch, to me and to Beethoven.' He couldn't hardly get over how she always called him Mr. Welch.

He had looked on Miss Pringle as a kind of angel. Father Tim said angels are real and walk among us. She even brought hot soup down to th' basement when he was sick as a cat. He counted Miss Pringle an' Lace Kavanagh his personal angels, along with his mama who passed when he was four or maybe five, an' Miss Downs, the schoolteacher he'd chopped wood for in th' holler.

He would admit—but only to hisself—that he used to have what you call feelin's for Miss Pringle. But he'd put a stop to that foolishness. Him in his late sixties an' hardly five years in a unpainted school stuck back in th' piney woods? He'd never let on to nobody that he used to git swimmy-headed over Miss Pringle, who was no spring chicken her own self.

Th' box was empty of squashes. All that was left was starch-based peanuts. At Meadowgate, they dissolved starch-based in water, then poured that mess down th' drain or flushed it down th' toilet. Th'owin' peanuts in th' garbage wadn't good for th' planet, Lace said.

He carried th' box to th' basement sink. He'd pour th' peanuts into th' sink then run th' water in. An' he'd break down th' box an' carry it to Mitford next time with th' recyclin'.

He tipped th' box an' poured. Landin' on top of th' peanuts was somethin' wrapped in green paper. Looked like a present without a bow.

He laid it to one side as he heard Jack comin' down th' steps. Jack's cowboy boots was a little big so they was sendin' up a clatter.

'Can you make a spoon rack?' said Jack. What with wearin' his sheriff's badge an' that ol' cowboy hat pushed back on his head, Jack looked serious as a heart attack.

'I ain't never done a spoon rack.' He'd never heard of a spoon rack or laid eyes on a spoon rack.

'Mom said she wants a spoon rack. She said that to Dad.'

If anything was to be made around here, he was th' one makin' it. Dooley couldn't make no spoon rack, he was handy with people an' animals.

'Let me see now, Sheriff. What *is* a spoon rack?'

'A spoon rack holds spoons. When y'all dug up that trash pit, there were a lot of ol' spoons an' broken dishes down in there. Mom says they're important *artifacts*.'

This was Lace's boy, all right, usin' such words as that. He squatted down an' hoped he could git up. 'Why you got to have a rack for holdin' spoons? You can lay spoons in a drawer jis' as good.'

Jack lookin' at 'im with them big brown eyes. If he never done another thing in this life, he would make this young'un a spoon rack.

'These are historic spoons,' said Jack. 'They date from th' nineteenth century. You can't see 'em in a drawer.'

'Let me think about it.'

'You could maybe see how on YouTube.'

Jack couldn't have his own devices 'til next year. He didn't have none, either, but Willie had a iPad that was old as dirt. If you had time to climb up to th' barn loft to git service, it might work pretty good.

'One way or another we'll git you a spoon rack.' His daddy had kep' knifes an' spoons in th' lid of a shoebox layin' on th' table. 'When you lookin' to git this spoon rack?'

'Before Christmas so I can paint it and get it wrapped. It'll be a surprise from me an' Sadie. But I have to paint it first. Blue is Mom's favorite color. Dad says you have paint.'

'If we ain't got nothin' else, me an' Willie have got paint. I can find th' blue we used in th' downstairs hall.' He high-fived th' little booger. 'I'll git back to you.'

That face breakin' out in a grin full of teeth, them boots clatterin' up th' steps. He'd sure like to build this young'un a treehouse out by th' corncrib. But yours truly wadn't gon' mention that time-consumin' notion.

He grabbed th' edge of th' sink an' pulled hisself up an' inspected what had fell out of th' squash box.

Ain't no way Ray an' th' ol' mayor was sendin' him an' Willie a present. Th' tape lifted up slick as grease. He reached into th' green wrapper an' pulled out a book. Studied th' cover. A cow on a couch. Poems, it said.

DOOLEY AND LACE KAVANAGH

It was hair-brushing time. Rain pecking at the window; bed feeling good; Charley snoring in the corner.

'Sorry I bit your head off this morning,' he said. 'Felt like crap about it all day.'

'It hurt.'

'I know. Hurt me, too. I'm sorry.'

He remembered when he couldn't say I'm sorry. They had both paid a price for that. With a lot of therapy and personal experience, there were four two-word sayings he'd come to respect: *I understand. Thank you. I'm sorry. Love you* was finally learned in his second year of vet school—that one was now total default.

His mother had waited a long time to say she was sorry, if she even really meant it. Damage had continued to pile up during the wait. Damage to her, damage to him and his sibs. But mostly, his stuff with his mother was manageable now. Manageable.

He didn't know how manageable for Sammy and Jessie. Jury still out. But the old stuff still hurt them all. When he thought about it, he prayed he'd be able to let it go. And he would let it go—then the anger would circle back. Not sadness, not bitterness. Anger. It was anger he dealt with.

He looked at Lace in the lamplight. Soft. Beautiful. Open. He could never be thankful enough for this woman in his life. In the flesh, given to him, and the slow, easy brushing of her hair. My God, he thought. My God.

He was in love with somebody essentially educated by the contents of a rural book mobile and a high-end scholarship at UVA. Sure, she'd had some grade-schooling but not a lot. She'd created a one-woman learning academy under her run-down house in the Creek district.

When she was ten, her dad and brother totally lost it to alcohol and her mother became bedridden with an incurable blood disease. Always on the brink, her family slid whole-hog into poverty.

He and Lace had both survived poverty and the loss of parents. He remembered stealing a pork loin to feed him and his sibs and he didn't know how to cook and got it all wrong. You can't cook pork in a pot with creek water, over a fire built with sticks and newspaper. They all nearly died.

His first contact with Lace came through his dad while he was still a working priest. His dad caught her stealing ferns from Fernbank. Dealing in botanicals was what a lot of mountain people did; it was a way to help feed herself and her mother.

When the school drop-out police came looking for her, she went on the run under her derelict house. She rigged an off-grid refuge down there where she slept when her deranged dad was home, read a ton of books, studied by flashlight, and filled sketch pads with her drawings. It was also a hideout from her father, who he hoped he'd never meet in person. One look at the crazy drunk who had kicked Lace in the stomach when she was a kid and he, Dooley Kavanagh, would be headed to prison for life.

The first time he saw her, she was wearing the beat-up hat he despised; he had hated that hat instantly—she seemed to be hiding under there and it creeped him out. Soon after their first meeting, he snatched it off her head and ran with it. When his dad forced him to return it, she'd busted him in the gut with her fist.

She got right up in his face. 'You really don't want to steal my hat again.'

Her punch hurt like crazy but something opened in him—he was maybe thirteen. She may be some kind of mean hillbilly savage, he thought, but she was incredibly beautiful. Mean was fine, he could handle mean, but her beauty had scared him. He was only thirteen, what did he know about beauty?

Not long after that, she was adopted by the town doctor and his wife, two great human beings. So, zero biological parenting, poverty, and adoption into amazing families for both of them. There were times when he could hardly believe the way their lives had worked out.

'We haven't prayed in a while,' she said. 'Not together anyway.'

'Where would we even start?'

Praying took discipline, and he'd spent whatever discipline he had today at the practice. He'd gone over the books with Amanda, cut a benign tumor off the spine of a three-hundred-pound pet pig, stuck his arm up the ass of a braying ass, cleaned and sanitized the kennel because Blake was down with the flu . . .

'Why don't we start with two of our most cherished assets?'

'Th' practice, th' farm . . . ' he said.

'Jack and Sadie.'

He was quiet; she was quiet.

'You want me to go first,' he said. He could tell when she wanted him to go first.

She paused the brush; took a deep breath; let it out through her mouth. He did the same. She was the one who reminded him to breathe, to drink water, to take a bathroom break instead of holding it in because he was too busy. He liked it better when she went first; he could find stuff she left out and pray for that, sort of fill in the gaps.

They hadn't really connected in weeks—talked on the run, yes, but not connected. They were both exhausted, and still pretty broke, not to mention overwhelmed—even with Harley and Willie taking care of the animals and the property, Lily Flower helping with the house, his mom and dad pitching in with the kids, and Blake and Amanda in the clinic. It was amazing how much help they could burn through and still be exhausted.

The clinic was a success; her mural business was a huge success.

Why did they always feel like they were running behind?

He didn't want to pray, he wanted to talk. 'It looks like the perfect marriage on the outside,' he said.

'It is the perfect marriage on the outside. We just don't know right now how to make it work on the inside.'

They needed to subtract something from their lives, but they couldn't figure what. There was nothing they could afford to let go.

'We look rich out here in th' boonies,' he said. 'Big farm, cattle, updated practice. You work your tail off, I work my tail off, and what happens? We're not in debt, thank God, but we're broke.'

'It takes time,' she said. 'We're getting there. And because we're feeding the college fund, it's going to be so much easier when the time comes. And look at your piggy bank. It's a big one and since I gave it to you, it's almost full, even though we mostly use credit cards. That's the way it works, Dooley. Penny by penny.'

She put the brush down. 'If Miss Sadie hadn't left you all that money, where do you think we'd be?'

'Maybe in a two-room apartment in eastern Carolina?' he said. 'Close to the beach. I'd be waiting tables or assisting in a vet clinic or laying brick—who knows?'

'We've got to stay focused, Dooley.'

'You're better at that than I am. And you're putting more into the upkeep of this place than I am.'

'Does that bother you?'

'What bothers me is the toll it takes on you.'

'Remember the toll bridge that first summer we were a couple?' she said. 'Neither of us had the money. The toll keeper was a godsend, he took it out of his own pocket, and we went our merry way. Do you know what a miracle it was that he would do that? When the toll gets paid, you get to move onto the next stretch of highway and it takes you where you're going. This is a toll station for us. It's not forever.'

So why're you crying, he wanted to say. He sat up and took her in his arms. 'What makes you so much smarter than me?'

'What makes you smart enough to know I'm smarter than you?' she said, laughing through the tears. 'Our lives are asking a lot of us right now. But we can get through it because we're young. That's what our parents tell us all the time. We've just got to hang in there. We need to pray; we haven't prayed together in ages.'

He rocked her in his arms, took a deep breath.

'Lord,' he said, 'I've got a list, I'll try to keep it short. You know what we need, so maybe this is just a reminder.

'The clinic really needs new X-ray equipment, you know how bad dentition can affect an animal's health. And new treatment tables would be great. You know we started out with a lot of used stuff, so I don't think I'm bein' unrealistic.'

Charley yipping in her sleep.

'We talked a month or two ago about Harley and Willie, how to help them handle their retirement. That's on my mind a lot, Lord, and I'd appreciate some thinkin' from you before we initiate that talk with them.

'So—I hate to bring up a new Bush Hog, but the old one is slippin' really bad. Harley and Willie have done everything they can, they're not magicians. I mean, basically you gave us a lot of acreage that needs bush-hoggin', even with th' cattle grazin' down a good bit of it.

'Okay I've tried not to whine, and I thank you in the name of Jesus, amen.'

He crashed back on the pillow.

She wouldn't remind him that God isn't Santa Claus.

'Dear Jesus, thank you for my wonderful husband who works so hard for all of us, and is redeeming this fragile old place as a refuge for birds and foxes and deer and all creatures great and small. Thank you for our precious miracle children, Lord; they're beyond anything we could possibly ask or think. Thank you for our sweet parents and their good health and for giving my dad his lifelong mission to help others no matter where he has to go to do it, and for Mom standing by him all the way.

'Thank you for this creaky old house that's our first real home, and for Harley and Willie and Blake and Amanda and Lily Flower and all the beautiful animals who live in our keeping—and the geese I hope my husband will give me for Christmas.

'Thank you for the big heart you gave Miss Sadie so we can have such an amazing life on your good earth. Most of all, Lord, thank you for your goodness and mercy and grace in which we all flourish and try to give shelter to one another. We love you, amen.'

The sound of their breathing, of rain at the window, of Charley moseying out of the room and across the hall for the second half of her nighttime vigil.

'You didn't ask for anything,' he said. 'You just thanked.'

She smiled, laid her brush aside.

'Why are you crying again?'

'Because I'm happy.'

'I didn't know I'm giving you geese for Christmas.'

'Three,' she said. 'One gander.'

'Lucky guy.'

She leaned down and kissed him. The scent of her hair.

'God knows I don't deserve you,' he said.

'So true. But I love you like crazy, Dools.'

'I love you like crazier,' he said.

They held each other, rolled over in the bed. One knot of human flesh for better or worse.

CYNTHIA

The memory came as she was driving to Meadowgate. She didn't prompt or invite it, there it was.

She was walking with Alice through the shaded places of the garden at Hollyhock Farm. The Blue Ridge Mountains seemed close enough to reach in a single leap. In the cote, the cooing of a dove.

She had made the right decision. Here she could do what had to be done.

'What took you so long?' Alice asked.

She didn't answer because she didn't really know. There had been shame in waiting to leave Elliott, in putting it off and denying the truth, though with Alice, shame had minor agency.

They strolled into the broad, sunny places where the hollyhocks were rampant.

'Twenty varieties,' said Alice with something of maternal pride. 'This is where you might think hollyhocks go to die, except hollyhocks never die—they self-seed and are the brave pioneer of all stalky things. Drown a hollyhock in an evening storm, trample it by cattle, move its root across country to foreign soil—you can't break the spirit of the hollyhock.'

She was no hollyhock. A peony maybe, bending helpless to the ground in a spring downpour.

She had come to stay with old friends, Alice and Jeffrey, both academics, on their hundred and sixty acres in western North Carolina—hardwood forest, meadow, and apple orchard surrounding a two-story farmhouse and a sublime garden. She and Alice had been roommates at Smith; they liked the same books, the same art, borrowed each other's clothes—they were comfortable in their old friendship.

The entire upper floor would be hers for as long as she wished; the only rent being the occasional watercolor she might render of the garden. Artist friends had covered a downstairs wall with images of the hollyhocks, the dovecote, and a twig pergola massed with Seven Sisters roses.

Here, her problem was not a painful blur, it was sharply defined.

The problem was, she could not blame Elliott. She would have to blame herself—for staying too long for all the wrong reasons, for not paying attention, for giving in when she should have been digging out.

As for the red flags everyone is supposed to look for in relationships, she had, early on, sensed his frantic need for assurance—she had some of that herself. He would do anything for assurance; it was his anxiety med. She knew she would not be able to bear children and had confided this to him upfront. It didn't matter, it wasn't important, they could adopt. But they didn't adopt. It took years to learn he preferred making his own children.

She saw two of the three children at a lawn party on their twenty-fourth wedding anniversary. Elliott was running for governor. She had retreated behind a trellis off the patio to catch her breath, able to see through the clematis their two hundred guests in celebration mode. She was feeling pleased with the caterer and hoping her fatigue didn't show, when she sensed someone standing near as if waiting to be acknowledged. A tall man in dark glasses and a seersucker suit.

He said nothing. She was caught off-guard but determined to be the gracious hostess. 'You're southern,' she said.

'I am.'

'It's the seersucker. I hear it's how southerners survive the summer heat. I'm Cynthia.' She assumed he would know she was the senator's wife.

He reached inside his jacket, withdrew two small photographs, and handed them to her.

Elliott with a young girl and boy and a blond woman. They were all beautiful, shining. It was, in fact, the woman and two children she met earlier, they were now standing by the pool. The woman was laughing with Elliott's campaign manager. The children, Ariana and Jeremy—she remembered their names—looked impatient.

In the photo, Elliott was beaming, his arms around the two kids and their mother in bathing suits; in the background, palm trees against a blue sky. She had forgotten to breathe and gulped air.

In the other photo, a beautiful dark-haired woman, possibly Latino, and a young boy in front of a restaurant in Provence. Le Poivre d'Ane, she'd been there with him. Her husband had gathered the woman and boy into his arms, looking insanely happy.

Her heart pounded with a kind of violence. She placed her hand on the wall of the house to steady herself.

'Are you all right?' he said.

'Yes.' But she wasn't.

He looked around but saw no one approaching. 'With these photos, you can destroy his political career. Something you may enjoy doing.'

She was suddenly furious that a perfect stranger would open this cruel wound, and at a party she'd worked on for months to get the right people on board.

'The opportunity is being offered out of regard for your goodwill toward the people of Massachusetts, and for a personal favor you did for a friend I can't name.'

Now her teeth were chattering. 'What do you want? What?'

'We want nothing in return.'

'Why?' she said.

'He doesn't deserve you. Thank you for not calling out your security people.'

The security people could still be called out; she saw two of them chatting each other up by the rose hedge.

Meadowgate coming up. Thank God for a familiar sight and people she loved at the end of the driveway. She turned in and stopped the car and sat for a moment to deal with this raw memory.

She recalled the overwhelming sense of coming apart. She had been shaking so intensely that she dropped the photos. Something inside her was collapsing like a wrecked building, timber by timber, stone by stone.

He picked up the photos; she could barely whisper.

'No thank you,' she said, as if declining a cup of tea. The photographs went back into the breast pocket of the seersucker jacket. He gave a curt nod and walked out to the allée of English box and was gone.

All that had happened before had not broken her. But the perfectly beautiful children, seeing their faces—that had broken her into a thousand pieces for all time.

On her second day at Hollyhock, she set up her easel in the garden. She must not waste these days. Elliott had not wasted his; he'd married soon after she left. The new wife, the one who had stood by the pool, was blond and petite, as was she, so it may have appeared to some that nothing at all had changed in Elliott's life, except for his failed bid for governor.

Her most recent Violet book had been published four years ago; she had lost momentum and would see if by some miracle she could regain it. Perhaps being in this beautiful place would inspire her to choose bright thoughts again. Perhaps the imaginary children who once gathered around her love seat would return; maybe she had a chance after all.

She would paint the pergola because the cloud of roses would be a challenge. She wasn't sure she had the patience for hundreds of blooms, all deserving at least a nod to Manet. But off she went, sweating through the first couple of hours with the sun at her back, hoping for what had so long been elusive, that moment when the painting began painting itself and she was along for the ride.

Had she loved him? He was smart, he was charming, he could be as fiercely bipartisan as he was partisan. In the beginning, he was easy to love. She'd never had anyone to love except a remarkable schoolteacher and of course her mother and father, though neither of them seemed to love her back. She believed they wanted to love her; they may even have planned to love her someday.

What she appreciated most was, she could count on Elliott to be there. She had never had anyone to count on for being there, yet after a very few years, he was rarely there. In the house on occasion, yes, and out with her to political affairs, but divorced from the rhythms of the relationship. She watched a man whose political career demanded visibility fade from her life. Whether the pictures were made public she didn't know or care; no media sought her out and she rarely read newspapers. Alice had informed her of his heavy losses in the political arena and the metastatic brain tumor that killed him.

She had contemplated suicide once before but was saved by a single known truth—she was happiest when making a book.

She loved the alchemy of it—conceiving it, typing or scribing the words, weaving the plot, illustrating the elemental scenes, emotionally splashing around in the paint colors, inhaling the paint odors, all. So far, she had three books out there that children were crazy about.

A favorite way to entice a story had been to lie on her old love seat with her legs dangling over the arm. In this inner gazing, she had seen children gathered around the love seat. She was not reading to them; she was drawing in the air and the drawings had voices speaking to the children, spinning out the story as she hatched it word for word. She knew when they were laughing and when they were paying attention and when they were distracted.

But children didn't gather around anymore. She had become completely frozen, barren of stories—an apple without a core, a window without a view. The books had not saved her.

She had come to Hollyhock to end her life and yet there she was, pouring her heart into painting the endless festoon of blossoms, and disappointing herself with the result. She had put the brush down and burrowed into the deep shade of the pergola. This was why she was here. Not just to put an end to living but to savor the pleasure of sitting in a cathedral of roses, and marveling at the number of guinea fowl speeding toward the back door of the house where Alice was scattering meal-worms.

Why did she keep hoping for more? Could there ever be any more than this?

Agitated, she looked again at the canvas, at the sketch of the pergola. Of the challenging mass of blooms, she had managed to render only three.

HARLEY

'So what you do,' he told Willie, 'is take this basket of squashes to Miss Pringle. Go around to th' back. If she's not home, set th' basket on th' back stoop. Th' front door's f'r her piano teachin' b'iness.'

What he was doin' was sendin' Miss Pringle a dozen squashes. She was a real good cook who learned all she knowed about cookin' from her granmaw, who was a French woman.

Miss Pringle, when she was tellin' stories, she sometimes forgot an' broke into speakin' French. He couldn't make out even one word but he liked hearin' it an' she liked hearin' him talk. So there you go—it was as good a swap as anybody could git.

'An' here's this,' he said.

He'd put th' book an' envelope back in th' green wrapper an' dropped it in a paper bag for Willie to take to th' bookstore. He figured a bookstore was a good place to send a book since that's where it would of come from in th' first place.

'Just drop it off,' he said, 'an' don't stand around chewin' th' fat. If Hope an' them is in th' back, leave it by th' credit machine.'

He'd left things from Lace by th' credit machine before if they was workin' in th' back with their mail order.

'If you see Hope, tell 'er it turned up at our place by mistake. You need to say that. *By mistake.*'

'What is it?' said Willie, lookin' in th' bag.

He wanted to say it's none of y'r business. 'It's a book.'

He'd rather powerwarsh a barn than trouble hisself with th' knick-knacks of everyday livin'.

TIM AND CYNTHIA

The first fire of the season was a primary event, and the night they generally got their ducks in a row for the holidays.

Cynthia came downstairs prepared for the Iditarod. Socks. Flannels. Fleece. A blanket.

'It's warm out there,' he said. 'Sixty-eight degrees!' But she was happy. And if she was happy, he was happy.

She settled on the sofa; he set out glasses, bites of sharp cheddar, a stem of white grapes, and a port recommended by Avis. He had acknowledged her sublime culinary genius and praised her linguini, though sixty grams max was his limit due to The Joy Killer, aka diabetes.

He sat, patted the sofa. Gus leaped onto his spot, turned around twice, and crashed.

'This meeting is called to order,' she said. 'To review—we'll have eighteen here for Thanksgiving. We talked about who's coming, but I've just received news of two surprise guests. I'll send you the list in a text.'

'Send an email. I don't know how to print a text.'

She had been his tech for eons but was currently leaving him to his own devices, so to speak.

He was thinking that leftovers would be as essential as the main act. After the Big One at two o'clock, he and Cynthia would provide Meadowgate with sandwich-makings for the following day and for those traveling. Food distribution must also include whatever leftover dark meat he could scavenge for Cynthia. A few leftovers for soup wouldn't hurt.

'I'll do a turkey and a ham,' he said. He was somewhat renowned for his baked ham; he liked to think people expected it. As for the bird, he was no Ina Garten, but he could muddle through.

'I'll do two gravies,' she said. 'Jugs of my tea, a gazillion lemon squares, and yeast rolls. Pauline's bringing a pumpkin pie. Kenny and Julie, asparagus from a friend's greenhouse. Lace, mashed potatoes with an illegal amount of butter and cream, to be done onsite. Cranberry relish from the Local. Jack is doing his specialty.'

'Popcorn balls!' He was a fan.

'And Dooley's baking two cherry pies.'

'One for him, one for us.'

'To conclude. Sweet Stuff is delivering a two-layer OMC. Whatever is left will be going out of this house immediately.' She drew a deep breath, exhaled. 'End of report.'

'You're amazing. All that reckoned and on paper, well ahead of the game.'

'Lace says I'm the family matriarch. Planning ahead is what matriarchs do. Whoever dreamed I'd be a *matriarch*? I always thought matriarchs looked like Queen Victoria in her golden years.'

To think that he shared a bed with this supersonic creature. Out of silent gratitude, he rubbed one of her sock feet resting in his lap.

'So about the surprise guests,' he said. 'Are you hoping I'll beg for a reveal?'

'I was, actually, but I'm over it. Sammy's coming and bringing a girlfriend!'

Sammy. With a girlfriend! He loved that bright, broken, pool-shooting genius. Though Sammy was on for Christmas at Meadowgate, no one had expected him for Thanksgiving on Wisteria Lane.

'She's an older woman. By four years.'

'Who?'

'Sammy's girlfriend. All I know is, she's a NICU nurse. And she has a little boy Jack's age!'

'Great! Wonderful!' Nobody dead, nobody lost and wandering. Plus the bonus of a girlfriend with a son *and* a wonderful job. There were times like these in families, times so good that hardly anyone stopped to notice, *We're all here! We're all vertical! The marvel of it!* Because other times also come to families, times when everyone stops to notice, and to grieve.

'Pauline, Buck, Jessie, Pooh—they'll all be here, of course, and Lace wants to invite Henry and Lucille for Christmas. Do you think they would come all the way from Miss'ippi?' She pronounced the name of his native state as he liked to say it.

'Let's give it a try.'

'Dooley asked if you could make your Rector's meatloaf for those arriving at Meadowgate the day before Thanksgiving. Harley would drive in to pick it up. Lace says he'll owe you big-time.'

He felt a dash puffed up; he hadn't expected much of his thrifty bachelor's meatloaf, but it had become something of a dark horse in the family.

'I'll put all this in your email. So, let's bring Henry and Lucille up as a Christmas gift. I just got my advance for *Violet Goes to the Met*.'

'They'll want the train,' he said. 'Fifty-fifty on first-class tickets and done. Brilliant! And congratulations on the advance, which means you'll be residing on another planet for how long?'

'The usual eternity. Sometime in January, I'll go up and make sketches at the Met, then I'm pretty full-on because there are paintings to finish for the hospital auction. But you'll survive, sweetheart; you always do.'

His wife drifted away when working on a book. There in the flesh, but missing in action—staring out the window; looking at him but not seeing. He would at times catch her gaze and say, 'Hello, anybody home?' That would call her back and they would laugh and he would hold her hand really tight, as if she might ascend like the red balloon of Albert Lamorisse.

He patted her leg to confirm that he would survive. 'I'll talk with Henry,' he said.

'Isn't it wonderful, Timothy? Your *brother*!' She never had a brother, half or otherwise. Or a sister or even a cousin. And now she had in-laws again—the good kind.

A few years ago, her husband had gone home to Holly Springs, where he'd grown up an only child in a marriage of misery. He learned several truths long in coming—among these, he had a half brother, Henry, younger by ten years. This life-changing news was followed by another astounding revelation—unless he, Timothy, would agree to donate stem cells to Henry, his brother would die. That simple and that complex, all at once. The chance of a match was five percent. Timothy had been a match. And Henry was alive and well now and married at a late age, just like her husband.

'So that's a wrap?' he said.

'Just one further morsel.'

She took an envelope from beneath a sofa cushion and handed it over. 'An early Christmas gift,' she said, 'from yours truly. I love you, and so does the rest of humanity.'

He read the note aloud. '*This certifies that Thanksgiving dinners with all the trimmings will be provided in the name of Father Timothy A. Kavanagh to the Children's Hospital maintenance crew, staff, patients, and their families on November twenty-second at noon . . .* '

He was an infernal weeper, always had been.

'I signed us up to be there,' she said.

Firelight, the scent of resin from the pine cones they added to the blaze, her feet in his lap. If this were in fact heaven, he would settle.

'I can hardly believe I'm married to a woman who knows how to make me happy.'

She gave him a sweetly philosophical look. 'I can hardly believe I'm married to a man I'm not afraid to love.'

DOOLEY

He wheeled onto the half-frozen track and entered the winter woods. The Gator engine was too loud for the woods; leaf mold and fungi wanted the moccasin foot.

In the clearing, he killed the engine and closed his eyes and listened to the sound of the place. The call of a cardinal. A crow. A red crossbill. The roiling of creek waters a few yards away.

Good light at two o'clock. A canopy of old hardwoods planted in front of the house in a crescent. He turned up his jacket collar, put the lunch baggie in his pocket, and walked around.

A couple of years had passed since he'd visited this neck of their woods; the place was bad then, but this was worse.

The roof, a goner. A derelict front porch pulling away from the house. Zero gutters.

It had been a rental during most of the Owens's ownership of Meadowgate, but nobody had lived here in nearly a decade. Early on, he and the guys had talked about taking it down, but that was no longer on their radar. Harley's advice was to 'Give it a while and it'll take its ownself down.'

At the rear of the house, a stash of old tires, hubcaps, rusted car fenders, Old Crow pint bottles, dead tree limbs, a busted-up cattle gate, bear scat. The least they could do was haul this mess to the county dump.

He took his peanut-butter-and-banana Elvis wrap out of the baggie and ate it as he checked the foundation. As far as he could tell, and he was no expert, it looked pretty good.

Flooring unsalvageable in two of the five rooms; warp in the other rooms. Framework solid. Dry wall mildewed, stone chimney needing hours of tuck-pointing, the job would require scaffolding. Toilet no, sinks no, firebox no, but yes to a walnut mantelpiece, fancy for a humble house like this.

Chicken bones, a dead squirrel, and a couple of dead birds in the fireplace. Former occupancy had included human vandals, one of them his biological father who'd been no credit to mankind. As far as he knew, nobody had grieved the passing of Clyde Barlowe a few years back.

Plumbing, sewage, and electrical would likely be total do-overs. He would ask Mink Hershell to take a look; Mink had been a home inspections guy. And who knows? Maybe Mink would think it's a tear-down and that would delete the whole craziness from his mind.

The idea of bringing the place back was a wild card; he hadn't mentioned it to Lace. Where would the money come from? His grandma Jacks used to say you cain't get blood from a turnip.

He and Lace were turnips. Living well and seeing light at the end of the tunnel, but turnips.

He could already feel the stress of unraveling the knot of this place. The best thing to do was salvage the walnut mantelpiece and let the house take itself down.

BUT HE COULDN'T get it out of his head.

'What do you think, Dad?'

'Pay attention to each of these three words from the missionary Hudson Taylor. If you decide to go ahead, here's what it will be.

'Impossible. Difficult. Done.'

HE'D LIVED OUT those three words one by one—in going to vet school, working his tail off, and pretty much passing with flying colors.

There were times when school had seemed impossible and he doubted he would make it. And yet, here he was and it was done.

He didn't have the time, he didn't have the money, he didn't have the bandwidth for this. He knew that if he launched into rehabbing the house in the woods, he would have to trust God totally.

Back in the day, he had prayed only when he happened to think about it. He had stepped lightly around God.

Then came Jack and Sadie. If having the responsibility of a vet practice and a start-up cattle farm didn't do it, having kids sent him straight to the throne—he couldn't afford the risk of stepping lightly anymore.

WILLIE

Harley said it was a book an' it looked like it might be a book by th' shape of it in th' green wrapper. Bein' educated, Miss Pringle would naturally like a book.

He could not pull up in his head th' exact instructions Harley give him. He'd been accused lately of not listenin' an' maybe that was right—he hadn't listened close enough to remember exactly which place th' paper bag was to go to.

Down at the bookstore, they had a whole buildin' full of books, they did not need another book. What Hope an' them needed is fresh garden produce because they was workin' all th' time an' could not manage a garden theirself.

So that was th' way all that was supposed to go an' he'd make Miss Pringle his first stop. He tried to call Harley on his cell to see how things was goin' with th' steers, an' ask a'gin what went where. But all he got was heavy breathin' an' *Leave a message.*

Miss Pringle come to th' back stoop dressed up for teachin'.

He never knew what to say to a woman who could make a actual livin' playin' a musical instrument. Ol' Harley thought she hung th' moon, but she made him feel shy as a fawn.

'Bonjour, Willie!' she said, lookin' happy to see him.

'Yes, ma'am, I hope you're doin' all right.'

'Indeed I am, thank you. And you?'

'Real good,' he said, in a hurry to get done. 'Harley wanted you to have this,' he said, holdin' out th' paper bag. Harley had some kind of attachment to Miss Pringle for sure, but he'd never asked what kind.

'Oh!' she said, lookin' down in there. 'Merci beaucoup. Thank you very much, Willie.'

'It's a book,' he said, proud to know.

HARLEY

Willie had went out an' looked at th' steers an' said they was all right. They had cooked a good dinner an' eat it on th' porch as it was a warm November day.

Willie hadn't said nothin' about his trip to town.

After they cleaned up th' kitchen they was settin' in th' livin' room watchin' th' History Channel. He worked th' remote because it was his TV.

He muted a commercial an' went for it. 'What did Miss Pringle say about 'er squashes?'

Willie give 'im a sharp look.

'Did she thank you?'

'She did, she did,' said Willie.

'Did you say they was from Harley?'

'I did. I said this is from Harley is what I said.'

'So that was th' end of it?'

'Right there was th' end of it. Looked like she was dressed for teachin'. I seen Grace Murphy comin' in as I pulled out th' drive. It was a quick visit. Real quick.'

Willie motioned for Unmute, and there went a bunch of people diggin' around in a pharaoh's tomb. Talkin' to Willie tonight was as satisfyin' as talkin' to a broom handle. He waited 'til th' show was over and powered off th' History Channel.

'Miss Pringle didn't ask how I was doin' or nothin'?'

'Nossir. Didn't ask nothin'. A real quick visit.'

Clock tickin'. Willie starin' at th' wood stacked at th' fireplace.

'Did you ask 'er how she was?'

'I did. I sure did. Said she was all right.'

If livin' with Willie was anything like bein' married, he was glad he'd never gone down that road full of roofin' nails.

'What did Hope an' them do with that book I sent over there? Did you tell 'em it landed out here by *mistake*?'

Willie's hearin' was goin' bad, he could tell. Willie got up quick as he could an' went to the kitchen an' started Swifferin.' Some people chew tobacco, some drink whisky, some gamble. Willie Swiffered to relax hisself.

ESTHER

Marcie had called before they could even get th' coffee goin'.

'Mama! Happy anniversary an' many more! Daddy found you th' cutest card, he took forever pickin' it out an' writin' th' message. Hope you like it!'

Th' way th' girls knew everything goin' on over here you'd think there was hidden cameras in every room.

She an' Ray were sittin' in th' nook next to th' kitchen. In honor of their seventieth anniversary th' TV was on Mute an' they were lookin' at th' OMC on th' kitchen counter. It could not be cut before the girls came over after school with two great-grans an' three great-greats.

'They say if you're stubborn you live longer,' she said, makin' conversation.

'Stubborn as you are, Sugar Babe, you'll live to be two hundred plus change. But I'm gon' have to go on without you 'cause no way I'm hangin' around for th' scenery.'

'You've been prayin' to go first, I know you have—it's your only way out of livin' with me.'

He laughed. 'Awww, now. What you want on your headstone?'

'She ruled.'

'You been thinkin' about that, I can tell.'

'What you want on yours?' she said. 'It'll be right next to mine.'

'She ruled.'

She did not laugh; th' girls had spoiled him to death by laughin' at his wisecracks.

'I'll be glad to go when th' time comes,' he said.

'Glad to go? Not me.'

'You're scared to go,' he said. 'But there's nothin' to be scared of.'

'That's what they say.'

'You're caught up with th' Lord, right?'

'As caught up as I'm gonna be,' she said.

'If we eat a piece of that cake, both of us havin' diabetes, we could practice what it's like bein' dead.'

'Why I bought that cake I do not know. Just to look at, was one reason. But th' girls are comin' an' they'll take home th' leftovers an' it'll be history by five-thirty, so have a good look.'

'That's a fine howdy-do,' he said. 'We get to look at it sittin' on' th' counter all dolled up with a sprig of whatchamacallit an' we can't eat it?'

'Let's just look at it,' she said. 'We don't have to *eat* it to enjoy it.'

'Ain't nobody sits an' looks at a OMC,' he said. 'This is makin' me nervous.'

'Get over it. Learn to bloom where you're planted or whatever.'

'There's no way I can look at that cake an' not have a piece. No way.'

'Step out to th' porch an' get ahold of yourself. Look what it did to Father Tim back in th' day, he was in a diabetic coma for cryin' out loud. I think he pulled a doozy an' had two comas. One from this very cake.'

'We could scrape off th' frostin' and just have half a coma. How's that?'

It was makin' her nervous, too. She heaved a sigh, gripped th' arms of her recliner, an' noticed her knuckles were white. 'So cut us a piece an' we'll share it. If you go in a coma, I'm goin' with you.'

'That's th' spirit,' he said. In honor of their anniversary, he hauled himself up from his chair without groanin'.

'You know what, Dumplin', I deserve a medal for puttin' up with you for seventy years.' He cut a slice, put it on th' plate, an' licked th' knife blade.

'I deserve a medal for puttin' up with myself,' she said. 'It's hard to be old an' out of whack.'

'You're old, Honey Bun, but you ain't out of whack, I can tell you that.'

'Don't mess up another plate. Let's eat it off th' same plate. Two forks.'

'Oh, mercy,' he said, takin' a bite. 'Mercy, mercy.'

'It's her original recipe, bless 'er heart. Th' deal is, Sweet Stuff bakes it exactly by th' recipe or Esther Bolick herself comes back an' haunts th' place. She's gone, what, five years now?'

'Sounds about right,' he said. 'This little town didn't have room for two Esthers. One had to go.'

'She made a difference with that cake,' she said, takin' a bite. 'Carried one around to everybody an' his brother.' Took another bite. 'Lord help, this is sinful. Old Man Mueller livin' out yonder in th' sticks an' there she was on his porch in th' dead of winter with a two-layer that cost a hundred dollars to make.' She handed off the plate.

'Not a hundred,' he said.

'Close to it. You remember that porch, it was fallin' off th' side of his house. Stop lickin' th' plate.'

'I was raised to lick th' plate. A compliment to th' cook.'

He shuffled to the kitchen, put th' plate an' forks in th' dishwasher, an' took somethin' out of th' knife drawer.

He handed her an envelope.

There was his strong, back-slanted cursive, which he used for special occasions.

Doll Face

She grinned. Doll Face was what he called her the first time they laid eyes on each other. They were sittin' on that quilt at th' church picnic, she was wearin' a little sundress with cherries on it. She had shown her arms back then. She had been so happy eatin' his fried chicken an' coleslaw an' there he was, tall as a tree an' so good-lookin' it was painful. A man who's good-lookin' is one thing, a man who's good-lookin' an' can cook is a whole other thing. Th' real miracle was, he was single.

Doll Face

Th' word she'd seen on that other envelope was way too poetic for reality. Life was not poetic. Life was anything *but* poetic.

She opened th' envelope an' took out th' card, which had a Snoopy on it, an' read th' message.

I must have been drunk when I asked you to marry me. Could we rethink this over supper tonight? Fried chicken and coleslaw.

Still yours for better or worse—mostly worse but I can handle it.

She knew she was askin' for trouble but she couldn't help herself. 'Come over here an' give me some sugar,' she said.

He pulled a dinin' room chair next to her recliner an' sat down an' leaned over an' did exactly what she told him to do.

'Happy anniversary, you ol' scalawag,' she said.

'Happy anniversary, you ol' battle-ax,' he said.

That's th' way it had always been with them.

HELENE PRINGLE

She would tidy up from the lesson and have a cup of tea and see what Mr. Welch had sent from Meadowgate.

The previous item from Mr. Welch had been a pumpkin, which she displayed on the front steps next to a pot of marigolds. Later she had cut open the pumpkin—not an easy task at all. In truth, she would never attempt such a thing again. A hammer, a meat cleaver, a screwdriver; it had taken half the contents of her kitchen drawer to get it open, but it had made several pies, which she had frozen to give at Christmas. One to the Kavanaghs next door; one to Mr. Welch; one to Avis Packard, who delivered groceries to her in bad weather; and one for herself. She rarely kept her baking for herself and looked forward to the luxury of a pie sitting on her own counter. It would be festive.

She put the cozy on the teapot and set the pot on the kitchen table. She continued to be amazed by her students. Grace Murphy, for one example. Only weeks into her lessons and she had a most beautiful sense of rhythm and timing.

Grace was a refreshment, the real coin, *la vraie pièce*. And writing a book! Buzzing along on page forty-seven, she said. About a widow who collects homeless people and has an interest in small-town skullduggery. She went further to confide that the widow had a forever friend in a gentleman, but she could not reveal more as it would be a spoiler. When she inquired what a forever friend might be, Grace said, 'Nothing romantic, just two people who have a special place in each other's hearts forever.' She looked forward to Grace's twice-weekly lessons as she had looked forward to recess as a child.

She waited for the Earl Grey to brew and poured a cup. Though her sense of smell was not what it used to be, she held the cup close to inhale the steamy fragrance. How did anyone exist without their tea?

She peered into the bag from Meadowgate.

A book from Mr. Welch!

She removed it from the bag and displayed it on the table next to the teapot. Wrapped but no bow. And rather loosely wrapped, as if by a distracted child. Of course, Mr. Welch was a man, and how often are men trained to wrap a gift? That it was a book was wonder enough.

She did not, of course, feel any shred of romantic love for her former tenant—he was uneducated and toothless. But she had certainly allowed herself to feel a warm and possibly maternal affection for his easy laughter, quick wit, and untainted heart.

Especially delightful—poignant, really—was his story of going to a one-room schoolhouse in what he called 'a holler.' A woodstove heated the schoolhouse, which was also the living quarters of a young teacher from Boston. Boston! Her own hometown after the years in France.

Mr. Welch had said she was very pretty, this Miss Downs.

He couldn't hide his fondness, even now, for the young woman from whom he learned cursive and simple arithmetic.

It turned out that the man paid to maintain the unpainted schoolhouse and split Miss Downs's firewood had fallen ill. Mr. Welch took on the task himself. Twelve years old and splitting wood for his teacher and starting the morning fire!

She sipped her tea.

He had walked to his one-room school every morning with a sweet potato just off the coals of his father's hearth. He rolled it up in a rag and carried it under his jacket, he said. It helped keep him warm on his long walk and would later serve as lunch.

She could just see the young teacher greeting the ragged little creature who, one morning in winter, had walked to school wearing one shoe.

Harley, she said, did you lose a shoe?

No, ma'am, he said. I found one.

And what was his opinion of that grinding hard time in his life? 'Them was th' good ol' days.'

She smiled, sipped her tea, then loosened the tape and pulled the book from its green wrapper.

A cow on a sofa. A book of poems by someone named Billy. Odd that the poet hadn't used the more formal appellation of William for a book of verse, Billy seeming better suited for a writer of fiction.

She was reading the end flap when something slipped from between the pages.

She noticed her sharp intake of breath and the need to sit down. But she was already sitting down. She leaned back in the chair, gathering herself. Something like a shock wave had swept over her, she couldn't explain it. The word on the envelope. . . .

This couldn't possibly be from Mr. Welch. And she was most assuredly not Mr. Welch's beloved! Not under any circumstance. She leaned forward and studied the envelope.

The ink, the graceful slant of the nib, the silken paper stock, the watermark . . .

There must be some mistake. This was utterly unlike anything he might have penned. And yet Willie had said it was from his friend Harley. Should that be true, had she tempted him in some misleading way? No! Never! Not in the least!

First of all, Mr. Welch would not trespass into the arena of such language. Indeed, he couldn't comprehend such language. Or was there something in him that she didn't know?

Mon Dieu! The thought was alarming.

Surely there was nothing sly or hidden about Harley Welch; he was as plain and transparent as they come. He had never given her cause for concern about his character. Quite the contrary. But the book had been delivered to her from Meadowgate, and Willie had plainly said . . .

He had always called her Miss Pringle, never Helene; she had never given him permission to use her forename. As an alumnus of Dana Hall, she felt a distinct responsibility to practice common courtesies so lacking in today's world.

She stood and walked briskly to the living room and around the Steinway and through the little pantry and back to the kitchen. She was trembling. If the book reflected the sentiment written on the envelope, she did not wish to look inside the book.

The tea wasn't working its dependable consolation. Something sought to present itself to her conscience, but she was denying it. The whole business was affecting the rhythm of her heart.

And what if this were a joke? But the costly paper stock and cultivated handwriting and the word itself could not be a joke. These elements reflected a refinement unpossessed by the coarse mind of a joker. Could he have paid someone to do this, as Cyrano had been engaged to write Roxane?

Her tea had grown cold, the light was fading. She had no appetite for the simple dinner she had put together after today's lessons.

She realized she was trying to deny what happened the moment she spied the word. Her heart had been instantly alerted—and if she were honest, dangerously warmed. The sight of that word inscribed on the crème stock had struck her with uncommon force.

In that one moment, she perceived that word to have been written for her. She had felt herself beloved.

Like a branding, it had happened quickly; she had no time to prepare or defend herself. She had seen the word through the lens of an unguarded heart and was altered in a way she could not understand.

She had been thinking of leaving Mitford—where she would go, she hadn't decided. But such thinking had been that of a loveless woman, which she had been only minutes ago.

As some people before death see their lives flash before them, she saw her future. She knew now that she would not move away—she would go out into the world in which she found herself—this strange yet utterly familiar village of Mitford. She would bloom, as the refrigerator magnet commanded her to do, where she was planted.

In past years, she had gone only so far with God—happily turning over a certain portion of herself and thinking that was enough. Wasn't that enough—a portion? Why should God have it all? If he had given her free will, as she had been told, surely he wasn't expecting every tidbit, scrap, and trifle.

And yet she was beloved, every crumb of her beloved—for reasons she couldn't know. And why her? She hadn't stood out or made a noise in the world. And there was that dreadful time she acted as a common thief and stole the bronze angel from Father Tim. To make things very much worse, she had sued him. Sued him!

She rarely revisited that memory; it was humiliating, grievous. That was not who she was at all; she had somehow stepped outside herself and been desperately wrong.

She had withdrawn the lawsuit, of course, and returned the angel. He had not only forgiven her, but—*merveille des merveilles!*—given her the angel for all time. Kindness was one thing, but kindness-upon-kindness was another.

Only now did she fully realize what pain her behavior must have caused both Father Tim and Cynthia. That she had done such a thing to decent human beings to whom she owed so much was proof that she was undeserving of God's love.

And yet, in one single, startled moment, she knew she was loved. A gusher had fallen upon her. A baptism.

She must abide with this epiphany, let it distill. She could not go rushing about, stuffing it into her spacious compartment of Reason. With Reason, all that just happened could be dismantled entirely.

She went up to her bedroom and stood before the mirror over her grandmother's bureau, staring at her reflection. She expected some other countenance to stare back, yet there she was—hair in a bun, the tidy collar of her dress, the small pearl earrings, her eyes gray-blue.

She remembered having the opportunity to be beautiful in the way she presented herself to the world. But the idea of being beautiful had frightened her, and she had stood away from it and pulled her hair into its severe knot.

She had tightened her body as someone might tighten a drawer knob. She had annulled a certain languor in her gait and tried to walk like a woman of great purpose. As a child, she had made friends with purpose, but great purpose had eluded her.

In the mirror's reflection, also—the two windows of her bedroom, her grandmother's fragile curtains, the chaste bed with its French linens—everything appeared to be the same. But she was different. And she must not be afraid.

She pulled down the shades, removed her clothes, and slipped into a loose gown. She had never, unless ill, taken to her bed in the light of day.

She lay still, trying to translate the language of her beating heart.

DOOLEY

They had disappeared into the storage room of the clinic and latched the door. Lace was unpacking sandwiches and chips; he lugged over a couple of wooden crates.

'So what do you want for Christmas?' he said.

'Sleep. That's all. No, wait. Sleep and French fries, aioli, please.'

'Me, too. Double ditto.'

'We've got twenty minutes,' he said, checking his watch. He was a little jittery about the splenectomy he'd be doing on Harvey, a beagle that had competed in the Westminster Dog Show. The little guy's entire family would show up, parents and seven kids, with a lunch basket and homework. They would set up a virtual household in the waiting room while the deed was being done. They adored Harvey; everybody adored Harvey. Like so many dogs these days, there was a mass. Maybe cancer. But maybe not.

His schedule and Lace's had been intense. He needed this break behind a latched door that nobody could walk through in need of something.

Fried baloney. Yes! Double slices crispy around the edges and still warm—with mustard on white-trash white bread. His favorite.

Lace tore into her sandwich like he tore into his—famished, in a hurry. He remembered how their life could have gone. She had finished school before he did. During a hard time in their relationship, she was planning to live in New York. She would paint murals in rich people's apartments, she said.

A couple of times they drove up together and 'rehearsed' the city as a place to live and work. He'd seen her on those insanely busy streets carrying her huge art portfolio. She hailed taxis as if she already lived there, as if he was a country dude who didn't know from hailing taxis. In her cropped jeans and beat-up UVA blazer, she was a star.

All through school, they usually saw each other twice a month. A lot of craziness had been hammered out during that long run of time together. No way could he finish the boot camp of vet school at UGA and run back and forth to New York City. The very thought was killin' him but he kept his mouth shut—he'd learned that much.

Then she got the offer from the Chapel Hill nonprofit. No money to speak of—teaching art to kids she fell in love with was enough. In two weeks, she was settled on home ground, with just five hours and a couple of speeding tickets between them. Teaching the kids had saved their necks.

'You took a chance on me,' he said.

'You took a chance on me.'

'Any regrets?'

'None that I could ever in a hundred years think of,' she said. 'Why do you ask?'

He patted her knee, grinned. 'Just checkin', babe, just checkin'.'

Five minutes. Not a good time to bring it up. He would wait.

'Found a home for Ruby,' he said.

'Thelma's old mare! Ruby must be twenty-five years old by now.'

'Twenty-seven, twenty-eight, easy. The new living arrangement comes with thirty acres and a mule. And two kids who'll treat her like the grand old lady she is.'

'You're the best, Dools.'

But he couldn't wait. If you really looked at the situation, waiting wasn't an option.

'What are we gon' do about Harley and Willie?' he said.

'Meaning?'

'They're gettin' up there. Harley's knees, Willie's back, that old shoulder injury. I didn't want to talk about it yet, but it's on my mind a lot. We need to start thinkin' about it together.'

'They're family,' she said. 'I think about it, too. I just don't have any idea . . . '

'We'll still need somebody to live on the place. Somebody young.' He sighed, couldn't help it. He shouldn't have mentioned it.

She got up and moved her crate back where it came from. 'Okay, we can't figure it out right now because right now, you've got to go in there and save lives and carry on your mission of rehoming, and we can talk about it this weekend—which is when we'll work on the Christmas party plans.'

He stood up and moved his crate into place. He didn't look forward to planning a family get-together that included his mother. Drama. Always drama. But they always included her because it was the right thing to do.

'I'll go out and love on Harvey's family,' she said. 'I saw cookies in their lunch basket. Peanut butter. I'll snag one for you, doc.'

He grabbed his scrubs off the hook. 'Clyde Perry dropped by this mornin'.'

'Our stand-up farmer comic? How's Peggy? Did she get a good report?'

'Yep. Good report.' He shucked out of his khakis and long-sleeve T-shirt, pulled on his scrubs. 'On the home front, a couple of financial windfalls. He said they sold their vacuum cleaner.'

'Why?'

'Peggy said it was just gatherin' dust. Better yet, he sold this year's entire corn crop to a pirate. He got a buccaneer!'

They cracked up. Even bad jokes were good when you lived in the boonies, twenty miles from a decent French fry.

'What are they doin' in there?' Blake asked Amanda.

'Livin' th' good life,' she said. 'Smellin' th' roses. Bein' in th' moment.'

ESTHER

She went for compromise, which she'd done plenty of as mayor.

Th' girls an' their families would be havin' dinner at their own houses, then comin' to Mamaw an' Papaw for pie an' ice cream.

And, she wrote in an email to Marcie, cc'ing the rest of th' girls, the grown-ups will be expected to have fruitcake in addition to pie and ice cream. I have not been faithfully pouring Wild Turkey on that humongous doorstop for nothing.

Th' husbands, th' grans, th' greats an' great-greats would collect their gifts of a ten an' a Hershey. Th' girls would get gift certificates to Cracker Barrel in Wesley, which would give them a good outing with their grans.

As for gifts outside th' family, Father Tim would get a Hershey, which he could share with Cynthia, plus ten bucks. Rumor had it that Cynthia made a killin' off those little cat books so they didn't need th' money—so th' ten was a *token* for all th' times he'd helped her out. He could at least buy a Starbucks hazelnut latte, her personal favorite, an' know it was from Esther an' Ray.

Who else? Lord knows she could hardly keep up these days an' no, it was not old age. Everybody blamed everything on old age. They say you fall because you're old. You do no such thing. You fall because you're not payin' attention.

As for old age bein' th' cause for memory loss, not true! Look at her girls.

Charlene could not keep up with her readin' glasses, Marcie could not keep up with her dentures, Tammy Leigh could not keep up with her Bible study notebook, Mona could not keep up with her triflin' husband, an' none of 'em could keep up with their grandkids.

If she an' Ray could take their RV out like they used to, they would not be in Mitford thinkin' about Christmas, no way. They'd be at their campground in Pensacola—cookin' all-beef hotdogs on th' grill, wearin' their baggy travel pants, sittin' under th' awning that pulled out from th' side of Goldie, which is what they named their RV, bein' short for Golden Oldie.

But th' Goldie years were history. Ninety-three is no time to be out on th' asphalt with a cardiac arrest an' no doctor for a hundred miles.

Th' problem with bein' housebound was you had too much time to think. In her case, she thought about th' relationship with her girls; it was what Tammy Leigh called 'fraught.' She had to google that.

Father Tim would be the closest thing she could think of to a shrink. He would listen, he would not judge, an' he would not go blabbin' all over town whatever you told him.

She would just come right out with it an' not beat around th' bush. 'I think I failed with my girls,' she would say.

After he got through tellin' her what to do about it, she would definitely remind him what she didn't fail at.

'What I didn't fail at,' she'd say, 'was mayorin' this town for sixteen years.' In case he'd forgotten, she would tell him again what everybody knew.

'First thing I did, I founded th' merchants association an' handed 'em a broom. Every merchant, fourteen to be exact, got a broom—out of my own pocket, mind you. An' what did they do? They started sweepin' their sidewalks an' washin' their display windows like they *lived* in this town, like they were proud to *be* here, for crap's sake.'

'I remember you makin' us pick up trash,' he might say. 'That was memorable.'

'Th' mayor's office said to people, "This is *your* town, these are *your* streets, these are *your* tax dollars at work. Show some *pride*!"'

He would nod; he'd been a big supporter. 'You wouldn't want to be seen walking past a piece of trash without picking it up and putting it in the bin,' he'd say.

'Absolutely!' she'd say. 'An' you remember what else happened.'

'I do, I do. Your invaluable mayoral vote broke the tie of your fellow town leaders and determined the destiny of our community—that was the famous vote that kept the box stores out of Mitford and saved the day for all time.'

Th' only person besides Ray Cunnin'ham who had totally appreciated her hard work for th' town was Father Tim Kavanagh. She would consider givin' him a twenty with his Hershey.

TIM

When it came to matters of the table, discipline was not his long suit. His long suit, defined in childhood, was flaky biscuits with a crunch onto salty ham and homemade mustard; pan dressing with its savory crust around the edges; potatoes mashed with a cooked turnip, heavy cream, and a lawless gob of butter. Not to mention yeast rolls, of course. No, not to even mention the decadent, featherweight Mississippi yeast roll.

If that wasn't enough to send a diabetic to his Maker, he had also been conditioned in his youth to love pumpkin chiffon pie and coconut cake, preferably served with a detonating blast of chickory coffee, which he learned to drink at age twelve. The childhood consolations of the table could be pretty ruinous for the grown-up.

The holydays were of course a nonstop carousel of carbs. That said, he must be choosey. He would allow himself a gain of four pounds over the upcoming weeks. Not three, not five, just four. And he'd do it with a clear conscience. He would join the rest of the overprivileged to repair the damage in January.

Meantime, he'd relish one of the great gifts of retirement—being off-leash for Christmas. Did he miss priesting? He did. But selfish as it may seem, the freedom to simply be a child of God at Christmas was wonderful; he liked being loosed on the wider world, splashing in the occasional mud puddle.

TIM AND LOUELLA

'Doc Wilson says I'm good to go 'cept for my bad knees an' my eyes givin' out with th' macular.'

Louella had combed her hair, put on lipstick, and was shielded from dark forces by her well-worn prayer shawl.

'He said I could be livin' a long time yet. But whenever th' good Lord calls, I'm ready to go an' lookin' forward to it. You still gon' preach my funeral?'

'As well as you're comin' along, maybe you'll preach mine. And don't be shy about passin' th' plate; th' church needs th' money.'

They never missed a chance to laugh.

Nurse Kennedy peered into the room. 'What y'all doin' in here?'

'Talkin' 'bout bein' dead,' said Louella.

'I'll prob'ly be dead myself, after this shift. It's been a cattle-call today. Enjoy your supper—it's chicken an' dumplin's. You want th' kitchen to send you up a plate, Father?'

'My wife is making dinner as we speak, but thanks, Kennedy. Go home and get some rest.'

'No rest for th' wicked. I've got two Yorkies at home—ten weeks old.'

'You don't even like dogs,' he said.

'It's a long story!' And away went Kennedy, Head Nurse and Chief

Bottle Washer, who saw him through two diabetic comas during her former years at Mitford Hospital.

'She babyin' them little dogs. People's got to have somebody to love. You still gon' preach my funeral?'

'Absolutely. If I can keep from bawlin'.'

'I hear you preached a sermon that wadn't nothin' but bawlin'.'

'Hate to say it, but that's true.'

'Just stood up there in th' pulpit in your priest robes crossin' yourself an' cryin'.'

'Couldn't help it.'

'All 'cause of that preacher who went and tried to kill hisself.'

'He's out there somewhere, healing, I hope.'

On the windowsill, her small clock ticking away.

'Ever'body got tears,' she said. 'Some people afraid to let 'em out. You can get sick holdin' 'em in. What you gon' say 'bout Louella Baxter Marshall?'

'Gon' say I loved you like an aunt or a big sister, like blood.'

She chuckled. 'What else you gon' say?'

'Gon' say you were brave. And good. And exceptional.'

'Brave an' good is enough right there. Wish I could hear it when you preach my funeral.'

'Maybe you can.'

'I hope you'll give me some hand-clappin' gospel music. Gospel reach down to th' deep waters of th' soul an' turn tears to joy.'

'We'll do our best; you have my word.'

He knew about tears and gospel music. He was ten years old and devastated when Peggy left and couldn't be found. He often hid in the bushes at her church, watching who went in, then watching who came out laughing and happy. Maybe he would find her there, just a mile up the dirt road, living her life as if she'd never been the one to wipe the tears he couldn't hold in, the one who believed him to be good even when he was bad.

All those hours in the bushes with his suffering, he could hear the music in the church like it would bust the roof off. He associated his suffering with that music. When he visited her empty one-room house down the yard, he sniffed up all the smells of her—fried bacon, cold ashes, chickory coffee, as if he could store them somewhere in his lungs, close to his heart.

'Mountain people all white an' can't sing gospel. An' here I can sing them ol' dusty Episcopal hymns like I know what I'm doin'. Miss Sadie could sing 'em backwards an' forwards. She sang soprano an' I'd come in with alto an' that's th' way we'd go up to bed, stoppin' to rest on th' landin'. Long as she could still climb th' steps, we sang ourself up to heaven every night.'

'Were you lonesome for your people up here in these hills?'

'Oh, I was, yes, I was. In summer I got to know th' colored help who came with their white families. But winter was a different story.

'After th' leaves dropped off, I was th' only colored on this mountain. But it got so I could look right through peoples' skin an' get on th' inside—which is all that matters anyhow. I got along fine most of th' time. The rest of th' time we don't need to talk about.

'I left up here when I was sixteen so I had a lot of years with my people in Atlanta, with my wonderful husband, Moses, and my sweet dead boy an' my grandson. An' every day I remember my little mama China Mae, who stayed like a child all her life. She loved me as best she could. She was a happy little woman you wanted to be around.

'Somethin' I jus' realized when you aks me that question. Miss Sadie was my people, too. We was each other's people in th' true meanin' of that word; we was sisters under th' skin.'

He was on the board of Hope House; he knew the careful wording of Miss Sadie's last will and testament. Essentially, Louella Baxter Marshall could occupy Room Number One for as long as she lived and be accorded all rights and privileges of the House, including nursing and memory care. There was even a clause allowing her to enjoy rights to the kitchen, as cooking was her favorite activity and would be 'beneficial to her emotional health.' Until recently, Louella had baked biscuits and cookies for House events, which had put a further shine on her celebrity as *Number One*.

'You know 'bout my daddy, Soot. Do you git tired of hearin' th' stories 'bout my people?'

'That's one of the things friends are for—to listen to our repeat stories.'

'He drove his white folks up to Mitford every summer in that big Packard car. It had white sidewall tires. They say he had special gloves to wear settin' a fancy table, an' could drive any kind of a contraption they was—a wagon or a horse carriage or even a boat if you had one. What else was it he could do?'

'He could preach a sermon that would bring people to the throne, they said, and when he preached, his stutter went away.' He was proud to help her remember.

'Thass right. What else?'

'They said he could catch a mountain trout of considerable size and fry it for the governor over an open fire.'

'That's th' one I sometimes forget. My fav'rite is him flyin' down th' hill on his bicycle from up at th' ol' Boxwood place. They said his coattails would be jus' *sailin'* out behind.

'When people seen him flyin' to town in that black suit on a black bicycle—they knew they was *seein'* somethin'. They said my daddy was th' most excitin'est human bein' in these hills.'

'I believe it.'

'You know I never laid eyes on a picture of him. This was all passed down by mouth an' I see him good as if I was standin' right there in th' street, watchin'.'

As in music, a good story needs a pause. He sat silent, contented. The clock did its busy work.

'They say he loved my mama, really loved my mama an' wanted to marry her in th' little church he built up here for colored. You know white people didn't let colored git married unless you had a colored church to do it in. I hadn't been born yet but they knew I was comin' an' he wanted to take Mama an' me down to Atlanta, but Miss Sadie's daddy, he was a hateful man. A *hateful* man! He was gon' put my daddy in jail if he didn't git shot first. It was a ruckus in Mitford, people's guns come out. You don't want to know what a ruckus they say it was. An' the people up at Boxwood sent him back to Atlanta on th' bus with a shoebox of fried chicken. He wadn't allowed to take my mama. After that ol' Boxwood man died, Miss Bertie, his daughter, gave my daddy that Packard automobile. They say he come up to git it in th' middle of th' night so he wouldn' be caught. But that kindness was too little, too late.'

He handed her the box of tissues—at one time or another over the years, they had both needed it.

With her stories, Louella had passed along the gift of imagining her father. He, also, could see the tall, thin, blue-black man, coattails flyin', as if Tim Kavanagh had stood there watching.

He often came to Louella with stories of his own people and their doings—the way their hayfields smelled after the first spring mow, the spotted Moon and Stars watermelons they grew and sold, how gulls flew inland and pecked their Mississippi seeds from fresh-plowed earth.

Louella threw open the door of her imagination to receive his people—his daddy, his mother, Peggy, Louis, his banker when he was ten years old and opening his first savings account, his Baptist church and his Anglican church and how having both in his life had made him bigger somehow yet more confused, and how it felt to perform the sacrilege of climbing the water tower with Tommy. She listened to what his people cooked and how they talked and how their roads were unpaved and full of potholes and how it didn't matter, really, no use to call up the president of the United States and get your trousers in a twist like his daddy had done, it was enough to just ride to town over th' potholes, knocking around in the backseat of a Buick town car with a dime in your pocket.

And there he was, chasing his own memories and missing Louella's tribute to her maternal grandmother.

'. . . flog you like a rooster if you stepped out of line. But oh, honey, she could cook. I'd give a widow's pension for a taste of her little green limas an' her chick'ry coffee. That ol' coffee pot looked like a Army tank rolled over it, then backed up and hit it again. She give me that pot for a weddin' present when I jumped th' broom with Moses. Don't you wish you could have a taste of somethin' your mama used to cook?'

'My mama,' he said, 'worked a garden as big as Rhode Island, which was open to the public. So Peggy did most of the cooking when I was a kid. Peggy's gaining on a hundred and one now and in good health. She was my second mother, as you know, 'til I was ten.'

'You got a black second mama, a black half-brother, an' you got Louella. Thass more black folks in yo' life than I got!'

'I'll share,' he said. He decided her laughter had grown deeper in the mezzo register, like molasses on a hot biscuit.

'My brother will be coming for Christmas with his wife, Lucille. We'll be up to see you. I know you don't like going out these days.'

'Too much trouble,' she said. 'Messin' with this wheelchair and my bad knees in this cold weather. But I ain't gettin' no knee surgeries, nossir, I'm too old for surgeries.'

He reached into his jacket pocket and handed her the small box. 'I brought you an early Christmas present.'

Louella possessed one of the biggest smiles he ever saw on a human face. 'Goes nearabout ear to ear,' Uncle Billy once said.

She untied the ribbon and rolled it around her finger. 'I don't throw away ribbon,' she said, putting it in the drawer next to her chair.

She lifted the lid of the box. 'An' look at this! I've used what you give me last year down to a nub. You know I wear my lipstick most every day. I have to be sick as a cat to not wear my Bright Cherry. I sure appreciate it, honey.'

'Remember how Miss Sadie scolded you for calling the village priest honey?'

They had a chuckle.

'What you givin' yo' sweet wife for Christmas?'

'She asked for a letter. Something . . . romantic. She likes that sort of thing.'

'Of course she do. All us do.'

'So I wrote it and it just . . . disappeared.'

'Disappeared?'

'I think I remember leaving it on my desk, and haven't seen it since. You fell that day and I ran up here to check on you.'

'I'm sorry 'bout that foolishness. I tripped over th' scatter rug at th' bathroom door yonder, an' by evenin' my scatter rugs was all gone. Not even a bye-bye. But yo' letter. You gon' find it.'

'You really think so?'

'I'm gon' pray on it.'

'Thank you. It means something to have . . . you know, written it.'

He stood to leave and she looked up at him with affection.

'Ever'thing gon' be all right,' she said.

He stooped and kissed her cheek. She smelled like Coty's bath powder. His mother had used Coty's bath powder and had given Peggy a box of Coty's. When he was coming up, all women smelled like Coty's, and that was a good thing. Evening in Paris was another womanly smell of his boyhood. It made his sinuses drain.

He was whistling as he crossed the parking lot and took the steps down to Church Hill Road, heading home. Louella was his people; he was her people.

He loved it when she called him honey.

TIM

The orders had gone to the Feel Good kitchen, and he presented his burning idea.

'A newspaper editor, a retired Realtor, and a priest walk into a bar.'

Mule laughed.

'Don't laugh yet,' he said.

'I'm an editor *and* publisher,' said J.C.

'One or the other, buddyroe. Gotta keep it simple.'

'Publisher.'

'An' take out th' retired part,' said Mule. 'I'm a Realtor. Once a Realtor, always a Realtor.'

'So tell th' joke,' said J.C. 'I could use a laugh.'

'That's all I've got. Just the opening line. I thought maybe we could come up with the rest of it by Christmas. What do you think?'

'I never wrote a joke,' said J.C. 'I never even *considered* writing a joke. Furthermore, I'm way too *busy* to write a joke. What a waste of *time* to write a joke. Time is *money*, Tim, time is *money*.'

'Don't look at me,' said Mule.

'Come on, guys. Loosen up. Go with me on this and I'll grab the check today.'

'It's about time,' said J.C. 'I grabbed th' check a while back.'

'I must not have long-term memory,' said Mule. 'I don't recall you grabbin' th' check a while back or any other time.'

J.C. wadded up his napkin and gave his face a once-over. 'Okay, okay, I'll give it a go. But only if we finalize it right here at this table, with a reward for gettin' it done.'

'Like?'

'I've been the poster child for healthy eating since July fourth, when I ate two racks of ribs and ended up in the ER. Because Adele thinks I'm killin' myself with th' fork, I promised to hang in there with a sensible diet 'til December twentieth, which is my birthday. So when we write this joke about a priest, a Realtor, and a distinguished newspaper publisher, I get to pick th' reward. Tim, you in?'

'Never been a gamblin' man, but sure, why not?'

'Mule?'

'I don't know. Depends on what th' reward is.'

'Bacon,' said J.C. 'Anything with bacon. Or just bacon without anything. A bacon rodeo.'

'I'm in,' said Mule.

He arrived home from the board meeting at Children's Hospital to a wife who had painted all day in her pajamas. When you consider these were pajamas with pink sand and turquoise water, not to mention exotic birds, why bother to dress?

He hung his jacket and kissed his favorite beach bum. 'A newspaper publisher, a Realtor, and a priest walk into a bar.'

She laughed.

'You're laughing in the wrong place. That's the starter line.'

'Only proving that I'm the best audience you'll ever have.'

He washed up at the sink. 'The Turkey Club is writing a joke.'

'Nice to know the Club is doing something for the betterment of mankind. So tell me the joke.'

'We only have the first line, that's why I said we're *writing* a joke. They were reluctant at first, but they came around.'

'When is your big reveal?'

'A few days before Christmas is our deadline.' He sat at the counter, selected a book of poetry by W. S. Merwin. 'We'll meet for breakfast at Wanda's and finalize the joke over something with bacon. Anything with bacon.'

There went her raised eyebrow. His wife—the diabetic's watchdog extraordinaire.

'In moderation, of course,' he said. He had been a reasonably good kid, an almost-straight-A student, a safe priest, a faithful husband—moderation was his middle name. But when it came to bacon . . .

TIM

He had nearly forsaken calling Henry Winchester by his Christian name. To both of them, the name Brother meant greatly more—blood, family, belonging. He had waited nearly a lifetime to have a brother.

Though a decade younger, Henry, too, didn't have forever anymore. Consequently, Henry spoke of matters of the heart—none of the rubbish of politics or the aches and pains of ageing.

Henry was many consolations, including a direct link to their long-deceased father, Matthew. Their father had been distant, removed, more vapor than man. That his, Timothy's, stem cells coursed in his brother's veins also created a type of intimacy with his father. Blood speaking to blood.

He sat on the sofa by the last of the evening fire and read Henry's letter. Handwritten in old-school cursive, his favorite.

Dear Brother,

We might have pulled the wishbone together but for Lucille's annual Thanksgiving extravaganza.

You cannot imagine the number of people who spring forth as blood kin, some of them surely imposters just here for the spectacular cuisine! Such laughter as you've never heard, such storytelling and leg-slapping as one will not see again! It's as if the dead have risen and for this one day must make up for all the chances missed while being alive. I usually require twenty-four hours to recover what remains of my faculties.

We hope you and Cynthia will put it on your calendar to join us next year in Holly Springs, as we do not wish to have any family member missing.

I appreciate your strong feelings about the loss of your letter to Cynthia, and am praying faithfully that you recover it. Your words in the letter were written from a place not always open and available, and to try to repeat what you wrote under inspired circumstances could be trying, if not impossible. Perhaps you could write another, and come at it from a fresh perspective. You never know what may spring forth; it could please you even more than the first! You asked me for candor and there it is, Brother. I do believe good will come of this.

As to your babysitting sideline, who but yourself would consider the difference poetry can make in the life of a three-year-old? You recall that Mama's husband, Packard, was a beloved educator in these parts. He took care to introduce Sister and me to poetry, an early favorite having been 'I have a little shadow that goes in and out with me . . . ' Thanks to Robert Louis Stevenson, I became good friends with my shadow!

I believe Countee Cullen was the most powerful poetic voice of my early youth. 'Hey Black Child' gave me license to ask all my questions. Packard never dismissed my questions and was therefore my richest blessing—he was the father who saved me. I don't believe I could have made it out there in the world without his devoted guidance.

Mama draws nigh to a hundred and one. Though a month or two short, she is already claiming this number, and no more do-rag for Mama, no. She bares the branded cross on her shining bald head as her personal flag for God Himself.

Though she finds the sermons somewhat lacking these days, she comes with us to church for the music. She is a mighty worshipper.

Mama sends her love, as do Lucille and Sister, to you and Cynthia. She is as proud of Cynthia as your own good mother would be, and brags on you both to all who will listen. The framed photograph of you and Cynthia stands with those of Packard, Sister, and myself in my porter's uniform. Btw, I'm fortunate to have a cousin (old and gray like yours truly) who served as a porter and we do have good times talking about those hard times.

Lucille is my world and I confess she is a woman who keeps me busy. She does not like to see me nodding off in my chair and will whip up a list in no time. 'I am keepin' you young,' she says, and so far, it appears to be working. My doctor, who is inclined to exaggeration, says I am good for another seventy, give or take a day or two. Praying that you continue to receive good news from your Doctor Wilson.

Am just coming up for air after rereading Ernest J. Gaines, and implore you to find time to seek him out. Though born and raised in rural Louisiana, he will take you behind our own Magnolia Curtain culture with his brilliant definition of southern character and landscape. I began my gallop through Gaines with A Lesson Before Dying, which I find a good place to begin or end a long examination of a profoundly great writer. I am always pleased to think of this little Black boy, one of thirteen, growing up in a rural parish and becoming Chevalier de l'Ordre des Arts et des Lettres!

Well, Brother, our chosen method of old-school correspondence via USPS is still the talk of the young people in the family. I'm exhorted to text you in order to 'speed things up,' but will continue to desist. I find joy in walking to the mailbox and finding your handwriting on the envelope.

Wishing you and all your beloveds a most happy and reflective Thanksgiving. We will include you in our table blessing, which is rendered by a retired AME preacher, who believes laughter is a praise offering. He met you at our wedding and looks forward to seeing you again, as do Mama and Sister. Lucille and I look forward to coming over to you for Christmas, details to follow soon.

Remember us to Lace and Dooley. I will write again when I finish Lucille's current to-do list, which includes everything but roofing; I am only allowed on the first two rungs of a ladder! I believe you will like the little room I added (with the help of a great-nephew) for Lucille's many quilting and sewing projects.

I remain
Your devoted brother

Henry was right, and what are brothers for if not to buck each other up? He would have another go at writing the letter.

It wasn't that he wanted the *approval rating* of doing it; he just liked getting things *finished*, out of his head. All the on-again, off-again of whether to give it a second try was torment.

He was eight, maybe nine, when he realized grown-ups could spend weeks, months, even years talking about getting something done without doing it. He would not bring it up to Louis, but how long had Louis talked about oiling the wagon springs? He was tired of hearing Louis talk about the squawking wagon springs.

So he oiled the springs himself, though Louis did not cotton to other people doing his job.

They were driving into town in the wagon and he was handling the reins. Louis was 'breaking him in' so he could one day take the wagon to town by himself. Outside town he handed the reins to Louis. It was bad enough to be seen in a wagon, much less driving a wagon. His father was a prominent lawyer and they had a 'spread' with hired hands and cattle, and he was taught that riding in a car or truck was the way to go. But if the wagon was the only way to get to town without walking, he'd take it and be glad to get it.

'What th' matter with this wagon?' said Louis.

'What you mean?'

'It ain't nothin' squeakin'. I cain't hardly tell we drivin' this thing.'

It occurred to him to keep quiet, but he had to say it.

'I oiled th' springs.'

He gave Louis the eye. He was learning to give somebody the eye so he could not be accused of saying out loud what the eye had to say. The eye was supposed to say it all—things like, *I am not fallin' for your tricks. Leave me alone. I don't need to hear this.* Or *I did it because all you did was talk about doin' it.*

There was a whole language to be spoken just with the face, with the eyes. But he was a novice and could not yet rely on that communication method.

'You crazy,' said Louis.

'It takes one to know one,' he said.

Louis hee-hawed. 'You been hangin' around wit' th' women, talkin' like that. Women says that'—Louis pitched his voice like a girl's—'it take one to know one!'

'Who else I'm gon' hang around with?' he said, mad as a copperhead. His daddy was hardly ever home, and when he was, he sure didn't hang around with nobody but th' field hands. Peggy and his mother did not allow him to play with th' neighbor kids a mile up the road because they were 'ruffians.' And because Tommy's dad was known to be 'a sot,' he wasn't allowed to play with Tommy, either, though he and Tommy managed to fix that more than a time or two.

He got up from the study sofa and poked the fire and did a brisk walk around the room. He was hacked off just thinking about the letter disappearing.

TIM

He was picking up shrimp for a scampi dish at the Local, and there was his mayor and friend, Andrew Gregory.

Andrew was earnestly squeezing an avocado. No, please! he wanted to say, don't squeeze the avocados. But he was no longer Mitford's interim grocer so he kept his mouth shut.

Upon sighting the tall, good-looking antiques dealer, he'd always been inclined to suck in his belly and stand up straighter. Andrew had, after all, been his primary competition in the pursuit of Cynthia. That he, the village priest, had actually caught her was flat-out proof of divine intervention.

Curious about the mayor's sole purchase of two avocados, but reluctant to ask, he was rewarded with a confession.

'Avocado mash on toast,' said Andrew. 'Making my own breakfast these days.'

'Your lovely wife . . . ' and she was indeed lovely, 'is away?'

'Has an early workout at the gym in Wesley.'

And there you go. The full reveal. Though known to have killed a cat or two, curiosity had endless rewards.

At Dora Pugh's Hardware, there was Miss Pringle buying a Phillips-head screwdriver. He was startled to see Helene looking . . . what? Radiant? Yes, absolutely. If she'd ever looked so before, he hadn't been there to see it. Always attractive and well-kept, but something had shifted. Piano bench yoga? A brisk walk around town?

He pried.

'Helene, you're looking beautiful! What has happened?' Blast, there were better ways of saying that.

She gave him a smile that wasn't exactly ear to ear, but a nice smile, nonetheless. Eyes bluer. Maybe contacts.

'I could say this only to you, Father. I saw a word. On an envelope.'

'Aha.' Maybe he wouldn't pursue that. Was she growing a bit—batty? Living alone can certainly be a culprit in such matters. He could have gone far battier than he naturally was if not for Cynthia, if not for being a man no longer flying solo.

He did not inquire why she was buying a Phillips-head, though frankly, he would enjoy knowing.

She indicated a brown paper bag clasped under her arm. 'On my way to the bookstore to drop off a book,' she said. On impulse, she held up the screwdriver. 'Just ran by for something to tighten my kitchen drawer knobs.'

He held up his intended purchase, one in each hand. 'Hinges for our screen door to the deck.'

Full disclosure. Life was good.

HELENE

She heard the faint sound of the vacuum cleaner toward the rear. Hope was likely in the mail order room, Coot was vacuuming, and it was too early for their college help.

She was fond of the Poetry section, somewhat hidden from view. It was always quieter in here except when the typewriter poets from the college showed up on Fridays.

People loved the typewriter poets. In order to help support a student who was almost certainly needing money for a decent meal, she had recently requested a Portrait Poem. She had felt awkward, even a bit fearful, asking for a poem about herself from a total stranger, but that seemed to be the point. The young woman had stared at her intently, then bent to her task.

She was still trying to unmask the meaning of the few words for which she had generously given five dollars, typed in less than sixty seconds on a Royal Manual.

```
Helene

In a black wood the crow
fades into the tree unseen
she has a very fine life
```

the wind fetches
seeds of dandelion from the fields
beyond the lake.
Her wings glisten.

The book and letter had lain for many days in their humble paper bag in the top drawer of her grandmother's bureau. She had read the letter and could hardly bear the depth of feeling it stirred in her. She had wept, overwhelmed by the power of language and proof that one human soul could so engage with another.

She would never mention any of this to Mr. Welch. The mystery of why it came to her was a lock to be picked by someone else.

She left the rumpled bag and its contents on the chair in the Poetry section, relieved that Margaret Ann was in absentia. She had sat there once and come away with a matte of cat hairs on her good black skirt. It was wool crepe from Jordan Marsh, her favorite store as a young woman.

She walked to the front door and opened it, the bell jangling behind her, and turned left on Main. As the street was deserted, she had not been seen leaving the store.

Though sunny this morning, it was bitterly cold and no one was lazing on the benches. She walked along Main to Sweet Stuff and stood for a few moments outside. She would steady herself before going in for a pot of tea and a profiterole—a bit of Paris in Mitford.

She had been anxious to be rid of it, and yet she felt bereft without it. The word on the envelope, altogether aside from the letter's contents, had been more beautiful than a tropical fish of a thousand colors.

Of course she had read the letter many times. Many times.

She could not have left it in the chair if she'd been referenced in the letter or in any way implicated. She had known somehow that she would not be implicated but knew she must confirm that. What she realized was disconcerting—she had the sure sense that she was supposed to read it. It was supposed to come into her life and work its mystifying power.

Altogether, it had been a hot potato that she tossed from hand to hand for days. And now it was out of her hands and into the hands of another. What better hands than a bookseller's in which to leave a book? And what better bookstore than the one in which the book had been purchased?

The letter had taught her many things. That such depth of feeling exists in the human spirit was itself a gift. It had never occurred to her that someone might love in this way. What she found in the letter was an example of surrendered love—love without fear of rebuff or loss of self. Though the writer spoke from the limits of his humanity, he spoke also from the liberty of the soul.

What a sight she must be, standing outside in winter, as immobile as statuary.

She adjusted her woolen hat and gathered herself and opened the door to the fragrant warmth of Sweet Stuff. Next to her own hearth, it was her favorite spot in Mitford. And Winnie's face was among her favorite faces—freckled, broad features, a smile with a choir of healthy, milk-fed teeth.

'Bonjour, Winnie!'

'Bonjour, madame!'

She enjoyed how Winnie's mountain accent sweetly flavored her morsel of French.

She gave her order—unexpectedly choosing something different by way of celebration. 'A pot of Earl Grey, as usual, Winnie, with a slice of *la quiche Lorraine.*' She always added *le morceau* of French to her order, which delighted Winnie.

She sat at the corner table, close to the heater, and removed her gloves.

She enjoyed seeing Father Tim today at the Hardware. He always instilled a sense of expectation in her, as if she'd been sleepwalking and was now awake to possibility. In truth, he was the very sort of person who could write such a letter as that just left behind at Happy Endings.

The thought, however, was discomfiting. If this were true, she would then know the intimate aspiration of her close neighbor, which could alter, if not entirely impair, the pleasant simplicity of their friendship.

She would choose to think it the work of an academic from the college at Wesley. Such people were known to be absentminded and could easily have lost the book and letter. But how it came into Mr. Welch's possession was a matter on which she could not speculate.

She really didn't care for speculation; it took a great deal of time and energy. But there was Andrew Gregory. He was an educated man with exceptional polish, though she couldn't imagine Mayor Gregory having even the rudiments of intimate expression. She sipped her tea. But why was she certain it wasn't he when he was married to a beautiful Italian woman who, according to rumor, knew how to laugh and drink wine? She could feel the heat rising to her face.

She sat up straighter in the plastic chair and poured the last of the Earl Grey into her cup. She must restrain herself once and for all. She did not need to know the identity of the writer who, in baring his soul to his beloved, had revealed it to an unknown spinster.

COOT HENDRIK

Over in th' Poetry section was a paper bag somebody left behind.

One thing he knew from workin' with th' public was people was bad to leave things behind. Raincoats, sweaters, schoolbooks, cell phones, umbrellas, he didn't know what all.

Sunglasses was a big thing to leave behind. If he had a nickel for ever' pair of sunglasses lost in this bookstore, he could be ownin' th' store. Not that he'd want to own th' store. He worried about Hope dealin' with a furnace gone south, th' college bookstore gettin' their own coffee shop an' café, th' economy slowin' down—nossir, he didn't want nothin' to do with ownin' a store.

But he liked his job better than anything he'd ever done in his entire life. He wished his mama was alive to see how good things was goin' for him—livin' upstairs over Happy Endings, keepin' th' place spotless, fixin' things in general, runnin' packages to th' P.O. An' gettin' a paycheck ever' other Friday.

Plus at Christmas, he got to dress up like a ol' bishop who was the first Santy Claus, an' give out candy from a sack. An' in th' parade, he was Santy th'owin' out candy to th' young'uns. Ever' once in a while he'd say, Coot ol' buddy, you have died an' went to heaven.

He picked up th' paper bag an' checked what was in there. Looked like it was a book in green wrappin' paper. As Chief Wrappin' Elf durin'

Christmas, he could just look at somethin' an' tell if it was wrapped professional. This was not wrapped professional. Ever' year, he trained part-timers from th' college to help at th' gift-wrap table. When they first come in, they didn' know how to wrap nothin' but a bun around a hot dog.

He took th' bag to th' sales counter.

Maybe he ought to look at what was in there to see if they was a name he could call.

No gift tag. An' this wadn't their store's gift wrap. Couldn't hurt to open it, seein' it had been opened already. He undid th' wrappin' in a way he could fix it back if he had to. It was that poetry book Hope and Grace liked, they was both crazy about this poet.

Out fell a letter with a word on th' envelope.

Haw. He'd seen that word on a book they kept in stock. He read th' word again, breakin' it into syllables.

Be lov ed.

Th' envelope was sealed and he did not feel like th' man to open a envelope with that word on it. He could tell it was not a trick by Grace Murphy, who was nine. She liked to trick him when she could.

One time he asked her, 'Why're you always trickin' me?'

'Because you're my friend,' she said.

'I'm gon' start trickin' you sometime an' see how you like it.'

'Okay,' she said. 'Tricking is fine when you like somebody. But bad if you don't.'

He was try*ing* to put th' *ing* on his words now, even when he was just think*ing*. Grace was teach*ing* him that. But he didn't remember to do it ever' time.

He'd been a mighty old dog to learn th' new trick of read*ing*. Father Tim had taught him th' main part of read*ing*, then come what you call a tutor, an' then Hope had stepped in an' you might say finished off th' job. His favorite read was Dr. Seuss. He had learned to spell the last name of the doctor and had about wore out all his Dr. Seuss books Grace had gifted him. One was comin' loose from th' spine, an' now Hope had moved him up th' ladder an' he was readin' chapter books but they could make him doze off here lately.

'I need to find you something gripping,' said Grace. She was always tryin' to school him.

'Find me somethin' what?'

'*Gripping*,' she said, like he was deaf as a pot handle. 'A page-turner. Something you can't put down.'

'Why couldn't I put it down if I wanted to?'

'Oh, good *grief*!' she said.

He looked at the book cover of a cow layin' on a green couch. Th' cow took up th' whole couch. He opened th' book. Somethin' about a dog runnin' in its sleep. Somethin' about a naked eye.

They won't one thing in this book that rhymed. Noth*ing*. An' th' poems, if that's what they was, was all short. Three or four lines. He could of wrote this book hisself.

These poems was way too short to qualify as poems when you held one up to, say, Mr. Longfellow. They had two of his books in stock but nobody ever asked for one. He had dusted Mr. Longfellow a hundred times. But he had personally never messed with poetry.

'You're scared of poetry,' said Grace. 'You don't have to be scared of poetry.'

'Haw,' he said. 'Poetry is scared of me.'

This was someth*ing* personal left behind, an' somebody would be lookin' for it. He stuck th' envelope back in th' book an' held his mouth right an' in a heartbeat that book was wrapped back up an' lookin' better than when he found it.

He put it in th' bag an' checked th' wall clock. He had to get out to th' P.O. an' over to Wesley for packin' supplies.

He set th' bag by th' credit machine. An' when whoever come in lookin' for it, it would be settin' right there in plain sight.

HOPE

It was leaning against the credit machine, which is where people often left things just for her. Though it was wrapped, she could tell it was a book. Oddly, people loved giving her books, though she would rather have cookies or a really crisp mountain apple.

She peeled back the tape and slipped it from its green shuck. She had sold this just days ago; their Happy Endings label was on the back. Father Tim had come in for it—he and Cynthia collected Collins's work. She loved it when a customer was a collector. That meant more income for the bookstore, but what she liked better is that collectors in general were *hooked* on reading and couldn't resist the visual allure of book spines on a shelf. What a powerful and seductive invention, the book! She never took books for granted, even though she saw them every day.

She remembered the harmless crush she had on Father Tim when she moved to town all those years ago. He was the only person she knew who had ever read so many of the books she loved, and could quote Wordsworth and George Herbert, for heaven's sake. Just for fun, the two of them occasionally used words most people never heard of, much less worked into a sentence. She had relished his love of books and learning; he had been a lifeline for her as a stranger in Mitford.

One of her favorites in this collection of Collins's work was the poem about wakefulness. '3 A.M.' it was called. It always made her laugh, especially as she was afflicted with insomnia.

An envelope fell to the counter.

Beloved

She was momentarily startled. The word inscribed in coal-black ink carried the sense of being more than just a written word.

Beloved? How could this be for her? It was not Scott's handwriting. Her husband and best friend would never use that word except in a sermon at Hope House, where he was chaplain. He would use his nickname for her, Freckles, though she had only four or five to show for it.

Beloved was another name for Christ. It was the name of the transformative Pulitzer Prize–winning novel by Toni Morrison. It was a word set apart from the daily grind of language.

Maybe it had been forgotten by someone overwhelmed with life in general. She tried Coot on his cell; he would know who had been in.

Please leave a message. She left a message.

She loved a mystery, having gone through a college diet of Agatha Christie in paperback. She hefted the envelope. Probably two pages by the feel of it. Not a card. A letter.

At least this was taking her mind off the furnace. God knows it would be a challenge to sell books in a creaky old building sliding toward thirty-four degrees.

She clapped her hand to her forehead with such force that she briefly saw stars. Of course!

It was his handwriting, she recognized it—old-school cursive. And the book he bought only a couple of weeks ago.

This was clearly a mistake. She wouldn't think of opening the envelope—which appeared to have already been opened and resealed. She would tuck the whole business back in its green wrapper, stick it in the well-used brown bag, and put it under the counter. She would give it to him when he came in to shop from his always-generous Christmas list.

But what if, for some really terrifying reason, he had actually meant it for her? How very distressing. She took a deep breath, held it, breathed out.

The front door. UPS.

Completely unprepared to see anyone at all, she shoved the envelope back in the book and went to show Warren where to offload the boxes.

Father Tim was a man of great feeling—she knew that, but this?

She stopped by the coffee area and had a cup of tea to calm herself.

He had said he was buying the book for Cynthia. So of course! It was for Cynthia. It was absolutely for her; he adored his wife. But how had it ended up here?

When she returned to the sales counter, she rewrapped the book and its contents in the green paper and slipped it back into the wrinkled brown bag. When she looked up, there were the Cunningham sisters wheeling the Old Mayor across the street.

They were coming for the annual Giving Thanks for Bookstores sale at five o'clock. She looked at her watch. Four-thirty! Mitford people were always infuriatingly early.

She heard Coot race in the back door to don his French apron and serve the wine and spiced tea with cookies. The Old Mayor would not touch a drop of wine, but her girls were a different matter.

She shoved the bag onto the shelf beneath the counter. She couldn't waste another minute on this book and its mystery letter! She would deal with it later.

TIM

He remembered losing a letter a few years ago. It had turned up beneath his old desk—Emma had a weekly gig with him at the time, and was working in the study.

The envelope had apparently fallen off the desk and somehow slid under its file side, which sat close to the floor. It was discovered later by Puny on a mopping mission.

His eighteenth-century desk was all French legs. Nothing could lie underneath that escaped the eye. Timmy and Tommy had no memory of a green package. He was deeply resistant to rewriting the letter. He could never express himself in just that way again; he knew his limits.

As small a matter as it may seem to others, it was not a small matter. He had somehow lost or misplaced what was extremely personal—a remnant of the heart, the soul, the gut, the sort of thing you would not wish sullied by other eyes. It was a frustration that gave him the random headache.

As he often did, he prayed the prayer that never fails. In one way or another, it always worked. And in this particular case, timing was everything.

He would take Henry's advice and try again.

HOPE

So my nephew's comin' for an overnight on his way to Tennessee to see his girlfriend who plays bass with a country band an' it's his birthday an' I asked him what he wanted an' he said a Stephen King book which he would share with his girlfriend or a jigsaw puzzle. He said make it a big one, I said th' book or th' puzzle an' he said th' book. So th' town library recommended *Th' Stand* which comes in at eleven hundred pages an' I hope you have it.'

'Let me check my inventory, Mrs. Skinner. I doubt that we have it in stock, I believe it came out in the nineties.'

'How come you might not have it in stock? You have a huge store just full of books.'

'I can't inventory everything. There are thousands of books published each year. Please hold.'

'Good Lord, thousands every year? There must be millions of books out there. An' I understand you can't stock everything ever written, that's for th' libraries.

'Back when I had my salon—which we used to call a shop, which my Aunt Nancy who had a shop called a beauty parlor—remember when we called it a beauty parlor? No, you're too young. There was also massage parlor, pool parlor, an' funeral parlor. "Parlor" was a big word back in th' day, anyway, I could not stock all th' hair products ever made, no way.

People said you mean you don't carry Redken like I had committed a cardinal sin, but no I did not carry Redken, like one little bitty salon in a one-stoplight town cannot carry everything ever produced in th' entire hair industry so I get exactly what you're sayin.' Hello? Are you there? Hope? Hello?'

'Yes, Mrs. Skinner, I just checked our inventory and I do have a copy of *The Stand*. It takes up a lot of room on the shelf, so I confess I'll be glad to see it go.'

'You could give me a discount for takin' it off your hands, just kiddin', I know a small business cannot afford to give discounts. I never gave a discount at A Cut Above. An' only once did I do a refund but I was not responsible, I did it because he was clergy. Like, Father Tim wanted his money back when I gave him a facial for date night and his face turned green which was not my fault. It was th' chemicals in his skin reactin' to my face mask in a way that was unique.

'So I'll have Mule pick it up. Just put it under the counter where you put my stuff when I order anything which is not often enough, right? And Mule will drop by for it tomorrow. I hope Mule won't get a hernia carryin' that thing to th' house.'

'Will do. And thank you, Mrs. Skinner.'

'Oh no, I should be thankin' you! I'm so glad you had it in inventory as my nephew will be over the moon about this book, he says his girlfriend loves to be scared by a book, can you believe that?

'I could have ordered a fun puzzle but a book is easier to carry with you, don't you think? I mean, to take a book with you, you just mark your place an' off you go, right? With a puzzle, oh my Lord, if it wadn't finished, you'd have to scrape that thing off th' table and start all over at th' next place, right?'

'Exactly. And I must . . . '

'I need to let you go, I remember when I had my salon, people would get me on th' phone and just blah, blah, blah a mile a minute while I had somebody tappin' their foot in my chair.

'But while I've got you, I've been meanin' to ask, do you read everything that comes in the store? I mean how do you know what to recommend to people if you've not read all your books? If somebody wanted a recommendation for a hair care product, I could just look at them and see th' problem—broken ends, color too brassy, thinnin' in th' back, flat at th' crown, dry scalp.

'But when a customer comes lookin' for a good book, there's nothin' to tip you off about what would be right for them, so you probably have to be a mind reader. Or you could prob'ly just say what kind of books do you like but what if they say I don't really know? Do you ever have that happen? They don't even *know*?'

'Mrs. Skinner . . . '

'Okay, I know you've got to go. Is there anybody shoppin' today? Some days I hardly had anybody in my chair. Bein' a small town, you're not always stacked up with people unless it's Easter or Thanksgivin' or Christmas or a weddin' but hardly anybody gets married anymore, they just, you know, anyway, so it's th' holidays that make great salon days.

'If we'd been in a bigger town, we'd of gotten a lot of business out of date night. Date night really brings people in, even married people because when you're married, date night is, like, more essential, wouldn't you agree? I mean, you kind of have to look new to your husband or whatever so it's really stressful, you know, havin' to put on somethin' besides your sweats, maybe even high heels. I will say this—date night with your husband is not th' night to try a new hair style of any kind. It could freak him out; I've known that to happen.'

'Mrs. Skinner . . . '

'I had one woman, she drove up every week from Holding, who wanted her hair dyed red for a big date night with her husband but he did not like it dyed red so she came back th' next day to return to bein' a brunette. An' what happened? You guessed it—all those chemicals burned up her hair an' a lot of it fell out. Honestly, it was not my fault, it was her doin' it twice in a row, so she ended up with a blond wig that didn't fit good but say la vee, life throws you a curve ball sometimes. Speakin' of, I hear your furnace broke down. Now *that's* a curve ball.'

'Gotta run, Mrs. Skinner. Under the counter it will be. Would you like it wrapped?'

'I ought to let you wrap it, but do not wrap it. Just stick it in a bag. We'll save a tree! And you've got my card number. Bye bye now, it was great talkin' to you!'

She had always wanted a place to lie down in the bookstore. Maybe one day, in the mail-order room. She would try squeezing a fold-up cot between the sink and the bookshelves.

HOPE

Though hidden beneath the counter, the book with its enfolded letter made her nervous. Father Tim had been in twice, and each time the store was busy or she'd been so addled by the furnace business that she forgot to give it to him.

She had rehearsed answers for likely questions: She had recognized the distinguished cursive as his. She could assure him that she hadn't read the contents. Why it showed up at the bookstore was a complete mystery.

She put Cynthia's books and puzzles in a box with their bookstore wrapping paper and ribbon, as Cynthia liked doing her own wrapping. His books and puzzles were in a separate box, already wrapped by Coot with sticky notes ID'ing the contents.

What if she slipped the Billy Collins book into Father Tim's box? She would like to rewrap it and put it in a nice gift bag, but that could be misleading and asking for trouble.

Say what you will about romance, the book and its envelope were worrisome. She had to get it out of her hands; she could not continue to be held hostage by a letter.

She stooped and looked on the shelf under the counter. Ran her hand along the back of the shelf—printer paper, old CDs, boxes of paper clips, a stack of rinsed-out yogurt cups they'd forgotten to recycle. She felt along the opposite end of the shelf. More printer paper, a nest of unclaimed items—sunglasses, a glove, a notepad, the usual.

The book and letter—not there.

HOPE

She saw the caller ID. She should *not* pick up.

She picked up.

'Hey, Hope, it's Fancy. What Mule brought home was anything *but* Stephen King. It's a little bitty book wrapped in green paper, I didn't even take it out of th' wrapper, I mean it's anything *but* Stephen King!'

'I'm so sorry, Ms. Skinner.' Dear God! She had stuck it under the counter as if it were a lost glove! And forgot completely to put the Stephen King under there. How could she possibly have done that? 'I'll send Coot with your book, he'll be right there. Give him fifteen minutes.' Her heart was thundering.

'Don't even think about sendin' anybody up here an' wastin' gas, Mule's goin' to town tomorrow, I'll have him stop by. He'll be headed across th' street from you to First Baptist, we're both lifelong Baptists, not Free Will or Full Gospel or anything weird, just regular, we've been fully immersed an' not sprinkled like th' Methodists . . . '

'There are customers in th' store, Mrs. Skinner, got to go, thanks for sending Mr. Skinner tomorrow—and goodbye.'

She hung up on Fancy Skinner. She had never before hung up on a customer.

She hadn't realized the book and letter were missing. To even think of how things could have gone . . .

She sat down hard on the stool behind the sales counter.

She was not herself; it was the furnace. She was blaming everything on the furnace. Her fingers were stiff from the cold.

She searched for her water bottle and was astonished to see several people still browsing around her frozen store, wrapped to the gills in scarves, hats, coats, leggings, mittens.

Even with the heaters going full blast, her breath steamed the air. Surely they could get by 'til spring; she was praying for an early spring. As for voluntarily closing the doors and going home? *Never.*

She would go around to each customer and thank them personally for coming in. They were her lifeline. But first, she would call Hope House and speak with her chaplain, who just happened to be her husband. She almost never called him at work.

'Could you please remind me,' she said, 'that all will be well and all will be well and all manner of things shall be well?'

'With due respect to Julian of Norwich, I have a better line.'

'Could we hear it, please?' The tears were flowing, she stepped into the mail-order room.

'I love you,' he said.

'Thanks, but . . . '

'I'm not done. I love you because you're brilliant. I love you because you're a great mom and my best friend. I love you because you're an inspiration to the community. I love you because you care so much about everything worth caring about.'

'Thanks, you're . . . '

'I'm still going, you'll like this part. I love you because you're sexy, and soft. You're very soft, Freckles. Personally, I'm a big fan of soft. It helps with the hard stuff.'

She drew in her breath. 'I don't think other men talk like this.'

'They want to but they're scared to. I used to be scared to talk like this.'

'Then we nearly lost Grace,' she said.

'And everything shifted for us. I learned how urgent it is to talk like this. I learned how urgent it is to just talk. It took a full-on lightning strike to get me in out of the rain, and I thank God for it. We made it through, and look what we got. Grace Elizabeth Murphy—a kid who's smarter than we are.'

She laughed. 'Not all the time.'

'You called me for a reason.'

'You already helped me. I was calling to whine about the furnace and the fact that sometimes I do really dumb things. And you reminded me how it felt to know we could lose her. And how . . . we didn't.'

She knew that on the other end of the line, he was having his own moment.

'For Christmas,' he said, 'because she works so hard and does so well, because she loves us, Hope, just because . . . '

'What?' she said.

'Let's give her a piano.'

HOPE

Mr. Skinner would be walking over from their house four blocks away. Even in an essentially safe town like Mitford, anything could happen.

Easily distracted and not a man to look both ways when crossing the street, he had two streets to cross. Also, he could trip on that broken sidewalk in his neighborhood and end up in the ER with book and letter sailing down the hall on a gurney.

She felt fiercely protective of a letter that had dropped into her life like a small grenade. She sensed it was intimate, and intimacy frightened most people. If just anyone read it, Father Tim could be ridiculed or misunderstood. Out of fear, people's defenses were often scornful, with the mean laughter she remembered from grade school.

She had been a bookish country child, despised by town kids for her clothes, her odd packed lunches, her run-over shoes, her love of poetry, her good grades. Mostly, they could not understand her; she was not one of them and so they feared her and did all in their power to make her feel misbegotten. An actual arrow in her flesh could not have wounded more.

She walked to the store window and looked south for Mr. Skinner. He would be wearing one of his several fedoras and possibly an entire vintage outfit from a local yard sale. He once confessed that he hadn't read a book since high school; she suspected Happy Endings made him nervous.

There he came at a trot, looking like a man from the forties or fifties, one of the well-meaning people with prospects who settle in little towns, build a business, and prosper.

He never removed his hat when he entered the store, as men would have done in the heyday of the fedora. But as a gesture of respect, he did tip the brim when he came in. How on earth did this harmless man hook up with the likes of Fancy Skinner? Though merely a bookstore owner accountable to a bottom line, she was, after all, a woman, and couldn't help wondering such things.

She practically snatched the bag from his hand, peered inside to confirm its contents, and handed him the weighty King novel in exchange. He took it out of the bookstore bag and gave it a careful once-over.

'Good to go, Mr. Skinner?'

'Fancy said it would be humongous, so this ought to do it.'

'I'm so sorry you were given the wrong book.'

'I wadn't given the wrong book. Fancy said you sometimes put her order under th' counter 'til I can pick it up. So Coot was busy with a customer and since it was paid for, I looked around under there and way in the back was a book in a bag.'

'We do apologize. Many thanks for your time to bring this one back and pick up the real thing.' There were just no words for this tribulation. Why couldn't she manage this book and letter? They were like a runaway horse.

Mr. Skinner cleared his throat. 'I just thought of somethin'. You're an educated woman, right?'

'I think you could say that. Depends.'

'So maybe you could help us out with somethin'. Father Tim an' J. C. Hogan an' me, we're tryin' to come up with a joke. You know, made up from scratch.'

'I don't think I can help you with that.'

'Here's th' opener. A highly *successful* . . . *longtime* . . . real estate *sales leader and dedicated community volunteer* . . . along with a priest and a newspaper guy . . . walk into a bar.'

She smiled, nodded, waited.

'That's all we've got so far. Thought I'd just put it out there. Maybe you could help us come up with th' rest of it.'

'I really don't think so, Mr. Skinner. But I'm honored that you asked.'

He touched the brim of his fedora and fled with roughly ten pounds of dystopia.

Now that the book and letter were safely back in her hands, she should text him to stop by. Since she found the bag by the credit machine, she'd been overwhelmed—by the holidays coming on like a bullet train and the college expanding its bookstore and adding a full-on café.

She told Grace about her quandary.

'Mama, just *give* it to him and get it over with. It's making a journey through you for a reason. He'll be glad it was you and not somebody who would, like, tell the whole world he wrote a mushy letter to his wife.'

'How do you know it's mushy?'

'Beloved.'

'That's mushy?'

'Totally.'

It was always surprising to realize that her best friend was only nine years old.

DOOLEY

He was way ahead of the lunch crowd at Crossroads.

'Haven't seen you in a while,' said Jake. 'All work an' no play.'

'I busted out of there for a little peace and quiet. How's it goin'?'

'Sugar's gone to visit her mama in Kentucky, wanted to give me a taste of how valuable she is as chief cook an' bottle washer. Guess you heard we got th' tech crowd comin' in over at Wesley. Got th' college expandin' with a big cyber security department; they'll be in a buildin' mode. Gon' get an economic boost out here in th' sticks. I keep up with this stuff, you know. I'm a county commissioner, in case you forgot.'

'And we thank you, buddy.'

'Want your sandwich an' fries to go or eat here?'

'Here. And double-dip th' fries. Two of th' same order to take out.'

He got to be hero of the day when he supplied lunch. Lace was on the scaffold, Lily Flower was feeding the kids and getting the closets ready for holiday company. Since they rarely spent money on clothes, why were their closets crammed full? He didn't get it.

'I'm thinking of doin' a project at Meadowgate. Rehab an old house in the woods. May need some cheap labor.'

'You're lookin' at it,' said Jake. 'But I'm not cheap.'

'Yeah, well, don't quit your day job.'

'Not cheap, I'm free!' said Jake. 'You know I help with buildin' stuff out in th' community an' I'm lookin' for th' right project. That's my way of givin' back.'

'I didn't know you did it as a volunteer.'

'That's th' only way I do it.'

'So what can you do?'

'Drywall, floorin', chimneys. I can knock out a deck in a heartbeat. Helped raise a barn one time but I'm definitely over that. One day a week. Eight to four. Get back to me with th' details, but hurry up, I'm popular.'

Jake lifted the fry basket from the roiling grease and gave it a shake. 'I got a new music system, practically any country singer you can think of.'

'George Strait,' he said, picking up his tray and a couple of napkins.

His favorite booth ahead of the lunch crowd, plus fries and 'I Cross My Heart.'

Life was good.

TIM

As Henry suggested, he was trying again.

What had the salutation been?

All he remembered about the salutation is that it included Bookend, a term of affection for their mutual taste in literature and their somewhat similar heights, she of the five-four-ish and he of the five-nine-ish.

He did a warm-up in his notebook. *Dear Bookend. Dearest Bookend. My dear Bookend.*

Come to think of it, why a salutation at all in this iteration? Why not just jump in? He looked out the enormous window of the study, aptly called a picture window, and realized that he had absolutely nothing to jump in with.

While the original letter was written at a creative boil, today he barely generated a simmer. He could replicate nothing of that spirit and nuance, though he definitely remembered his riff on the fragrance of summer grass crushed beneath the cloud watchers.

He would do as Henry advised and write from a fresh perspective.

He observed a male cardinal in the leafless maple; watched a young squirrel that was still hoarding—did this forecast a breaking-news kind of winter? A half hour had ticked by when he realized he didn't have a fresh perspective.

If he were a man for the drink, a double single-malt Irish whiskey straight up—or maybe an old-school Kentucky bourbon? Being Irish from the American south had its conflicts of interest.

He was done with this failed attempt. His gift would be the oral recital of the whole aggravation.

HOPE

'What if you were to come down on Christmas morning and find a piano by the tree?'

'Oh, Mom! A *piano*? That would be the best thing in the whole wide *world*. It's hard to practice on the school piano, it's always so busy in the auditorium after school, and, like, the old thing hardly stays in tune.'

'I've been thinking about something. My question is, would you share the piano if we were to have one?'

'Share it? Are you going to take lessons? You always said you might!'

'Sassy Guthrie also needs a piano.'

'Sassy Guthrie? Why can't she get her own piano?'

'She's trying. She has a notice on the community board, hoping to find a piano in playable condition. But that may not be the best way to get a piano.'

'Mom! Think about it. Sharing a piano would be a very intimate thing, like letting somebody wear all your favorite clothes. I don't really like Sassy Guthrie. She's very bossy.'

'Well, it takes one to know one.'

'Am I bossy?'

'A good bossy. Look how you kept after Coot to expand his reading and fall in love with books, and how you bossed that shy young man into dressing up as Ernest Hemingway at Halloween. And lest we forget, how you talked Miss Phillips into giving you a whole curriculum to co-teach.'

'But Mom, Sassy is *really* bossy.'

'She is.'

'Is she smarter than I am?'

'Honestly, honey, I don't know anyone smarter than you. But you mustn't take pride in that. Not at all. That's a gift from God. You do not make yourself smart. It's your job to cultivate your intelligence and use it in positive ways. Not everyone is smart, but everyone has a gift and some have many. Miss Pringle thinks you may be gifted as a pianist. She also thinks Sassy may be gifted as a pianist. For a little town, that is a very high ratio of musically gifted. And you both need a piano so you can practice.'

'Why can't she, like, have her own piano?'

'I'm guessing that four kids to put through college in a few years may be constraining.'

A long silence.

'I don't want to share my piano,' said Grace.

'It wouldn't be your piano.'

'Why wouldn't it be? It would be in our house, in our living room!'

'But it would not be yours, and it would not be ours. It would just be . . . The Piano.'

'Mom!'

She really loved being called Mama, but she wouldn't complain. 'Yes?'

'I don't know what to even think about your idea. It's really weird. What if she plays better than I do?'

'I think you both play well, you just play differently.'

'Sassy has a temper.'

'Most people have a temper somewhere down in there. I believe I've seen yours, Love Bug.'

'What if we get mad at each other about the piano? I'm thinking ahead, Mom. You taught me to think ahead.'

'While you're thinking ahead, think how the really smart person does not cultivate pouting and sulking and revenge and all that messy business that can happen with young girls. Yes, there are pressures at school and even at home, and there will be certain pressures in growing as a pianist. And you will sometimes be tired and fretful and angry, just as your dad and I sometimes are. But angry disputes over the piano will not fly—or there will be consequences.'

'Like what kind of consequences?'

'I haven't thought that far ahead.'

They laughed.

'This is an unusual conversation, Mom.'

'It is. And you're handling it well, as I knew you would. So we could offer Sassy two afternoons a week for practice, and three afternoons before a recital. One hour each. Nothing for her in the evening, we've all worked hard all day and that's our family time.'

'So if I won't, like, share the piano we can't have a piano at all? Is that what you mean?'

'That's what I mean. We can't afford a piano for only one person. It's too dear a possession to have such little use. And you and Sassy would have to care for it. For example, if you ever have a dog, you, not your daddy and I, need to take care of feeding it and brushing it and all the things people must do to have a happy dog.'

'You're cool, Mom.'

'Really? Me?'

'I don't think other parents talk to their kids like this.'

Actually, she was not especially wise, and for sure not cool. She was praying all the time, and making up parenting as she went; she was flying by the seat of her pants.

HARLEY

It was turnin' cold, like Willie predicted, he was a reg'lar weatherman. They ought to be havin' a fire tonight but they was both too give out from a honest day's work to lay it.

Seem like Willie had somethin' on 'is mind.

'What we gon' do with that red oak up ag'in th' big house?' said Willie. 'It's rotten on th' inside is my thinkin.'

'Dooley said he'd have it took down.'

'It's me an' you ought to take it down. If we don't do it, gittin' a tree service out here'll cost big money. Because it'll cost big money he'll wait on takin' it down an' first thing you know, it'll be on th' roof—an' there'll be that to clean up an' th' roof to repair.'

Willie was not a man to look on th' bright side.

'So,' said Willie. 'You ever took down a big tree?'

'Nossir. Where I come from if a tree needs to be took down, we wait for it take its ownself down.'

Willie didn't never roll his eyes but it looked like he'd enjoy it if he did.

'You ever think about what we gon' do when we git old?' said Willie.

'Not yet. I'm in my sixties.'

'Soon you gon' be in your seventies, then you gon' be in your eighties an' next thing you know you gon' be pushin' up wire grass.'

He didn't know whichaway this train was movin'. Sometimes Willie made him nervous as a cat. Hisself, he was jis' tryin' to set on th' couch after a good supper, an' here was all this.

'What're you sayin'?'

'What I'm sayin' is, they need young people on this place. With my bad back, I cain't take down that red oak an' saw it up and clean up th' brush and haul it off an' all th' rest of it. I cain't even git up in th' trees to hang th' Christmas lights. An' with your bad knees, you cain't do none of that neither, which means Dooley's got to pay somebody to come out here an' do it. Then there's th' barn roof—I ain't goin' up there ag'in for nobody an' you ain't able to, neither. He'll have to git a roofer in from Wesley, just for a patch.

'An' how about th' bushhoggin'? That ol' tractor's about ruint my back, pullin' th' Bush Hog all day. An' with th' rain we had back in October, you'll see weeds come spring you never laid eyes on before. So this is what I'm sayin', Here in a little bit, we're gon' be costin' Dooley big money.'

Willie set back to let that sink in, then went at it ag'in. 'An' what about when things git so bad we need a walker or some such?'

A *walker*? 'I cain't believe you're talkin' like this.'

''Cause you don't take facts as serious as I take facts. Facts is what a man has to deal with in this life. Think about gittin' out in th' field with them steers when you're my age.'

'What is your age?'

'Seventy-five gainin' on seventy-six next May. So what I'm sayin' is, they're gon' need two young people livin' out here. In this house.'

It hadn't never crossed his mind that one day he'd be too old to git up in a tree or patch a roof. Two monkeys is what Dooley needed.

'When th' time comes, where you gon' live at?' said Willie.

'I ain't thought about it. Where you gon' live at?'

'That's what I'm sayin'. I don't know where I'll be livin' at if we cain't turn in a day's work on this place.'

Thunder in the distance. Maybe a storm comin' but Willie hadn't predicted nothin'.

'You got any savin's?' he asked Willie.

'Well now, that's my personal b'iness.'

'Aw come on, you know about my savin's, I ain't hid my personal b'iness from you. When that woman in th' early model Toyota invited me to Las Vegas, you an' me talked about money, an' I said I got four thousand put back, but that was a good while ago an' it's headin' to six an' a quarter.' Six an' a quarter! He'd come up poor as Job's turkey, an' now he had what his granpaw called a nest egg.

'You know how long that'll last in a nursin' home?' said Willie.

'A nursin' home?' Seem like his heart was beatin' offkey. 'What about a nursin' home?'

Willie give 'im a look. 'You don't take care of them knees, pretty soon you cain't walk. Then you'll be in a wheelchair an' then . . . '

'Jis' wait a dadblame minute. I'll take care of plannin' my own life if you don't mind. An' what about your back that you git down in? We gon' have to order *you* a wheelchair.'

If Willie got any crankier than this, he'd have to go live in th' barn. When th' Welch young'uns used to git cranky, his step-mama give 'em a dose of castor oil. Or if she was out of castor oil, she'd heat up some collards she'd canned an' add a little bacon grease to make th' medicine go down. That got things movin'.

'I'll bring us up some collards tomorrow,' he said. He'd canned collards last year, a dozen quart jars was in th' basement storeroom. He felt better havin' a plan. 'Maybe you'll bake us a cake of cornbread.' Willie's cornbread was champion; it was a hit with ever'body.

'I don't know that I'll be able,' said Willie.

'Able for what?'

'Bakin' cornbread. All that standin' by th' oven door to watch if it's brownin' on top. What puts my back out of whack is standin'.'

'It's all that dadblame sittin' if you ask me—drivin' th' truck to Mitford about ever' day with th' suspension system needin' work.'

'It's th' shocks an' struts, is all,' said Willie.

'I know about replacin' shocks an' struts,' he said.

'Takes about four to five hours to replace, they say on YouTube.'

'I don't need no YouTube. When I was runnin' 'shine, nobody but me maintained th' cars I drove.'

'So when you gon' work on it?'

'If it's on th' road to Mitford nearabout ever' day, how'm I gon' work on it?'

'Bad struts can be life-threatenin',' said Willie. 'I asked about it at th' Crossroads. So 'til you git all that replaced, I'll ask Dooley to send you to town.'

As much booze as he'd hauled, he'd never been a drinkin' man, but if Willie kep' up like this . . .

HARLEY

So him an' Willie was makin' their Christmas list while eatin' their supper of meatloaf with a sweet potato an' green limas. Th' list was short, with Lace an' Dooley at th' top.

'So I've got a idea,' he told Willie. 'Dooley said she wadn't cookin' ever' night after paintin' them big murials.'

'Takeout,' said Willie, forkin' in th' meatloaf.

'Th' only takeout we got this side of Mitford is a hot dog from th' Crossroads, which ain't even all-beef. You cain't run a place like this on a hot dog.'

Willie didn't look up. Buttered hisself a store-bought roll.

'Let's say ever' month, we switch a Spaghetti Night to a Pizza Night. An' we make two whoppers an' take one over to th' big house. That could be our gift to th' family this year is what I'm thinkin'.'

Willie eatin' like they wadn't no tomorrow.

'Th' personal touch,' he said. 'Handmade instead of store-bought.'

'I thought we was gon' git Lace an' Dooley two bed pillers.'

'We was, but this is a better idea. Her an' Dooley work overtime ever' day an' a good dinner comin' in th' door . . . '

He was wore out jis' talkin' about it. 'If we're too triflin' to do twelve pizzas, they ain't no hope for neither one of us. So how about this. I'll do sauce an' toppin's, but th' whole thing hinges on you doin' th' crust. I ain't never messed with dough.'

Willie sopped his roll around his plate, didn't say nothin'.

He put his last card on th' table. 'They give us a good place to live, a fair wage, an' a pretty good truck to drive, an' they like their crust thin an' crispy, not thick an' doughy.'

'You cain't be givin' people choices,' said Willie. 'Thin an' crispy, thick an' doughy, no pepperoni, nothin' *but* pepperoni, no peppers, just mushrooms, no sausage, more sausage. Th' only thing people ever agree on is cheese. I might be prepared to make th' crust but it's gon' have to be th' way I make crust, which is not thin an' crispy.'

Th' last of Willie's roll went down th' hatch. 'My style is thick an' doughy. It's always been thick an' doughy.' Willie leaned his way. 'People cain't look a gift horse in th' mouth.'

Willie pushed back his plate. 'I'm gon' git out of these clothes.' An' off he went down th' hall. In a little bit, he come back down th' hall in his drawers.

'Another thing,' said Willie. 'I was raised to eat whatever was set before me. I did not whine. I did not take a fit an' roll around on th' floor, I did not stomp off from th' table like some young'uns do today. So if I didn't do none of that, what do you think I done?'

He didn't know and didn't want to know.

'I et what was set before me,' said Willie.

An' off he went ag'in.

Th' collards wadn't workin'.

HARLEY

He'd been rode hard an' put up wet today. Re-pointin' th' stone foundation of th' corn crib was a job of work. In her spare time, which she didn't have none of, Lace was gon' put this ol' place on what you call th' National Register. Meantime, ever'body was pitchin' in to make it look spiff.

When he come in from work, they was a sign nailed up to th' right side of th' front door.

Geezer Cottage it said in black letterin' on a painted board.

He took off his jacket an' hung it on the hat rack; Willie didn't go for throwin' clothes ever' whichaway.

'Where'd that sign come from?' he asked Willie.

'Mink Hershell was about to drive off as I come up from th' barn. You know Mink, he likes a good joke.'

'I don't see a good joke as hammerin' nails in a man's house shingles.'

Willie was peelin' potatoes. 'There's no harm to it. He left us a card from him an' Honey, says th' sign is a early Christmas present. He said if we was ever to move, we could take it with us.'

If we was ever to move? Was that more nursin' home talk? He wanted nothin' to do with bein' a geezer.

'So I reckon you like bein' called a geezer,' he said.

'Looks like I am one, so it don't make no difference to me.'

'Wellsir, it makes a difference to me. I ain't never cared for that word, it's f'r some gray-headed ol' dude who sets around in a rockin' chair whittlin' a squirrel from a piece of hick'ry.'

'You wouldn't whittle no squirrel out of hick'ry, hick'ry's too hard a wood for whittlin'. You'd want you a nice piece of sycamore, sycamore'd be dandy. You wouldn't whittle no squirrel from hick'ry, I can tell y' that.'

'Whatever,' he said, mad as a hornet. It was hard livin' with somebody who knows it all, all th' time.

'You might want to heat you up a bowl of collards,' said Willie, havin' hisself a laugh.

CYNTHIA

At Hollyhock, she'd known one thing for certain. She wouldn't end her suffering in a way that would cause Alice and Jeffrey trouble to clean up.

She would not be the guest who ruined the carpet or the floor with blood stains that no amount of scrubbing could remove. There was always something for those left behind to mop up or carry away.

A great-aunt by marriage had hanged herself from a peach tree. If you must do this, she could imagine someone saying, do it outside and away from the house. She had been a child when this happened to one of her father's relatives whom she never knew. But the story handed down was so vividly told that she felt she had been there, seeing the old aunt's bedroom slippers slide from her feet into the orchard grass.

Alice was impatient with nonsense, including her own nonsense of oversleeping, being unable to get dinner on the table before ten o'clock, and allowing perfectly good books to lie out in the rain.

Suicide was of course looked upon as sin. But did she not govern her body? Could she not do as she pleased with it? What was free will for, if not to be used and useful? The great-aunt had written a note and slipped it into the pocket of the apron worn over her house dress. *I can't take it anymore.*

That might have been her own mantra. I can't take any more emptiness, anguish, not knowing.

She remembered something she came across in her sophomore year at Smith. She had no reason to be interested in what a sixteenth-century French clergyman had to say, but she copied the quote onto the flyleaf of a notebook and never forgot it.

Every saint has a past. Every sinner has a future.

She was not one to think in terms of sin but liked that the word called out a particular weakness or brutality. She supposed that she may actually be a sinner to willfully leave behind a life that could be happy if only she worked harder to make it happen. Perhaps there would be points in her favor for having tried.

As she had always sought a saving of some kind, death continued its pledge to be the kindest.

LACE

She could not make an apron or even a potholder for her mom and Cynthia or a ballerina skirt for Sadie. She had no magic with a needle. But she hated ordering things that would come in boxes with styrofoam and all manner of wrappings to be recycled. Bought gifts were impersonal. As poor as she'd been before Olivia and Hoppy adopted her, it seems she would love gifts of any kind, especially bought, and she had tried to love all that, but couldn't.

Her mother never had any money at Christmas but would send her to the woods with an old hatchet that could hardly chip kindling. She would drag the little tree home—a white pine smelling of its delicious, sticky resin. They would set it in a blue bucket with river stones placed to keep it standing. Its presence completely changed the feeling in the room, it no longer felt barren like the pictures in *Let Us Now Praise Famous Men*, which was one of her favorite books from the bookmobile.

Sometimes they had electricity and when they didn't, they used a kerosene lamp handed down from her grandmother. They always lit the lamp at Christmas, to see shadows of piney branches on the walls. The house felt safe then, and she wanted that feeling to never end.

Before her mother was dying with the blood disease, they would sit at the little table with its oilcloth covering and cut shapes of bells and angels from construction paper; she had been proud of those tree ornaments.

The last time her brother came home, he had at least brought firewood up to the porch for the stove. But the logs were too big to use in the stove. Harley lived down the way then and taught her how to use his splitter, and helped her whenever he wasn't working. So they always had a fire in the stove at Christmas, and a kettle on the boil with a cinnamon stick in it.

Before she was really sick, her mother would put something for her under the tree on Christmas morning. She remembered the simple, hand-stitched blouse made from a white shirt gone gray with age, but bleached white again with lemon juice and sunshine. It was crisp with her mother's homemade starch and good as new. She went to school for three days in a row so it could be seen under her scroungy jacket.

She rarely thought about those days, because it had been a desperate time. Soon, she and Dooley and Jack and Sadie would be making happy memories of Christmas. And all the family would be under one roof, all at the same time.

She heard carols from the radio in the laundry room where Lily Flower was ironing. Her mother's old radio had been taken by her father ages ago so she and her mother had sung what carols they knew, and prayed that her father would not come home for Christmas.

JACK

He ran up the stairs to Heaven, which is what his mom and Granny C called the room where his mom painted murals.

He and Charley were both out of breath. 'I ran all th' way from Harley and Willie's in forty seconds! This is important, Mom. I just remembered to tell you—don't get a spoon rack!'

'A spoon rack?'

'You told Dad you wanted a spoon rack. I hope you didn't already get one.'

'I've hardly thought about it again. Why can't I get one?'

'Don't order one online or anything. I can't tell you any more, it's a secret.'

'I'm crazy about secrets. Anytime you need to tell a secret, you can tell me.'

His mom was painting another huge picture on a sheet of canvas nailed to the wall. When she finished, he and Harley and Willie would help her roll it up and send it off on the UPS truck. They knew the driver, Otis, who sometimes brought them plum jam his wife had made, and his mom gave Otis stuff from the garden.

Charley's tongue was totally hanging out. He sat on the floor with his dog and looked up at his mom. She squatted down because there wasn't a chair on th' scaffold. When she squatted down to talk to him, he knew she was payin' attention, which made him feel great.

'I know what I'd like for Christmas if anybody needs to know,' he said.

'I need to know.'

'A horse.'

She, like, raised her eyebrows but didn't say anything.

'But we would keep Scooter. Scooter is the best pony in the whole world. Dad said we can always keep Scooter. Besides, Scooter can be Sadie's pony when I have a horse.'

'We don't have money for a horse this year. In the meantime, you have a wonderful pony. You have a bike. You have a Gator.'

'Willie an' Harley are always using th' Gator; I hardly ever get to use th' Gator.'

'But when you do get to use it, it's special. It's special when you get to drive all around the place looking for mushrooms and Indian pipes and rocks for the garden. So it's good that you can't have it every day, because then it wouldn't be special. And Scooter loves you. You have a relationship with Scooter. You can't just walk away.'

'I wouldn't be walkin' away. I would be teachin' Sadie to ride Scooter. Sadie's three, which I researched and, like, three's not too young to have your own pony. I just want a horse, Mom.'

'Not this year, sweetheart. We don't always get to have what we want when we want it.'

He heaved a sigh, lay on his back, arms outstretched. He was not givin' up, he was just lyin' down.

There were plenty of horses around. He saw horses in people's fields all the time—just standing there, not doing anything. There was a horse that lived on the Hershells' farm next door that he liked a lot. It was mainly brown with, like, big white splashes on it. That horse would eat a carrot in a heartbeat. One time it ate five carrots from Willie's garden that hadn't even been washed.

His research said if you're asking for something you really want it should not be all about you.

'So, Mom, here's th' other thing. The really, really important thing, okay?'

'Okay.'

'Th' really important thing is, Scooter is lonely. He needs a companion besides donkeys and cats. He would be happier with a companion, even healthier with a companion. I researched it. Lucas Shaffer said his mule Toby was depressed and they got a Great Pyrenees to guard th' goats and Toby is fine now, which is what I'm sayin'. Did you know it's the same with humans, that we're better with a companion?'

'I understand, I promise I do. But we can't afford a horse this year. Next year things may be different. And here's something else to consider. A horse is a lot of work.'

'I can do it, Mom. I promise I can do it. I've practiced on Scooter since I was five. I feed him, I ride him, I brush him, I muck his stall. I can do the same for a horse.'

His mom was probably ready to get back to painting a hundred million leaves on a tree in th' picture.

'Let's talk about this again. With your dad. The three of us.'

'Another thing to think about, Mom, is th' donkeys are, like, bonded an' sometimes aren't very nice to Scooter. So a horse would be perfect for everybody, even th' barn cats. Everybody needs somebody, Mom.'

'You're so right, honey. So right.' She sat on the scaffold with her legs hanging down. That meant she was not through talking.

'But whatever happens, you're still th' world's best mom.'

'Awww. Thank you. I'm just crazy about you, too, Jack Kavanagh.'

'Do you remember when I was five and I asked if we could be best friends? We were layin' in th' grass . . . '

'*Lying* in the grass.'

'An' you said okay and so we stayed best friends since I was five.'

'I remember that. We were looking at clouds.'

'So, what if I had a best friend at Mitford School?'

'That would be wonderful. Absolutely!'

'But does it mean you can't be my best friend anymore? Miss Thomas said there can be only one best of anything. You can have all the betters you want but only one best.'

'That's the rule, but I actually have three best friends. Your dad is one and Sadie is one and you are one. When it comes to best friends, I think you can't play by the rules.'

He sighed. Rolled over. Sat up.

'If you and Dad could be glued together, you could be one big best friend.'

'That might be fun for a few minutes. Are you leaving?'

'I'm taking Sadie for a ride on Scooter. Harley's comin' with us. An' Davey's meetin' us on his pony. Before you say it, I'll take care of Sadie, I promise.'

'Let me come down there and give you some sugar.' She liked saying that to scare him, it was their favorite game since he was a kid. She got up like she was for real coming down to give him some sugar.

He ran down the stairs, yelling really loud. He heard her laughin'. He did not want anybody givin' him some sugar, except th' one or maybe two times he let her catch him.

TIM

The community notice board at Happy Endings didn't have much plot, but there were plenty of characters.

Mule Skinner was looking for a used Weed Eater, hoping that since it was winter, the owner might give it away.

There was Percy, hoping to help finance their twelfth cruise by selling household detritus—a cannister set, a transistor radio, a framed quartet of paint-by-number views of the Swiss Alps. He had once sat in their kitchen; it had been like going back in time by say, thirty or forty years. After decades of getting up at four a.m. to open the Main Street Grill at six, Percy and Velma were in a hurry to wring their money's worth from retirement.

A Medley of Blow Dryers was Fancy Skinner's offering from her years as a salon owner. As he had so little hair to blow, he was not a prospect.

Wanted please—a free piano that really plays and is not broken. Thank you very much. Sassy Guthrie, 11 years old. . . .

The two sets of Guthrie twins had spent a few of their early years at the rectory while Puny carried forth their housekeeping. He was the twins' unofficial Granpa on their mom's side, though he rarely saw them these days. A full roster of after-school activities kept them busy.

He pinned his notice to the community board.

Free. Crate for large dog. Water and food bowls included. Call . . .

Coot closed his Cheetos bag with a paper clip and stuck it under the counter. 'See any*thing* you cain't live without, Father?'

'Nossir, but if you get yourself a big dog, there's a real bargain on here. Check it out.'

He buttoned his jacket, turned up the collar. The store was on the chilly side, though the small army of heaters was going full blast.

'How's the Santa suit fitting this year?'

'I tried it on last night,' said Coot.

'And?'

'I'm gon' have to give up somethin' to git in it.'

'You have a little time to go before the parade. What's your plan?'

'I could give up my ice cream, I et a pint of Chunky Monkey last night. Or I could not eat th' bun on my chili dog I have at lunch. Or I could give up drivin' to th' UPS place an' start walkin' is what Grace said. Which would you give up if you don't mind me askin'?'

'I see you have carefully thought this through.'

'Yessir.'

'Well, a chili dog down th' hatch with no bun is nothing to look forward to. As for the ice cream, I'd do a cutback there, for sure. But bottom line, I'm with Grace.'

'Walkin'.'

'Afraid so. But here's a thought. You could give up the hot dog and the ice cream.'

'All at one time?'

'Cold turkey.'

'Nossir, I cain't do no cold turkey.'

'Ah, well, you'll figure it out.' He gave Coot a clap on the back. One of his favorite people.

Before leaving, he dropped a cash offering in the jar marked Furnace Fund. While the contents of the jar were growing, a whole new heating system was not something the citizens of Mitford were prepared to wrangle.

COOT

He watched th' Father walk up th' street and out of view.

A big dog. If he got hisself a big dog, it might not git along with Margaret Ann, th' store cat. When he come to work at Happy Endings, Margaret Ann ignored him for two or three years, which suited him fine. Then one day she started sleepin' at th' foot of his bed.

'Go *on*,' he said. He did not want to be sleepin' with a cat. 'Git!'

But Margaret Ann wouldn't git. She laid there like a rock with him kickin' around under th' covers and hollerin'. Night after night, she rooted in there.

He did not like her thinkin' she owned th' place. Take th' way she left cat hairs on th' chair in th' Poetry section. Hope had had that chair re-covered for a hundred an' forty dollars. It was their *best chair*! He used th' hand vac on it twice a week.

One thing about a big dog is it could scare people in th' store. An' if a big dog jumped on you, it could knock you down. Plus a big dog would have a big bark. That would send people flyin' out th' door, an' Hope wouldn't go for that by a long shot.

He pulled at his chin like he seen people do when they're thinkin'. It would be nice to have a big dog for company in his upstairs apartment at th' bookstore. It would be somebody to read to in th' evenin's when th' store was closed an' people gone home. Most of th' time he read out loud to hisself. He remembered that Father Tim used to read to his dog, which was big as a Buick, an' it acted like it understood ever' word.

A big dog would prob'ly like Dr. Seuss. A dog would want a book to have action in it. A cat, on th' other hand, acted like it didn't need nobody to read to it, it had already read ever'thing in th' store by its ownself.

He walked around an' nodded to th' customers an' said, 'Thank you for comin' in,' an' kep' on thinkin'. It seemed like th' worst problem with a big dog was that it'd be big.

He walked over to th' community board an' read what th' Father had pinned up, then read it ag'in.

Somebody told his mama, we like your boy, but he's not th' sharpest knife in th' drawer. He didn't have to be th' sharpest knife in th' drawer to figure out what jis' dawned on him:

Gittin' a big crate did not mean he had to git a big dog.

He could have a little dog in a big crate. An' a little dog could eat out of big dishes as good as little dishes.

It would be puttin' th' cart before th' horse, but he reached up and took down th' Father's notice before anybody else took it down. All he had to do was talk to Hope and prob'ly Scott and definitely Grace.

As for Margaret Ann, he would cross that bridge when he come to it.

HARLEY

It was crazy even to think about, but him and Willie thought they'd give it a shot.

'Foundation solid. Shell good,' said Mink. 'Needless to say, the roof's totally shot. You'll want three replacement beams for your roof deck. Three out of five of your floors are ruined.

'Chimney's got to be repaired, big time. It's leanin' south. If you gon' use th' fireplace, you need you a new firebox, new mortar inside an' out, new flue. Don't even think about buildin' a fire 'til that's done an' inspected.'

'What if we jis' board it up?' said Willie.

'I don't believe in boardin' up a fireplace,' said Harley.

'My people always boarded up a fireplace,' said Willie.

His people never boarded up nothin'. They was proud to have a fireplace. But he let that pass, since this was a dream. They was jis' what you call feelin' it out.

'You want to put a porch back on?'

'A man's got to have a porch,' said Willie.

'Forty-five hundred, you'll have you a nice porch. Then there's your heat. That ol' boiler hadn't been used in a coon's age. Me an' Honey like boiler heat. I could prob'ly tune it up for you, but y'r pipes an' vents'll have to be replaced. If it's shot, you'll need around ten K for a decent system.'

He was gittin' swimmy-headed. He wanted to set down but they wadn't no place to set as th' porch was leanin' into th' grass an' th' steps didn't have no treads.

This could go on 'til th' cows come home. 'How much for the whole shebang?' he said. His hands was shakin' so he put 'em in his pockets.

'I'd say thirty-five grand. That's based on y'all doin' a good bit of heavy liftin'. You an' Harley could handle the carpentry, th' floors, installin' your sinks, your toilet an' all.

''Course your drywall has to go. Rip 'er out, boys, I'll give you a hand. Been meanin' to tell you my oldest boy is movin' home with his bride come spring. They'll be lookin' for extra work. Meantime, me an' Jake'll pitch in to help clean up around here. You gon' need a Dumpster if they can get it down your washed-out road.'

Mink stood back from the house and looked it over again, worked a toothpick between his molars. 'First off, make sure your roof is tight and your doors hung so if you have to stop work you can close it up and keep it dry.'

He sat down on a rock. If he'd been hit in th' head with a two-by-four, he couldn't feel more knocked out. Thirty-five grand. He'd never dealt with that many zeros. Willie set down on another rock, both of 'em knowin' they'd have trouble gittin' up.

'A little at a time is how I like to do a project,' said Mink. 'Get your roof on. When th' weather's good, do your cleanup outside. When it's bad, work inside. Get your floors down an' covered, an' wait 'til spring to get on with it.'

'I might not make it 'til spring,' said Willie.

'I'd give you a hand with th' roof beams,' said Mink, 'but Honey won't let me get on a ladder. I'm limited to th' kitchen stepstool. After Christmas, I'll give you my Saturdays 'til spring, then I'm slammed at my place.'

'Much obliged,' said Harley. 'Much obliged.' He was wastin' his breath, there wadn' no way they could pull this off.

'What's Dooley sayin' about this?'

'Best not talk to Dooley jus' yet,' said Willie.

'Don't wait too long, boys. This ol' place cain't handle much more bad weather. It's fish or cut bait.'

HARLEY, WILLIE, AND DOOLEY

Him and Willie went back a few days later to look around. They knew it wadn't gon' happen, it was all a dream. But they both liked th' notion of livin' in th' clearin' an' puttin' in a big garden.

They had rode over in th' Gator and parked out front of th' house an' was lookin' around. A man could set out in th' yard and get hisself some rays over here. It would be a good place to grill out an' have th' neighbors over. An' a swing, they could hang a tire swing off of that maple. Its lower limb was jis' waitin' to be swung from.

They heard it comin'.

'It's hittin' th' fan,' said Willie. 'Don't admit nothin'.'

An' there was Dooley ridin' up in his truck.

'What y'all doin' over here?' he said. 'Lookin' for that snake to climb out on a limb?'

Willie scratched his head. They had to step up to the plate sometime. Why not now? They didn't have a plan, just a notion, just a dream—that was th' problem. But this wadn't NATO. They didn't have to set down at a big table like visitin' dignitaries.

Dooley turned off the truck engine. How to say it to the guys was the problem. How would y'all like to live here? How about if this was Geezer Cottage? How about if we all pitch in and pass the hat and work on it ourselves and just get it done? You leave for any reason it turns over to the farm.

Maybe he needed a lawyer to look at this harebrained scheme, but that would cost money and why couldn't they just wrangle it themselves—they were decent people.

'Jus' wanted us a breath of fresh air,' said Willie.

'Right,' said Dooley. These guys were up to something, he could read them like a traffic ticket.

HARLEY

On the way back to the barn in the Gator, he asked one more time.

'We cain't move ahead one way or another,' he hollered over th' clamor of th' engine, 'if we don't know what you've got saved up. So how much you got saved? Like I said, I got six an' a half an' I don't need no sermon on how I could've done better, I was bad off a few years back an' couldn't work.'

Father Tim an' Cynthia let him move into the rectory, into their guest room. It was like God Almighty had done him a personal favor. Two pillers, a warm blanket an' a flowered spread, a hot shower, an' a readin' lamp. He'd never had a lamp to read by. Th' doc had put him on what they call bed rest. It like to drove him crazy but he got well.

Then he got a job at Lew Boyd's an' Father Tim let him move to th' rectory basement, which was as fine a place as th' upstairs. He had mowed, limed, fertilized, worked on their cars, cleaned out th' garage, painted this an' that, built a deck, an' done whatever he could to help 'til he could pay a little rent. Then Father Tim an' Cynthia moved over to her house next door an' Miss Pringle rented th' upstairs right over his head at th' rectory an' th' piano playin' started. Saved hisself th' cost of a radio.

Th' ruts in th' road was flingin' him an' Willie ever' whichaway.

'Money's a private thing!' yelled Willie. 'Like religion an' politics, you don't go around blabbin' about it.'

Why did he even think about shellin' out hard-earned cash to live with this bonehead?

'Six!' said Willie.

They hit a hole.

'Six an' a half is what I got!'

Another hole.

'How much did you say?'

Willie give him th' eye. 'Seven!' he hollered. 'An' not a penny more.'

HARLEY

It was meatloaf an' mashed potatoes with green beans at the kitchen table in th' big house. It was what him an' Willie called their NATO meetin' with Dooley. They had cooked at their place an' brought it over. Lace was puttin' th' young'uns to bed.

'So, guys. Great minds think alike, right? We were fallin' all over each other lookin' at that old place.'

'When you drove in there an' caught us,' said Willie, 'we were jus' dreamin', no idea we'd be settin' here tonight, right, Harl?'

He was so bowled over, he could hardly talk right now, so he nodded.

'Lace and I are good to go if y'all want to go. We agree it would be good for everybody. Right now, we don't know how we can make this happen, it might take a miracle, but there are plenty of those up for grabs and we're ready. I can't pitch in any cash right now, but I'll give each of you a day off every week to work over there. Every Monday, one of you will be full-time at th' old place and one at th' farm. You're on your own for the weekends.

'When we're loadin' cattle or whatever needs two men, you'll have to work around that and stick here.

'Mink and Jake and my dad will give us three days a week. None of these folks will get on a ladder, just so you know. We might rope in a few guys from our church, so the labor pool is lookin' pretty positive . . .

'But somebody's got to organize this thing. All th' labor flyin' around with different schedules and skills will be a can of worms. Willie, we'll need your organizational savvy, so you run the job. Harley, you'll be the wingman—nobody's as experienced as you in all th' trades. First things first. Line up your help to get the trash off th' place. How does this feel, guys?'

Willie saluted.

'Harley?'

'That'll work,' he said. There was a churn in his gut. Puttin' all his savin's in a scheme like this—he was pretty scared. But he was excited, too. He felt like he needed to throw up but held back.

'This will take a miracle,' said Dooley. 'It took a miracle for us to be sittin' at this table on a farm Lace and I could no way buy on our own. But we can do this, guys, we can do this. After Christmas, we'll meet right here at this table and go over our progress. Everybody in?'

They was all in.

'And when we pull it off,' said Dooley, 'when th' chips have fallen where they may, as Dad says, th' house will be yours till you pass.'

Pass! Here he was, an experienced, reliable, jack of all trades, an' already they was talkin' about him passin'. From a wheelchair to a nursin' home to dead as a doorknob in hardly no time.

They heard Lace barrelin' down th' stairs. She slid onto th' bench at th' table. 'Where are we?'

'Tryin' to grease this thing,' said Dooley. 'We've got to get our financial stuff together. It all needs to go in one account. Lace, you said you want to invest in what's goin' on.'

'Five thousand,' she said. 'As soon as I get paid for the mural.'

Seem like his breath was took away.

'That's eighteen and a half,' said Dooley. 'The miracle's already working. Willie, you and Harley and I can handle the bank stuff in town, and everybody with money in the game gets to see the cash flow—receipts, withdrawals, deposits. Everybody knows what's happening.'

'If you all were renting,' said Lace, 'your money wouldn't last long.

This way, you're covered for the rest of your lives. And we all get to be close by instead of split up all over the place. So what will you name your new house? Houses need a name.'

Head-scratchin'. Namin' hadn't been on th' list.

'Geezer Cottage,' said Willie. 'We take down th' sign we got an' carry it with us.'

'Great!' said Dooley.

'Perfect!' said Lace. 'What do you think, Harley?'

'Good to go.'

He wondered if this was how NATO worked, all them countries tryin' to agree on how to lay down th' law to other countries. Geezer wadn't his favorite name, but since th' sign went up at their front door, he'd sort of felt like a geezer an' it didn't feel too bad.

'Most people would've tore it down,' said Willie. 'Most people would look at this whole notion as crazy.'

Lace leaned in like she was gon' tell a secret. 'There's something an early poet said: "Start a huge foolish project like Noah. It makes no difference what people think of you."'

He felt suddenly proud of their huge, foolish project. Ol' Noah an' his boys must have got on a few ladders to whip that thing out.

Yessir, they could do this, they could do this.

DOOLEY

On the following Monday, he was washing up at the sink by the clinic window, his observatory.

He saw Harley's truck turn into the old road. Minutes later, there was the truck hauling the Dumpster, with Jake's busted-up Silverado wheeling in behind.

He did something his dad often did, something he'd never done before; he made the sign of the cross—touching his forehead, chest, each shoulder. He realized he'd done it without thinking and without even knowing what it really meant.

'Thanks,' he said. 'Thanks.'

JAKE, DOOLEY, WILLIE, AND HARLEY

Nothin' on a ladder. Nothin' on a roof. An' nothin' with a chain saw,' said Jake. 'That's Sugar's three no-no's if I sign up to help with any kind of construction.

'Here's my deal. I'll give you two Mondays a month. Eight to four with a hour for lunch—I'll run home for that. You pay one cold beer after work. Stella Artois is th' label. An' can't nobody be makin' fun of me for drinkin' what they can't pronounce.'

'That'll move us along,' said Dooley. 'You're mighty kind. Thanks, Jake.'

'Yessir,' said Willie. 'Mighty kind.'

'Much obliged,' said Harley.

'Y'all picked a booger of a job, I'll tell you that, most people would tear it down and keep goin'. But one more thing. Just like at th' store, no cussin'.'

'We cain't guarantee that, no way,' said Willie. 'But we'll do our best. Me an' Harley ain't bad to cuss unless we smash a finger with th' hammer.'

'Then it's whatever flies out,' said Harley.

'We'll owe you for this, Jake. Me an' Harley'll give you labor when you need it.'

'I don't aim to need it. I give a hand to pay back my community for their business. Thirty-four good years at th' Crossroads—middle of nowhere, soon to be somewhere when a couple of tech companies get goin'.'

'They's angels droppin' out of th' sky ever' whichaway,' said Harley.

TIM

He almost never put his feet up. But here he was, unshaved, in his pajamas, and sock feet on the coffee table.

'All this comfort,' he said. 'All this luxury and ease. I feel like I haven't done anything for anybody for way too long.'

'If it's any consolation,' she said, 'this is Saturday. Isn't this what people do on Saturday? I've worked all week; I'm thrilled it's Saturday.'

Her hair uncombed, barefoot; she was happy. He needed to buck up.

'Do you realize,' she said, 'that you say this sort of thing at least once every year? Every year! You're terrified of hanging out. Your son said it in plain English, remember?'

'He said I need to learn how to chill. It seems selfish, somehow.'

'Selfish! You don't have a clue how to be selfish. So, listen to me, okay? Are you listening?'

'Sort of,' he said. He rather enjoyed it when his deacon started preaching. He liked watching her when she was getting up steam as she was currently doing. One credit he could give her, she was honest, she would level with him. The caveat was, he'd already heard what was coming. Several times. Many times.

'You have poured out and dug in for decades,' she said. 'You deserve a break. A long break. Putting your feet up for *five minutes* does not qualify as a break.'

'Yes, but name one meaningful thing I've done . . . '

'If not your very self, who was that guy running up and down the mountain for all those months supplying in Holding? All those days of writing new sermons because you dislike repeating yourself! And you ask what you've done that's meaningful? Here's the real answer. You fixed the screen door!'

He liked this particular heckling from his wife; she had a streak of the cheerleader. He patted her knee, sipped his coffee. 'You know—if I had it to do over, I think I might be a teacher.'

'You are a teacher. What is a preacher if not a teacher? Anyway, I love seeing you with your feet up. Hold on. I'm taking a picture. This is historic.'

'Please,' he said. 'I haven't combed my hair.'

They had a laugh as she grabbed her phone and framed him against the background of the small fire on the hearth and the portrait of Dooley over the mantel. Never fond of the camera, he gave her a fake grin.

'And in case you're looking for a legacy, honey, you already have one. How about the family you put back together? Scattered to the four winds and now together again with their feet under our table in just a few days. Enjoy that, revel in it.

'And if that's not enough, may I remind you that you've been an absolute staple of consolation at Hope House and the hospital for a quarter of a *century*? You ran a bookstore for nine long months so it wouldn't go out of business, you managed a grocery store and kept a black bottom line. And as soon as the holidays are over, what then? You'll be going out to a construction site to help redeem a house that Mink called a tear-down.

'Now listen to me, Timothy. While we're on the subject, you are not to get on a ladder. Or a roof. Or any other high place. Will you promise?'

'This is verging on a homily,' he said, 'except you're leaving God out of it.'

'For God's sake, Timothy, no ladders and no roof. Is that a promise?'

He might have saluted, but that would not be a good idea. She had her soft, albeit ersatz southern side, but at the core she was a damn Yankee all the way.

'So how did I do?' she said over a lunch of leftover pasta with her marinara sauce.

'With your dictatorial about ladders and rooftops?'

'Yes. Did I scare your pants off?'

'Almost. But not quite. I will get on a ladder. But I will not go above the second rung. How's that?'

They high-fived. Oh, Lord, if only the halls of world government could work like this.

TIM

He stopped by Happy Endings for a go at yesterday's *Wall Street Journal*. Hope was out, Marcie Guthrie was in. Marcie floated among the town merchants, subbing at retail, bookkeeping, and, like her mother, the general bossing of any available staff. On his way out, he searched the community board for Sassy's piano plea—still up. Mitford was not known for homes with pianos.

His mother had tried to get him interested in the piano but since the piano teacher was eight miles roundtrip and gas was rationed, he took a few guitar lessons from Tommy, who had a beat-up Martin N-20. This had been a barter deal. For each lesson of undetermined length, Tommy required a frog. He was going to be a marine biologist.

The deal was a hassle. Slippery didn't come close to describing a frog. It was no sooner in his hands than it was out. He tried Louis's frog net with zero success. As for a gig, that was for people who got in a boat in the pitch-black dark, drank bootleg hooch, hollered all over the place, and fell out of the boat. When he got three frogs behind with Tommy, he quit and turned over a quarter and a dime to settle.

With just three chords, he could butcher '(Ghost) Riders in the Sky.' At the end of the lessons disaster, he was given a verbal summary of the whole affair. 'You ain't got rhythm,' said Tommy, who was never afraid of raw truth.

That he had no rhythm was concerning. When he tried dancing to Louis's radio music, which was mostly static, Louis looked at him and shook his head. 'You dancin' white,' said Louis, who proceeded to show him how it was done.

He had never seen Louis all hunkered down an' poppin' his fingers and shaking himself around. If that was dancing, he would never be able to do it. And so he never did it, except at the ball at Fernbank, but that was box step and didn't count. Box step was merely an excuse for having conversation in a good-looking outfit.

He was obviously different from other kids. Like he couldn't tell anybody he loved poetry, no way. They would have beat the snot out of him. They didn't know what poetry was, exactly, just that it was foreign. He could, however, do recitations from Scripture for their priest, who appeared overjoyed by his memorization skills.

But whatever else may come or go, he could play softball and he could build a fort like nobody's business. The fort he built with Tommy would have won a blue ribbon in the state fair if they had a Build Your Own Fort competition.

He would keep his hands off the space station Jack and the neighbor boys planned to build in the spring; he would be only, let's say, a mere consultant.

COOT AND TIM

He had talked hisself out of a big dog, but that's what he really wanted. It's what he kep' picturin' in his mind, him walkin' down th' street with his big dog an' people sayin', Coot, that is some kind of a big dog you got there, or somebody else'd say, What'll you take for that big dog?

Th' people at th' feed store in Wesley had a big dog. It laid around on a feed sack and let people scratch behind its ears and give it snacks an' whatall an' it didn't bite nobody or even bark.

It was true that a big dog usually had a big bark but think how yappy them little dogs could be. He didn't want no yappy dog. Hope wouldn't take to that an' Grace wouldn't neither.

He saw Father Tim comin' in, which was th' perfect time to git this thing rollin'.

'I taken down your notice,' he said.

'Why is that?'

'I aim to git a big dog an' thought I better take it down 'fore somebody else gits your crate an' dishes.'

'Good thinking. Okay with Hope, I presume—getting a dog?'

'Long as it's a retail dog, yessir.'

'A retail dog?'

'Don't bite. Don't do its b'iness on th' rug. Don't bark at customers. Don't jump on nobody. Don't have fleas.'

Right there was a good laugh. 'I'm not sure such a breed is out there. Might take a while to chase that one.'

'Me an' Grace are gon' train it.'

'If Grace is in on this, consider it done.' He got excited about anybody's hunt for a dog. After Barnabas passed, he hadn't dog-hunted at all. He'd had the best of dogs, he would never have another, and now look—he had a dog!—albeit one with the occasional flea, but he could give you a grin and bark with a ball in his mouth.

'Ahead of gittin' th' dog is it okay for me to come git what your notice says?'

'So you're sure you want a big dog? More expensive to feed, more brushing, can be hard to get in and out of your truck if you're going to the vet. Just a thought.'

'Yessir, I'd like a big dog.'

'So come around tomorrow afternoon and move everything to your place. The crate's a whopper, but you've got your truck. And when you find the right dog, you'll have the right equipment ready to go.'

Coot lit up like a Christmas tree. 'Much obliged, Father. I thank you, I sure do.'

'Because it's you, Coot, I'll throw in a blanket. Clean, with good years left in it.' He felt his eyes mist. Barnabas had loved that blanket; he had no idea he'd be able to let it go. But the time was right.

Coot was obviously overcome by flat-out joy. They shook hands with vigor.

Coot reached under the counter, opened the bag, and held it forth. 'Have a Cheeto!' he said, by way of celebration.

COOT

Hope said it would have to be on a trial basis.

Right off th' bat, a dog would have to pass th' Margaret Ann test. Along with th' dog bein' house-trained, not barkin' at customers or jumpin' on anybody, it could not have fleas. Fleas could get in th' Poetry section carpet an' that would be a breedin' ground.

Bottom line, his dog would have to be what you call 'properly trained.' If th' dogs their customers brought in was any example, they wadn't any dog on th' planet that was properly trained.

Grace added her two cents' worth. 'It especially can't bite, and it can't let kids make it nervous. It has to like being petted, and people will bring it treats, which it can't have because they are not organic.'

Maybe he didn't need a dog. Maybe a parrot like his teacher brought to school one time. Th' teacher said to th' parrot, What's worse than findin' a worm in your apple, an' th' parrot said, Findin' half a worm. Teacher said, What's th' smartest insect? An' th' parrot said, Th' spellin' bee. He had never seen such a show as that; his mama had thought he was makin' it up.

But he wouldn't want to put anything with wings in a cage. He had gone this long without a dog; let some other person deal with th' torment of gittin' a perfect dog.

But Grace was excited about him gettin' a dog an' said she would help train it. Th' problem with that was, she'd have it wearin' a clown suit an' walkin' on its hind legs in th' parade. He didn't know if he wanted anybody else trainin' his dog, but he did know this:

To turn any kind of a dog into a retail dog, he would need all th' help he could git.

TIM

When the letter popped into his mind, he tried to shut down the frustration, even the anger, that flowed in. Sometimes he stewed before he realized he was stewing. Over and over—how could it possibly have disappeared like that? What clue to its whereabouts was he missing?

In any case, he needed to give her a gift. People in Mitford liked to know what you got for Christmas, plus who gave it to you and how you liked it. If hyperobsession over gifting could be defined like dog breeds, Mitford would be a terrier.

So what could he give her that would bring out that great laugh of hers, the sheer delight he loved to provoke? They hadn't slipped to the point of giving each other a flat nothing.

He wouldn't undertake the sensitive mission of finding her another white cat. Her last Violet, a life model for her book illustrations, had passed a year ago; she would be illustrating the Met book sans a living model.

In any case, she didn't need the affections of an adoring four-legged companion right now. While pumped by painting for the hospital auction and mapping out the Met book, her chief delight was being an on-call Granny, a role not likely to be shed until the grans left for college. If ever.

Nothing would do but the letter.

TIM

A wind was up. Yesterday's coupon page of the *Muse* flew by on his walk to the Local. He checked his pocket—he was one of the few Local customers allowed to give Chucky a dog biscuit.

For several years, Avis had gotten away with keeping a dog in a no-dogs-in-grocery-stores ordinance zone. Therapy dogs with their owners were of course free to come and go as they pleased.

Back in the spring and with Avis's approval, he argued this sensitive point before the town council who, every year or two, got tough on the Chucky business.

'Time to put it to rest,' said the council, which was chiefly composed of cat people. Thanks to a dog clocking in every day at the grocery store, the Town of Mitford was flat-out breaking the law and this time, the party was over.

Forty years in a pulpit had never completely fixed his pre-talk jitters.

He had sat in the front row in the town meeting and noticed that the council members were avoiding eye contact. He hadn't exactly organized it or anything, but a group of supporters had shown up to root for Chucky.

He opened his remarks by noting that Avis had endured a hard year a while back, and Chucky had helped him completely recover from a life-threatening pneumonia, hyperanxiety, and depression. Chucky was, in fact, good medicine.

The crowd of supporters supported that, waved their signs, chanted, 'Chucky, Chucky, Chucky!'

He leaned into his science bit. 'Having this well-behaved dog that does not bite, scratch unnecessarily, or jump on people is also good medicine for everybody who comes into the store. Scientific studies show that interaction with a dog can lower blood pressure, lower cholesterol, and elevate levels of serotonin and dopamine, which can calm anxiety.

'Further, it is essential to Avis's well-being that Chucky not be left home alone during the workweek. Chucky has been diagnosed with a disorder known as separation anxiety, and Avis may be unable to fully serve his customers under the stress of these concerns.'

Though seldom one for bucking the system, he found this plea a dash on the side of exhilarating. His concluding remarks were delivered in his pulpit voice.

'Chucky is a total therapy dog,' he said. 'Not just for Avis but for an entire community.'

'Chucky, Chucky, Chucky!'

'In my ancestral homeland of Ireland, I never, not even once, saw a dog that required a legal permit to get in the door. Where there were people there were dogs. In the pubs and restaurants, in the cafés and hotels—even on the beaches! For whatever that's worth.' Which was nothing, he was pretty sure.

'I have researched what's needed to go legit and it is a can of bureaucratic worms—entirely beyond Chucky's skill set. I appeal to the council to allow Chucky to remain in place—in his crucial role of personal and social therapy dog and valued community morale booster. Thank you.'

The council remained mostly heads down, taking notes and squinting at phones held with zero discretion under the conference table. Indeed, they were pretty rattled by a town citizen coming in with twenty-some people behaving like a protest mob.

The MPD chief stood, dressed in full regulation gear, Glock, radio, baton, the works. He adjusted his tie and stepped to the lectern.

It didn't hurt that their police department was partial to Chucky. Representing the entire force of three men and one woman, Joe Joe Guthrie gave the council his two cents' worth.

Avis, he said, had been out there as 'a longtime dogless bachelor' whose lonely life was changed for good when Chucky personally chose Avis as his forever companion.

Joe Joe went on a good bit about Chucky's beneficial effects on Avis's psychological and physical state and ended with a reminder that would have 'brought tears to a glass eye,' as Council Secretary Mary Jo Bean later remarked.

'May I remind you,' said Joe Joe, who, like his grandmother, Esther Cunningham, had a dramatic flair, 'how many times Avis Packard, in *all kinds* of foul weather, has come to the aid of th' sick an' shut-in of this town?

'Think about haulin' up some of these steep driveways in winter—ice, snow, hail big as golf balls, power out, house cold—an' here comes Avis's truck up th' hill, got a cherry pie in that bag, an' a little pack of firewood an' a quart of hot soup and a pound of deli meat an' a loaf of bread an' a jar of Duke's. Think about that.

'Any of you remember Old Man Mueller out there in th' cornfield in that house with the cold wind whippin' though th' cracks? Imagine him layin' in there under a pile of quilts in th' dark, preparin' to go home to his Maker, an' who drives up? It wadn't Santy Claus. It wadn't th' town council. It wadn't a church van or even th' MPD. Who was it?'

This was not a rhetorical question.

'*Who was it?*' said Joe Joe. 'I want to hear his name spoken in this room, ladies and gentlemen.'

The council looked at one another. The mayor spoke first.

'Avis Packard!'

'Avis Packard!' said Council Secretary Mary Jo Bean.

'Avis Packard!' said the council members in unison. Unable to help themselves, they burst into applause, as did everyone else.

'Let th' man have 'is dog in th' store!' said Joe Joe, and walked out of the meeting. They heard the siren on his car as he scratched out of the parking lot, headed to lunch.

The meeting ended with a uniformed Girl Scout troop passing out cookies and giving voluble testimony to Chucky's popularity. His popularity was 'humongous, amazing, and totally awesome.'

Scout spokesperson Grace Murphy said if the town made Chucky stay home, there would be pushback from the kids at Mitford School and even some of the teachers, but maybe not the principal, who was a cat person.

He had high-fived the Scouts and split a caramel chocolate chip with Grace.

The wind slammed the door behind him as he blew into the Local. Chucky was at the ready for his peanut butter dog biscuit.

'Still breakin' the law, you guys!'

'If th' law comes after us,' said Avis, 'they'll have to catch us, right, Chucky? We'll head out west an' pan for gold, we'll get th' Father here to run th' place.'

'I'd rather take a whippin',' he said, and they had a laugh.

While Avis was hospitalized a few years ago, yours truly had managed the Local and was totally cured of fooling with perishables.

'Here to pick up our Thanksgiving order.' Three days out on a ticking clock. Once again, he told Avis the number of guests; he was proud of the number. 'Eighteen,' he said. 'We'll have eighteen at the table.'

'You got a fourteen-pound turkey—it's a dandy, I can promise you that. An' your ham is as fine a ham as I've seen from th' Valley in a long while.'

'My culinary reputation rides on your ham.'

'My supplier's good to 'is hogs. Keeps 'em warm an' dry on clean straw. So eighteen people, five of 'em young'uns, you'll have plenty of leftovers both ways. You're good to go, Father, I'll just step in th' back an' get Otis to wrap up your order.'

He pulled out his billfold.

'Nossir. Put that back in your pocket. This is on th' house.'

'Now, Avis . . . '

'I was laid up in th' hospital with my chest feelin' like a block of cement. All I lacked of bein' dead was th' news gettin' out. Who was gon' run th' store? I had good people, but they couldn't run th' store. Thanksgivin' was comin'—my biggest time of th' year. If I had to close th' doors, this place was a goner.

'An' you stepped in an' we didn't have to close an' we had a good bit of profit out of all that. I remember layin' there listenin' to you pray—you might've thought I was pretty drugged up, but I heard a whole lot of your prayin', Father. All that time settin' by my bed, an' all that work you done when you didn't have to. Nossir, this has been a good year, an' your Thanksgivin' turkey an' ham are on th' Local.'

'Avis . . . '

'An' what all you've done for me don't stop there. Remember that woman who come in here an' stole my dog from under th' nose of th' *po*lice captain? So who went lookin' for Chucky? That would be you, Father. And when he come home, whose door did he run to for a square meal and gettin' his paws doctored? Plus you got 'im off th' hook with th' council.'

'Not just me, I had support . . . '

'So nossir, you're not payin' a *dime* for your ham an' turkey. An' I'm throwin' in th' oysters y'all need every year for your Christmas pie. They'll be in th' cooler by December nineteenth.'

'Avis, that's . . . '

'There'll be a pound with your name on it. As you like to say, consider it done.'

'But you . . . '

Avis leaned over the counter, looked him in the eye. 'You know what you need to do, Father? You need to let people do for you once in a while. It gives us a blessin'.'

'My wife wouldn't say I don't let others do for me. But I hear you, Avis, and I'm grateful. Very grateful.' He was pretty good at giving, but receiving was another matter. Resistance to receiving was what his bishop had half-jokingly defined as a personality disorder.

Avis straightened up, and with a firm look summarized his point. 'You cain't hog all th' blessin's, Father.'

He shook the hand that fed Mitford. 'Thank you, my friend. Thank you. Way more than generous. As my grandfather used to say—much obliged. Much obliged.'

Avis's long face was well supplied with a big grin. After decades of dishing out recipes, his grocer was dishing out cures for personality disorders.

He loaded the star attractions of the Thanksgiving table into the trunk and foraged in the console for his knit hat. He put it on and pulled it over his ears and crossed Main to Happy Endings.

His Christmas books and puzzles order was in and he was picking it up, each gift already wrapped. This was definitely the way to do the holydays. Shopping early cleared the path through Advent and tamped down the haste of the season. Cynthia's order would be ready next week—unwrapped, she said, to give her a little vibe of seasonal stress.

Business was brisk. Four typewriter poets at their laptops, two with a small queue. Ha! There was Mule Skinner. Mule in a queue for a typewriter poem? He would take out his phone and shoot this phenomenon, but he didn't want to embarrass anybody.

He dug into his billfold for his credit card.

Hope shook her head. 'Please put it back in your wallet, Father. This is our gift to you.'

'Hope!'

'No protests. Look at all you've done for me, and for the first time Happy Endings is able to do something for you. You must allow us this pleasure.'

'Have you by any chance been talking to Avis?'

'I'm always talking to Avis.' She gave him a smile. 'At least as far as gifts go, you'll be free as a bird to enjoy the holidays.'

'Hope, please . . . '

'No, Father. You must let others to do for you as you do for us.' She looked at him fondly. 'You can't hog all the blessings.'

Was that their official mantra for this caper? He smacked his forehead. 'You and Avis . . . cahoots!'

'The butcher, the baker, the bookstore maker,' she said. 'Oops, bad me. I didn't mean to mention the baker. Please don't tell Winnie I goofed.'

'You're all in this together!'

'We are,' she said. 'A conspiracy long in the coming.'

He took out his handkerchief and wiped his eyes. 'See there? See what you've done?'

'To thank you even a little for the love you give us,' she said, 'it takes a village.'

HOPE

She had actually remembered the book and letter, but it seemed out of place to give it, and explain why she had it—all that, along with trying to give him a gift for all he had done for the store. She would give it to him after the lighting of the tree. Yes, after the lighting.

TIM

He was headed to the car with the book box when Mule caught up with him.

'Lookit this!' Mule held forth a sheet of paper, hassled by the wind.

'What?' he said, still walking. The box weighed a ton, and they were walking against the wind.

'I paid two bucks for this poem, cooked up in thirty seconds by a total stranger who's workin' his way through college.'

'I hope you gave the kid a tip.'

'Are you kidding? I worked my way through college and nobody gave me a tip. I can't make heads or tails of this. You're always quotin' some poet or other, maybe you can tell me what it means.'

He kept walking. The heavy box was a killer, thanks to the tome on vintage cars. 'Read it to me.'

'*Truth*,' said Mule, '*is a silver bullet*

'*Allow it to enter the heart*

'*And shatter the bone*

'*Of worldly attractions*.'

'That's it?'

'That's it. I don't get it.' Mule was panting from the walk to the car. 'Is this supposed to have some meaning about my personal life?'

'I don't think it's like a fortune cookie.'

He opened the trunk, placed the box of books next to the Thanksgiving comestibles. Alleluia! Ahead of the seasonal madness—everybody's dream.

'It doesn't even rhyme,' said Mule. 'Plus there's no bone in th' heart as far as I know; I hope this kid's not in med school.'

The wind grabbed the poem, whisked it along the street, and sailed it over a lamppost.

'Whoa! There goes your literary investment!'

'An' good riddance!' hollered Mule.

TIM

Out of habit, he checked the community notices.

Sassy had scored a piano! Her plea was no longer on the board.

'Someone from the college,' Hope said. 'A professor retiring to a cabin in Montana. All he's taking is a fishing pole, an iron skillet, and *The Oxford Book of English Verse*. Not even his wife.'

'Whoa.'

'She'll follow when she retires next year. The rumor is, she'll take curtains, dinner plates, and a case of cabernet.'

'The amenities.'

'It's not a Steinway,' she said. 'But because Sassy's an eleven-year-old with special talent, the professor had it tuned.'

The bell jangled as the door blew open and a virtual passel of fourth-graders blew in. 'Back here in ten minutes!' Miss Everhardt commanded as her pupils split off to the toilet and various book racks of interest.

'Father!' said Miss Everhardt, shaking his hand. 'Great to see you!'

'Miss Everhardt! Even better to see you. What literary marvel is up for today?'

'We're reading the Newberys this year. Finishing up *Shiloh*. A heart-warming story about a dog that's being abused but finds a forever home.'

'Something a seven-year-old might enjoy?'

'Absolutely!'

He added it to his tab while the kids assembled in the Poetry section.

Compared to the amount of gifts he received as a boy, the modern Christmas was a tsunami, way up from the trickling creek of his youth. The bag of marbles when he was seven? Olympic gold. The horse Louis made from a hickory stick and a bit of wood with leather ears, hand-painted? Beyond!

What if everybody got just one thing—the one thing they really wanted? 'The caveat,' he said to Gus as they drove home, 'is that a lot of people don't know what they really want. Right?'

Gus looked his way, clearly thoughtful.

He was resigned to telling Cynthia what he really wanted, using the time-honored oral tradition. He was over the angst of the loss, and after the fashion of Lady Macbeth, was washing his hands of the whole business.

He would go online and look at cardigans with pockets.

HOPE

Heaters galore, borrowed and bought.

One blazing away in the Poetry section; one by the coffee maker; one in the History section; another by the hot chocolate table; the one with the rattle behind the check-out counter; and the big one at the front door where a chill blew in with every customer.

Due to a glitch on the town calendar a few years ago, the Christmas parade was traditionally held a day ahead of Thanksgiving. At two o'clock, Coot had appeared on the fire truck as Santa; now he was walking around the store as Old Saint Nicholas of Myra. He had thirty minutes to get in full character; this was his warm-up. She loved to eavesdrop on what the kids had to say.

A freckled boy was dubious. 'Are you Santy Claus?'

'Nossir. I'm ol' Saint Nick. Santy Claus modeled hisself after me.'

'Where's your red suit at?'

'I ain't got no red suit. This here's a green suit.'

A curly-haired five-year-old whose academic parents were browsing the Gardening section gave him a look beyond her years. 'It should be red if Santa modeled himself after you.'

She'd been promised that peppermint sticks would be given out of a sack somewhere. She did not see a sack and was getting impatient. 'Aren't you supposed to say ho ho ho?'

'Saint Nick don't say no ho ho ho, that's Santy that says ho ho ho; you seen him today on th' fire truck. Saint Nick was a ol' bishop who give out candy an' whatnot to kids who was poor.'

'I'm poor!' said the freckled boy. 'You can give me some!'

'I'm poor, too!' said his sister, holding forth both hands.

'You are no such thing!' Their mother pulled them away by their coat collars. 'Your daddy works at th' post office and I do everything but mop floors at th' college. We are *not* poor! Of all things to say!'

'Just for tonight,' wailed the boy, who was banished to the Children's section with his sister.

Since the store added Saint Nick and upscaled the refreshments, people were coming to the annual Happy Endings event from other small towns. Last year's front page of the *Muse* was posted on the community board: 'Local Bookstore Brings Visitors from Afar.'

'Afar is where them Kings of Orient come from,' said a great-grandfather along for the ride from Wilkes County.

The store was fragrant with the aromas of spiced tea and hot chocolate. It was Happy Endings's biggest day of the year; their economic Holy Grail. She missed her sister, who had helped her out in a time of need, but Louise was in Arlington, Virginia, madly in love with the trumpet player in a jazz band and making a small fortune in an accounting firm.

This season, a spruce occupied the twelve-foot floor-to-ceiling upstairs window. Though hung with hundreds of colored lights and ornaments mostly given by customers, it no longer belonged to the bookstore; it belonged to the people.

When its lights were turned on at five-thirty, the craziness, joy, and marvel of Christmas would be official. That Thanksgiving was tomorrow and clearly out-of-sync couldn't be helped. 'It is what it is. C'est la vie,' said a council member who had been to France in high school.

Meanwhile, people were filling the shops and a customer reported a hungry line outside Wanda's Feel Good. Wanda left her smoking hot kitchen, they said, and with the door fanning out the ravishing smells of Tex-Mex, walked the line, serving little cups of hot ponche.

Scott estimated that four hundred people had poured into Mitford. Not counting the thirty-voice ecumenical choir in front of the store, steaming up the air with carols. They had a trumpet this year.

'Shepherds why this jubilee?
'Why these songs of happy cheer?
'What great brightness did you see?
'What glad tidings did you hear?'

Parking was a total disaster; even with a couple of hires from the college, their four-member MPD was grossly overworked. She heard that Chief Guthrie announced, as he did every year at this event, that he would be taking early retirement. A customer told her he'd just hollered, to nobody in particular, 'I mean it this time!'

At precisely five-thirty, Scott was at the bookstore light switch; Coot was ready to make-believe. And across the street on the sidewalk, lined up two- and three-deep, were people from both near and afar.

The choir director lifted his baton for the countdown.

'Everybody!' he shouted.

'Ten!'

'Nine!'

All those voices in unison, all those expectant faces turned up to the dark window.

'Eight!'

'Seven!'

Everyone believing the light really would shine forth and save them from darkness.

'Six!'

'Five!'

Whatever you give us, Lord, she prayed, whatever is out there for the holydays ahead and for the coming year, we're thankful, we're grateful, we're blessed.

'Four!'

'Three!'

She felt Grace close beside her, and put her arm around her daughter and drew her close.

'Two!'

And here came the moment they both loved best, that evanescent moment before the final count when the promises of Christmas became suddenly, vitally real.

'One!'

Cheers, applause, colored lights splashing onto the street below—red, gold, purple, green, stained glass on common asphalt.

'Love divine, all loves excelling
'Joy of heaven to earth come down . . . '

Her husband giving her a thumbs-up from the switch box, and her daughter hugging her, the daughter she could have lost, her own miracle baby among all the miracle babies of the world.

'Jesus thou art all compassion
'Pure, unbounded love thou art
'Visit us with thy salvation
'Enter every trembling heart . . . '

Christmas had come to Mitford.

Furnace or no, they would remain grateful and carry on.

TIM

Priesting had refined in him an alert system that took root when he was young. It told him who he could trust, who was safe, and who was not. He could not trust his father or grandfather. He could not trust the man who delivered their ice or the male teacher who kept him after school in seventh grade.

He could trust his mother, though she was particular about how she gave her love. He couldn't understand why she continued to love his father, who appeared to love only his rage and himself; he felt he got a divided love from his mother. Sincere and devoted, but divided.

Peggy and Louis had loved him all the way, as he loved them. Peggy and Louis would have gone to the mat for him, risked everything for him. Even Peggy, who disappeared from his life when he was ten, would have stayed to save him if she could.

When he heard Buck and Pauline coming down the hall with Jessie and Pooh, something shifted; he sensed it. Gus barked. Coats, scarves, hats, gloves were stuffed into the hall closet. A basket with Pauline's pumpkin pie, Jessie's brownies, and Buck and Pooh's cranberry relish was handed off to the kitchen. There was laughter but he could feel it—the air was different.

He embraced the big guy who once lobbed a chair at him, the hopeless, alcoholic overachiever who later headed out to Mississippi but turned around and came back, all in one long, desperate drive into the heart of God.

Buck eyed his wife. 'I hope this is headed in a good direction, Father. We talked before we came over. I don't know, I hate to be negative . . . '

Perhaps they'd all come expecting the best and feeling guilty for dreading the worst.

Dooley embraced his mother; it was well-meant but cursory. Kenny did the same, unafraid to look into his mother's eyes as he drew back and took her hand. Then the two brothers hurried to their kids.

Though still beautiful, grief had torn away her mask—he thought Pauline looked unusually aged. Pooh watched, on alert as he'd been since a kid; Jessie got busy at the jigsaw.

Pauline turned and saw Sammy standing with Carolina by the tree. 'Sammy! My son! There you are!' Sammy took Carolina's hand; they stepped back.

Pauline opened her arms, but Sammy moved farther away and pulled Carolina with him.

'Who is this?' she asked Sammy.

Carolina extended her hand; Pauline dismissed it. 'My name is Carolina.'

'Do we know you? Why are you here?'

'I was invited.'

Buck turned to him. 'Jesus,' he said. 'I'm sorry. I . . . '

'L-leave us alone.' Sammy's voice was quiet; he had trained for this. But here was a surprise—his mother coming for him as if to eat him alive. He held Carolina to his side. 'Just l-leave us alone.'

Pooh went to his mother. 'Mama.' Buck took Pauline's arm. 'Leave 'em be. Let's go over here with th' kids an' put a piece in th' jigsaw. You've always been handy at jigsaws.'

Pauline weeping; the usual. 'They could be decent to me, Buck. I'm his mother. Th' other kids are decent to me.'

Sammy left the room; Carolina went to the kitchen and was welcomed by Cynthia and her sous-chefs. Standing near the oven, he was able to hear Julie whisper to Carolina, 'It's the family acceptance test.'

'You passed!' said Lace.

The turkey—moist and tender, reigning over the board and already carved. The glazed Valley ham delicious, and both of Cynthia's gravies perfectly seasoned.

He relished wielding his razor-sharp carving knife and seeing the slices of ham fall away from the blade with military precision. He would give up his day job to do this. Would he ever just buy a presliced ham and get it over with? No way.

He was not a fan of people helping themselves with the turkey; he liked to serve it. That way, he could keep the bird looking presentable even while being decimated.

After a blessing offered in the kitchen, the plates were passed to him with requests from the troops: not too much; pile it on; white meat, please; dark only; worth the drive; woohoo; et cetera.

Though the kids' table was having a heyday, the air was a little fraught. But people were hungry and ready to move on.

Apparently, the worst was over and he was giving unspoken thanks.

But it wasn't over.

During the grand finale of dessert, Dooley told how he'd demolished a cherry pie while hiding from the Sugar Police—namely his wife.

Pauline interrupted Dooley's story.

'Sammy! I hope you an' Caroline will come visit us while you're here. You know we live just two blocks up th' street. You've never been to visit, not even once. It's about time you came to see us, you're my son.'

Sammy looked up. Carolina took his hand. 'Thank you, Mrs. Leeper. That's nice of you.'

'So we'll look forward to seein' you this trip. I'll fry you some chicken.'

'Mom,' said Jessie, 'it's a busy trip for them.'

'But he's my son!' Tears again. 'I've never got to fry him some chicken! He's never once come to th' house.'

Under the table, he patted Cynthia's knee, code for 'hang in there.'

Sammy stood, pushed back his chair. 'I'm n-n-never comin' to your house. Never. Not this trip, not the next trip, never. And while you're at it, h-h-hear this. I am n-not your son. I have never b-been your son. You turned me over to a freak, remember? I was f-f-five years old.'

As clergy, he was the official counselor in the room and also the host. It was his job to intervene. 'Pauline.'

Dooley gave him a look. 'Let th' family handle it, Dad.'

He sat back, losing his breath for a moment; the incision was clean and to the quick. He excused himself and went to the garage; Cynthia and Gus followed.

'I'm sorry,' she said. 'I'm so sorry.'

They held each other.

There was only one person in the world who would really get what just happened. Thank God he was married to her.

CYNTHIA

He was pacing the bedroom floor as he paced the study when voicing a sermon. She had never seen him like this.

'Let the family handle it? Have I been so wrong to think I was a member of this family? Or are we talking about another family split? The Barlowe crowd goes one way and we go another way? Or do we all pitch in and go the same way?

'Dooley Barlowe came to me and said what gave me great joy in this mortal life—I'd like to have your name. As the sign in front of the clinic clearly states, Dooley *Kavanagh* is the vet—and the cohead of a whole family of Kavanaghs. And now I, a Kavanagh, am not part of the family? I have no voice, no feelings, no rights? All that has suddenly changed?

'They wish to break away from what we've been thrilled and privileged to consider family—break away into their own tribe and even now, that tribe is splitting apart, that one small wounded fragment is scattering in all directions, nursing their wounds, reluctant to give up anything so darkly familiar as their wounds, and headed to places from which they may not find their way back.

'This is where it hits the fan, Kav'na. This is where we all cut and run or stay and figure it out. It will not be easy. It will be painful. Why invite more pain into a family raised on pain? Because pain can serve as a passageway to joy. It's that dark tunnel that goes through a mountain and dumps us out on the other side where the light is.

'Do we want to be people who looked forward to being with family, only to get here and find a bunch of fakes trying to *act* like family? Is family just for the holidays? Or for all time? I never signed up to be family that meets once or twice a year, I signed up to be family even when we're hundreds of miles apart, family who's here for each other when prayer is needed, family who's here for the tears as well as the laughs. If we're family, we're here. We show up.'

Her husband was destroyed by this, she hadn't seen outrage in him even once before; it was scary. Strokes and heart attacks come from the terrible force of spilling it all out. But, no. What gives people strokes and heart attacks is holding it all in.

'Years of damage, years of not sitting down and really talking, years of hoping that time will do the healing so you don't have to work to make it happen. That's the bloody problem.

'It sounds like what's being said is let's put a Band-Aid on this thing, fake it through the rest of Thanksgiving, and get back to wherever we came from. Then at Christmas we can round everybody up and do the fakery all over again.'

'You need to say this to them, Timothy.'

'They may take it as just a big whine for being pushed out—me, the blasted savior of the family who rescued them from the destruction of their mother's addiction, their father's abandonment, I put it all together again and want some payback—like actually being seen as part of the family.'

'It's all true. You did put it back together. By the grace of God.'

'They're leaving God out of this.'

'You need to put God back in.'

'They'll think I'm using God as my foil; that I have God on my side and they don't.'

'Say all this to them, Timothy. Don't second-guess what they'll say or think. My own guess is that Dooley is feeling like a heel right now. He knows he hurt you. He'll call and apologize.'

'It doesn't matter.'

'Of course it matters.'

'You know what I dislike? That one person—one!—refuses to get help and continues to sow bitterness among an entire group of people. This estranges you into the bargain. Suddenly the woman who's been so loving to her son-in-law, daughter-in-law, her grandkids, to all the Barlowes—you're not family, you're thrown out with me. And the grandkids? This toxin impacts them, too. So the dominoes keep falling, no end to it. All this ruination from the grief and destruction that one person continues to foist upon this family.'

'Speak the truth to them, Timothy. Risk your neck, like you'd be asking them to risk theirs by hearing the truth. Someone has to do it.'

'Why is it always me?'

'It just is,' she said. 'It just always is. You put broken pieces back together. The Nativity figures, sweetheart—all that brokenness, you put it back together. That's what you do.'

'If we don't know how to love as a family, how can we fight to save ourselves as a family? This is where the Enemy has a heyday. Give in to the Enemy this time and there may not be a next time.

'Do we want the same thing all over again? Let's call it the Barlowe Effect—do we want everybody scattered all over the place, again? Do we want to be torn apart over every blasted thing? Or are we moving through this together?

'I've said it before and I'll say it again. I did not put this busted-up family together. I have no idea how to do that—God put us together. I did some legwork, okay? We've all done legwork or we wouldn't be here.

'This is God's family. God pulled all us crazy, frustrating, headstrong people into a single unit called family. Every time we're together we're practicing the awesome rite of being a family. When we get it wrong, the last thing we need to do is scatter. No more scattering, Kav'na. No more scattering. There's got to be a way.'

He came to her and took her in his arms. 'Lie down with me,' he said. 'Let's just hold each other. That's what I need.' He felt old. Old and hollow and foolish. He didn't have all the answers.

'I love that you know what you need and can ask for it,' she said. 'If people could learn just one thing, it's to know what we need and how to ask for it.'

TIM

Pooh called early and invited him to breakfast the day after Thanksgiving.

He didn't want to let Pooh pick up the check, even though he and Cynthia were primary donors to his college fund. But it was a grown-up thing to do to invite him to breakfast; he was flattered. And he didn't wish to whine to a kid who had lived through more pain in his twenty-some years than most people do in a lifetime.

Grown-up was definitely the word for Henry, who he often, out of affection, called Pooh. He hadn't noticed until now just how mature this wonderful boy had become. It was as if it had happened in secret and today was the reveal.

'How can so many people, so different in temperament, ever come to anything even resembling unity?' said Pooh.

'What God was thinking when he pulled our motley crowd together, I can't imagine. But here we are, with still some assembly required by the One Who loved us first.'

Henry smiled. Like Dooley as a boy, Pooh didn't often smile. 'There should be an intervention for people who get clean but remain addicts, like Mama is addicted to grieving for herself.'

'You could pursue that avenue in your studies. You know we keep up with your grades online and they're a real dazzle. Great job, Henry. You're going to make a difference in this world.'

Blushing was currently unpopular in today's culture; he savored the faint hue of modest pride on this young man's face.

'We want to be healed of this, Father. As for what Dooley said to you, he's pretty sick about it. We're family all the way, he knows that, we all know that. Mama knows it, too. She can't totally handle it, but she knows it.'

He was still smarting from yesterday's wound. 'Our faction will just step over there and handle everything and get back to your faction? Not gonna work. With or without Cynthia and me as part of it.'

'The world seems to model division,' said Pooh. 'And maybe our family can't be repaired. Maybe our family will stay divided, and what we have to do is leave it split and learn to forgive over and over again. Like on the T-shirt in the portrait of Dooley—*Love is an act of endless forgiveness.*

'None of the kids except Kenny and I can really forgive Mama. Kenny was raised by believers; he gets what forgiveness is and can do. I was able to forgive her because I saw there was no way she could help herself. I knew she loved me. What hurt was that I couldn't help her out of the trauma; I didn't know how to stop the bleeding. All I could do was be there, just be there. It was . . . it is . . . it . . . Sometimes I have trouble with words, Father, finding the right ones.'

'Join the club,' he said. He loved this gangly, redheaded Barlowe who was schooling himself for a ministry to the spiritually sick and hurting. What was it about these Barlowes, anyway?

He was walking home when his phone buzzed. Dooley.

He could take it. Or leave it.

He took it.

'Dad.'

'That's me.' That, by God, is something Dooley Kavanagh couldn't walk away from. Not without legal fees.

'I'm sorry, Dad.'

'Yes, well. Me, too. Cynthia, too.'

'I guess I lived for a long time thinking the kids and I were on our own and we could handle it without help.'

A lousy excuse. But he wouldn't say that.

'What was it really about, son?' Why did you discount me? Us? What was really at the root of it? He could hear the indrawn breath, feel something like fear at the other end of the conversation. He would not settle for fake.

'I was scared.'

'Of what?'

'I guess I've held on to some of the power I felt I had as a kid, when I took care of everything for the others. They still kind of see me like that, like somebody who can handle the hard stuff. So when you started to deal with Mom, I felt the sibs would see me as weak. You would be the wise one who takes over and fixes things, the one who always gets things right.'

That hurt, too. He didn't like that image of himself and the possibility that Dooley was right. He stopped to sit on a low wall in front of a neighbor's house. He couldn't walk and breathe and be real with his son all at the same time.

'There was nothing that could be fixed,' he said. 'I just hoped to turn the temperature down before it reached the boiling point. Within any family unit, the members have separate and individual homes. This was getting out of hand in my home, it was happening at my table. We all bring different baggage to the table, Dooley. The baggage the kids bring right now can set off the worst in your mom. I was taking care of Cynthia's and my territory within the family unit. I had no intention of being seen as an autocrat attempting a family takeover. That's my story.'

'I understand. I really knew that all along, Dad, but right then—I lost it with you because . . .'

Dooley was struggling with this. A good thing for them both.

'Because?'

'Because it's safe to hurt you if somebody has to be hurt, because you forgive, because things don't fall apart with you. I didn't realize I even thought like that 'til I went over it with Lace last night. But mostly, I didn't want to lose my place in the family as—for a lot of years, the only grown-up. Which is stupid. Because half th' time I'm no grown-up. Even with two kids, I'm not always the grown-up. Just forgive me, Dad. Please. I love you.'

'I love you back. Are we family?'

'We are. God knows. Forever.'

Dooley had suffered, too. Plus, Lace had probably half-killed him.

'Why don't we forgive each other and call it a wrap?'

'Deal, Dad. Yes! Thanks. Thanks.'

'Caveat,' he said. 'Cynthia and I get permission to sit the kids for two nights so you and Lace can get out of there at your early convenience. I recommend Asheville. Should be some decent fries over there.'

Dooley laughing. Cackling. Or maybe shedding a tear of relief. Sooner rather than later, they needed a talk about Dooley's very mistaken notion that he always gets things right.

HELENE

When walking about town on errands, she collected snippets—a snippet while buying a croissant revealed that Cynthia had been courted by Andrew Gregory prior to his election as mayor, and how some thought the handsome antiques dealer might win the day. But Cynthia's affections had turned to the priest.

While the ordinary person might consider Father Tim an ordinary man, it was plain to her French instincts that he was a romantic—thoughtful and refined of feeling. She could understand why he had held the winning hand.

Several years ago, she had overheard Father Tim console and edify someone on the telephone. Miraculously, she, too, had been consoled and edified. Indeed, she had found a semblance of peace—by partially surrendering her heart to God.

Mr. Welch had referred on occasion to being 'saved,' but he had never said what that meant precisely. Perhaps she had been saved.

Or perhaps not.

She had settled into her spinsterish life in college, practically living in the library and the music department, looking inward and seeking to preserve memories of her young life in Provence.

She had been happiest when 'hiding' beneath her grandmother's dough table, the baptism of flour sifting upon her head through cracks in the wood. She had loved crawling from beneath the table and hearing her beautiful grandmere's exclamation. *'La fee est nee!'*

That was her cue to run out her grandmother's door and into the garden, flapping her arm wings around the big vegetable bed, flour blowing into the air. She had been a real faerie, with real faerie dust falling on the lettuces.

To clean the table, her grandmother scrubbed the wood with a cut lemon dipped in sea salt, a smell loved with all the other aromas that cosseted her as a child—peonies in May, filling vases throughout the house; fresh lavender beneath her pillow; onion soup with its crusty edges; bouillabaisse simmering on the immense iron stove. All this had defined happiness for a lifetime. Nothing ever replaced that deep sense of security, nothing could.

She had thought herself a woman of character, fulfilling her grandmother's most fervent prayers for her *petite fille*. And then, after a long career as both librarian and piano teacher, she had moved to Mitford to steal from Father Tim what she believed to be rightfully hers.

During her long confinement in the prison of inward gazing, she hadn't once considered God to be a factor in her life. She had, however, sensed the vacuum in herself and had pondered ways to fill it.

And then she had overheard Father Tim's phone conversation with someone searching for God. God, she realized, had been standing behind a sort of curtain in her life. There but unnoticed, there but disregarded. Yet there, in any case, for the first time in her cognition.

Things had shifted with that phone call. Something softened in her, though not entirely. She knew better than to let down her defenses entirely. To rest on the hope that God may be real and living? Yes. But that God may move from behind the curtain and swallow her life into his? Unthinkable.

Since seeing the word on the envelope, she felt a sense of relief that was ecstatic and painful all at once—a transfiguration in which the life of a spinster—not even a speck on the map of humanity—became more than it seemed.

TIM

Wanda was out with the annual Mitford Crud, J.C. was in a better mood, and fish tacos were the special. Life was good.

'So I'm working on the joke,' he said. 'Nothing major so far, but a start. How about you?'

'Zero,' said Mule. 'One of my handicaps in writin' this joke is I've never been in a bar.'

'Whoa. Wait a minute,' said J.C. 'Never been in a bar?'

'Well, maybe once. Or twice, I believe it was. But that's it. No big deal.'

'I know you're a Baptist, but this is looneytoons.'

'I was never young an' foolish like some people.'

'Come on. Out with it. Give us th' truth. We can handle it.'

'Fancy don't like me talkin' about personal behavior.'

'So you've been in a bar two times.'

'Let's see. There was that time in Nashville, I forgot about that. Actually, I try not to remember that at all.'

'We're up from zero to three bars an' countin',' said J.C. 'Keep 'em comin', buddyroe.'

'So, Tim,' said Mule. 'How many bars have you been in?'

'I didn't count.'

'They say that's where th' sinners are. Lined up for easy pickin'. A perfect place for clergy to hang out.'

'J.C.,' he said, 'how about you? Any movement on our joke?'

'I've got Vanita workin' on it.'

'Ah, Vanita, bless her heart. But that was not the plan—that we would call on others to do it for us.'

'It was my plan,' said J.C.

'Now that we have a plan,' said Mule, 'mine is to get Fancy on board.'

He could, so to speak, smell the bacon. His great idea was going off the cliff.

HARLEY

Lace was upstairs puttin' th' kids to bed an' him an' Willie was settin' by th' kitchen fire with Dooley. Somethin' was on Dooley's mind.

'I've got a cat to rehome,' said Dooley. 'ASAP.'

'Don't look at me.'

'Don't look at me, neither,' said Willie. 'I break out in a rash, go to sneezin', coughin', even throwin' up. I ain't a cat person.'

'You're around barn cats all day,' said Dooley. 'I never heard you complain.'

'Barn cats are different. You're not closed up in a house with barn cats. I ain't a cat person.'

'Spread the word when you're in town. This is a special kind of cat, a Ragdoll. Four years old, high maintenance, we've got to get it out of here. Amanda will make you a bunch of signs to put up at Wanda's, th' Hardware, th' bookstore. We have zero room for this cat.'

'What kind of a cat did you say?'

'Ragdoll. We put a notice in the clinic sayin' We Don't Rehome Pets, and that's when they really started flyin' in. Just since Wednesday, th' cat, two bantam roosters, a one-eyed bluetick hound, and then we found a mule tied up out front this mornin'.'

'What's his name?' he said.

'He didn' tell us an' we didn't ask,' said Willie, who squawked like a settin' hen when he laughed.

Him an' his granpaw had plowed with a mule when he was a boy. An' it was a known fact that Junior Johnson plowed with a mule before winnin' all them NASCARs. 'Seem like we could use a mule,' he said.

'You know what it costs to keep a mule?' said Willie. 'You take your feed, your vet meds, your man-hours to train, work, groom, feed up, an' you've got an investment of more'n two hundred a month. That's twenty-four hundred a year. Minimum.'

Willie looked pleased with hisself. '*Minimum*,' he said ag'in.

Willie had made that up, he could tell it wadn't no scientific study.

'Plus,' said Willie, 'they can live up to fifty years. Run that through your calculator at twenty-four hundred a year.'

'We can't keep takin' on other people's responsibilities,' said Dooley. 'This is not a dumping ground. Next time you're in town, pick up a camera for the driveway and one to go over the clinic door. Meantime, turn him out with Scooter and th' donkeys. Put a blanket on him at night, feed him good. I'll check him after lunch tomorrow.'

Dooley kicked a log layin' on th' hearth. People dumpin' their animals made Dooley plenty mad.

'What's so special about a Ragdoll?' said Willie, knowin' when to change th' subject.

'Extra soft, fluffy, blue eyes, follows you around like a pup.'

Miss Pringle! She had a cat that died a while back. Chances are, she'd be up for a new cat. 'How come it's named Ragdoll?'

'When you pick it up, it goes limp like a rag doll. Likes to cuddle, they say.'

This was soundin' good. A single woman livin' alone? Throw that in with fluffy, likes to cuddle, an' follers you around like a pup.

Only thing was, she hadn't said nothin' about th' squashes he sent over there. He hadn't talked to Miss Pringle in a coon's age an' he felt like it wadn't his place to call. But if they had a cat to talk about, that'd be a whole other deal.

'Put a hold on that cat,' he said to Dooley. 'I'll git back to you in th' mornin'.' His heart started beatin' in his ears when he said that.

Willie give him th' evil eye.

'This better be good,' said Dooley. 'No returns, buddy. Period.'

'What's its name?'

'It's a doozy. Dolores.'

Dolors. 'Could you write that down f'r me?' he said.

His hands was so clammy he didn't know if he could hold on to 'is phone, which was second generation an' goin' south anyway.

He went out to th' barn in th' freezin' cold where he could git pretty good reception. He wouldn't want to talk in th' house; Willie was bad to hang around an' listen.

His fingers was too numb to punch the numbers, so he give a extra fork of hay to Scooter, who had his winter blanket on, an' th' same to th' donkeys. Which caused all seven barn cats to come runnin' for a extra handful of kibbles.

He'd told Willie he'd take care of th' mule that was standin' over in th' corner with its head down. That was th' saddest-lookin' mule he ever seen. He didn't much fool with th' livestock on th' place; he was th' plumber, th' carpenter, th' jack-leg electrician, th' roofer, th' painter, th' brick layer, th' stone mason, th' gutter cleaner, you name it.

All he knew about mules is they'll lay down to sleep but like donkeys, they like standin' jis' as good or better. They sleep for about two seconds at a time. An' sweet feed is likely to mess with their gut so stick to hay. Dooley kep' a little field of timothy for th' pony an' donkeys so he dropped a forkful in front of the mule. Th' mule turned his head to th' wall.

'You got a name?' he said. Pedro come straight to his mind. Pedro! Why, that was as good a name as a mule could ever git. 'Pedro!' he said, an' he'd be dogged if that mule didn't turn his head around an' look him in th' eye.

He left the forkful in Pedro's corner, an' propped th' hay rake ag'in th' wall, an' looked at his breath fog up. He'd done all he could to put off makin' this call. But he hadn't put no blanket on Pedro, so he done that.

Pedro give him a little snuffle.

'Ever'thing gon' be all right, Pedro.'

He give Pedro a neck rub. Yessir, this was one sad mule.

Then he set down on a hay bale an' practiced what he had to say.

'Miss Pringle, how you doin'? This is Harley. Harley Welch. How you doin'?'

Whoa, he already said how you doin'.

If you took a animal offa Dooley, you could not bring it back. He was headed to town tomorrow, but if he delivered Dolors to Miss Pringle without checkin' he could be haulin' Dolors home to Geezer Cottage. His daddy had talked about th' Second World War bein' hell on earth an' that's what it would be if he took Dolors to him an' Willie's house.

He could not set out here all evenin' in freezin' weather with a pony, two donkeys, a mule, an' seven cats. Fish or cut bait.

'Good evening. This is Helene Pringle.'

His heart stopped, he could feel it stop.

'Miss Pringle?'

'Yes, this is Helene Pringle.'

'This is Harley. Harley Welch.' He was short of breath, as if he'd run after a steer gittin' loose.

'Oh, Mr. Welch. How nice to hear your voice! It's been a long time. How are you faring?'

Faring. 'Pretty good for a . . . for a ol' geezer. An' how about you, Miss Pringle? How're you farin'?'

'Very well, thank you.'

'How did you like th' squashes Willie brought over a while back?'

'Squashes? I don't believe I received any squashes, Mr. Welch.'

He felt like somebody'd throwed a tub of dishwater on 'im. But he had to keep movin'. All of a sudden a idea hit him—he wouldn't use th' word 'cat'; he would talk about a surprise. Lace liked surprises, an' th' pretty teacher he chopped wood for liked surprises.

'Miss Pringle, how would you like somethin' with blue eyes that's soft an' fluffy an' likes to, you know, what they call cuddle?'

He waited. Had th' phone gone dead?

'Miss Pringle? Are you there?'

'Yes, Mr. Welch, I'm . . . here.'

'Miss Pringle, I would like to bring you a early surprise Christmas present. Tomorrow. If that would not be an inconvenience.'

'How kind of you. Any hints, Mr. Welch?'

'No ma'am, this would be a surprise. Like Santy Claus. He never told us what he was bringin', he jis' brung it.'

'And I will have a surprise for you as well,' she said.

'You don't say!'

'I do say,' she said, laughing.

Lord A'mighty, he was glad to hear her laughin'.

It was th' middle of th' night an' he couldn't sleep. He sat up, scratched his head. Seem like somethin' was tryin' to git through to him.

Wait a dadgum minute. If Willie hadn't delivered th' squashes, did he git mixed up an' deliver that poem book an' letter?

Seem like he could feel his hair standin' on end. Whatever it was, she didn't act mad or nothin'. She told 'im she had a surprise for him. Said she was happy to hear his voice. Yessir, she had said that very thing—Oh, Mr. Welch. How nice to hear your voice!

They won't nothin' to worry about. He laid down, pulled th' covers up around his neck. Him an' th' cat was leavin' out of here at eight o'clock sharp in th' mornin'.

If he could get th' shocks done by a little after lunchtime, him an' Willie was goin' to th' woods with Jack an' stake out a big tree for th' big house an' a little tree for th' little house. It was gon' be a good Christmas.

He had a dream in th' night. He was at th' Wesley mall when he seen what looked to be Saint Nick that Coot Hendrik dressed up like. In a real loud voice, Saint Nick said, 'Harley Eugene Welch, what do you want for Christmas?'

He didn't even have to think about it.

'I want to make Miss Pringle happy,' he said.

HARLEY

He had to pump hisself up about this. As he brushed his dentures, he went over th' positives. They wadn't many.

She as good as said she'd take whatever it was.

She said he was kind.

An' she laughed.

He emailed Dooley a reminder that he'd git th' cat at eight o'clock. Then he'd run to Wesley an' pick up what he needed for th' shocks an' pick up lunch for ever'body at th' farm as it was Amanda's birthday, an' stop by Miss Pringle's to deliver Dolors. He'd say, I cain't stay long, don't you know, it's a birthday at th' farm.

He had pressed his khakis last night to wear with th' plaid shirt she said she liked a while back. He'd carried th' ironin' board to his room without Willie seein' it because Willie knew ol' Harley never ironed nothin', which would be a tip-off to somethin' irregular.

HARLEY

Amanda brung th' cat to th' front desk in th' carrier Dolors was brung to th' clinic in. Amanda said th' woman who raised th' cat was a rich lady from Grandfather Mountain. She heard Dooley was a excellent rehomer an' drove a hour to git here.

Th' woman was movin' in with her daughter in Birmingham who was allergic to cats. Th' cat liked canned salmon an' garden peas if they was cooked to a mush. Gerber had a nice mashed garden pea.

'Where are you takin' Dolores?' said Amanda. 'We need to fill out this questionnaire.'

He did not know they was paperwork.

'Takin' her to my former landlady.'

'You have a farmer landlady?'

'Former,' he said, 'I said former. Back in th' day.'

Amanda wrote that down.

'And what is her name?'

This was gittin' personal. 'If anything goes wrong, I'll be liable,' he said. 'Mark me down as liable.'

'This is a Louis Vuitton carrier,' said Amada, 'so we need to have it back. It does not go with the cat. Okay?'

When he answered th' rest of th' questions, Amanda asked him to sign an agreement that th' cat would not for any reason be returned to th' Kavanagh Animal Wellness Clinic. He was scared to ask if this was a actual legal document.

Amanda went off to th' back an' brought out a box with a dozen little jars of Gerber peas.

'Compliments of the previous owner,' said Amanda, flashin' him a big smile. 'Dolores is an *exceptional* cat, Harley. She's a Ragdoll and very affectionate. Ragdolls will follow you around like a puppy. I'm sure your former landlady will be over th' moon.'

He hauled a copy of th' agreement an' th' box of peas an' th' carrier—this cat weighed a ton—out to th' truck. He set th' carrier on th' passenger seat an' laid th' paperwork an' th' peas on th' floor. Th' cat let out a howl, which made him jump.

He felt swimmy-headed just thinkin' about Miss Pringle's face when she seen this *exceptional* cat, never mind th' free mashed peas.

'Harley, ol' buddy,' he said to hisself, 'you must be livin' right!'

TIM

Saturday, and he was headed out of town to Meadowgate in his babysitting-poetry mode. He would be leaning today on rhyming and was pretty excited. Both Jack and Sadie had an ear for rhyme.

He noted the sign in the window of the Local.

Father Tim's
Italian sausage
Store-made
$4.00 a pound
~This week only

Some people get streets named after them, or entire states, or even cities—Lincoln, Nebraska. Madison, Wisconsin. He was a sausage brand.

While filling in as a grocer for Avis, he'd put together a batch of Italian sausage made from his mother's family recipe. The point was to spice up sales. And it worked! Sausage made from the recipe had continued in local favor and was often used as a special promotion.

While it was no threat to Jimmy Dean, Mayor Gregory had given it a great review in the *Muse*. 'Father Tim's sausage captures a magic repris-ing simpler times.'

There were legacies far worse. And at four bucks a pound, the price was right.

He parked at the curb and bought two pounds for Willie and Harley's proposed Christmas gift to the big house.

CYNTHIA

What if she went into the woods for this, lay down with the leaf mold and wild geranium? But there would be people and dogs searching the property. They would be dragging the lake, combing the woods. The serenity of Hollyhock would be violated at every turn.

As in life, death is best kept simple.

Dear Alice and Jeffrey,

In asking your forgiveness, I may be asking too much. I have considered every option, and I am truly sorry for this sordid business under your roof.

My affairs are in order. You will receive my royalty stream and copyrights, and there isn't much else to leave. Here is the ring you always loved, dear Alice. A note with the phone numbers of my editor and trust attorney are in the night table.

You know that Elliott's nephew David is dear to me, but he is wandering about in the world, as I once did, trying to find answers, and I no longer have any idea how he may be reached. He would not have any legal right to contest what I'm leaving in your good hands.

Thank you for being faithful and caring friends. If there really is a God who presents himself to me in what may or may not be an afterlife, I will find a way to tell you.

She had no idea how to sign it. *With love* seemed an insult, for who would leave the shock and inconvenience of a lifeless body to someone they loved? *Thanks for having me* was hardly an option. She wouldn't sign it. The identity of the writer would be perfectly clear.

She had taken the sleeping tablets one by one, saying her goodbyes. Goodbye, starry nights. Goodbye, old fears. Goodbye, weeping, wanting, losing, leaving. Goodbye, scent of lilacs, of garden roses, of her own sour sweat as she hefted bushels of apples onto the bed of the farm truck. Goodbye, goodbye.

For someone who enjoyed research and did it often when writing, she hadn't looked into the details of dying by sleeping tablets. She only knew she mustn't stop taking them as long as she was conscious. She shook a handful from the pill container.

Along the way, she had come across Thomas Edison's last words. *It's very beautiful over there.* She wanted to believe that. The catch was, she didn't know if she would end up over there. She remembered her father's dour remark. 'Like life, death is a dice roll.' How did he know what death was like? But he had convinced her, and especially her mother, that he knew everything.

She had been groggy then, and felt the need to hurry. She put the tablets in her left hand in order to add a P.S. to the letter.

My carry-on which you thought to be fake is an actual Louis. Just so you know.

That would appeal to Alice's ironical sense of humor. She felt no pity for herself, no shame. Perhaps because she'd shut down what remained of her feelings.

On Friday, she and Jeffrey had been loading apples for a farmer's market.

'Are you all right?' he asked.

'I'll be fine.'

He grinned. 'Yes, but when?'

Sometime during that nearly fatal night, she'd been called. Not by voice or sound, it seemed an inner alert. If not her own flesh and bone, something like her spirit rose up without alarm and stood by the bed. There was a soft radiance, like candlelight, where she stood and held forth her upturned hand. The hand of another was indefinite, mostly surmised, as the bloom of a white bellflower was placed on her palm. The frilled blossom was weightless, a whisper, and was given with an unspoken message.

You are loved.

Stunned by a wave of feeling, she lifted the bloom to find if it had scent and was staring at her empty palm. She stood for a moment, then went back to bed feeling completely safe, not wondering whether she was alive or dead, nor questioning whether she deserved unbounded love. It was simply hers, a gift. Somewhere in her reflections, she realized the room was love, her body was love, she was formed by love.

Though embraced by a vast darkness, she found it very beautiful over here.

DOOLEY AND JESSIE

'So about Christmas at th' farm,' said Jessie. 'Are we goin' through all that Thanksgivin' crap again?'

'We are,' said Dooley. 'It'll just be different crap this time.'

'How long do we have to do this charade?'

'As long as it takes.'

'Mom is always going to be a horse's ass.'

'I'm always goin' to be the one who hogs the dark meat. You'll always be th' one who figures how to get people out of a jam like you did at snow camp. Sammy will always be th' one who beats us at pool. Dad will always be the one who loves us no matter what.'

He shrugged.

'You could quit doin' Christmas at Meadowgate. Father Tim and Cynthia's Thanksgivin' would be enough for most families.'

'It's not enough for this family. So we're doin' Christmas at th' farm, Jess. Live with it.'

'It won't matter. Christmas won't matter. Because nothing ever gets settled.'

'Yes, it does. We can't always see it, but something gets settled every time.'

'What're we tryin' to settle, Dools?'

'Ourselves, not each other. Just ourselves. We want to know we're capable of love and capable of loving. That's all. Lace taught me that. Trust me, I didn't have a clue what that meant. Then Jack and Sadie happened. You learn from havin' kids. I've seen pure, unconditional love not just from God and my dad, but from my kids. I didn't know that existed on this planet. Maybe you'll have a relationship someday, Jess, maybe you'll have kids.'

'I think I'm gay, Dools. I can't tell anybody. I don't even know.'

'We love you, Jess. That's all I know.'

'I'm afraid of a lot of things. Afraid to go to college, if I could even get in. Afraid to try to be pretty because I'm totally weird looking.'

'You could be pretty if you wanted to be.'

'I want people to think I'm pretty just like I am.'

'People won't think that, Jess, without something from you. Comb your hair, wear some decent clothes. It's not that hard. Whatever it takes.'

She wanted to hold his hand for a minute but didn't know how.

'Well, thanks for the free consult, brother.'

'I love you, Jess.'

'I love you back, Dools. But I'm different.'

'We're all different. Each one of us, totally different. You don't get the big shiny trophy for being different in this family.'

They hugged—a tight wraparound hug that counted for something.

HARLEY

It was a bumpy ride from th' farm over to Wesley to pick up parts for th' suspension system. He'd been fightin' th' wheel ever' minute to hold 'er in th' road. Willie hadn't said things had got this bad.

He was thinkin' this rig cain't make even one more town trip before th' shocks blow out.

Then they blowed out.

Th' wheel was jerked plumb out of his hand. Th' truck pitched to th' right an' him hollerin' to Jesus, an' rolled over two huge bumps that rattled his brain an' down in th' ditch they went, cat an' peas ever' which-away. He heard th' toolbox in th' truck bed slam up ag'in th' cab winder.

Thank th' Lord th' airbags wadn't workin', he was scareder of air bags bustin' out in his face than of a wreck itself.

'You all right?' he asked th' cat. Th' cat let out a wail that give him goose bumps, but it didn't sound like she was hurt, sounded like she was mad as a snappin' turtle. Her carrier was stuck upright between th' seat an' th' dashboard so he let it be.

His uppers had been knocked out but he seen 'em in th' console with what was left of th' loose change, a rabbit's foot, an' Willie's earplugs.

He felt around on hisself an' he was fine. No blood or nothin'. He hadn't been th'owed into th' windshield, but his chest had hit th' wheel plenty hard, an' looked like that was th' only damage done. He'd been wearin' his seat belt.

He was pretty shook up.

He looked to see if they was any farther th' truck could fall, but it was a clean nose to nose with th' bed of the ditch. He wiped his uppers on his khakis and popped 'em in. But they didn't exactly pop in. He looked at hisself in th' mirror an' faked a grin. Yessir, his uppers was in, but not in right. He made an adjustment but in toward th' back somethin' was wrong. He left 'em in. He pulled out his comb an' run it through his hair in case somebody stopped to give a hand. He heard th' traffic up on th' asphalt but wadn't nobody stoppin'.

He dialed th' Exxon an' talked to Bud, who'd been with that gas station a hundred years. Bud was breakin' up but got across that th' tow truck was in Holding so it'd be a while. Th' truck would have to head back to Mitford an' drop off a SUV that had took a bad hit by a Mack. Then they'd get out to him.

'Where you at, Harl?'

He didn't know; he was addled. Seem like it was about a mile north of that curve where Sammy totaled Father Tim's Mustang back in th' day.

'Jis' look for my red truck. Head down in a ditch. You don't reckon it could explode?'

'Naw. It ain't gon' explode if it hadn't already.'

Th' cat give another air-splittin' howl.

'I'd come get you but I'm th' only one here today. Best to stay with your vehicle. Hang in there,' said Bud.

He was pretty much hangin' because they was pitched foremost into th' ditch. He tried to open his door but it wouldn't open, they was a embankment right out th' door.

'I got to speak to Dooley,' he said to Amanda. His wages might be docked for the tow truck, as vehicle maintenance was him and Willie's responsibility, but mostly his'n.

'Dooley's out to a cow givin' birth to twins as we speak,' she said. 'Twins! That's totally rare for a cow.'

Th' cat was soundin' like a male in heat.

'What's that awful noise?' said Amanda.

'Gotta go,' he said.

'Hush up!' he hollered, which caused his uppers to fly out to th' floor. He could've said any bad words he wanted to out here in th' middle of nowhere hangin' head down in a ditch, but with respect for th' person th' cat was goin' to, he let it pass.

It was cold as whiz in the cab. He didn't know what might happen if he turned th' heater back on. The cars he'd drove when haulin' shine mostly didn't have no heater.

He put his arms on th' wheel and his head on his arms. If he'd knowed about all this when he got up in th' dark this mornin' he would've went back to bed.

Taptaptap.

Big face lookin' in at him.

'You all right in there? Open your window.'

He rolled it down.

'State patrol. Sergeant Webster. What's goin' on?'

'I ain't drinkin', Sarge. I've got bad shocks and they run me off th' road.'

'Be glad they run you off here 'cause half a mile down, it's a two-thousand-foot drop.'

'I got a tow comin'.'

'When's he comin'?'

'Said they're in Holdin', it'll be a while.'

'You need water?'

If he drank water, he'd have to— 'Can you open my door?'

'Nossir,' said the trooper, 'this door's not gon' open, your rig slid in right by a bank, I'm layin' on it to talk to you. How about th' other side?'

'I ain't got over there to find out,' he said.

'I'm gon' write this up an' have you sign it—just for th' records, an' I have to keep movin. I'd take you to town, but I'd be breakin' th' law. I'll see about your other door. I got a candy bar in th' car, you interested?'

'Yessir, I am.' He'd et half a pack of Nabs this mornin' as they wadn't nothin' to speak of in th' refrigerator, tomorrow bein' their day to food shop.

'It's a Snickers,' said the trooper.

He managed a fake grin. 'My lucky day,' he said.

WHEN THEY ARRIVED at the Exxon in th' tow truck, he called Blake at th' clinic. Blake would pick up lunch at Jake's, not to worry, an' Honey Hershell had baked a chocolate cake for the birthday celebration. Did he need anybody to come git him? No, he'd git th' shocks changed out an' be on home.

'You're going to miss the big doin's,' said Blake.

'What big doin's?'

'I'm proposing to Amanda at th' party.'

'You ain't!'

'We'll tell you all about it. You ought to get you a nice lady, Harley.'

'They ain't enough cash money to make me do that,' he said. He couldn't even deliver a cat to somebody.

SO NOW ALL he had to do was hustle a ride to Miss Pringle's, with a person who'd wait while he handed off th' cat. He hadn't heard th' cat's name but twice and it was mumbled. Dolors was th' best he could make of it. He would give Miss Pringle th' name Dooley wrote down, he had it in his shirt pocket.

He was worried about his uppers. If they fell out in front of Miss Pringle, he'd never be able to look her in th' eye ag'in. But he had to go through with this because he couldn't take Dolors home, thanks to Willie throwin' up and breakin' out in a rash, end of discussion.

At th' Exxon, Bud hitched him a ride to Miss Pringle's with a tattooed guy from Atlanta, Georgia.

'Passin' through,' said Bud. 'Seein' America. He don't mind waitin' at your cat drop-off, says he's got all th' time in th' world.'

'That's some kind of a rig he's drivin'.'

'Ram Laramie. Goes for around a hundred K. Don't git many of them through here.'

A man needed a ladder to git up in this truck; he took ahold of th' grab handle an' pulled hisself into th' cab with a radio playin' what you call praise music.

'Name's Reginald!'

Th' guy was bald as a doorknob an' tattooed all over his head an' arms.

'My mom calls me Reggie, but most folks call me Reg, said like edge.'

'Harley Welch,' he said, shakin' hands. 'Th' boys around here call me Harl.' Th' guy's hand was tattooed an' big as a cured ham, an' his forehead said God is Love.

Him an' Reg buckled up.

'You visitin' family, Reg?'

'Just passin' through. I did a gig with Delta for twenty-four years, aircraft maintenance supervisor. Had my time in th' air lookin' down on this country. I'm out here to see Mother Earth up close, but mostly to spread th' word of God's love to us badass humans.'

Reg seen him gawkin' at th' tattoos.

'Bodysuit,' said Reg.

'What'd you say?'

'Full-body tatts. Called a bodysuit. Scares a good many people. They think I'm a nutcase, which is only partially true. They can go for a heart on somebody's arm that says Mama, but you ink full-body an' it mostly hits th' fan.'

He was what you call blowed away.

'If you think I'm crazy now, you should've seen me before God turned me around. I was doin' drugs, anything I could lay my hands on, this is my way of payin' it back to th' good Lord.

'Some people, they'll stand an' read me like th' Sunday mornin' funny papers. On th' subway in New York City, I'm ridin' th' One train, it's summer an' I'm wearin' a tee an' just hangin' on to th' strap, an' people are gettin' more of th' Word from my tats than they'll get in a lifetime.

'Look at my right arm there, Harl. Philippians four-thirteen. You can believe it, you can take it to th' bank; it'll turn you plumb around if you need turnin'. But I've about run out of canvas. I ought to show you th' soles of my feet.'

It prob'ly wadn't a good idea to jump from a movin' vehicle, but no way was he checkin' out this guy's feet.

'Left foot, first John four-nineteen, "We love because he first loved us." Amen to that. Right foot, first John four-seven, "Beloved, let us love one another because love is from God."

'I like layin' on th' beach in th' summer. Kids'll squat down an' read my feet if their parents ain't lookin'.'

Him an' Reg had theirselves a laugh.

'A few people, if they're shortsighted, they'll get up in my face an' read my forehead, an' we'll start talkin'. They open up to me, because I'm their people. An' they're not afraid to maybe just think about God, and God bein' love. Do you know God loves you, Harl?'

'Yessir, I do. I surely do.'

They high-fived.

'When I kick th' bucket,' said Reg, 'I hate to waste all this ink. So I'm havin' a open casket. My daughter's handlin' that. We'll rent th' casket long enough for everybody to visit th' deceased. To give th' full effect, I'll be wearin' a Speedo.'

'That'd be a sight for sore eyes.'

Him an' Reg cracked up.

'Just kiddin',' said Reg. 'I'll be fully dressed from th' waist down, but my upper torso will be mainly first John. When they've read my front, they can flip me over and read my back. Psalm thirty-four, fully freehand. Doves, lambs, angels with trumpets, what they call cornucopia. It's a masterpiece.

'Then my daughter will have me cremated, an her an' my two exes—they're from Texas—will carry my ashes down to Ocracoke where I like to fish. They'll wait for a good stiff breeze an' open up th' box an' I'm outta here. Gone with th' wind!'

Willie wadn't gon' believe this.

BUT MISS PRINGLE's car wadn't in th' driveway an' she wadn't answerin' his knock. They hadn't set a time.

Th' note stuck in th' Christmas wreath said:

Mr. Welch, I am at an unexpected meeting with a pupil's family and will join them for dinner. So sorry to miss you if you come by. I hope you will call again soon.

Helene Pringle

Th' cat let out a holler. She was mad. Or hungry. Or needed to use a litter box. This was totally nerve-rackin.'

He took th' carrier back to Reg's truck an' popped it in behind th' passenger seat. Reg had his phone out, lookin' for Cracker Barrels on his route up to Roanoke.

'She ain't home. Do you have anything I could leave a note on?' If this wadn't th' worst day of his life, he didn't know what was. His chest felt like he'd been hit with a two-by-four.

'Got you covered,' said Reg, pullin' a card an' pen from th' console. 'All I got to write on is my tat guy's card. It's blank on th' back.'

They wadn't hardly enough room on th' card to write his name; he printed because printin' was his thing. His teacher he chopped wood for had said, 'Harley, you're a young genius at printing!'

Miss Pringle, I have got you a big surprise. Will try again. H. Welch

He had to git them shocks changed out an' do somethin' about lettin' th' cat do its bui'ness an' git back to th' farm while it was still daylight enough to cut trees with Willie an' Jack.

He looked at the th' other side of th' card. It had a huge phone number an' a big arm with a muscle that said, *TATTMAN*. Lord only knows what Miss Pringle would make of that.

He remembered what Father Tim liked to say an' once explained to him: They ain't no balm in Gilead.

He stuck his note in th' wreath, right by th' red bow so she couldn' miss it.

CYNTHIA

She was in their bedroom, rubbing lotion on her wintry hands, when he came barreling up the stairs. He stripped, then stood over the heat register to pull on his long johns, his corduroys, an undershirt, a turtle neck, a flannel shirt, a puffer vest, and heavy socks.

'Give me a hint,' she said.

'Very important to get out there before somebody beats me to it.'

She followed him downstairs, where he stopped at the hall closet and finished the job. Boots. Hat. Scarf. Gloves.

Sometimes he told her everything, sometimes he told her nothing.

She looked on, arms akimbo. 'Where on *earth* are you going? The Arctic tundra?'

'To see a man about a dog.'

She watched him reverse-zoom out the driveway. Her father used to say what her husband just said. But when James Coppersmith went to see a man about a dog, he didn't come home for days and never came home with a dog. No, Timothy Kavanagh would come straight home from his mission, famished and half frozen. As for his mission, whatever it may be, it would be accomplished.

TIM

Smoking out the perfect dog for a friend had put a certain shine on the day. Never mind that the cloud cover was dense, with temperatures still in the thirties.

Coot was on a ladder, shelving books.

'I've found your dog!'

Coot looked cautious. 'Is it a retail dog?'

'Checks every box but the barking box. The fleas are zapped.'

'But th' barkin' . . . '

'You have Grace in your corner. With training, I'm sure the barking will soon be history. You'll never find another dog that meets so many of Hope's standards. This, my friend, is a *superlative* dog.'

Coot got down from the ladder. 'Somebody said look at 'is ears. Are his ears all right? They can git infections in their ears, plus what you call mites can be a problem. An' I forgot Hope says it cain't shed.'

This was not the fun part of finding somebody a free dog. The prospective owner at some point becomes picky. Never fails. He had found this dog to be so perfect for Coot's needs that he'd signed an agreement that said he couldn't return it and shook Dooley's hand, which was code for 'done deal.' He would pick the dog up tomorrow after a complete examination.

As Coot had repeatedly referred to a male dog, he needed to get that issue on the table.

'Elsie, by the way, is a beautiful, healthy female.'

'Who's Elsie?'

'Your dog. She's a female.'

The look on Coot's face was that of a kid whose ice cream just fell out of the cone.

'Actually, a female is likely to be less highly strung around customers.' He didn't know if this was absolutely true, just likely. And probably politically incorrect, no matter what.

'And—you'll be surprised how *little* this loving, fully vetted, *friendly* dog will cost,' he said.

'Oh, nossir.' Coot took a step back. 'I'm lookin' for a free dog.'

'It will cost you, my friend . . . a cherry pie!'

'Haw! I cain't cook a pie.'

'Sweet Stuff,' he said. 'Three doors down! Easy as fallin' off a log. I bring th' dog, you donate th' pie. It's for Dooley. He likes to get a pie for a dog.'

'What if th' dog don't work out? Do I git my pie back?'

'Not in th' deal. But guess what? Just for you, this healthy, good-looking, friendly *companion* dog comes fully vetted—*spayed, all shots and vaccines. Two years old. House-trained.* Top that for a free dog.'

That should do it.

'What breed is it?'

'Multi. Like you and me and all the rest of humankind. Primarily golden retriever—a good-natured, protective, and gentle breed. You'll love her, Coot. I daresay there won't be another chance like this. So, I can bring her to town tomorrow afternoon; she's at Meadowgate, I've just checked her out personally. Has Dr. Dooley's full approval as an *exceptional* dog.'

Where was the joy in the man who, a very short time ago, was eager for a dog? Why had he, the meddler extraordinaire, acted in such great haste? Because Elsie would have been taken in a heartbeat by another dog-shopper. The opportunity had presented itself, and he had jumped on it.

'Whatever dog I git, it's got to do a trial run with Margaret Ann.'

He had forgotten to ask Dooley about Elsie and cats. And obviously, none of the carefully curated adjectives and multiple free perks were working. Where was the fun in this?

If Coot decided not to keep Elsie, Tim Kavanagh would be stuck with this beautiful, loving, sixty-five-pound exceptional dog that sheds all over the place and barks at the drop of a hat. His wife would not like that, not even a little.

When Dooley rehomed an animal, he did it thoughtfully and he did not take it back. There was no room at Meadowgate to house all the creatures, great and small, dropped off at the road, left at the door of the clinic, or stowed in the bed of Dooley's truck while parked at Crossroads store.

He'd once gone with Dooley for a burger at Jake's. When they got home to Meadowgate, they discovered the local vet had been duped again.

Deposited in the truck bed was a box of eight kittens. Eight!

HARLEY

It was goin' on four o'clock an' he still wadn't through changin' out th' shocks. His chest was hurtin' pretty bad where it was knocked ag'in th' steerin' wheel, an' all he'd had to eat was a half pack of Nabs an' a Snickers.

But somethin' was naggin' him an' he didn't know what.

He was wipin' his hands on th' rag when he realized what it was.

He'd forgot an' left Dolors in Reg's truck.

ESTHER AND RAY

They were sittin' in th' livin' room they hadn't visited in a hundred years. It seemed like another planet. Even when th' girls came over with their multitudes, everybody hung out in th' kitchen an' th' nook, with its humongous TV screen. This year, they would start a new tradition an' spread out to th' livin' room an' no gangin' up in th' kitchen.

It was nice with th' tree lit, thanks to th' girls who did all this th' day after Thanksgivin'. She liked th' strings of popcorn an' cranberries made by th' kids, loved th' old colored lights—th' whole caboodle was just like her childhood. Except for th' wallpaper, they could be sittin' in her mama's front room.

Ray reached over an' took her hand. Hand-holdin' an' kissin' had always been her favorites. She squeezed his hand.

'Merry Christmas, Cupcake.' He leaned her way. 'Give me some sugar.'

'I just gave you some sugar.' She should not have squeezed his hand.

'When was that?' he said. 'Surely it's somewhere in my long-term memory. Halloween, I think it was. Yessir. Halloween. And here we are, gainin' on Christmas!'

She tried to remove her hand, but he held on like a puppy to a sock.

'Do you know how much time you have left on this green earth?' he said.

'I do not. Do you?'

'I don't know th' numbers, but I do know this—we don't have forever anymore. And if you can't give your old man a little lovin' we may not be spendin' eternity together.'

'That might be refreshin',' she said. Seventy Christmases with this ol' booger.

'I'll be up there enjoyin' th' streets paved with gold an' learnin' how they built th' Pearly Gates. I've always wondered; that had to be an architectural feat.'

'You'll be busy as a bee.'

'Busy lookin' down at th' Other Place an' all th' women who were too stingy to give their husbands a little sugar.'

He got up, which was not easy these days, an' grabbed onto his cane an' there he went up th' hall.

Her husband was not th' type to get up an' walk away. 'Ray Cunnin'ham!' she hollered, 'in case you've forgotten, I'm ninety-three!'

'An' I'm ninety-two. You should be flattered.'

Him bein' younger, she thought. That was th' problem right there.

'Hold on!' she hollered.

Gettin' up was tricky. She would continue to skip th' knee replacements everybody was so over th' moon about.

She caught up with him mid-hall.

'I have a great idea,' he said.

At least he was still speakin' to her.

'Let's race,' he said.

'Let's *what?*'

'Race. A man needs to have a little fun in this life, Esther.'

He never called her Esther. Never. 'You mean *us*? Race up th' *hall?*'

'It'll be fun,' he said.

'Is this th' fool notion you had in mind when you took up my scatter rugs?'

'I'm gon' say ready, set, go, an' when I say go, we go.'

'What if I fall?'

'I'll catch you,' he said.

It was not dementia, it was psycho.

'We're not runnin',' he said. 'Just walkin'.'

She'd wondered when A-fib would kick in to her medical conglomerate, an' there it was, right on time.

'Th' *girls*, what about th' *girls*?' Mentionin' th' girls would nip this in th' bud. Four girls keelin' over like dominoes when they heard their mama an' daddy were bein' airlifted to Charlotte.

She practically hollered. '*What would th' girls say?*'

'Ready. Get set. *Go!*'

An' there went Grandaddy Long Legs movin' out like a colt at th' Derby. She rolled in behind him to catch th' draft.

It looked to be ten miles to her recliner. This house was *not* teeny-tiny. But her legs were pretty good, an' if she picked up speed, she could move around him in th' left lane. He was pretty much ridin' th' rail on th' right.

'There's Buttercup comin' up on my left!' he hollered. 'Buttercup is lookin' good, folks, neck an' neck now with Ramblin' Ray! Looks like a dead heat, ladies an' gentlemen, a dead heat, Buttercup an' Ramblin' Ray crossin' th' finish line in th' same split second! Th' crowd's goin' wild, what a race!'

She fell into her recliner, huffin'. He pulled up a chair, grinnin' like he hung th' moon.

'How was that, Baby Cakes?' His chest was heavin' just like hers.

She caught her breath an' looked at her husband. Was she dreamin'? His color was better. His teeth whiter. His eyes bluer.

He gave her a wink; she reached for his hand, squeezed it. Was that little race number what the girls meant by spicin' things up?

She couldn't help flashin' th' smile he was always lookin' for.

'Lean over here an' give me some sugar,' she said.

DOOLEY, LACE, AND JACK

'We should let him do it, Lace. Let him speak for himself.'

'Okay,' she said, not meaning it. She didn't know much about horses except they're big, very big. And smart. *You can't pull the wool over the eyes of a horse*, is what Mink once said.

'Mink can't get over 'til late afternoon, but he's coming,' said Dooley. 'It's his idea; he's all in to do this. We'll sit on th' bench at th' corncrib while Mink cuts th' deal with Jack. Our job is to just be there.'

She wondered what would have become of her, and of Dooley, if their parents had ever, even once, just been there.

'I AIN'T GIVIN' you my horse,' said Mink. 'Nossir. I like this horse, his name's Daniel. I rescued him out of th' lion's den, you might say. He's a quarter horse—that means he can run faster for a quarter of a mile than any other horse breed, how 'bout them apples? You say you like Daniel?'

'Yessir. I visit him at th' fence. I like his big white markin's.'

'Those markin's tell you Daniel's a paint. He comes down from English an' Spanish breeds that crossed with Chickasaw an' Mustang breeds—Indian horses! You look at pictures of th' ol' West, you'll see warriors ridin' paints.'

'Wow.' Warriors! He didn't know this was such an important horse. He had told this horse some stuff he'd never told Scooter, without even knowin' the horse's name. Daniel had listened; he had felt him listening. 'He's really nice.'

'One of th' things makes him nice is I take care of him. He gets fed, watered, brushed, talked to, loved on, stabled in a clean space, an' rode. Gettin' rode is important to a horse. You cain't just leave 'em out with nothin' to do but crop grass.'

Mink gave Daniel a nose rub. 'He gets about everything but his own room in th' house.'

'He'd be sittin' in your chair watchin' football.'

'Yep. With my wife knittin' him some socks over in the rocker.'

They cracked up.

'But we wouldn't be watchin' no football, right, Daniel? We're soccer guys.'

Daniel blew horse noise out his nose.

'Here's the deal, Jack. You're a good kid. I know because I've watched you come along out here in th' sticks an' you've got everything a boy could want. A great mom and dad, a baby sister, a pony, two ol' geezers who think you hung the moon, an' you ain't too afraid of hard work. You've got it all. Except for one thing.'

'What?'

'You ain't got a horse! I was a boy once, pretty much like you, and I cain't even tell you how bad I wanted a horse. I wore my mama and daddy to a nub beggin' for a horse. An' when did I get a horse? I was about fifty-four, fifty-five years old. It's criminal that a boy has to wait that long to have a horse. So here's what I'm willin' to do. I got three good horses over yonder at my place. I cain't ride but one at a time. I'm gon' loan you Daniel for six months. I'll bring him over at Christmas. This here's a audition.'

When he was six, he fell off the barn ladder and it knocked out his breath. That's what this felt like.

'But there's a string attached. I'd like to have visitation rights.'

'What's visitation rights?'

'That means I can come over an' give him a handful of sweet feed or just rub his nose and tell him he's good-lookin'. If at any time I see Daniel's not gettin' a good deal over here, back he comes. This is a one-time-only offer an' I'm glad to do it. Y'all got clover over here and Daniel likes clover. You got timothy and lespedeza and he'll eat those like candy. So I think he'll be pretty happy at your place. You're a smart kid, Jack. You should go for it.'

'Does my dad know?'

'I know, and it's okay,' said Dooley. 'Mink's a fine friend to do this.'

'Mom?'

'I know, sweetheart. We're excited for you. And we'll help you get into the swing of things.'

He felt tears tryin' to come; he rubbed Daniel's nose. 'It's me, Jack,' he whispered.

'Why don't you get up there and we'll walk you around,' said Mink. 'We'll see how you look ag'inst a Carolina blue sky.'

It was what Willie called a far piece to Daniel's back, different from jumpin' on Scooter. He was so excited and so scared he could throw up in the weeds.

'How do I get up there?'

Mink braided his fingers together and stooped next to Daniel. 'You're gon' put your left foot right here in my hands an' I'm gon' lift you up an' you throw your right leg over Daniel's back like you do with Scooter an' that's it. Good, great. You're home. That saddle's comin' with th' loan, it belonged to my oldest boy; I'll show you how to take care of it.'

Even in the dim light he could see all the way to the tree line where the cows were lyin' down. Maybe he could even hear better up this high, because th' brayin' of th' donkeys was really loud. His head was buzzin'.

'Hold your bridle like you do with Scooter. We'll just walk around for a few minutes, okay? If you still like th' idea of a loan, we'll shake on it. How's that?'

'That's really good!' Jack wiped his eyes on his jacket sleeve. 'But we don't have to walk slow, I go fast on Scooter. You could turn us loose!'

The sun was shaking out its colors—red, gold, coral, blue. Dooley put his arm around Lace, who was intent on the moving silhouette of Jack and Daniel and Mink against the winter sky.

'There goes our boy,' he said. 'Into the sunset.' He was pretty choked up, actually.

He kissed the top of her head. 'Merry Christmas, World's Best Mom.'

Six months to find the money for a horse. They would figure it out.

HARLEY

He had depended on Dolors to let out a yowl that would git Reg's attention, an' that's what she'd done as Reg headed to Virginia. Reg said it scared him to death, but he couldn't afford to jump out of his skin.

When he seen th' Ram pull in at th' Exxon, he'd broke down an' cried an' forgot an' wiped 'is face with th' rag and there he was, a grease monkey like you never seen—wore out, hungry as a nanny goat, an' bawlin'.

He'd thanked th' Lord that they wadn't no worser wreck than they had—th' truck grille wadn't even dinged. An' he'd been happy as a pig in mud to eat two hot dogs all th' way at Jake's on his way home. Now he thanked th' Lord as he took a hot shower in the basement bathroom. When he crawled into th' princess bed where he started out at Meadowgate, he was glad to look up at th' ruffled pink canopy.

Dolors had used her litter box borried from th' clinic, she had eat her mashed peas, with mashed tuna donated by Lace, and was in a borried crate, sleepin'. He did not turn her loose, he couldn't handle a cat jumpin' on th' bed in the middle of th' night, no way.

Tomorrow first thing he'd head out to Miss Pringle's, but he'd sure call first.

He turned off th' pink lamp that used to play a little nitey-nite tune before th' batteries run out, an' hoped Dolors didn't mind him snorin'.

TIM

At ten o'clock, he picked up Elsie from Meadowgate and dropped her off with Coot, who was waiting on the bench outside the bookstore. Coot did not look thrilled.

At three o'clock, he had heard nothing. He didn't swear by the adage that no news is good news. No way. He called the bookstore.

'It's a zoo,' said Grace. He held the phone away from his ear—barking in the background. Sounded like three dogs barking, including a yapper. 'Customers just came in with their dogs, and one of our gift-wrappers is totally scared of Elsie.'

'Ahh. How is Margaret Ann taking all this?'

'She's on top of the refrigerator in Coot's apartment.'

He was afraid to ask. 'And your mom?'

'She locked herself in the mail-order room.'

He was too . . . what? Too terrified to ask about Coot.

'I really like Elsie, Father, but I think she's beyond my skill set for training.'

'So . . . '

'So I think you could come get her if you don't mind. I was just going to call.'

'What would, ah, Coot say about that?'

'About you coming to get her? He would be totally thrilled.'

On the short walk to the bookstore, he made a mental list of candidates for the perfect dog. Rehoming Elsie should be a piece of cake.

Lew Boyd once said he missed having a dog. Puny's twins had begged and bawled for a dog, but Puny had stood her ground—no dog, they shed. No cat, a smelly box. No horse, too much upkeep. No snakes, end of discussion. Possibly Elsie could change her mind? Father Brad! There was a wide-open guy. In fact, it was a wonder he didn't already have a dog. Definitely a call to Father Brad.

He couldn't think of another soul. That was the problem of being retired; he didn't have a parish anymore. He didn't have a hundred and thirty-four people, only sixty percent of whom were at all active or would even read the newsletter, to help him out in matters such as this.

He prayed the prayer that never fails. Aloud.

He and Elsie had a moment in the garage. He sat on a bench, she sat at his feet, looking at him with what he might define as expectation. He had confided in Barnabas, read poetry and Scripture to Barnabas, run his sermons by Barnabas. Dogs enjoy a little conversation, albeit one-sided.

'Now listen, Elsie. There's a little guy in there who wouldn't harm a fly. Try not to queen it over Gus, okay? Be nice to Gus, and Gus will be nice to you. No need to make enemies. Go in with a good attitude. I have a special chicken dish for you tonight. Vet approved, Gus approved, and I have personally checked it out. Delicious. Now. One more thing. Do not shed, and do not bark unnecessarily.

'Got it? Be nice!'

It was Gus who wasn't nice. He snarled, he stalked, he barked, he nipped. Elsie leaped onto the sofa and peered down at the witless creature.

'Does she shed?' asked his wife, who was obsessively protective of their recently reupholstered sofa.

'She does. Down, Elsie. Down, girl.' He pointed at the floor. Elsie sat on the sofa and surveyed the room. 'Down, Elsie.' This was hard; before the new upholstery, they had been dogs-on-the-sofa people.

'Elsie,' said his wife, 'down! Now!'

Gus barking. Gus, too, had his walking papers about the sofa. The best that could be done was a towel on the third cushion and permission to watch *60 Minutes* on Sunday evening.

'Where is she sleeping?' said his wife.

'Ah. I hadn't gotten around to that. I gave Coot the big crate. So. Maybe a blanket by the fireplace?'

'Does she roam?'

'Roam?'

'Through the house. All hours of the night.'

'I do not know this dog's entire résumé. She has Dooley's full approval; she is a superlative dog, checks all the boxes. I thought you liked dogs.'

That was a mistake.

'No, I *love* dogs. Didn't I give Gussie a hugely warm welcome when you brought him home *unannounced*? I've *always* wanted a dog, but things never worked out. And Dooley's just *shoveling* dogs your way because he doesn't have time to home every canine on the planet. And so now we have a big *surprise dog*!'

'I told you I was bringing a dog home. Just for the night.'

'You did *not* tell me that. You *thought* that in your *head* and forgot to *verbalize* it! *Down*, Elsie! This *minute*!'

Elsie jumped down. Gus was exhausted and stalked to his bed, furious.

He hadn't told her? Something more dangerous than a senior moment must be going on. No matter what, he'd have to rehome this dog tomorrow, no excuses.

He got out the chicken and rice dish and warmed it up and put it in one of his mother's Spode soup plates and set it by the kitchen door with a bowl of filtered water.

'Bon appétit!' he said to Elsie.

That was currently the only *bon* in this fiasco.

LEW BOYD'S WIFE, Earlene, was allergic to dogs; they were cat people.

Father Brad was traveling back and forth to Boston to move his new wife to Mitford and their unfinished kitchen. Not a good time for a dog.

Puny laughed, convinced he was joking.

No need to call Hal and Marge, who were traveling too often to have a dog. Same with Hoppy and Olivia.

Their priest in Wesley! If ever a man's disposition could be *vastly improved* by the company of a dog, it would be their man in Wesley. He made a call, got the wife, whom he met just once at the coffee hour, and introduced himself. Her husband was not taking calls, he was setting up his new electric train and village on the living room floor. They had trains all over the house, and you had to be careful where you step, which certainly wouldn't work with a dog. But thanks for asking and they were totally cat people, anyway.

'Oh, and a question,' said the priest's wife. 'Are you by any chance the bald person who sits on the gospel side six rows back?'

'No, ma'am,' he said, 'I'm the bald person who sits on the epistle side two rows back.'

No balm in Gilead.

Zero.

HARLEY

He'd took a tack hammer to his dentures and tapped 'em back in place. He'd shaved an' used his after-shave lotion, he'd cleaned his fingernails with his pocket knife, he'd pressed his pants, he'd parted his hair in a straight line.

They was a note on her back door stuck in a Christmas wreath.

Mr. Welch, I hope you have time to sit in the kitchen and enjoy a cookie just out of the oven. I will soon be finishing up with Ms. Pope.

He set Dolors's carrier on a kitchen chair. As th' note said have a cookie, he done that. It come off a whole plateful of oatmeal-raisin, his favorite.

He was nervous. He'd never broke out in a rash, but this would be a good time for a rash if he was what you call prone.

Miz Pope was half-killin' that piano. He knowed her from changin' out th' brakes on her Chevy Malibu; her an' her car was both a booger.

He wondered if he should put th' carrier out of sight. Him bringin' a cat in th' first place would likely be enough of a surprise. But—if th' cat was hid when she walked in th' kitchen he could say Miss Pringle, close your eyes!

Yessir, that was th' way to go. He stuck Dolors under th' table, which made Dolors give a howl. He checked his watch, he paced th' floor.

All of a sudden there she was. He'd never seen Miss Pringle so got up. She looked a lot younger than last time an' she was smilin'.

'Miss Pringle, close your eyes!'

'Don't let anything jump out at me, Mr. Welch!'

'No, ma'am. Scout's honor.'

He wanted to git Dolors in Miss Pringle's hands before Dolors done anything he'd be responsible for.

He slid th' carrier from under th' table an' held it up.

'You can open your eyes now!' His heart was beatin' like a kettle drum.

Miss Pringle opened 'er eyes an' said 'Oh! Oh!!' an' clapped 'er hands. 'Oh!'

'Merry Christmas!' he said. But words kep' comin' out. 'Happy New Year! Happy birthday! It's a cat! An' many more!'

If he never done another thing to make somebody happy, handin' Dolors to Miss Pringle would be th' topper.

To celebrate, she had turned him loose to eat as many cookies as he wanted while she rustled up the litter box from her cat that died. Then she asked him to join her in a cup of tea.

She was settin' at' th' table with Dolors sprawled in her lap like a dish-rag. Miss Pringle was wearin' a black dress an' they was white cat hairs ever whichaway but he didn't say nothin'.

'Scarlatti was a great composer,' she said. 'We're told that a cat walked across his keyboard and the sounds that resulted inspired his Sonata in G Minor.'

'You don't say!'

'Indeed, I do. I hope to play it for you someday; it's a modest four minutes of delight, proving that cats can be very inspiring creatures. All that to say, you've given me something I've longed for, Mr. Welch—a companion that I didn't have the get-up-and-go to go out and get. And of all things, a Ragdoll, the princess of the cat kingdom! Look at those eyes. How could anyone resist those blue eyes?'

He felt like a rag hisself—so relieved he could about melt off in a puddle.

'And what is her name?'

He pulled Dooley's scribble out of his shirt pocket and handed it over. She laughed an' said th' name two times like it was a beautiful name.

'Now!' she said, 'I have a surprise for you! If you'll just bring that basket over from the counter; I have a lapful of cat.' She was strokin' Dolors's head an' Dolors was lookin' at him like *I'm good, you can go now, Mr. Welch.*

He set th' basket on th' table.

'Do you remember when you sent over the pumpkin, and I used it on the porch for décor?' She took a napkin off of what was in there. 'Well, here it is in a pie, just for you, and maybe a slice or two for Willie.'

'That's a fine-lookin' pie, Miss Pringle! A fine-lookin' pie.' An' it was all his'n, even if he did have to give a slice to Willie. 'I sure do thank you for it.' He set down.

'You're very welcome. I've been thinking, Mr. Welch, and I have an idea. You've been so thoughtful to me over the years. So very kind.'

'An' you've been mighty kind to me,' he said.

'In many simple, lovely ways, you've given me happiness.'

He felt his face heat up. She hadn't never talked like this.

'What if we made a promise to each other?' she said.

He had never noticed her eyes was gray with a little blue.

'I would like you to consider me your forever friend,' she said.

He didn't know exactly what that meant. But he could trust Miss Pringle. He knew he could trust Miss Pringle. Maybe it was like Jack comin' to live at Meadowgate an' Lace an' Dooley got to be his forever family.

'There are no strings attached to our friendship. If you never offer me another kindness, you've already done enough to be my forever friend.

Perhaps such a promise between us will be a reminder—that there's always someone there for us, no matter what.'

He swallered. 'I'm proud to be your forever friend, Miss Pringle, an' I thank you for bein' mine.'

He hadn't never seen a woman shine like that.

TIM

Scott called at six-thirty to ask if he could get over to the bookstore. No details save 'a miracle on Main Street.'

The bookstore lights were on, the mayor's Audi and a police car were parked at the curb.

The bell jangled as he came in from the cold. He saw Andrew Gregory holding a champagne bucket, the MPD chief holding his hat over his heart, Scott holding Hope while she—what?—bawled?

The guys were as mute as clams but they were grinning. Hope gave him a hug. 'What?' he said. '*What?*' She wiped her eyes, handed him a letter. Typed. A familiar letterhead. He needed to sit down for this.

Margaret Ann saw him coming and jumped from the chair; he sat on her warm spot and adjusted his glasses.

Dear Hope,

I have instructed my attorneys to have this letter delivered to you on the day following my death.

It was my dream as a little girl growing up in the great Everglades Swamp to own a bookstore. I imagined it in a little town where people needed the companionship of a good book.

My father supported our family through his business of venom extraction, working primarily with the Florida cottonmouth and

Eastern diamondback rattler. Father was not a licensed herpetologist, but like many at that time, he was enterprising.

At the early age of seven, I was trained to become his assistant and remained so until the age of fourteen when I left my home and moved to Naples, where I lived on the street until my aunt took me in.

During the years in which I learned and practiced the skills of venom extraction, I was bitten but once, and nearly lost my life. It was the Everglades' deadliest viper—the diamondback.

Many people in Mitford have thought of me as venomous. I am saddened to say they were right.

Indeed, I learned early on that if I were to survive, I must protect myself by striking others before they struck me. It was behavior which I profoundly regret. But a housefire coupled with brain trauma proved to be a baptism of faith.

God has chosen to acquit and forgive me. I can now die in peace and enter fully into a state of grace. What a marvel is his love, and how long it has taken me to come alive to this transforming truth.

Allow me to enter your dream, which was once my own, and ask one consideration. Though I didn't always properly care for my real estate holdings, I would ask you to do differently. Please be as kind as reason permits to the historic structure that houses so much more than a bookstore. Under your wise and steady direction, it has become Mitford's flagship of culture and community.

I have long received reports of Happy Endings's activities, and am grateful for all you do and how you apply yourself. To put it plainly, dear Hope, I am giving you the building free and clear for as long as you operate a business therein. My trust will settle your county and state taxes for the duration of your ownership.

May God bless Happy Endings to thrive, and grow its important outreach to a mountain people who were often kind to me despite my unkind behavior toward them.

Your mortgage is forgiven as of today's date. You will have a return of mortgage payments, retroactive from July of this year, to make needed repairs and updates. My attorneys will contact you within two weeks to make the dream fully your own.

Remember me.

Yours very truly,

Edith Mallory

He returned the letter to Hope. She was in full let-down mode, sobbing. He was about to pitch in with his own let-down mode. The stark sorrow in this letter. The gravity, the joy, the amazement of it.

'July,' she said. 'I was born in July. She must have known that. So it's also a birthday gift.'

That did it. 'Blubber away!' Scott told his wife. 'The store just got a new furnace—for starters!'

'And more poetry readings,' said Hope, 'and more author events, and more reading lessons for adults and summer activities for kids . . . '

'I came by to pick up a book,' said Andrew. 'And managed to horn in on the best thing to happen since the man in the attic confessed at the altar. Found a pretty good champagne in the store fridge.'

'I delivered th' letter,' said Chief Guthrie. 'Th' delivery guy is new, he stopped by th' station to get his bearin's an' I said I'd take it over as I was headed this way for a jigsaw.'

'A jigsaw,' said Andrew.

'Puzzle,' said Joe Joe.

'Claiming somebody else's express delivery,' said Scott, 'is probably illegal, ol' buddy.'

'Prob'ly,' said Joe Joe, looking pleased with himself.

Andrew handed around paper cups of champagne and looked to their onsite priest for a tribute.

'Should we be doin' this?' said Joe Joe. 'Drinkin' when somebody's just passed?'

'The Father is Irish,' said Andrew. 'This is a mere soupçon of what goes down the hatch when the Irish get at it. Right, Father?'

'Pretty much,' he said.

'Hard to think about what she went through as a little kid.' Joe Joe shook his head in wonder. 'She was tough as barn nails, now I know why. Yet she went out of here givin' money away for a good cause.'

Andrew lifted his cup. 'Which is cause for celebration if ever there was one.'

Hope glanced at the ID of her caller. 'Winnie? What is it? What's happened?' Hope's look, the little agony of joy. 'Me, too. Us, too! Congratulations, Winnie! Yes, yes, we love you back! Thanks be to God! Oh, Winnie. How wonderful, there aren't any words! Talk tomorrow!'

Hope looked at them, astonished. 'She did it for Winnie, too.'

A few years ago, Edith had sought to erase Sweet Stuff Bakery from the town map. And now look. Edith Mallory's story of redemption would be told in Mitford for years to come. He didn't want to shed a tear if he could help it.

They lifted their cups.

'To Edith,' he said. It was absolutely all he could manage.

'To Edith!'

Hope was smiling now. 'Thank you for your years of prayer, Father. Just look what's happened.'

'*Soli Deo gloria*,' he said. '*Soli Deo gloria*.'

He did shed a tear, mainly because he couldn't help it.

HOPE

She was trembling. From the cold, yes, it was freezing in here, but from excitement, too, and the suddenness of Ms. Mallory's letter. For a moment last night, she had thought it a hoax.

This morning, she still couldn't, not yet, completely believe it. How ironic that today she would have written the mortgage check to Ms. Mallory's company in Florida—she always splurged and sent it two-day, just to be safe.

She hadn't slept well at all; her insomnia was growing worse with age. There was so much to get done, and Ms. Mallory's letter had sent her thoughts flying in all directions. One of the directions had made itself known after everyone but Scott left last night—she needed to move the Billy Collins book and letter.

She would have given it to him at their champagne moment, but they were all celebrating the miracle that had fallen to her and to the town. It would have been awkward to do it then.

How did it come to you, he would have asked. And how did you know it belonged to me? And there would have been her assurance that she hadn't read it—no, she wasn't the one who previously opened the envelope!

When they all left, she had gone to the mail-order room and pulled out the top file drawer with its burden of paid invoices. In the space at the rear of the drawer was the book wrapped in green paper.

The blue backpack was hanging on a hand-forged nail that came with the building. She had bought the backpack weeks ago, hoping to offload her old beat-up backpack into the new one, but there hadn't been time for that. She would put the book and letter in there because it would remind her to switch out her old backpack and get the letter in his hands once and for all. She would feel more secure about this than a vulnerable file drawer. She would even go a step further and cut herself some slack—she would give it to him when she could catch her breath, be more herself. Soon. They were so busy now. Before Christmas for sure.

She checked the time. The HVAC people would be answering their phone in ten minutes, at eight-thirty. The owner was the mayor's pro-tem—because the bookstore needed a huge turnaround on the furnace, she would let him know that Mayor Gregory was a friend of the bookstore.

Happy Endings could now afford extra help for the rest of the Christmas season, she must begin making calls immediately.

Each year, the crowd grew, many coming to buy, some just to absorb the wonder of Christmas in what a southern magazine once called 'a cute little town on the side of a mountain.'

This was Scott's day off at Hope House and he was here to help her shelve a huge order and tidy up after last night's impromptu gathering. The brut had definitely gone to her head last night. One glass—or was it two—and she was all over the place when what she had really wanted was to lie down.

The choir! She hadn't written the director to thank him for the marvelous gift of their music at the Lighting. That wonderful ecumenical choir! Where to even begin?

She gave her husband the job of calling the HVAC company; he was magic with people. If he couldn't get central heating up and running in five short days, then it couldn't be done. Real, actual central heat for the rest of the winter would save their year.

Poor Ms. Mallory. What a heartbreaking account of her life as a little girl whose dream was to own a bookstore. Happy Endings needed to acknowledge this sea-change gift in some very important way, but she couldn't think about that now, she just couldn't.

HELENE

The snippet this morning at Sweet Stuff had been one of keen interest to the town. Edith Mallory had died.

She had not known Edith Mallory, only that she had been intensely disliked. There had once been a dreadful rumor that Father Tim was seen riding about with her in a town car with dark windows. If the windows were dark, how could anyone identify who was riding in there? She had flown to his defense when told such a thing. She didn't say it, but didn't the Christ himself mingle with profligates and tax collectors?

TIM

The postmaster shifted the bill of his Red Sox cap.

'Mornin', Father. You heard about Miz Mallory?'

'I did, yes.'

'Good riddance,' said Julius Harper. His former parishioner at Lord's Chapel was in line behind him.

'We must let her go without contempt, Julius. Her life was changed a few years back.'

'Whatever that means,' said Julius.

He would not defend Edith with the news of her generosity to Hope Murphy and Sweet Stuff. That was not his news to put out there.

'She became a committed believer, something to celebrate.'

Julius gave him a disbelieving look. 'If you say so, Father.'

He bought a sheet of stamps and walked toward Sweet Stuff to congratulate Winnie.

Edith Mallory had been quite the albatross for a small town—and for a small-town clergyman. She had harassed the lessees of her several town buildings with unfair rent hikes and no structural repairs in kind. She had pursued him with everything from casseroles to significant church donations to a panicked experience with her in a moving car and again in a locked room.

Then the roof had fallen in—literally. He wouldn't forget the horror of the night he looked up to the ridge and saw flames devouring her enormous house and gardens. Everything at Clear Day had been destroyed because the fire trucks couldn't pass through the dense canopy of trees and rhododendron. By the time they hacked their way in, it was too late.

Smoke from the destruction had hung around town for weeks; even in his sleep, he smelled the torment of that catastrophe.

Edith had sustained a severe injury to the head but escaped alive, thanks to the quick work of her aide, Ed Coffey. Years later, she returned to Mitford in a wheelchair pushed by Ed. Up Main Street and down, they stopped to greet everyone they encountered. To each person who would listen, reluctantly or with astonishment or both, she spoke the only words she was able to speak then—three words she had cobbled together with great difficulty.

God. Is. Good.

Of the roughly hundred and seventy thousand words currently in use in the English language, he thought those three sufficient.

PAULINE

She stood on the brick stoop of the yellow house, tryin' to get up the nerve to ring the doorbell. She should have apologized sooner but she had to work up to it.

People in Mitford didn't pop in. They called first. It was a close town; everybody seemed to know everybody and even some of each other's secrets, but it wadn't a pop-in town. Visiting was generally done at the post office, the Hardware, Wanda's, the Local, at church—a little ol' timey, but she was glad of it. She wouldn't want people poppin' in on her.

She was scared of Cynthia—beautiful, artistic, upbeat, and very smart. She'd been to college, Father Tim said, and had done all those cat books. She seemed perfect, which was also scary. But Cynthia would tell her the truth. Buck would tell her what she wanted to hear, Jessie would tell her nothin' at all, Henry Pooh would tell her he loved her no matter what, that she'd done her best an' given all she had, and that was true. Except it hadn't worked. Anything she'd tried to do to know her children since she got sober had been hurtful to them and to her.

She'd got clean twelve years ago in a rehab down the mountain. When she hadn't died from the torment of it, she expected life to just sweep her along in some kind of dream world where everything got fixed—her kids would forgive her and love her, her husband would stop bein' afraid they'd both relapse. But bein' sober had turned out to be hard work. Work she had no idea how to do; she'd been drinkin' since she was eleven. If she'd grown up in the opioid crisis, she wouldn't be standin' at this front door, aimin' to ring the bell. She would be dead.

CYNTHIA

When the doorbell chimed, she was so immersed in her work that she forgot she was in her pajamas.

'I'm so sorry,' said Pauline. 'I should have called, but . . . could we talk, please? Would it be too much . . . '

'Yes, yes, come in, come in and get warm, it's freezing out there.' Pauline! Of all people.

'I'm so sorry, I really am, it's just that, I don't know, it's just . . . '

She looked directly into Pauline's brown eyes. Dooley's mother was terrified.

'I'm glad to see you, Pauline. Thanks for coming out in the cold. Let's have a cup of tea.'

On their way to the study, they stopped in the kitchen, where she put the kettle on. She was shaken, hoping for wisdom, beyond apologizing for pajamas at two o'clock in the afternoon. This was the woman who wrecked their Thanksgiving dinner and walked out into the night, her stricken husband and son following on foot. This was the woman behind the firestorm of her husband's fury and grief. She had forgiven Pauline but she hadn't taken her selfish behavior lightly. Not by any means.

She set out the cups while Pauline went to the study and looked at Dooley's portrait over the mantel. Both she and Pauline were as silent as Carmelites.

She gathered the honey, the lemon, the tray, trying to summon even a shred of social chatter. Having been surprised while working intensely and feeling vulnerable in her pajamas, there was no small talk in her.

They sat in the study, Pauline grasping the chair arms as if ready to bolt. Dooley's mother had not come for small talk.

'I'm sorry about Thanksgivin'. Really sorry. I don't even know how to say how bad I feel for doin' that to you, to everybody. I should have said this sooner, I'm sorry . . . '

'Thank you for saying it now, Pauline. You're forgiven.'

'I feel like you're the only person who'll tell me the truth.'

'I will tell you the truth. As I see it.'

Pauline sat back in the chair as if exhausted. 'What's it goin' to take for me? What's it goin' to take?'

When Paul counseled the Ephesians to speak the truth in love, he must have known it would take some doing.

'I'll be coming from places of pain in my own life, Pauline. Let's start with Thanksgiving. You were distressed that Sammy wouldn't allow you to hug him. If you really look at your son, you'll see he's not ready to hug you or come to your home for a visit. He's not ready to trust you, and you must respect that. You can't push him to love you.'

She felt the tease of anger as Pauline looked tearful. For far too long, her tears had held them all hostage.

'Please, Pauline. No tears. We're trying to speak the truth. Please don't burden it with tears.'

At the cold hearth, Elsie lifted her head as if alerted.

'I feel your tears demand that we feel pity for your suffering. Your tears are all about your hurt, your pain, your grief. They tell us your pain is more important than the pain of your children. You're not the one who was hurt most deeply, you're but one of six who were hurt most deeply. It's not all your pain or all your anguish. The pain and anguish must be shared with those who were wronged by your choices.

'Let me put it this way. Each time you weep for yourself in the presence of your children, you abandon them all over again. It's a way of insisting that your pain is greater than theirs, more worthy. Can you hear that, Pauline?'

'Yes.'

'Have you ever imagined, one by one, how it was for your wonderful children?'

Pauline drew back. 'Please don't talk about that. Please.'

'It's the only way I can speak the truth, which is what you asked me to do.'

She was silent for a time, pouring tea.

'Okay. All right,' said Pauline. 'Okay.'

She could see the struggle to hold back the tears.

'I'm praying that you'll turn your eyes on your children and truly see them. Seeing only yourself will not bind anyone's wounds, including your own.

'We know you were in the grip of hell, but you're sober now. Your kids are all alive and all here now. That could easily be considered a miracle, Pauline.'

'They won't want me there at Christmas.'

'Here's more miracle. They will want you there. Deep down, they'll be glad to see you, because each time you're there, there's hope that you'll see them and actually love them. Not love them in a hindered way, but in a way that can only come with really seeing the courageous and amazing people they are.

'Did you really see the little boy you traded for alcohol? Or have you wiped him out of your memory because you can't bear to look at that?

'And what about the little guy you sent to live with his father? How old was he? What color were his eyes? His hair? How tall? Any freckles? Did you ever really see him? And Pooh, who stood by you even when the insane boyfriend tried to burn you down like a barn, Pooh was there for that horror, Pooh was there for you. He's loved you unconditionally, no matter what. No matter what, Pauline. Who loves us like that other than God himself?

'And Dooley. Have you ever thanked him, just thanked him, Pauline, for stepping in at the age of ten—ten!—and doing his best to look after the kids, stealing food to keep everybody going, and Jessie still in diapers. When you thank him for that heroic feat, you're seeing him, you're acknowledging that you see his sacrifice, his courage, that he's worthy and wonderful. All that agony really happened, Pauline. And not just to you.'

This was crucifying for them both. She was reminding Pauline of what the alcohol had helped her ignore, forget, toss aside, cover up.

'Your dear Jessie. She's still hoping you'll show her how to conduct herself in this difficult world. Look out and see her, Pauline. Please. See this bright, capable young woman eager to know, from you, that she's worthy and can make it out there with what God has given her.

'Honor the pain of your children. Be the grown-up!'

She was killing herself with a kind of sudden grief; it was overwhelming. And now she was weeping. For Pauline, yes, and even for herself—the little girl whose parents had forgotten her birthdays, forgotten to pick her up from school, forgotten to tell her any good or decent way to live this complicated life. Her tears were also for the boundless grace she'd been given, for the love of her husband, for the love of Jesus, who made the pain a blessing, for the Barlowe kids and their courage to amount to something extraordinary.

She went to Pauline, who stood and embraced her, and they held each other.

She had never spoken so frankly to anyone other than Timothy.

Pauline's tears were a river, but she sensed the river had a fork now, and flowed also in the other direction.

They wrecked a box of tissues; finished their tea.

'You're good to tell me what I know is true. Thank you. Thank you, Cynthia.'

Pauline had never before called her by name.

'I feel so much shame for ruinin' Thanksgivin', so much shame for everything. How can I see them at Christmas? How can I ever fix that?'

'You can't. Don't even try. Instead, try to see them as God sees them—bright, gifted, loving. And your darling grandchildren. Think of that,

Pauline! There'll be six of them this time! You'll meet Carolina's son, Taylor, the same age as Jack. He's blind, Pauline, as most of us are in some way or other. Yet he's courageous and positive, eager to face what comes. More grace poured into this family.

'Just soak up the joy of having all these lovely souls around you. Don't ask for pity. Don't ask for anything. And sooner or later, their love will come to you.'

'That's a lot to try an' do. But I want to do it.'

She took Pauline's hands, looked into her brown eyes. 'I'll stand with you.'

'You will?'

'I will. All you really have to do is be there. Just be there.'

ESTHER

Every Thursday, Ray read th' *Muse* to her in a radio voice he reserved for the occasion.

Th' *Muse* had hit th' porch this mornin' at nine o'clock sharp. With th' kitchen cleaned up an' coffee grounds dumped in th' pot of philodendron, it was Cunnin'ham Mornin' News, live.

'Listen at this, Cupcake. *Edith Mallory, formally of Mitford, dies at eighty-two.* She's bein' buried in . . . no way . . . th' Everglades? That's a weird place to be buried.'

'An' good riddance!'

'Now, now. Don't speak ill of th' dead.'

'That was a mean woman an' you know it.'

'She cleaned up her act toward th' end. You remember I personally saw her on Main Street in her wheelchair, she could speak only three words an' was shakin' hands with people sayin' God is good. After that ceilin' come down an' busted her head, she was a different person, Father Tim said.'

'Yes, well, Father Tim would hunt for good in th' devil himself. I call a spade a spade.'

'Whoa. Looky here. In this piece by Vanita Bentley, it says, *Mrs. Mallory has bequeathed the historic building in which Happy Endings Bookstore is housed to current bookstore owner and manager Hope Murphy, with state and county property taxes to be paid by the Mallory estate as long as Ms. Murphy operates a business there. Mrs. Mallory's last will and testament is rumored to recognize another of her local lessors with a generous gift which is not yet known to this newspaper. Stay tuned for the breaking news!!!!!'*

Ray laid th' *Muse* on th' kitchen counter. 'This is big.' He rooted around in his pocket and pulled out a wad of napkin from Chick-fil-A. 'This is big for our little town.'

'All done so she could pass with a clear conscience,' she said.

'She was right,' said Ray. 'If she could only get three words out there, that was th' right three words.'

An' there went her husband wipin' a tear.

As for herself, she wadn't wipin' any tears about Mona not bein' home for Christmas. Let her have some space. She, Esther Earlene, had never had an inch of space anytime or anywhere 'til she was too old to enjoy it. She and Ray couldn't discuss Mona as he'd go off on a tangent. He liked th' other husbands enough to step out to th' porch when they smoked or whatever, but he wouldn't give you two cents for Jimmy Watson.

TIM

He dropped by the small office where he had administered the affairs of Lord's Chapel for sixteen years.

Father Brad was his pick for the poster child of Most Desirable Priest—young, virile, fair-minded, authentic, the energy of a team of horses. He was 'out there' in the best sense of the term—whitewater rafting, corralling runaway youth, climbing mountains, leading troops of young people into old-growth forests, studying mushrooms and tree bark, raising gardenias, and praying as if God was everywhere, all the time, just as the Almighty vowed to be.

He loved Father Brad and so did the parish. Sometimes he felt the smallest jealousy. Why couldn't he have been as agile, youthful, pumped as Brad? But no way could that have happened to the bookish Mississippi boy who had grown up shy and uncertain.

The Church hadn't been thrilled about Tim Kavanagh's retirement from the Chapel of Our Lord and Savior, aka Lord's Chapel, and the deal he cut with the bishop. The rule was, the obedient priest must move from his old parish, leave it entirely to the new priest, and never, ever meddle in the politics of the former parish.

But he and Cynthia wanted to live in Mitford; it was their hearts' desire, the perfect fit. And so he managed to wrangle his way into a retirement he could love, not merely tolerate. Not some warm clime with palm trees, not some retirement village in a strange land, not back to his roots, just here. At home in Mitford.

They absolutely could not, of course, be parishioners at Lord's Chapel. That would be rattling a chain to rankle the whole clerical caboodle, and casting Tim Kavanagh as a serious troublemaker. No, troublemaking was not his sin. His sin was meddling. In any case, they had gone over to Father Pittman's Anglican church in Wesley. He made Father Pittman nervous, he could tell. Pittman's gaze from the pulpit sometimes searched the epistle side, and when spotting the Kavanaghs two rows back, gave him a look that said quite plainly, So there you are *again*.

Father Brad was himself today, as most people generally are. Vivid. That was the word for his friend.

'Timothy! Just the man I'm looking for to help me kill this fresh pot of coffee.'

He rarely drank coffee these days, and killing a pot of freshly ground full-bore with Brad would keep him awake 'til the twelfth day of Christmas. But it would be worth it.

Happily, both of them disliked politics. But what would they spend the morning discussing? Politics. It was everywhere, in everything, the church most certainly not excluded.

They would pray that God tidy up the horrific state of governance in general and show them how to better do their part. They would struggle with the fact that whatever their part may be, could it ever be enough? Bottom line, God, not man, must be the one to judge whether it is enough.

During their four-alarm caffeine blitz, Father Brad offered to give a hand with the cottage in the woods. And what did the mountain-climbing, snow-camping youth leader have to offer the world of down and dirty rehab?

'Kitchen countertops,' said Father Brad. 'I love doing all-wood countertops. I can cut you a deal!'

They were thankful to have each other, thankful for the license to speak what needed to be spoken without judgment, thankful they could, on occasion, cut each other a deal.

ESTHER

Ray had gone off to get a haircut without sayin' 'bye. She had picked on him this mornin' an' she could see he was at his limit.

She shifted herself in the recliner.

Why was she always pickin' on her husband? He had th' patience of Job, worked a big garden every year, was a good church-goin' member of th' community—you name it. For a man on a cane an' sometimes a walker, that was pretty much a miracle right there.

Ray had been her mama an' daddy's pet. They thought he hung th' moon because he made everybody laugh. 'Don't be bringin' any more candidates home,' said her mama. 'Your daddy an' me are done. It's Ray all th' way.'

At th' end of th' day, as some people liked to say, she did not deserve Ray Cunnin'ham. Everybody said so, especially her daughters. An' it was th' bloomin' truth. He was the best man God ever put on this green earth, not a jack-leg bone in his body.

She closed her eyes an' tried to picture what surprise gift she could put under th' tree for her husband. Blank, blank, blank was all she got.

She didn't know if she should bother the good Lord with such a small matter, but Father Tim said you can pray about anything. She knew for a fact that her husband prayed every night, she could hear him mumblin' around gettin' ready for bed. She hadn't prayed enough to amount to anything in a good while. She had offered up little sentence prayers all through her mayorin' career but stayed too busy to be regular.

Think about it. Who had kept the box stores at bay? Esther Earlene Cunnin'ham. Who had kep' th' tax base low for nearly two decades? Ditto. Who promoted th' little gardens between th' stores an' made th' merchants sweep their piece of the sidewalk? Who showed up at every ribbon cuttin', political barbecue, hospital gala, all-church Thanksgivin', Bane an' Blessin', an' even a few Dollar General sidewalk sales? Who had seen to it that Miss Rose an' Uncle Billy had oil in their tank? Or Old Man Mueller had a bite to eat now an' again?

Who had time to pray?

Okay. It was time.

She shifted in her recliner, patted her hair to see if she'd run a comb through it today. Should she put on lipstick? No.

She would pray out loud to confirm that she was actually doin' this.

'Lord Jesus.'

The words sort of came loose an' gathered in th' air around her chair. She felt good about gettin' that far.

'Creator an' savior, you are th' big Gift.'

She might have gotten that line from a prayer by Father Tim. He had prayed with them many times in this very room, which he didn't actually have to do since Cunnin'hams had a history of bein' Baptist.

'So I ask you, Lord, to help me with a little surprise gift for my husband. I'm reminded that you gave me Ray an' th' girls an' th' grans an great-grans an' you've helped us along all these seventy years. I know it was you helpin' us along because we ourselves could not have done it. No way. So what can I give my husband that would be a surprise an' a blessin'? It has to be a blessin' to him or there'd be no use doin' it.'

Maybe that was it. But it seemed short.

'I thank you, Lord Jesus, for layin' on my heart what to give Ray an' for standin' by us an' all th' kids, an' hope you'll help me do a better job of stayin' in touch. Amen an' thanks for everything.'

After she said all that, she must have fallen asleep. She did not mean to doze off an' was glad Ray wadn't here to catch her droolin' all over th' place like an old person.

She was haulin' herself out of th' chair when she had an idea. It just popped out like her number four, Charlene, had popped out.

She wadn't exactly good at stuff like this, but it would be personal, which he would love; it wouldn't cost a dime, which he would also love; an' she didn't have to wrap it.

She would write him a letter.

HARLEY

It was th' Saturday before Christmas, an' he went over to th' big house to see if th' oven was still workin' after he fixed it.

Dooley was long gone to th' clinic, Lace would be paintin' her murial, Sadie would be down for her mornin' nap, an' Lord knows what Jack was doin' 'til Lily Flower roared up in her 2001 Toyota Tacoma.

To his mind, Lily Flower should not be babysittin' young'uns. She was way too high-wired for young'uns. You would not see Lily Flower down on th' floor playin' dolls or trucks or whatever like Willie said some babysitters do. Pretty soon, Lily Flower would have th' young'uns marchin' around th' room like military an' hangin' up their clothes. Plus, wadn't nobody allowed to say *ain't* around Lily Flower, who had went to tenth grade an' knew all they was to know. He would not want to be babysitted by Lily Flower, no way.

When he come in th' kitchen, there was Jack walkin' in a circle, arms stretched out in front with his eyes squeezed shut.

'What's up, Sheriff?'

'I'm bein' blind.'

'How come you bein' blind?'

'Taylor is blind an' I need to know how it feels.'

'How does it feel?'

'Weird.' An' there he went, crashin' into his dad's rockin' chair. 'Blast!' said Jack, usin' his granpaw's cussword.

HARLEY

Willie walked around it, looked it up an' down. 'Prob'ly a whole lot better-lookin' than when it was built.' As Willie didn't give out compliments like Santy gives out candy, this was big.

Lace come out an' took pictures for th' National Register people. 'A masterful job,' is what she said. *Masterful.* He could feel his chest swell up.

When they'd went their different ways, he wanted to tell somebody what they said about his job on th' corncrib. After supper, he surprised hisself by goin' to th' barn to tell Pedro. He'd told Pedro a good bit about hisself. Like how he started serious drivin' when he was twelve—trained by his first cousin, Davy, on his daddy's side.

People was blowed away by how good a driver he was as a young'un. He was th' talk of th' holler. At thirteen, he was Davy's backup if Davy took sick or went to jail. Because he was a little young'un, he didn't put much weight on th' axle like some of th' drivers. He drove for two years settin' on a couch cushion; his legs was pretty long for his age.

Hisself, he run liquor but didn't make none. At th' age of fourteen, he was a paid driver for a one-eyed man name of Hoke Taylor. Th' trade was goin' down th' drain around that time but a good many moonshiners was still in b'iness.

Hoke could make liquor but couldn't haul it—he was scared of drivin' with that glass eye—so he hauled for Hoke in a Ford Model A outfitted with a 85-horsepower flathead V-8. He mostly run shine in 'is fender tanks or, dependin' on his route an' where th' law was hangin' out, he could haul a hundred an' thirty gallons in th' trunk.

Back in th' day, all th' boys in th' Welch family was paid to run liquor but didn't make none. His oldest brother, Ralph, had him a Dodge Cor'net, his stepbrother Wayne run a Oldsmobile Rocket 88. Davy had him a flathead V-8 Ford with a engine out of a Cadillac ambulance.

'All them vehicles,' he had told Pedro, 'run like a scalded dog.'

Seem like it done Pedro good to hear about life back in th' day.

He went in th' barn through the little side door an' looked over to th' corner.

Pedro wadn' there.

He'd got used to Pedro standin' in th' corner. He'd been comin' out to th' barn of an evenin' to check his water bucket. Pedro was jis' gittin' comfortable with ever'body.

He walked up to th' shed where Willie was sodderin' th' handle of th' cow bell used for all big events at Meadowgate.

'Where's Pedro at?'

'He's over at Johnny Stokes's.'

'Why's he over at Johnny's?'

''Cause Johnny said he'd take 'im.'

He didn't like th' way Johnny Stokes's animals looked. He couldn' tell if they was half-starved or half-fed.

'Does Dooley know he went to Johnny's?'

'Dooley told me to move him along to a good home. That's all he said an' that's what I done. You can't git just anybody to take a mule. Johnny'll give him a pretty good home an' he's built his stock a pretty good run-in shed.'

He didn' want to argue with Willie. It wadn' no use stirrin' up a fuss—Pedro was gone an' that was th' end of it.

He felt sick about a simple fact that didn't always register with Willie—

They's a whole lot of times when pretty good ain't no good a'tall.

HELENE

As a young librarian in Boston, she had on occasion imagined the turns the rest of her life might take.

Living again in the Midi was a possibility she liked to explore. Teaching piano had not yet occurred to her because she was still a student, giddy with the love of music and the complexities of her new life in America.

She had adopted as her banner a line from a poem by Gerard Manley Hopkins: 'What is all this juice and all this joy?'

Marriage was a possibility she thought she should at least consider.

In that particular exercise, her imaginings took place at an oval table like the one in her grandmother's kitchen. The tablecloth was stitched with hand-embroidered iris. She saw a young husband on one side of the table and herself on the other. She never clearly saw his face, though she could plainly see he was wearing a proper tie; he was not a workman.

On the table was her iteration of her grandmother's baked chicken, her baguette, her potatoes with aioli and chives, and a salad of butter lettuce dressed in a lightly sweet vinaigrette with a pinch of *fleur de sel.*

There was always wine on her grandmother's table and so in these excursions into daydreaming she placed a bottle in the tableau—*rouge*, because it was said to be good for the heart. In or out of season, there was the vase of cornflowers, in remembrance of her grandfather, who perished in the Battle of Verdun.

If she conversed with the husband, to whom she'd given the name Andre, she talked of what she was reading—Rimbaud in the English translation, perhaps—and the Debussy she was struggling to play. She sensed that Andre was interested and engaged but never knew this for certain.

There soon came a time when she couldn't conjure this imagined life. The young husband disappeared entirely and so did any thought of marriage. In her daydreaming, wedlock had been tidy. She didn't believe she could bear the living, breathing flesh of an actual person.

She wondered where the letter might be now—how it had moved from the chair in the Poetry section, and if it had found the writer or the one for whom it was written.

She knew with certainty that Mr. Welch had not written it or worked through a Cyrano or in any way had anything to do with it coming into her possession.

She thought of the time Mr. Welch rented quarters in the basement of the former rectory, which she rented from Father Tim. As her tenant, he was forever fixing things in the house or working in her garden. He also kept after her old car as if it were a Bentley—changing the oil, replacing the windshield wipers, taking it in for inspection.

After moving to Meadowgate, he faithfully sent or delivered garden produce and tins of his popular brownies. On one occasion, he cooked a pot of collards to introduce her to the food ways of his childhood.

She had learned about pot likker, or *liquer de pot*, and cornbread, and something he called livermush and she called *pâté*. And oh! How he tried to please her by liking her music. He'd sat frozen as marble when she played Clara Schumann but eventually gave way to a doze. When she played 'Für Elise,' he didn't fight sleep, but fell immediately into its embrace, sitting upright.

How might she really thank him for all he had done? Should she consider her friendship thanks enough? That seemed prideful. The pumpkin pie she gave him certainly helped; he was proud of that pie.

Dolores wound herself about her ankles, purring. The most important of all his many offerings! What greater gift could he have given her than Dolores?

Dolores leaped onto the cushion of the chair next to hers, blue eyes looking directly into her own. 'Dolores,' she said. '*Ma petite chou.*'

Something more than a pie; he deserved something more.

She was pleased with the idea that fell like a feather onto the careful plane of her imagination.

Yes, he would like that.

Mr. Welch would like that very much.

A letter.

COOT AND GRACE

FOR A LUCKY PERSON

Hey everybody. I have a big gov project out west and will be livin there for two years. I work in all aspects of refrigeration. I cant take my dog because dogs are not allowed where I'll be bunkin with a bunch of guys.

I'm pretty tore up about givin my dog away. His name is Hey Dude but we just call him Dude.

Dude is a pretty big guy. Mixed breed including German shepherd. About four year old and kind of ugly but Lord help he's a sweet bugger. He is as good a dog as you'd find anywhere on the planet. And he's FREE. All shots.

I have a few questions for anybody that wants to take him. But I'm on a short leash and have to leave out of here on the 22nd so give me a holler ASAP. I'm puttin up a copy of this notice all around Mitford and I flat-out guarantee you Dude will get gone in a heartbeat.

Alvin

Will deliver.

Here's my cell . . .

Alvin Bush arrived at Happy Endings Bookstore at four o'clock in a three-quarter-ton super-duty diesel with crew cab. Dude was standing in the passenger seat. Grace and Coot couldn't get a good look at the dog as they were being interviewed by Alvin Bush from the driver's side. Alvin's window was rolled down, the motor was running, the heater going full blast.

'So any of y'all smokers?'

'No way,' said Coot.

'Dude don't like tobacco smoke. Any of y'all drink alcohol?'

'Do we look like it?' said Grace.

'You never know,' said Alvin. 'People who hit the bottle can forget to feed a dog, forget to put water down, you name it. Are y'all th' ones who'll be lookin' after him?'

'Yessir,' said Coot. Nobody had told him there would be all these questions with the motor runnin'. His knees was shakin' pretty bad; this was real but it was like a dream. He was gettin' a dog he hadn't even laid eyes on as they couldn't see anything but ears stickin' up over in the passenger seat.

'Is this where he'll live at?' said Alvin. 'In this bookstore?'

'Yes,' said Grace. 'In a nice warm apartment upstairs.'

'What if you get busy and he has to, you know, do his thing?'

'We'll take him out,' said Grace. 'It's not like we want him to poop on our floor, which is a hundred years old and historic.'

'Will y'all keep water down at all times?'

'All times,' said Grace. 'We understand dogs.'

'Our customers bring their dogs in ever' day,' said Coot. 'We forgot to ask this on th' phone—does he jump on people? 'Cause if he does, we cain't take him.'

'I myself have personally trained Dude to not jump on people. But if you come in th' house with tenders from Chick-fil-A, he will jump on you. He likes honey mustard.'

Dude barked. It was a deep, rumblin' bark. Him an' Grace both stepped back from th' truck.

'Okay, no more questions,' said Alvin. 'Dude's ready to move on. Y'all look like good people. Come around to th' other side and he's all yours.'

'Not to be rude,' said Grace, 'but could we see him first?' She did not like the way this was going. What if they were getting a pig in a poke—which was a saying she'd just used in the book she was writing.

'You can take 'im out of th' truck and look 'im over but in five minutes I'm headin' on to th' other people who're interested.'

Coot looked at Grace.

They walked around the front of the truck and looked in. Dude mashed his face up to the window. Yessir, this was a ugly dog all right. A really ugly dog.

Then he barked. A lot.

'I ain't openin' that door,' said Coot.

Alvin rolled down the window a few inches. 'That's his happy bark! Let 'im out, he's got on his leash.'

'You have to open the door,' Grace said to Coot. 'He'll be our dog, but he's your dog the most. So you have to open the door.'

He was scared of this big dog jumpin' out and doin' he didn't know what. He made hisself open th' door.

Dude bounded from the truck and stood looking up at them with his tail just goin'. Big brown eyes. Big pointy ears. Big dog.

'He's beautiful!' said Grace. 'And what a gorgeous coat!'

'You gotta brush it,' said Alvin. 'Prob'ly th' shepherd in 'is mix.'

Grace stooped and gave Dude a hug. She loved his hot dog breath on her cheek. She loved the crazy thumping of his tail against Coot's leg. And his face. His face was beautiful, too—and so funny, she laughed.

'I love him,' she said to Coot. 'He's perfect for us, for everybody!'

He wouldn't want nobody to see him this happy. He stooped to touch the wonder that was happenin' in his life, as Dude turned his head and looked up—eye to eye, tail beatin' his leg, dog breath makin' little clouds.

It was like somebody was pourin' warm chocolate all over his insides.

'I bought him a burger no onions as a goodbye,' said Alvin. 'So y'all need to take 'im for a spin around th' block here in a little bit.'

'Yessir,' said Coot. 'An' we sure thank you.' He wanted to say somethin' like Father Tim would say, like this is a answer to prayer, but he didn't know how to say that.

'Thank you,' said Grace. 'We love him.' She wanted her next book to have love in it. Love at first sight would be a good kind of love to write about. 'Merry Christmas! Have a good trip out west! You can visit Dude when you come home, right, Coot?'

'Right,' he said, pretty tore up.

Alvin wiped his eyes on his jacket sleeve. 'He's a good dog,' he said. 'Merry Christmas.' Then he rolled up the windows and was gone, the exhaust pipe of the diesel smoking the cold mountain air.

CYNTHIA

She remembered a searing headache and the realization that someone was holding whatever was attached to the end of her arms. Hands. Her hands!

She was fascinated by the feel of the hands holding hers—both palms rough and vast, a landscape of hills and valleys. Was she alive? Her throat was damaged, scraped. She opened her eyes to a blur, perhaps the interior of a cloud.

'You *ridiculous* person!' said a husky voice. Alice kissed her forehead. 'I'm keeping the Louis bag but will give the ring back!' Alice-Who-Never-Weeps, as her husband called her, was 'giving it a shot,' he later said.

When she could see again, Jeffrey appeared much older, trying to hold together his long-cultivated stoicism. 'So were you far enough gone to see God?'

She was afraid to speak of it; it could be taken from her. But she wanted them to know.

'Yes,' she said. 'Yes. Yes.'

As her mother had done, Uncle Joe lived far longer than the doctors predicted. She remained Star Boarder at Hollyhock for months, cherishing the isolation and reading about the radical thing called faith. C. S. Lewis, Dietrich Bonhoeffer, Frederick Buechner, Henri Nouwen, Augustine, Francis of Assisi, Elisabeth Elliot, Corrie Ten Boom, Chesterton, Julian of Norwich, Catherine of Siena, Hildegard, the New Testament, the Old, Wendell Berry—she free-ranged, not knowing what to read in any formal way, generally following her instincts and the guidance of a wonderful librarian named Zelda, who went on the hunt with her.

She spent days by the big window at the town library, on the bench beneath the twig arbor, on a favored stone in the middle of the orchard. She helped out with farm chores for her daily bread—Alice would not accept money—and on occasion she submitted a watercolor of the garden.

Alice sometimes picked up one of the library books, then put it down, bemused. 'This faith of yours,' she once said, 'it's so . . . challenging!'

Eventually, she moved from Hollyhock to a little town in Pennsylvania, seeking something more of the One who had waked her from the death sleep.

Why did God love her? Why had she been chosen in a way she didn't understand? What was she to do with what had happened?

She found a small church, unpacked her Holy Word, chased God for all she was worth. And discovered that people could be heartfelt, caring, real. She'd been frozen for years and was thawing, something that would have been terrifying before the night of the bellflower. All she wanted now was more of this powerful, transformative love in her life.

She began writing and painting again; the outpouring was as devouring as the famine had been. There was a small art store nearby; it was her joy to help keep them in business. A bookstore two streets over in a former bakery that smelled faintly of rising yeast invited her to give a talk. Thirty people came and brought their children and sat on the floor with her as she told them stories and knew she was becoming whole in a way that let others in, that defied the Enemy, and that could outlast fear.

ESTHER

Christmas was four days away, or was it five? A recliner was a drug, an' she was overdosin'.

She needed to get out of this chair, change into a decent outfit, an' go to town if one of th' girls would take her. She would even put on her lipstick, which was down to a nub, an' shop for a surprise gift for Ray. She would like to get the surprise-gift business off her mind an' let somethin' else park in that space. Maybe th' letter she was goin' to write would be surprise enough, but she wadn't sure a letter could be a gift.

Mostly, she needed to get out there an' show people a thing or two about th' vitality of old age. She just read on her iPad that Rita Moreno, who she loved in *West Side Story*, was gainin' on a hundred—an' still winnin' Grammys an' Oscars.

Ray came in th' back door lookin' like he'd been hit with a two-by-four.

'*What?*' she said.

'Gettin' that stump out of th' garden is killin' me.'

'What stump?'

'From th' ol' apple tree I've been tillin' around for twenty years. Should've rotted out by now, but no way. Dug all around it, gettin' it ready for th' chain saw.'

'Chain saw!' She cranked herself upright. 'You are ninety-two years old on a walker an' a cane, an' talkin' *chain saw*?'

'It's either that or rent a stump grinder.'

'When we have a son-in-law who's all about stump grindin'? A *relative* who's in th' *business* of stump grindin'?'

'That's just th' thing. He's in th' business. He would consider it a freebie for old people. I'm not goin' there.'

'Freebies for old people is *exactly* where I'm goin'. If Tammy Leigh knew what you were up to when Larry would happily grind that bloomin' stump, she'd be over here in our face in a heartbeat.' Ray Cunnin'ham was scared of Tammy Leigh; she often used her second daughter as a threat.

'You're pale as death,' she said. 'Sit down! Drink some water! Make yourself a little crackers an' cheese!'

He gave her a look. 'Which should I do first? Sit down, drink water, or make myself a little crackers an' cheese?'

Ol' upbeat, back-slappin' Ray Cunnin'ham could be a smart-ass, somethin' his fan club of four daughters never seemed to recognize.

He took off his jacket an' pulled off his work gloves an' plopped into his chair. It was forty-four degrees out there, it said this mornin' on her iPad. If he wanted to commit suicide by chain saw or just freezin' to death, so be it. Lord knows, she'd rather have a toddler runnin' through th' house wreakin' havoc.

'I'm goin' to town to shop,' she said. 'If I can get one of th' girls to take me.' She dug her cell phone from her housecoat pocket.

'No use callin' over there,' he said. 'Th' girls left this mornin' for Arabia or wherever for their Sisters' Getaway.'

'Oh, shoot,' she said. 'I forgot.' Th' girls had never gone on a getaway of any kind but they said times were changin' an' off they went. Every husband was left with a fully stuffed refrigerator to keep him alive durin' th' four-day getaway.

'You sure you want to go out in this cold?' he said. His skin looked kind of grayish; she'd never seen him look grayish.

'I stay home too much. People think I'm dead.'

'I'll run you to town. Go get yourself together.'

Her husband was not one to run to town without a list of things to do.

She was suddenly excited, as if they were goin' on a date. 'I think I'll wear that pantsuit I wore for th' parade a few years back. Th' navy blue if I can still get in it. Is that too dressy for town?'

'I'll put on a decent shirt an' a sport coat,' he said, a little short-winded. 'We'll both be too dressy for town an' have lunch at Wanda's.'

That idea seemed to bring a little color back to his cheeks.

She did not want to risk comin' up with a dud, so she might as well ask. 'If I give you a little surprise for Christmas, what would you like it to be?'

'You give me a surprise every day of my wakin' life. Besides, if it's gon' be a surprise, why're you askin' me what it should be?'

'I have racked my brain an' can't come up with anything.'

'Rack it another time or two, you might hit on somethin'.' He went in th' kitchen an' started makin' a cup of coffee. He was not in a good mood, but th' coffee an' a nice lunch would take care of that.

She made her plan goin' down th' hall. She would wear that blouse with th' ruffles at th' neck. Marcie told her she was too big a woman to wear ruffles, which would make her look fluffy, but she got compliments on that blouse an' wadn't that what it's all about?

After lunch they'd go to th' drugstore, which had some nice gift items, an' th' Woolen Shop, where they'd have a doodad or two that might work. She heard th' angel lights were beautiful on th' lamp posts. With all th' cloud cover today, th' lights would shine way before dark; town would be festive. She would remind people how they got th' angel lights everybody was so crazy about—it was one of th' top achievements of her mayoral career.

Maybe his own iPad! He liked goin' on th' internet when she wadn't on it herself. But th' surprise in that notion would be th' cost. He would not like a surprise from her that cost an arm an' a leg. If she had it to do over, they would have separate bank accounts so he couldn't track every nickel an' dime.

At their age, surprises were not a good idea in th' first place. You could keel over from a surprise. Her grandmaw had done that very thing.

Her grandpaw Justice had given her grandmaw Iris a baby pig in a sack when what she expected was a Collie pup. He plopped th' sack in her lap an' out jumped th' squealin' pig, which caused her grandmaw to keel over. She lived for three or four years after, but everybody knew it was th' pig that came shootin' out of th' sack that put her on an edge she never got off of.

She remembered her grandpaw sittin' by th' oil stove after th' funeral, elbows on his knees an' his head in his hands, just bawlin'. 'It was th' pig, I shouldn't've give her th' pig when she wanted a Collie dog.'

Because 'little Esther' had been her grandpaw's pet, Aunt Flore trained her to say it wadn't th' pig that killed her, Granmaw's heart bein' mortally offbeat is what did it. She was to rub th' top of her grandpaw's bald head an' say over an' over that it was Granmaw's heart, not him, which seemed to help.

She listened for Ray comin' down th' hall to put on his clean shirt an' whatnot.

She had not seen him dressed up since they quit goin' to church a while back. After gunnin' their walkers across th' gravel lot to th' church door in hot weather an' cold, they'd both be out of breath an' ready to go home. So Father Tim or Father Brad or a lay person came up now an' again to give them Communion an' have a bite of lunch. Fried chicken when Ray was up to it, an' she always mashed th' potatoes an' made biscuits. They liked cookin' for clergy.

Maybe Ray had forgotten he was goin' to town. She hurried up th' hall, still shocked that she'd been able to fit in th' navy suit. Proud of this outright miracle, she had added a touch of Evening in Paris, which the girls ordered out of th' Vermont Country Store catalog.

An' there he was in his chair, asleep, wouldn't you know. If they didn't head out of here in five minutes, they would not get a table at Wanda's.

ESTHER

They had whizzed him up th' hall for tests an' brought back what looked like another person on th' gurney. Her tall, strappin' husband who had chopped wood like Paul Bunyan looked as defenseless as a house cat under that blanket.

'Overmedicated,' said th' doctor, who was ten years old if he was a day. 'Or possibly dehydrated. One or th' other. Or both. I see it all th' time.'

'My husband has never overmedicated. You have got that wrong. Back up an' start over!' She stomped her foot out of natural frustration, it was not intentional.

'Geriatric patients often overdose on their anti-anxiety meds,' said the doctor. He was standin' up straighter now that she'd put her foot down.

'He does not take anti-anxiety meds. He has *nothin' to be anxious about*!' She had just hollered. Hollered so loud she scared herself! Th' doctor gave her a forced smile—she could tell by his teeth he was a smoker.

He waved his clipboard like a Glock an' pointed it at her. 'Time will tell,' he said, an' walked away.

She didn't know doctors had given up scrubs an' were now wearin' old T-shirts with Smokey th' Bear.

She sat down, out of breath; a nurse came in.

'You need to fire that doctor,' she told the nurse. 'He is both underage an' a smart-ass, who's dressed like he just slopped th' hogs.'

'Oh, no, ma'am, that was not a doctor, that was your ambulance driver. He was just leavin' an' stopped by to say hey. I'll speak to HR or whoever about that. I'm sorry.'

Where were th' girls when you needed them to tell you what to do? When you didn't need 'em, there they were, swarmin' like house flies—tellin' you *exactly* what to do every single minute an' throwin' out your scatter rugs left an' right.

At this terrible moment when their daddy's life hung by a thread, where were they? Piled up at some place she couldn't pronounce that wadn't even in th' United States of America! She had googled 'sisters weekends' on her iPad an' was dumbfounded. Wine out th' kazoo. Chocolate fountains *in th' room*. Dancin' in sarongs. Flirtin' with airline pilots. You name it.

Dwayne had driven her up to the ER because it was illegal to ride in th' ambulance with her own husband. She had momentarily forgotten who was runnin' this town, but as soon as she remembered, she would file a complaint.

An' why wadn't Dwayne here now, by her side? Th' girls told their husbands if anything happened to Mamaw or Papaw while they were in wherever, the most available husband was to *stand by their side*.

Further instructions were to call th' girls only in an emergency, not to ask stuff like which one borrowed th' floor waxer an' hadn't brought it back.

This checked all th' boxes of an emergency. But none of th' girls would pick up if it was her caller ID. Dwayne would know how to get through, but Dwayne had taken his starvin' self down to th' cafeteria to 'get a bite.' He was halfway down th' hall when he remembered his manners an' came back an' stuck his head in. Did she want a bite?

No! All she wanted was her husband of seventy years to get through whatever this was turnin' out to be. She had never once thought about losin' him; she was convinced she would go first. Obese, two strokes, high blood pressure, diabetes, bunions, you name it, she had it. An' now look what a fix she was in.

If she had poured him a glass of water an' *handed* it to him, this wouldn't have happened. Same with th' cheese an' crackers—she could've fixed him a little cheese an' crackers easy as fallin' off a log, but what did she do? She as much as said, fix you own dern cheese an' crackers!

A man who'd been *grindin' a stump* had to get his own water, fix his own cheese an' crackers, plus wash an' fold his laundry. He'd been livin' like he was campin' out. An' all because of that mean streak th' Lord had given her to deal with in this life. We all have a cross to bear an' that mean streak was her cross. She knew very well th' Lord did not take kindly to a mean streak, though he had obviously put it there as somethin' for her to struggle with an' hopefully overcome.

She would not want to live even a day in this world without Ray Cunnin'ham. She would run him a glass of water ten times a day if th' good Lord gave her another chance. She would get her rear end out of that recliner an' cook her husband a decent meal an' give him some sugar when he asked for it, or even when he didn't ask for it an' . . . Wait a minute. She was carryin' this thing way too far. She would figure how nice to be to her husband once th' doctor got ahold of what the problem was.

She looked over to see if he was breathin'. As her eyes were not what they used to be, she pushed up from th' chair an' bent over him to look. He was possibly in a coma or maybe even . . .

He opened his eyes an' gave her a big smile. 'Honey Bee,' he said.

She lost it. 'You're not dead! You're not dead!'

'Not yet,' he said an' closed his eyes.

She grabbed his hand an' kissed it. Kissed it again, wet it with tears. 'Oh, Blue! I love you better than life, I do, I really do! I don't want to go on without you, you hear me? I wouldn't go off an' leave you like this, so don't you go off an' leave me, you hear?' But he was snorin' an' thank th' Lord hadn't heard that ridiculous mush.

She sat down, winded. Who was she, anyway? If she was to die right now, sittin' up in this bad chair by her husband's hospital bed, who would know she had mayored this town for sixteen years? Who would know they could be lookin' at th' roof of a box store instead of th' mountain?

These children runnin' around in their scrubs didn't know her from Adam's house cat.

Her prayin' had been skimpy, knowin' that Ray was keepin' up his end, an' one per family should be enough.

She would kneel down right now by his bed an' say what was on her heart—but since she couldn't get up, that was not an option.

She had never felt so alone.

'Change me, Lord.

'Not change Ray, not change th' girls, just change me an' please hurry because we don't have forever anymore.'

SHE HEARD THE text ding in but she was hangin' on to Ray's hand and didn't look to see who it was.

> Mama, Jimmy begged for months to get me to come back to him but I finally said no. No! Can you believe it? I have found myself Mama and I am courageous!!!
>
> I'll be home for a visit soon but want to live at the beach for the rest of my life.
>
> Courageous, Mama! Courageous! The family mouse! Tell Daddy!
>
> Love
>
> Mona

HARLEY

He didn't know how many letters he'd got in his life, jis' that he could count 'em on one hand.

His hands shook as he opened the envelope with his pocket knife. He was thankin' th' good Lord that him an' not Willie had picked up th' mail today because you could tell who this was from, it had her address on it. He hoped she wadn't givin' back Dolors.

Th' letter was a page long an' he set down to read it. He could feel th' heat in his face an' he'd got short of breath. He didn't know what to make of gittin' a letter from Miss Pringle.

Miss Downs had wrote him a note, which he kep' for years in his billfold 'til it wore out. He could still say it by heart. He looked around, but wadn't nobody listenin' so he said it out loud to settle hisself.

'*Dear Harley, you are a sweet boy. I thank God for you ever' day an' th' way your chopped wood heats you twice—once while you are choppin' it an' once while it burns in our school stove. It was Mr. Henry Ford who said that quote about heatin' you twice. You did well at your studies this year. Keep up th' good work. Learnin' is a life-changin' adventure.*

'*Your friend, Miss Downs.*'

He had hisself a deep breath an' read th' letter.

Dear Mr. Welch,

I am dismayed to realize that you have never been thanked on paper for all your kindness to me.

My gratitude is especially due for your wonderful gift of Dolores.

She is a great comfort, and being a Ragdoll, sets high standards for her keeper. Indeed, she is a cat of particular tastes! I must feed her just the right amount of Scottish salmon that Mr. Packard gets for me, and speak intelligently to her. Neither she nor I enjoy baby talk so it is an adult conversation about the marvels we see on PBS, especially those having to do with space travel, music, and the many indigenous tribes in the Amazon.

Please know that my gratitude for Dolores does not diminish my gratitude for the times you repaired my car, took it for inspection, changed the oil, moved the tires around whatever that is called, and washed and waxed it for Easter Sunday.

For all that and very much more, I thank you. May God bless you at Christmas and throughout the new year.

With sincere regards from your forever friend,

Helene Pringle

HE'D NEVER GOOGLED much of anything but a spoon rack, so he went to th' reception desk an' asked Amanda.

'Can Google tell somebody th' meanin' of words?'

'What words do you need to know the meanin' of?'

He handed her th' words he had copied out on a piece of paper.

dismayed
indigenous
diminish

'You can ask Siri,' she said.

'Who's Siri?'

Amanda snatched his phone out of his hand an' went to talkin' in it. 'Siri, define "dismayed."' A woman went to talkin' on th' other end. 'Feeling consternation and distress.'

'Define "indigenous,"' said Amanda. An' th' woman on th' other end went to talkin' ag'in. 'Originating or occurring naturally in a particular place.'

He snatched back his phone. 'Much oblige',' he said an' got out of there. If you had to do all that to learn th' meanin' of words, he'd jis' enjoy th' letter and let it go at that.

He read it over an' over 'til he stopped feelin' swimmy-headed an' started feelin' happy. He didn't hardly know how to take such a feelin' so he walked down th' hay road an' seen th' moon big as a dinner plate, then went back to th' house an' commenced foldin' th' letter half by half.

One. Two. Three, four times. An' that was all th' foldin' it would take.

He put it in his billfold next to the picture of his mama. It had been took with a Kodak Brownie when she was expectin' him an' you could tell. She was standin' in th' yard by th' black iron warshpot where she done their laundry with a warshboard. *This is me* was wrote on the back in pencil. *1946*. She was a pretty little barefooted woman with a good head of hair; he was proud to carry her around.

ESTHER

Christmas was right around the corner; she had to get a move on.

Dear Ray was a consideration.

There was not a romantic bone in her body, so th' idea of a surprise letter might be a dud. Her husband was th' romantic in th' family if Baby Cheeks an' Cupcake count as romance.

When th' girls were little an' she had a minute, she read Barbara Cartland, who was Princess Di's step-grandmaw. Now, there was romance for you. Barbara's books were a cut above what they called bodice rippers, but not much of a cut. Barbara Cartland lived to be ninety-eight years old, provin' that romance is good for your health.

Though she'd never use this particular salutation in a hundred years, it wouldn't hurt to just see how it looked on paper . . .

Honey Bunch

That's what her Aunt Flore had called everybody. Otherwise, her people never talked like that. Little Esther took after her mama, Big Esther, who bossed th' chickens, th' cow, th' mule, th' cats, th' house, th' garden, th' car, th' outdoor spigot, th' mailbox, th' barn, an' her daddy. Th' only Dumplin' or Sweetie Pie around her place had been when Aunt Flore came to visit, smokin' Pall Malls unfiltered.

Ray was twenty-four when he came back from over there an' they met at th' picnic. He tried for a long time to forget th' way he was treated when he came home—like a criminal, not like a solider who'd had boots on th' ground of a bloody war. He didn't talk about Nam. At th' picnic, she didn't even know he'd been military.

Th' sniper bullet had gone into his right backside an' out th' front, missin' his intestines, his spine, an' everything else it needed to miss. Otherwise, he would not be here to write a letter to.

Because he never talked about th' war, it was easy for her to forget it. But back in the day, tryin' to make up somehow for what had happened, she'd used her best lotion to rub th' little pooch of a scar where the bullet went in an' he liked that, it meant a lot. There wadn't much of a scar left on th' front where th' bullet came out.

She gave his back scar a name. They called it Blueberry, because it had a bluish color to it. An' sometimes when things were goin' good, she used to call him Baby Blue or just Blue for short. Th' nickname had been a secret just for them to know. She did not use it around th' girls, it had been her way of sayin' mushy stuff.

They'd had their ups an' downs. He'd been jealous of her bein' mayor an' other people gettin' most of her time, but he got over it an' was proud as a rooster with three hens of all she got done while in office.

Ray Cunnin'ham had been her biggest cheerleader. Through all those grindin' years of tryin' to knock some sense into th' heads of this stubborn little mountain town, there was Ray—hangin' in there, Velcro'd to her bossy self.

Had she ever thanked him?

She took a deep breath.

ESTHER

Dear Blue,

You know I am not a mushy person.

The Good Lord is helping me write this so if you have any complaints talk to him.

The girls said to give you a surprise gift this year so I am writing you a letter which I know will be a surprise because I have never written you a letter but you have written me letters and I am sorry I have not written you one. So that's my story.

I know you just love it when the girls boss you around but I do not love it when they boss me around. But I do think a surprise letter is a good idea and they would approve though I am keeping it a secret. Thinking of something to say important enough to go in a letter is a problem. But I would like you to know in case you have not noticed that I think you are a real . . .

A real what? This letter was tryin' its best to get mushy. Cutie Pie? No, that sounded like him talkin' to her.

A word she hadn't heard in years popped into her head. Guy Lombardo sang about it, or was it Lawrence Welk? Back in th' day, it was a very popular word to call somebody that made you swimmy-headed. So, yes! It was the perfect description of her husband, who was still tall, handsome, an' a great laugh at th' age of ninety-two! Back in th' day, girls had wanted to scratch her eyes out because she was th' first to get to Ray Cunnin'ham, who was th' perfect definition of that word!

What did she have to lose to use it? She had nearly lost him; he could've died right there on that freezin' cold gurney, an' didn't he deserve to be called somethin' special?

Here he was, asleep in his chair right next to hers, snorin' like a sawmill. It was music to her ears. She had hated it for sixty-nine of their seventy years, an' now it was music! If that wadn't a miracle, she didn't know what was. She filled in th' special word an' would also use it on th' envelope. She was totally excited—writin' this letter was kind of like runnin' uphill without breathin' hard.

Thank you for putting up with me. I know I am not perfect but who is? Anyway, I sure do love you. And I thank you for all the years you helped me mayor this town. If it wasn't for you I don't know if I could have been such a hit with everybody.

It needed something more.

It gets better every year . . .

That was true. But lately, that had changed.

. . . and better every day.

Would tellin' him this stuff give him th' big head? She would just go for it an' let th' chips fall where they may.

She signed off.

Cupcake

She folded the letter written on two sheets of blue stationery an' put it in an envelope.

Makin' sure she didn't mess up, she wrote . . .

Dreamboat

CYNTHIA

She would have missed an endless list of grace and gratification—

Her husband with his good humor and generous heart.

The village and its people, some of them quirkier than herself.

The joy she found in her work; the books she'd written and illustrated; the books she'd read; the redemptive faith she'd chosen.

And what of her studio, with the best light she ever worked by? And Elsie? She would have missed Elsie.

As if by some unknown communication, Elsie got up from her rug at the fireplace and trotted to the sofa. She glanced up for permission but found she no longer needed permission. She jumped into place and put her head in a lap that felt like home.

'This is my last thought on all that, Elsie. I'm forgiven and must let it go for all time.' It had been hard to forgive herself for attempting to take a life that wasn't hers to take. And yet the attempt had changed everything. Everything.

And now this—the mountain spruce with its colored lights. The fire in the grate. The benediction of this Christmas Eve morning . . .

'*Soli Deo gloria*, Elsie.'

Elsie looked up at her.

'*Soli Deo gloria*.'

TIM

One more time. One more desperate, last-minute time; Christmas was upon them. Some people performed better under stress and he was definitely stressed, so he grabbed the pen and paper.

How many times had he said it was the last time? How long would he torment himself with even thinking he might be able to spin off another version? And here he sat, furious all over again. No. No. No. This was it, he was done. Quoth the raven, once and for all.

After whipping around the block with Gus a couple of times, reading Psalm 37 and a few lines of Billy Collins, he felt better.

TIM

Eight-twenty a.m., thirty-six degrees, the walk from home brisk. J.C. was already seated at their table.

'I've got it!' said J.C., who was wearing a suit with a vest.

'Got what?'

'Th' *joke*. Th' joke about th' prominent newspaper editor and publisher, th' preacher, an' th' Realtor.'

'You said you'd never write a joke, and look what happened.'

J.C. gave his face a wipe-down. 'Don't believe everything you hear.'

The priest in him liked stuff to go as expected, though it seldom did. He'd envisioned several lunches to be devoted to writing the joke; he'd definitely conceived it as a team effort. No team effort had been forthcoming, yet he had strived away and had a copy in his jacket pocket.

'I haven't seen you this cleaned up since Uncle Billy's funeral.'

'I dressed up to tell this joke. As soon as Mule rears his pointed head.'

Wanda paid them the tribute of visiting their table, a stuffed Santa in a sombrero riding on her hat brim. 'So where's th' other turkey?'

'Out peckin' on people to give a donation to th' historical society,' said J.C.

'Mr. Skinner, who squeezes a nickel 'til it hollers, is now squeezin' money out of innocent people?'

'It's a trick he learned from you, Wanda. Come on—nine bucks for an omelet with fries? Eleven bucks for huevos rancheros? An' about th' cheeseburger. You want to charge me extra for th' *cheese?*'

Wanda gave J.C. the smile she reserved for dishwashers who don't show 'til closing time. 'Only if you want a cheese other than cheddar, as the menu plainly states. Now, a question for you. Would you like your steamin' hot coffee in your cup or in your lap, Mr. Hogan? Think about it. So, Father, are you totally back on caffeine or just foolin' with th' notion?'

He slid his cup toward her. After the aggravation of kicking his habit and switching to herbal tea, it looked like he was back on caffeine. C'est la vie.

J.C. CLEARED HIS throat, loosened his tie.

'So, three guys walk into a bar. J.C., a prominent western North Carolina newspaper publisher and editor; Tim, a priest; and Mule, a Realtor. The bar is empty except for the bartender, who brings 'em three cold ones and a couple bowls of mixed nuts.

'J.C. takes a sip of his beer and a voice says, *Enjoy your beer, J.C., your editorials are gems of practical wisdom!*

'They all look around to see where the voice was comin' from. Nobody there but the bartender polishin' glasses at the end of the bar.

'Mule takes a swig of his beer and th' voice says, *Mule, anybody with real estate to buy or sell would call you first—you're the best!*

'The guys still can't figure out who's talkin'. So Tim takes a swig and the voice says, *Father, your sermons have changed the lives of everyone who ever heard them.*

'Again, they look around, totally bewildered, 'til the bartender notices and says, "Oh, that's just the mixed nuts talkin'. They're complimentary."'

No laughs from th' Realtor, but the priest in the joke was cracking up.

Then he leaned back and laughed some more. Slapped his leg. Didn't take much. 'Hilarious!' he said. 'Great job. Hats off, buddy.'

J.C. grinned.

'I don't get it,' said Mule.

'No surprise,' said J.C.

'Plus I don't drink beer,' said Mule. 'Never have, never will. So take out that part. Maybe a little shooter of 'shine at Christmas, if I know who made it, but nothin' serious.'

'It's a *joke*,' said J.C. 'A *joke*. It doesn't have to be factual.'

'Right, but people might think it's factual.'

'So, J.C., how did you come up with it? It's pretty funny.'

'How I came up with it was to tell Vanita to google *three guys walk into a bar*.'

'Aha. I thought we were going to do something original.'

'It's original to somebody. Whoever did it, it was original to him.'

'Just remember,' said Mule, 'that I've been elected to th' board of th' historical society, so put in I'm a distinguished volunteer community leader.'

Wanda sent over her wingman, Jose, a new hire with muscles. A male server was a novelty in Mitford; the town had arrived in the twenty-first century. As J.C. didn't mess with muscles, breakfast would be peaceful.

'Bacon,' said J.C. 'Two servings with toast.'

'Bacon,' said Mule. 'Two servings with toast.'

All eyes were on the preacher. Jose leaned forward, pad at the ready. 'You, *señor*?'

'Bacon,' he said, lingering over the word, glad to even speak it. 'With whole wheat toast. Thanks, Jose.'

'Wait a minute,' said J.C. 'This is not a bacon rodeo, as promised. This is a bacon tea party. What's with all th' *toast*? I'm sick of toast. Let's make it a cheeseburger, guys. Double bacon, double cheddar, onions, pickles, th' works. All th' way! Our wives will never know.'

He looked at his watch. 'It's *breakfast*,' he said.

'It's Christmas! If push comes to shove, Jose here can be our pall-bearer.'

'Medium rare,' he said.

HOPE AND TIM

Happy Endings was open ten to two on Christmas Eve. He walked over to give a hand. Both Coot and Melissa were out sick, and Grace was committed to helping her dad with the Christmas play at Hope House.

Business was brisk. He made a conscious effort to not feel smug for having done weeks ago what these good people were desperately doing now.

During a lull at one o'clock, he and Hope made a pour-over and split a sandwich from Sweet Stuff. It had started to snow and was sticking on the bench facing the store.

As they were closing up at two, Grace called with a report and a question.

'Everyone wanted to have their cookies and cake before the play, not after. So Dad said great, you know Dad. As for what to do after, we were, like, stuck, so we decided to tell jokes.'

'Always a good idea, honey. I'm putting you on speaker so Father Tim can hear what's going on up there.'

'So, Mom—how much did Santa pay for his sleigh?'

'Umm.'

'Nothing! It was on the house.'

A crowd pleaser.

'Merry Christmas, Father Tim! What do you call Santa's helper?'

'Let me get back to you on that.'

'A subordinate clause!'

Applause for the clause.

'So, I have something to put under your tree, Father. It's my book. I printed it out and stapled it and illustrated the cover and I hope you and Cynthia like it. I'll bring it by this evening, it has a happy ending. And just so you know, the very *best* Christmas present is . . . a broken drum—you can't beat it!'

'That was a shot in the arm,' he said when they hung up. 'We're flattered to be getting her book.'

'You're in it,' she said. 'I think you'll recognize yourself in the Inspector. She was going to cast you as the milkman but thought you deserved better pay.'

He'd never appeared in anybody's book before; he was pretty excited.

'Grace is growing up fast. Only weeks ago, she was calling me Mama and now it's Mom.'

He remembered the day Dooley first called him Dad. It had been a stunning breakthrough, one he'd hoped for but never expected.

'Look!' she said, gesturing toward the store window. The seat and arms of the bench were being upholstered in snow. The lamppost angel lights came on in the dusk of cloud cover.

'There's a question I've always wanted to ask you, Father. You once said that some see no miracles at all, but you see too many to count. Do you say that because you really believe in miracles? Or because it's what a priest is supposed to say?'

'I absolutely believe in miracles, and I'm as grateful for the little ones as I am for the big stuff. My wife, for a good example of the big stuff, is a total miracle. There I was, sixty-two years old, a diabetic confirmed bachelor, and hardly a candidate for a successful, good-looking woman. Add a son, grandchildren, and a brother? Miracles galore!

'And while we're at it, Hope, you're a miracle. I've seen your challenges in pushing this bookstore to live up to its name. Thank God for the little girl who extracted venom in a snake-infested swamp and grew up to know the one great truth. You've received a building out of that truth.'

'After years of scraping by,' she said, 'the doors are still open, the lights are still on. What some may call coincidence or luck, you call miracles. I'm climbing on board with that.' She smiled all over herself, as Grace liked to say. But deep down, she felt the sick twinge of guilt. She had searched the file cabinet and the new backpack and the entire mail-order room. She was devastated by shame and remorse. That she had lost the book and letter seemed a kind of crime. She would most likely never tell him. Time could heal most anything, including guilt.

He pulled on his jacket, scarf, and hat for the walk home. 'The world is definitely turned upside down, but the good news is, we can still expect good things to come.'

'On board with that, too, Father. In the new year, let's plan a tribute to Edith, something involving the whole town. A kind of healing.'

'Count me in,' he said.

She was grateful for her friend, customer, counselor, and fellow book lover.

'This town,' he said, 'this time in our lives, this holiness of being—it's the flat-out best of all worlds, in the scheme of things.'

Two friends laughing and talking in a village bookstore on the side of a mountain in the midst of winter. What could be better, she wondered—in the scheme of things?

ABE EDELMAN

Abe Edelman secretly loved snow and icy mountain air, and was glad not to be in Florida. How could he be Jewish, his Jersey brother asked, if he wasn't nuts about Florida? Since the thirties, their family had a tradition of spending the season in Florida, retiring to Florida, getting a tan in Florida, and sending postcards to everybody forced to molder in Newark. Was Abe some closet Gentile? When was the last time he'd even seen his yarmulke?

The truth, though his brother didn't deserve to know it, was that he was having the most stupendous sale of his career as soon as the snow melted.

Then he would hook up with the mishpocha in West Palm.

HELENE

She had listened this afternoon to Schumann on her record player, and only occasionally to the weather report. The snow was probably getting deep, but she couldn't wait another moment. It was suddenly something that must be done at once.

But what if it stirred an old wound in her neighbor? What if he was done with the whole business and enough was enough?

She could wait, of course, until the snow melted, there wasn't any hurry. But no, there was hurry.

She thought of Marie-Louise, her plump, no-nonsense grandmother, and a particular story she told of the German occupation. There was a military camp of three thousand Germans two miles from the village. During the plague of occupation, gardens were raided, livestock was stolen, cellars were robbed, homes were occupied. There were, of course, circumstances too alarming to reveal to a young child, but overall, her grandmother said, the occupation was 'bearable.'

A general occupied the house next door. He was known by villagers to be respectful—he asked permission, he proffered thanks, he stood when an elder entered the room. To the point, he was fond of her grandmother's haricots verts, sweet onions, and in particular, her tomatoes.

Came the day when a German soldier drove his cargo truck into the vegetable garden of Marie-Louise Arlette Dubois. Furious, she stormed through the cabbages and approached him as he stepped down, gun in hand. Into her torrent of French, he inserted a raw German insult. At that, she slapped his face. With force! A German with a Luger! He would have shot her on the spot but for the general, who came running from the neighboring house, shouting, '*Halt! Halt, du Narr!*'

If Marie-Louise Arlette Dubois could look down the barrel of a Luger P08 and slap the face of the enemy, Helene Marie-Louise Pringle could go next door to right an inexcusable wrong.

HELENE

She selected a box from her recycling bin and wrapped the contents to fit snugly inside. In case she should slip and fall, the gift would not be damaged. In truth, it couldn't be called a gift. It had belonged to him, not to her, all these years. It would be a travesty to gift-wrap it.

'I'm going out, Dolores, and will return soon. Do please stay off the table.' She quoted a snippet from Heinrich Heine, which seemed a favorite with her blue-eyed cat. 'Your eyes are like sapphires, so lovely and sweet!' She had always flattered her cats.

She removed a pair of heavy socks from the boots by the back door, shook them out in case of spiders, and sat on the bench to pull them on. The boots that stood by the kitchen door had been worn only twice. She rarely went out in weather and had never thought of snow as recreational.

She layered her cardigan with a fleece-lined vest, a wool jacket, a warm scarf, and added a knit toboggan and gloves. Grace Murphy had given her the toboggan just days ago; she'd been cheered by it.

It was still snowing. Fat, powdery flakes, but daylight was still left to see by. She was careful on the steps, holding the box tight against her side and gripping the rail with her other hand. It took a moment to realize the steps had been cleared. Who might have done such a thing? She hadn't heard any rummaging about outside. Everyone knew she used her back steps for daily coming and going. But who, she had to wonder, would have left their warm hearth for a woman who does so little for others? Mr. Welch would not be on the road in falling snow in fading afternoon light.

And it wasn't just the back steps. There was a shoveled pathway leading through the hedge to the Kavanaghs' side door, as if someone knew she'd be going there.

She knocked, setting off a burst of barking inside.

'Helene!' Father Tim was clearly astonished to see her. 'Merry Christmas! Come in, come in! You're out in *this*?' He took the box from her. 'Cynthia, it's Helene! Put on the tea kettle!'

Father Brad had just stopped by, and now here was their neighbor, looking unpredictably rosy-cheeked. People were obviously out all over the place. All day he'd meant to groom himself and here he was, caught again in the act of looking like a rough sleeper. At this point, he didn't bother with an apology.

They gathered at the kitchen island as the kettle built up steam. 'We have fruitcake and lemon squares galore,' said Cynthia, 'but the best thing in the house is your pumpkin pie, Helene. By divine intervention, there are two slices and a sliver left!'

It was gratifying to know that a pie baked with her grandmother's recipe was touted as 'the best thing in the house.'

'I told Dolores I wouldn't be long,' she said, in case they wondered about the length of her visit.

'Cats,' he said, devouring the sliver, 'do not care how long you'll be out. Such desperation is left entirely to canines.'

Gus and Elsie sniffed her boots, saw there were no treats coming from this person, and resumed their naps by the fire.

She felt flushed, happy, eager to do what she'd come to do. 'Thank you for shoveling the path through the hedge, Father. And clearing off my steps. How did you know I'd be coming over?'

'A path through the hedge?'

'It must have taken a good bit of force!'

'If I were a better person, Helene, I would have done the shoveling, but I am not your man. I haven't stirred from the good company of my wife in roughly twenty-four hours. In days of yore, if I had a church service to perform during a heavy snow, I picked up a shovel and dug myself out. These days, I wait for it to melt.'

It was good to laugh; that and the tea gave her courage.

They moved to the study, where her hosts sat together on the sofa. She chose a chair on the other side of the coffee table, where the box sat waiting.

Just a few paces from her door, she had entered another world—the fire on the hearth, the sleeping dogs, the tree with its colored lights, the infant in the manger. Perhaps such loveliness was the cup from which married couples drink in the soft times to sustain themselves in the hard times. This room, this moment, these people—this was the cup of joy.

She nodded toward the box. 'It isn't a gift,' she said.

He took the box into his lap and lifted the flaps and pulled forth the contents, enfolded in several editions of the *Mitford Muse*. He took his time, pensive, as he unwrapped what he somehow knew it would be.

It was the bronze angel, with its complex history of love, betrayal, and a mistaken Atlantic voyage.

He was moved, she could see that. He didn't look up for a long moment, and then he looked up and smiled at her.

'It has always belonged to you, Father. I apologized to you once but never as fully as you deserve. And you, Cynthia, had to suffer my behavior as well.' She didn't weep easily but could barely restrain her tears. In this act of contrition, she was removing armor, baring herself.

'I'm sorry for the disappointment you must have felt when I stole it from this very room. It's yours entirely now. As it should be.'

'It was supposed to have happened this way,' he said. 'It was cast, produced, and directed by God, Helene.'

'Do you really think that?'

'Without a doubt.'

'God wanted me to steal?'

'God wanted you to understand how it feels to be the one from whom something is stolen.'

'I acted as a common thief.'

'What did you learn from being a thief?' he said.

'Suffering.' She wanted to be plain. 'And then I sued you, Father. As if it were possible for me to be an even worse human being.'

He laughed a comfortable laugh. 'You certainly pulled out all the stops, but you know you're forgiven. Long ago. Your lawsuit was withdrawn, no harm done.'

'That was painful, too, to know you both forgave all that and still allowed me to live in your house, to remain your nearest neighbor. You could have canceled my lease, ruined my teaching practice, but instead . . . '

He grinned.

'It's your Debussy, Helene, that lets you off the hook—especially in summer when our windows are open and the peonies are in bloom. The Mozart helps, too, of course.'

Cynthia leaned forward and took her hand. 'We love you, Helene. You're an important addition to our little town. Would your many pupils know the joys of the piano but for you? Most likely not.'

'I have an idea,' he said. 'Miss Sadie gave me the privilege of going through her possessions and taking what most appealed to me. I chose the angel. Then you took it for a while, and later, back it came to me. Sometime after that, I gave it to you, and now you offer it again to me. We've shared it in this neighborly way for more than a decade.'

'If it weren't pure bronze,' said Cynthia, 'you two would have worn off the finish!'

The bit of laughter, the goodness of these people in her life . . . she felt as if her very bones were thawing.

'We'll enjoy seeing it on the mantel again,' he said. 'But next year at Christmas, back it comes to you, Helene. We can do this merry exchange until . . . until the cows come home! How would you like that?'

'We would certainly like that,' said Cynthia.

She took a handkerchief from her cardigan pocket. How could she not like that? How could she not?

SHE HADN'T INTENDED to stay so long, and now, *c'était la nuit*!

'You must hold on to his arm,' said Cynthia. 'It's getting icy out there.'

'If one of us goes down, the other follows,' he said. 'It's a quaint hazard of the buddy system.'

Off they went with a battery-operated lantern, through the hedge and up the steps to her door. They stood for a moment in the pelting snow. 'A question, Father. Who could possibly have done the shoveling?'

'Maybe it was your Christmas angel. I've had a couple of those myself, and to this day I have no idea who they were.'

She went in to her warm kitchen, to the old faience plates on the wall, and the books stacked by her reading chair, and the embroidered French tablecloth worn thin as a moth's wing.

With war raging around the world and suffering everywhere, how extraordinary, how beautiful this life could be. There were no words, really. No words.

None.

TIM

He closed his eyes, and for one last time tried to retrace in memory his handling of the book and letter.

He'd put the sealed envelope in the book at page 110, marking the poem he thought she'd especially like. Then he went to the hall closet shelf where they kept the box of wrapping paper and ribbon, took out his favorite dark green paper, the Scotch tape, and the scissors. He would add a ribbon later, she liked ribbons.

He'd gone back to the desk, wrapped the book, remembered turning down the flaps at either end and taping them. He put the wrapping paper, the tape, and the scissors back in the closet, and returned to the desk as his cell phone rang.

'Hurry, Father, hurry! It's Miss Louella, she took a bad fall! She's askin' for you!'

The wind went out of him as if he'd taken a blow. The car, Cynthia had the car!

He couldn't remember much from there. What would he have done with the book? Put it in the drawer, of course, taking no chance that Cynthia would come home early and find it lying about. He did not lock the drawer; he knew that for certain.

He'd thrown on his jacket and left the house immediately, thankful to be wearing the old sneakers he wore around the house these days.

Roughly a year since he gave up running, he ran uphill to Hope House. He would never do that again.

When the poking, praying, and general alarm were over and all seemed well with Louella, he had walked down the hill he'd run up, feeling buzzed instead of exhausted. Gus had been walked and fed, Puny would be there, so instead of heading home, he headed to Wanda's, taking his chances on who would be around to share a table.

Over the last weeks, he had opened and closed the drawer several times, reenacting the likely scenario. It was a desk with a generous surface, thus the drawer would likely be of greater than usual length.

Now, for the first time, he ran his hand the full length of the drawer bottom, until . . . there was no bottom. The rear part of the drawer bottom was missing.

His heart seemed to stop for a couple of beats. It was an eighteenth-century desk; he'd put almost nothing in it, knowing that antique drawers can't always be trusted with weight. He'd had no reason to pull the drawer out to its full extremity and no idea the drawer was missing part of its bottom.

In his haste, perhaps he had slammed the drawer shut? The book could have slid to the rear of the drawer and dropped to the floor? But Puny hadn't seen it, the boys hadn't seen it. If it had landed on the floor someone would have seen it and picked it up.

The black cloud of obsession was coming for him. He said a word he hadn't said since he mashed his thumb with the hammer.

His wife would be down in minutes to put the oyster pie together. He'd just lost his appetite but would, no matter what, have zero trouble finding it again.

TIM

Her oyster pie had been, as it was every year, the best yet.

With dessert, they had the last swig of champagne, bottled by the vineyard that supplied bubbly to Napoleon and his marauding troops.

Midnight Mass at their church in Wesley was out; the snow was coming down fast. Alerts of church and business closings were crawling along the bottom of Mitford's TV screens; Lord's Chapel would be closed, also. He'd been keen to soldier through a little snow to the celebration of the Birth.

They didn't talk about the possibility of missing Christmas Day at Meadowgate because of the weather. There was a certain dread of tomorrow, of what Pauline may or may not bring to bear on the day.

'I hope,' he said, loading the dishwasher, 'that having Christmas Eve dinner in sweats isn't classified as mortal sin. If so, they forgot to mention it in seminary.' Somewhere around noon, their intention to get dressed in case somebody stopped by had gone completely out the window. Such loose living was pretty much a first for him.

'You may be learning how to chill,' she said. 'Dooley has been after you for ages to chill.'

He had always been, at his core, a mite on the uptight side. He couldn't precisely get the hang of chilling or hanging out. 'Hanging' was a word that suggested dangling, loose, as in one's legs over the side of a dock while watching sailboats breeze by.

'I'm praying we don't lose power and have to burn the furniture,' she said.

He put a log on the fire. 'If that happens, let's start with the chair by the window. I never liked that chair.'

'I thought you liked that chair. That's why it's still here.'

'I never said I like that chair.'

'But you sat in it,' she said. 'Isn't that some sort of approval rating?'

'Because late afternoon light is better over there for reading. But you'll notice that I don't use it now that we have a reading lamp by the sofa.'

'January one, that chair will go on the Geezer Cottage pile in the garage.'

'While we're at it, let the coffee table in the living room go with it. It came to the rectory with one of the bishops who probably received it from a parishioner's attic. And the table on the landing—what do we use it for?'

'Catching dust. Hoarding outdated magazines. It's been perfect for that.'

'Let's put it on the pile for the guys. A wonderful table, actually. Solid cherry! And the living room draperies. Put those on the pile.'

'I thought you were holding on to that living room stuff for life.'

'I was holding on to it out of, I don't know, respect for the past. Sort of a museum.'

'I think "mausoleum" is the word you're looking for, sweetheart. The Mausoleum of Old Bishops. So what if we put everything in the room on the pile? And I start a makeover as soon as the paintings for the hospital are done. Paint, wallpaper, natural light, alleluia! And Harley and Willie will be thrilled with everything we cast off.'

'The rug,' he said. 'Let's be sure to roll it up and add it to the pile.'

He felt some burden fly from his shoulders like a startled bird.

With Gus and Elsie at his heels, he went to the front door and opened it, but couldn't push open the storm door. He went to the deck door at the end of the hall. By force, he was able to open the storm door enough for the dogs to squeeze through. A bit of ice seemed to be mixing with the flaky stuff. But for two cases of flu, he'd never gone AWOL from a midnight Mass.

He wouldn't be giving her the book and letter; he would be giving her a story instead. A great story, really, maybe better than the book and letter because the story was infused with mystery, and who doesn't love a mystery?

The dogs skidded back in for their rubdown with old towels. Seven thirty. They would soon walk the Christ Child down the hall to the manger and read their cards and open presents.

Meantime, the very least he could do was go upstairs, shave, put on a pair of khakis, and comb his hair, in case anyone else in the village was socially inclined.

TIM

It had always been his job to plan the evening.

Reading aloud the cards and letters from friends and former parishioners was standard.

This year, they learned that George Gaynor, now married and known to Mitford as the Man in the Attic, had become the proud father of twins. Twins! A photo fell from the envelope.

Their innkeeping friends in Sligo wrote to say Evelyn had passed and William was declining. He and Cynthia were invited to come again, next time as their personal guests. A card from Peggy, gaining on a hundred and one and still able to sign her name legibly. She was part of his history, of who he had become.

The lovable crowd at Whitecap chimed in via Marian Fieldwalker, with a card asking them to come again anytime. *You are always in our prayers.* Morris Love's CD of Handel's organ concertos was enclosed. He knew that Handel left much of an organ score blank so the organist could improvise. *You must not miss Morris's improvisations,* wrote Marian. *Handel himself could learn a thing or two!* They no longer had a CD player, but he could listen at the bookstore.

From over the creek and up the mountain, Agnes Merton wrote to say that Holy Trinity was filled 'many a Sunday' with mountain folk, a few having come over from the Baptists. She and Clarence sent 'abiding love.'

He was moved by the memories, grateful. How many lives had touched his, all of them divinely cast and directed?

Dinner was at six-thirty these days. It used to be at the fashionable hour of eight. But they were old now, or he was, and he usually had a hunger pang or two around four-thirty. He knew people who actually ate dinner at four-thirty, but he was not going there. Not yet, anyway.

After card-opening came the procession from living room to study with the Babe. He usually sang during the procession to the manger; 'Angels from the Realms of Glory' was a favorite. Shy about her singing voice, Cynthia hummed, which added pomp. Afterward, another trot to the study, with wise men and camels from the Orient of their bedroom armoire. Presents, mostly baked goods loaded with sugar, were opened as the spirit moved.

It had been a full and joyful day, punctuated by Helene's welcome visit, a drop-in by Father Brad, and a delivery by Grace, arriving with her dad on their snowmobile. She had taken a bit of time placing her novel under the tree, and tonight there would be a reading by Cynthia. As soon as Grace left, his wife pounced on the novel and claimed her end of the sofa.

'Listen to this! *The Temptation of Miss Nellie Inglethorpe: A Murder in Which Nobody Is Killed*, exclamation mark. A murder without killing somebody sets a very high bar for the writer. I would never attempt such a thing!'

In her read-aloud of the fourteen pages, he learned he was a retired detective inspector—with a mustache—in an English village. Cynthia, known as Rosemary, operated a chocolate shop, and they were, if you will, sweet on each other. They were assisted in their roles as secret spies by an overweight spaniel named Pudge. Miss Pringle was clearly Miss Inglethorpe. Louella was the duchess who had helped Jewish families escape via tunnels under her mansion. Coot was Geoffrey, a fellow presumed to have been murdered but who was in fact alive and well and causing trouble.

'She's been reading Agatha Christie,' said his wife. 'I can tell. Or maybe it's just the mustache.'

'As to the temptation of Nellie Inglethorpe,' he said, 'I'm uncertain. Those clues are missing.'

'She's only nine years old,' said Cynthia. 'Cut her some slack.'

It had taken decades, but at last he understood something of his father's passion for Christmas. As a working priest, he'd been harried by the demands of the holydays—uplifted and joyful yes, and yet—harried.

Since his retirement, this was the first Christmas in which he felt he was finally getting the kinks out.

DOOLEY

'So let's pile in our vehicles and go see Christmas lights.'

'Where?' said Jack.

'Right out here in th' boonies. Roads are clear, Willie's scraped our drive, we're good to go. Pizza at Jake's after.'

Six kids clapping, squealing, general commotion. Mittens, coats, scarves, boots, socks, hats. And no, Sadie couldn't bring the talking duck.

Kenny was driving an SUV so his crowd and Sammy's could fit in one vehicle. 'We'll be a caravan!' said Julie.

'Just so you know, everybody, this won't be any Christmas light extravaganza. A couple of places and it's over.' In his opinion, Meadowgate's fairy lights in the trees were as spectacular as anybody could get out here in th' county.

Down the road to the next-door neighbors and up the driveway to the 1950s ranch where a lighted Santa, sleigh, and team of reindeer arced from the roof into the night sky. Santa was waving, Sadie was waving. This was totally the star attraction in their little no-stoplight part of the world.

Mink and Honey trooped out into the falling snow, bundled. The neighbors coming to see Santa on the roof were mostly drive-bys, but this drive-by was by personal invitation.

'Merry Christmas! Y'all get down an' come in,' said Honey.

'We'll just cruise through,' said Lace. 'Showing our family your wonderful Santa and sleigh.'

'It was on an old cotton mill building,' said Mink. 'I fixed it up; took three years and considerable pocket change. But it's th' installation that's th' killer, had to hire that done.'

Honey passed two bags to Lace. 'For th' young'uns, I know you've got a houseful. Merry Christmas, Jack, Sadie! We love bein' y'all's neighbors.'

'Is this your special muffins?' said Jack.

'With buttercream frostin' 'cause it's Christmas.'

'Thank you,' said Jack. 'It's for us kids, say thank you, Sadie.'

'Merry Christmas!' said his sister, still waving at Santa.

Jack leaned out the window. 'Mr. Hershell, where's Daniel?'

'In th' barn where it's warm. He's excited to be seein' you tomorrow. His saddle's ready for you to put some mileage on it.'

'Hope you can meet us at Jake's in a half hour,' said Lace. 'Pizza with all the bells and whistles! Dooley says we have to keep our labor force fed.'

'Will do, much obliged,' said Mink. 'Thanks for stoppin' by. See you up there. Merry Christmas!'

Down the driveway to the main road, Kenny following, and a right turn to another neighbor.

'Can we have a muffin?' said Jack.

'*May* we have a muffin. In the morning, not tonight.'

'Okay, because it's Christmas, I won't beg.'

'Mr. Teague won't have lights,' said Lace. Everybody called him Mr. Teague to his face, but it was Old Man Teague to his back.

'Me an' Sadie . . . ' said Jack.

'Sadie and I,' said Lace.

'. . . don't want to go to that old man's house. It's dark an' scary.'

'We don't like it,' said Sadie.

One dim light in the small house set away from the road. Spud barking. The clinic had rehomed a feist/beagle cross with Teague after the loss of Redeemer.

'Give me a minute.' He got out and left the heater running.

He knocked, hollered. 'Mr. Teague! You in there? It's Doc Kav'na!'

A shuffle inside.

The old man opened the door, gave him a curt nod, the usual. He was carrying a lighted kerosene lamp.

'Merry Christmas, Mr. Teague. Anybody comin' to you for Christmas?'

'Never have, never will,' said Teague.

'How's Spud?'

'Still vertical.'

'My family's here, we're all goin' up to Jake's for pizza. How about meeting us there?'

'They doin' any dancin' up there?'

The old man was a legendary flat-footer.

'Once you get there, maybe so. How about we see you at Jake's in thirty minutes? They're keepin' the roads clear.'

Spud barked. The old man studied for a time. 'Much oblige',' he said. 'But no pepperoni. I cain't eat Eyetalian.'

'We're glad you didn't make him ride with us,' said Jack.

'He smells bad,' said Sadie, who knew the old man from his couple of visits to Meadowgate.

'We all smell bad at some time or other. Here we go. Last stop before pizza.'

'We're starvin'!' said Jack.

'Hang on!' He headed home and turned in through their open front gate.

'Why're we goin' back?' Whining from the crew cab.

'This is the best part,' said Lace.

The old farm track had undergone some work but was still rough enough to toss them around like corn in a popper. He switched off the truck lights, which the kids loved; Kenny kept his on. Stars galore.

Driving the truck around the farm without lights was one of his favorite things. At six o'clock on Christmas Eve, moonlight reflecting off the snow was plenty to see by.

'Why're we goin' to that ol' fallin' down house?' said Jack.

'That house,' he said, 'is not fallin' down anymore.'

And then the clearing, and a constellation of red, green, yellow, blue lights, gleaming along the fascia of the new roof, looped through the maple to the oak and around to the branches of a young hemlock with a lighted star on top.

The kids went nuts. Lace went nuts. He knew this was coming, but he hadn't seen it; he was blown away.

There was even a light in the window and a wreath on the new front door. Inside—still a wreck.

'Merry Christmas!' he said. No way could anybody ask for more.

But there was more. Harley and Willie opened the new door and came down the new steps hollering, 'Merry Christmas!' Harley was carrying a box.

'Can we go in, please, please?' said Sadie.

'There's no floor in there,' said Jack. 'You'd fall in a huge hole of monsters. All that would be left is toenails, which are hard to digest.'

Harley handed the box through the open window. 'It's m' brownies!' Whoops and hollers and thanks all around. From the crew cab and passenger seat, a flood of reviews on the lightworks. Magic! Better than the stars in the sky! As good as the lights in Wesley! And did the bathroom work yet because they both had to go.

When his wife and kids were happy, he was happy.

'Great job, guys, great job! Meet you at Jake's for pizza ASAP. How's that?'

That was good.

They sat with the heater blasting while Willie and Harley paid a quick visit to the SUV. They took a few shots with their phones, but mostly just looked, mesmerized. It was another world in the clearing, something to be remembered long past this night. They drove back to the main road, followed by the SUV and Harley and Willie in the farm truck. Though the cottage was no way ready to be lived in, they were practicing for when it would be.

TIM

Henry and Lucille had arrived late, delayed by weather but nonetheless cheerful. They had taken nourishment, exchanged gifts, and were up to bed by half past ten.

He and Cynthia had one gift left to open, and it was his.

A black Sewanee hoodie! The University of the South, his alma mater. 'I'll look like an *educated* burglar,' he said. How good to have someone concerned about his uncovered head poking into the elements.

He could see it in her face; his supercharged wife was not often exhausted. Executing a swarm of paintings for the auction, sketching the Met book, hosting a stressful Thanksgiving dinner, cooking for Christmas, prepping for Henry and Lucille, and, depending on weather, heading out tomorrow for Meadowgate—no matter that he'd done his best to help, it had all landed on her face in a pileup.

'We should get to bed now.' His story was rehearsed and ready to go, but it could wait.

'See what else is in the box.'

He adjusted his glasses, removed the card from the envelope. Holy smoke. She had funded fourteen urgently needed new beds for the Children's Hospital—in his name. What could he possibly say? He was pretty choked up.

'You're my favorite person,' he said. 'Thank you. I can never top this.'

'You're not supposed to. It would be bad manners.'

'You wanted a letter.'

'I did. I do. I love a good letter.'

'So . . . for tomorrow evening, would a really good story suffice?'

'You know I love a good story.'

'What don't you love, Kav'na?'

'The calories in French fries, the calories in the seemingly innocent oatmeal-raisin cookie, and going from a size six to a size eight in four short years.'

He kissed the palms of her giving hands and got up to tamp down the fire. Elsie and Gus immediately occupied his warm spot on the sofa.

The roads were cleared and everyone had arrived safely at Meadowgate. His brother and Lucille were upstairs, gaining strength for the morrow. And his wife was already snoring.

He stood for a time before the warmth of the embers, listening to the toll of the church bell. In his imagination, which was barely alive at this hour, he was the London watchman of yore, going from street to street, crying, All is well, all is well. Eleven o'clock and all is well.

LACE

The snow came in flakes that pecked at the windows of the farmhouse. She was glad to be awake to hear it, though exhausted from the evening in which they exchanged gifts with Sammy and Kenny and their crews.

She often dreamed of Meadowgate's hundred acres of fields and woods. In these dreams, she walked with her children by the pond and listened to the spring chorus of the frogs. She searched leaf mold like a child, seeking mushrooms and Indian pipes to paint in her murals. She danced through the woods, a feral thing with no scaffolding to climb or supper to cook, a filament floating over her bare skin.

The timber would not be cut in their lifetime, the cattle would be rotated among the pastures, and the pastures would not be treated with chemicals. They would continue to grow clover and alfalfa and timothy to improve pasture nutritive and provide nitrogen to the grasses. The pond and the creek would be kept as healthy as their human resources would allow, and if they could get the property on the National Register, the chances of its protection from alteration or serious neglect would be improved. What lay within the boundaries of their deed was all the conservation they could manage. Charity begins at home.

The snow was not an inconvenience, but a bonus for the moisture it would soak into the soil, for the insulation it would give the pasture grass. Every peck at the window was a gift to the farm.

It was possible that Father Tim and Cynthia and Miss Pringle couldn't make it out to the farm in the morning. That would leave a hole in things, as Dooley's parents were both quick to set any listing ship back on keel.

It also was possible that Pauline and Buck and the kids would be stuck in Mitford. And maybe that would be a good thing. She hated to even think it. She would never say that to Dooley, but she knew he would be thinking it, too.

She slipped out of bed to check on her sleeping children. Any heat generated on the main floor had the courtesy to climb the stairs at night, but there was not enough of it for the kids to sleep without cover.

She thought of her geese, safe in the corncrib, warm in their bed of straw with no icy drafts leaking through new mortar. How totally great to get something you really want for Christmas!

She crossed the hall to the room that Sadie and Jack were sharing.

Her kids were awake and talking to each other. At nearly midnight!

Jack was usually the spokesperson. 'Th' owl woke us up, Mom.'

'That old owl loves to wake you up, it's her favorite thing. Lie down now, go back to sleep. You have cousins to play with tomorrow.' She kissed the top of his head, and there was his barn smell. He'd been beside himself with joy today, cleaning the stall for Daniel.

'Do you like your spoon rack, Mom?'

'I love my spoon rack. Thank you a hundred times, it's exactly what I wanted. Let me cover you up, your fingers are icicles.'

'I wrote your name on it.'

'I know. I love that Mom is my name. It means so much that you knew I wanted a spoon rack and I didn't need to use Amazon because I have a son who's brilliant!'

He beamed up at her. In this old house with the creaking floors, there was room to keep every single thing her kids would ever give her.

She moved to the other bed.

'Sadie girl.'

'I brushed my teeth.'

'Good job, sweetheart. I love the bedroom slippers you gave me. I've hardly ever had bedroom slippers. I'm wearing them right now.'

'You can wear them to th' garbage can, too.'

'I will absolutely do that.'

'Daddy made me buy them.'

'He made you?'

'I had to spend my own money. I had twelve dollars and now I only have two.'

'That's the way things happen in this world.'

'Etta gave her mommy a bracelet and her daddy paid th' whole thing.'

'You're fortunate to have a daddy who lets you pay with your own money. When you see me in my slippers you can think, I gave Mom those slippers and she loves them! And I thank you again a hundred times. Okay?'

'Okay! I'm goin' to sleep now.'

She kissed her daughter's warm cheek. 'See you in the morning, I'll be wearing my new slippers!'

They said she could never have children. And then—she did.

There were no words for this love.

They were country kids, these two. Among their models were Harley and Willie, whose grammar was a salad of blunders. She was constantly correcting her kids' grammar and forbidding the verboten 'ain't.' At the same time, she was grateful that the people who worked and lived here were also modeling love and hard work and character and generosity.

Nearly all the income from her work as a muralist went into a college fund. She hoped that one day her kids would be enrolled at major universities. Because of their upbringing, they may feel different from kids raised in town with heaps of money. She and their dad had felt that way. But look what could happen.

She eased across the hall and into bed, 'as quiet as moss,' as Jack would say. Shivering, she put her arm around her sleeping husband, in need of his heat. He was the simmering fire, she the cool breeze. She hurried to his fire; he yearned for the respite of her breeze.

'Merry Christmas, Dools,' she whispered.

'Merry Christmas, yourself,' he said.

'You're awake!'

He turned to her, laughing his sleepy laugh. 'Aren't you glad?'

GOOSEY

The widow next door to Lord's Chapel, now elderly with her hands gone stiff against the cold, made herself a cup of tea and turned on the oil heater to take the chill off.

Unlike previous years with recorded carols playing on Main Street 'til midnight, there was now an ordinance: no music on the street after nine o'clock. She had liked the music and was sorry about the ordinance, but she could look forward to the music from midnight Mass at Lord's Chapel. She turned on the TV to PBS and saw the slow crawl at the bottom of people talking. Churches. Businesses. Everything closing. All because of a few flakes that were falling!

There was always the Tabernacle Choir that might be on somewhere if she surfed long enough. TV was still a mystery to her. If she touched the wrong button, off it would go to men driving trucks on ice—what foolishness!—or wrestlers covered with tattoos. She never knew where a misguided action might land and how to get back to PBS could be impossible so she saved the problem for when the church people came to check if she was still alive.

She napped a good bit 'til her tea grew cold, and at eleven-thirty she heard it. The organ music had started! Muffled as it was by the stone walls it had to travel through, there it was. She went to the window and watched for the people to come, bundled against the snow and shouting their 'Merry Christmas!' 'Merry Christmas!' then remembered the church was closed and there would be no people.

She drew her shawl close against the icy bit of air that seeped in around the panes. It was pelting down now. If snowfall could be anything like rain, it was snowing cats and dogs. A good amount had collected on the church roof and bushes, and there was Lord's Chapel lit up like a Christmas tree! Like it was expecting people to just flock in there. Maybe they hadn't heard they were closed.

She turned up the volume on the TV and they said six or seven inches were expected, then there was something or other about a Woolly Worm.

She would be pleased to hear the chime of her grandfather clock mark the arrival of midnight. All at the same time the church bells would chime their own twelfth hour.

If they lost power, she had quilts and blankets 'a foot thick,' as she assured her daughter in California. There was nothing to worry about thanks to the church people who checked her oil drum and brought food.

As a Covenant Baptist in childhood, she remembered church food as snap beans with ham hock, deviled eggs, fried chicken, potato salad, and cathead biscuits. But the people next door brought food from parties they had after their Sunday sermons. It was mostly donut holes, a few lemon squares, and pimiento cheese sandwiches with no crust. Because their bread dried out so fast, she scraped the pimiento cheese off into a plastic container and put it on her own light bread.

At Easter and Christmas, Mr. Packard brought her a gift bag of groceries she especially liked—always with a big jar of Duke's. This year he had added a fruitcake, saying it was from him and the church, but the granola he brought stuck to her dentures and she didn't have the heart to say don't bring it anymore.

Ida, the country woman who came to food shop, give her shots, and do the medicine box, would sometimes bring banana bread, but her favorite was Ida's juicy homegrown tomatoes in late July and August and the watermelon Ida cut up in little cubes. She would eat all the watermelon at one sitting, and Ida would rinse out the Tupperware and take it home. 'For cantaloupe next time, if it's any good after th' rain,' Ida would say. Ida also looked after the utility bills and drove her to the doctor and sent her grandson to mow the yard.

It took a good many people to look after her these days. Her seventy-four-year-old daughter in California paid her property taxes and talked to the Mitford drugstore about her medications. Father Brad came to sit with her now and again and it was okay if they talked or didn't talk, he prayed for her and called her by the pet name her daddy gave her as a child—Goosey.

They sent their deacon to give her the wafer and wine, though she made it clear she was raised Covenant Baptist. She also let them know she had been baptized in the south fork of the New River. Since actual wine for Communion was Biblical, she did not waste her time feeling guilty that it wasn't grape juice.

She apologized for not attending services. 'My knees' was all she had to say, which should be enough as most of them had a bad knee themselves. She had attended services over there a few years back and had never seen the like of kneeling—at the drop of a hat they would kneel, sit down, kneel, stand up, kneel, and sit down again 'til you were swimmy-headed.

If anybody had asked what she really wanted for Christmas, she would have said a piece of fried chicken. She would love to have a piece of fried chicken one more time; she liked the dark meat. And just one piece would be enough before the Lord called her home. The call could come anytime now that she was ninety-nine. But she did not want to ask anybody to bring her fried chicken because she remembered how much trouble it was to cook it and make it crispy.

Not a soul had passed into the church as far as she could tell, but the organ music had not stopped. The way the light poured from the church windows onto the snow was a sight to see—it was all blue and red and green and gold, blazing through the stained glass. Whoever was playing the music was glad to be there; the organ was going like a coonhound after a rabbit and loud as anything. It sent chills up her right leg.

She put her good ear to the window pane.

The music was generally different from what she was raised on, except for the song playing now. She sang along in her whispery voice, the words she learned as a child in a one-room unpainted mountain church that doubled as her schoolhouse.

'Go tell it on the mountain
'Over the hills and everywhere
'Go tell it on the mountain
'That Jesus Christ is born!'

She remembered when water would not run down to their cabin through a wood gutter from the frozen uphill spring. She remembered when the ground was too hard to bury a loved one and the digging was put off 'til the thaw in May.

It could be bleak, a mountain winter. But there was the comforting smell of their kerosene lamp and the homemade sausage frying in the pan. There was the apple butter she helped her mama put up in September and the hot biscuits. And there was the lost dog that became her best friend. Again and again the dog was found sleeping on their porch, then off he'd go 'til the next time.

Turned out the dog belonged to the dark-haired young man who became her husband. 'Scout run off,' Austin said, 'to lead me to you, Goosey. So let's go on an' get married, to keep th' dog at home.'

Austin was a wonderful husband who worked hard for his engineering degree at WCU. She had washed and ironed his overalls 'til his company gave him a promotion and he had to wear a dress shirt and nice pants. As for herself, she had studied at Lees-McRae to get her teaching certificate and taught the lower grades for forty-two years. She and Austin had brought three little ones into the world—one dead at four years of pneumonia; one dead at sixty-five of cancer; and one living in California in a house surrounded by palm trees, she had seen pictures.

She believed this was the Christmas hymn she especially liked from next door. They had given her a hymn book with the place marked and she had it out and open to the page. She put on her glasses—her eyes weren't as bad as some people's—and read it out loud while running her forefinger under the words.

'What can I give him
'Poor as I am?
'If I were a shepherd
'I would bring a lamb . . . '

There had been her and her three sisters in one bed and nobody cold because they kept each other warm, even if they did fuss and spite one another during the day. She also remembered the way she felt in her heart at the age of eleven, that God loved her more than she could ever imagine, and she could count on him to provide her needs.

And there went her clock chime and there went the church bells and there went the chills up her leg again 'til her hair fairly stood on end. There was no clamor like the clamor of church bells, with her clock keeping up as good as triple-A batteries can. She might not be here to enjoy such a thing next year.

Lights were being turned off in the church, but it seemed like the organ player couldn't stop. Hoarse as she always was these days, she whispered the words.

'If I were a wise man
'I would do my part
'Yet what can I give him?
'Give my heart.'

Even though the church, just like her house, was built of stone from this very mountain, music had a way of seeping through walls into the winter air and giving a mite of joy.

JOHNNY STOKES

A mile and half from Meadowgate, at three a.m. on Christmas morning, Johnny Stokes prepared to leave Farmer in the dust.

In the yard, his truck was warming up and the radio playing a Johnny Cash number. He'd wrestled chains on the tires last night, just in case, and packed his lunch—two banana and peanut butter sandwiches, a Snickers, two cans of Coke. In another bag, a pack of deer jerky and a pint of Johnnie Walker Red.

Hanging on a hook in the crew cab were a couple of jackets, with undershirts, a pair of jeans, and a pair of boxers wadded up in a Food Lion bag.

He had privately sold to a buyer all but one of his livestock, which he'd took from Willie thinking it would add to his price for the whole lot, but no way. He'd given the chickens to the neighbor—what was left of 'em after the fox—and dropped off the cats by the side of the road. An hour ago, he'd done what he had to do over at Dooley Kavanagh's place.

He knew there was a camera on him, he could see it plain as day attached to the underside of the clinic roof, so before he got back in his truck, he looked up at the camera, stuck out his tongue, and gave ol' Dooley a sign he'd taken a whipping for in first grade.

He had backed out with the empty trailer and turned the music up.

With all that behind him, he could leave his wife a note for when she came home from her mama's house in Haywood County. He took out a twenty and laid it on the sink top for the light bill. Then he found a pen and a scrap of paper.

The one he called the Other Johnny had already said it, so why bother to say it any other way? He scratched out a couple of lines.

Heaven help me be a man and
Have the strength to stand alone

Before the ink ran out, he added something original.

Try to miss me when I'm gone.

HAMP FLOYD

Hamp Floyd, Mitford's former fire chief, aka the Woolly Worm, slipped out of bed to bundle up and measure the snowfall on his flagstone patio. The snow had turned to a few flakes idly landing hither and yon. In less than a half hour, Mitford would hit the cool seven inches he predicted, on the date he predicted. This would be the second—or was it the third?—time he'd nailed it. He'd placed a few bets with the guys—enough for a fire pit at Lowe's plus four all-weather Adirondacks.

It was three forty-five a.m. when he made the mistake of waking his wife to share the great news. She had cooked all week for twenty-two people coming today for Christmas dinner.

He spent the rest of the night on the couch with two Rhodesian Ridgebacks, as the guest room was made up for company and he wasn't even allowed to look in there.

DOOLEY

They had rolled out of bed at dawn for a quick walk before six kids woke up and stormed the Fraser fir for a few gifts still under the tree. Weather prediction for the day: fifty-one degrees. Sunshine. Roads plowed. Snow melting.

They stopped near the garden patch at Willie and Harley's place. He wouldn't bring up the subject of their mom being out here today. Sammy knew she was coming; the chips would fall where they needed to fall.

'Remember the secret garden you had down the mountain?'

'I don't think about that,' said Sammy.

Sammy had lived with their dad then. A freak with a gun who forced Sammy to look down the barrel too many times.

'Always wanted a p-piece of land for a big garden.'

'There's no available piece of land in Chicago, buddy. I've been there and know for a fact.'

'If you put in a garden where we're standin' right now,' said Sammy, 'an' you stood up to ease your back, your eye would look across th' bean poles and tomato vines out to th' pasture, then to th' tree line where your cattle are lyin' in th' summer shade, then on to th' mountains, then up to th' Carolina blue sky. Layers, Dools. Layers make a garden. Th' tomatoes, th' timothy grass, th' cows, th' mountains an' sky, it's all layers in one huge incredible garden.'

He'd never had a chance to spend much time with Sammy. Was this a new Sammy, or an old Sammy he'd somehow missed? 'What would you grow in this patch?'

'Peppery radishes big as snooker balls. Spring onions with a little burn in th' mouth—you've had a spring onion grown commercially—no zing, no onion. Red an' yellow peppers. Sweet potatoes. Carrots—homegrown' with th' right touch, crisp an' sweet as honey. Garden peas. Snap beans. Asparagus. Red lettuce. I like lettuce—it can surprise you with th' shapes an' colors it comes in. I get pretty dopey at th' farmers market just lookin' at their stuff. Last week, I had a total crush on beets an' brussels sprouts. I roasted those guys three nights in a row.'

Sammy opened his arms wide. 'I can feel it in my bones, Dools. We're standin' in the b-best garden spot on th' freakin' planet!'

'So you *cook*?'

'For th' last couple of years, yeah. Can't all be about pool. My specialties—roast chicken, ribs, chili with a little heat. Taylor says, Make it hot, Dad. Him callin' me Dad means a lot, you know?'

He knew.

His brother was blowing him away. He could manage a deep-dish pizza and a cherry pie, but that was it, he was done. 'We're lookin' for a couple to live here. Young. Strong.'

'Where are Willie and Harley goin'?'

'We're wrangling a house for them over in the woods. Just got a roof on it. I'll show it to you tomorrow.'

'We've got to get out of here tomorrow. I have a couple of tournaments comin' up. Virginia Beach, th' Derby in Indiana, big money-makers if you hold your mouth right. Got to get back to my trainer, I'm in th' gym every day at home.'

'These tournaments, bro—that's all you do now?'

'No more shootin' pool for pocket change, that's for sure.'

'So you're a real Earl Strickland these days.'

Sammy had the Barlowe laugh, which was mostly a cackle. 'That's me, all right. No, Earl Strickland's a saint, a legend in his own time. He's not on th' tour circuit anymore, he's doin' exhibitions. You can get a class with Earl at five hundred bucks a pop, prob'ly with wine and cheese.'

'I had no idea about the money in this game.'

'Let's say I could win three out of four games at Derby, I could haul in maybe eighty grand. That would totally take a miracle, but I don't like to think about th' money. I keep my eye on th' ball, so to speak. Carolina and Taylor have changed everything for me. I want to give them a really good life, you know?'

He knew.

'You're the first to hear this—Carolina and Taylor and me are gettin' married in th' spring.'

Bear hug. Slaps on the back. Wow. His little brother. Gettin' married!

'Out here,' said Sammy. 'With y'all. If that would be okay.'

'We're total wedding experts. All we need is a tent, a cowbell, and somebody to let th' bull out. I'll talk to Lace, she'll be good with this. Congratulations.'

'Best man?' said Sammy.

'Best man. Honored. So, with the way things are going, sounds like you can live anywhere.'

'All I need is an airport.'

'What do you know about cattle?'

'New York strip, T-bone, rib eye.'

So much for that. What if he just said it, what was there to lose? He hadn't talked to Lace about this; it was crazy. Even with Kenny and his tribe living five hours away in Wilmington, the family would be together again, for better or worse. And how much worse could it be than it had been?

'What if you and Carolina and Taylor came to live at Meadowgate? Harley and Willie will be moving out of this cottage before too long, you could rent here instead of Chicago. Carolina could work at Hope House or Mitford Hospital—either way, two great places. Or Children's Hospital, a twenty-minute drive.

'They would love Taylor at Mitford School, and he and Jack would take the same school bus right out there at th' road. You could have the garden you've always dreamed about, Sam.'

The more he pitched this, the more he liked the idea. He watched Sammy's expression. Their mother living close by in Mitford would be an issue, but Sam was listening.

'And how about the regulation pool table right over there in our library? I mean, think about it, how many times in life do all the pieces fall together? And the airport situation is beyond perfect, as you know, because we don't have just one. We have two. Asheville, an hour and thirty minutes. Charlotte, where you flew in, under two hours. Family, bro. Family. We're sure not perfect, we've got a long way to go. But to go it together, that's th' real deal.'

The idea had literally gushed out; without realizing it, he'd already formulated a plan.

Sammy sank down and sat on his haunches in the snow, not saying anything.

The sun was rising fast, splashing a wash of coral on a cloudless blue sky.

He squatted beside his brother; there were tears on Sammy's face. They high-fived, interlocked their fingers, held on.

HARLEY

He thought it was th' donkeys he was hearin' but it sounded a little different. It was comin' from up around th' clinic where no donkeys was supposed to be at, so he walked up to take a look, an' there he was, tied to the clinic sign.

He would never in this lifetime tell nobody that Harley Eugene Welch busted out cryin' at th' sight of a mule.

DOOLEY

Breakfast. People in robes and pajamas, old T-shirts and sweatpants; a motley crew. Three rounds of full-bore caffeine.

At eight o'clock, Lace banged a saucepan with a spoon. 'Let the cooking begin!'

It was a unisex endeavor. Sammy would do the turkey and pan dressing, Carolina would handle the potatoes to be mashed with a cooked turnip, Julie would be on the green beans, Kenny on the cranberry relish, and Lace had dough rising for yeast rolls. The Mitford crowd would bring further contributions.

He realized he was half-killed from eating an entire cherry pie since Monday, but mostly from cutting a deal without asking Lace. He grabbed her from the fray and they went to the hall john and locked the door. She sat on the toilet lid; he sat on the laundry hamper and pitched it hard.

They would have the phenomenal benefit of a skilled nurse on the property, always a great idea with kids. They would share in a huge fresh food supply without having to rogue Geezer Garden. They would have rent money—which he could apply to the part-time hours worked by Mink's son and daughter-in-law. Sammy and Carolina were paying nineteen-hundred a month for a small apartment in Chicago; they could work out a deal that would be good for everybody. Mink's wife would be free to do cleaning and babysitting as Lily Flower was often employed elsewhere. Sammy was totally up for giving a hand around the place when he wasn't traveling, and—not to be taken lightly—Sammy was a cook! Think chili, roast chicken, barbecued ribs. Onsite! They could share meals once in a while.

All this could happen next year when Taylor was out of school and Harley and Willie were—hopefully—settled in their new house.

She had grinned the entire time; it looked like his scenario was getting positive reviews.

'So?' he said.

'I love this, and Jack and Sadie will be thrilled to have a wonderful cousin next door. I'll sign on. But only if Sammy will commit to stop going berserk when he's around your mother. Tell him to stand back and keep his cool. You and Kenny and Pooh can teach him how to do it. Starting today.'

All he'd ever stopped from going berserk were more than a few wounded animals. But he knew in his bones that Sammy would get it; Sammy could do this. Starting today.

GRACE

Her dad had already gone up to check on Hope House. He didn't have to because he had help, but he liked to wish all the people merry Christmas. It was just her and her mom, exactly like she planned, sitting at their breakfast table with cups of chamomile tea and, because it was Christmas, scrambled eggs and bacon.

She had delivered four of her books—one to Miss Phillips; one to Miss Pam, who cleaned floors at school and was on her forever support team; one to Father Tim and Miss Cynthy; and one to Coot and Dude. Coot was going to read it out loud tonight to Dude, who was in training to appreciate literature.

She was totally excited about putting her new book in people's hands. But her gift for her mom was the best gift she could possibly give in maybe her whole life. And she wouldn't even have to wrap it.

'Mom, you said more than anything you'd love to have peace of mind for Christmas.'

'So true, honey. I'm disappointed that I'm such a mess because my life is blessed beyond all I could ask or think. A wonderful husband, a sensational daughter and friend, a building we can call our own, your new piano. It's mostly about the letter I lost, how could I do that? I was trying so hard to be careful.'

'It's okay that you're not perfect, Mom. Really. I promise. So I will *tell* you your present, okay? This can't be wrapped.'

'It's so like you to give a gift that can't be wrapped.'

She had always liked her mom's smile; it just took over her face.

'I found the letter and the book.'

Her mother hardly ever cried, but when she did it was a little scary. Except this time, it was, like, for relief so it was okay.

'I took your blue backpack home to switch out your stuff because you haven't had time. That was going to be my main present, but the main present is—there was the book, in an inside pocket that's really hard to find because the zipper is hidden. It felt like the book was part of the construction of the backpack, and because your backpack is new, you probably didn't remember all the places to look.'

Her mom came around the table and hugged her so tight she could hardly breathe. 'Oh!' was all she could say. 'Oh!'

'But wait!' she said. 'There's more!' And her mom sat down again and was, like, hugely beaming.

ESTHER

As Christmas Day was all sunshine, th' girls volunteered to roll her out to th' porch, away from th' crowd who, as usual, were ganged up in th' kitchen an' th' nook.

'Let's get Ray to come out with us,' she said. To think she was scared of bein' by herself with her own children! There was no tellin' what they'd come up with this time.

'Don't bother Daddy. He's havin' a little schnapps with th' guys.'

'A little what?'

'Somethin' European,' said Tammy Leigh, not makin' eye contact.

'Somethin' to keep him from gettin' dehydrated,' said Winona.

All four were just cracklin' with what she called nervous energy. They did their boxcar lineup along th' porch railin'.

'Mama!' said Marcie.

Anytime Marcie opened th' meetin' it was bad doo-doo. Or voo-doo. Or whatever.

'We're gon' start leavin' you alone.'

'Leavin' me alone? What do you mean by *alone*?'

'We're gon' quit comin' over and bossin' you around.'

'You are?'

'We know you're thrilled,' said Charlene.

'Who said I wanted y'all to leave me alone?'

'You as much as said it a hundred times, Mama!' Winona had new hearin' aids an' talked way too loud.

'Well, don't believe everything you hear.' Of all th' underhanded tricks, this took th' cake. She had never said any such thing as leave me alone! Plus this would half-kill their daddy, who didn't want to be left alone for one minute.

'We love you, Mama,' said Tammy Leigh. Bein' a country songwriter, Tammy Leigh was not afraid to talk about love.

'You do?'

'We love Daddy, too. All we want is th' best for both of y'all.'

'I know you love your daddy, but I didn't know about me.'

'Why do you think we try to help you all th' time?' said Charlene. 'Do you know what can be really heartbreakin', Mama? Do you even know?'

Winona threw out her chest, which was a considerable chest to throw out. 'It's heartbreakin' that we want to help you but you hardly ever let us!'

There was a long silence, which scared her; there was never a long silence with this crowd.

'What if I start lettin' you?'

That took 'em by surprise.

'To put it another way, what if you keep comin' over like always but just stop bossin' us?'

They looked at one another.

'*What?*' she said.

'Daddy likes it when we boss him. He says that's our way of showin' love.'

'He said that?'

'Yes, so we'll continue to boss Daddy 'til he, himself, says otherwise.'

If she'd ever been speechless before, she had no memory of th' occasion.

'All right,' she said, gettin' ahold of herself. 'Keep comin' over like you always do an' keep bossin' your daddy if he'll let you get away with it. But don't boss me anymore, you hear?'

'Yes, ma'am.' When Marcie agreed, she agreed for herself an' the other three. It was what they called their 'protocol.'

'An' don't take advantage,' she said.

'No, ma'am, we won't.'

She wouldn't bring up th' scatter rugs, which was totally takin' advantage.

While they were rollin' her back in th' house, it came to her in a flash.

'I never did spank y'all. That's th' problem. I should have spanked y'all at least once or twice a day.'

'You tried,' said Tammy Leigh. 'But you couldn't catch us!'

CAROLINA

She went out into sunshine and melting snow and followed the several sets of boot tracks to the barn. Sammy's mother was sitting on an upturned washtub by a stall for what Taylor called 'the mule with a hurt foot.'

'May I join you?'

Pauline looked up. 'If you want to.'

'I do want to.' She found a bucket and turned it upside down and sat close to his mother. 'It's nice in here,' she said to make conversation.

'I love barns,' said Pauline. 'I grew up in a barn.'

'Really? You grew up in a barn?'

'My great-aunt had a barn. I liked th' way it smelled. I liked th' animals in it. Their warm breath. She taught me how to milk a cow. Sometimes I spent th' night in th' barn.'

'I don't know much about barns. Or even animals. We never lived in th' country.'

'Where did you live?'

'All over th' place. My dad couldn't hold a job more than fifteen minutes, but in North Carolina, he worked for the same trucking company for two whole years. I got named for where we lived the longest. Everybody but Sammy calls me Caroline but my name is Carolina and I like that better.'

'I'll call you Carolina. You can call me Pauline.'

'Thanks, I appreciate it.' The soft light of the barn was blurring his mother's wrinkles. She was a pretty woman, with hair the color most women wanted when they got older—not the flat, lifeless gray, but the silver gray, which was beautiful with her red coat.

'Where's your family?' said Pauline.

'Scattered. Minneapolis. Baltimore. North Dakota. I can't ever remember th' name of that little town in North Dakota. My brother's out there, he works on a cattle ranch. And my mom and daddy are buried down east in Duck, where Daddy ended up with a bait shop.'

'Are you close to your people?'

'My sister's in Baltimore, we talk every day. She wants us to move down there but I have a good job in Chicago, I can't just up and leave it.'

'I up an' left my job at Hope House. I worked in th' dinin' room.'

'What is Hope House?'

'It's a place for our elders. It was founded by th' person Sadie's named for.'

'Why did you leave it, if I may ask?'

'Because . . . I don't know why. I guess because I got mad at somebody. I wish I'd stayed. It's good to get out of th' house every day an' be with people. I liked my job. What do you do?'

'I'm a NICU nurse. It's really hard. But it's worth it. When we know th' babies are goin' to make it . . . that's worth everything. I love workin' with babies or old people—I never had much interest in nursin' people in middle age.' She laughed a little.

'I was talkin' with your son.'

'Taylor.'

'Taylor. He's sure got a beautiful smile. And he's really smart.'

'Yes, ma'am, and he's lovin' and kind and generous, too. He'd give you any of his toys or books if he thought it would make you happy. And

Taylor loves Sammy. Sammy's makin' a wonderful daddy and I'm so grateful for that.'

They were quiet for a time. A cat wound its way around Pauline's ankles.

'Mrs. Leeper . . . '

'Pauline.'

'Pauline, Sammy said I can tell you anything I want to.'

'He said that?'

'He trusted me to say whatever I felt like sayin.' I'd like to come into your family with things about me really clear. I mean, it will be better than things leakin' out one at a time. In my family, it seemed like everything was a secret. Us kids had to guess and most of the time we guessed wrong.'

'I hope what you're goin' to tell me is good. We're havin' a peaceful day, so I hope it's good or please don't say it.'

'It's very good. It's th' best thing I can think of to tell you. I had a drug habit.'

I had a drug habit like you, she wanted to say. She saw Sammy's mother go stiff as a board. It was good she heard it now and not later, and from her and nobody else.

'But I've been clean eight years. Sammy did drugs, but it was messin' with his game and with our relationship and I wouldn't allow that around Taylor. We both know it's insane to use, and Sammy's totally clean for four years. Th' game is Sammy's drug and his medication. It's what calms him down when he gets anxious.'

'Did you have to say all that?'

'Yes, ma'am, I had to. I guess the only other thing I wanted to say is that I love your son with all my heart, and here comes th' shockin' part.' She hoped Pauline would find it funny, as most people did. 'I'm a whole four years older than Sammy!'

At that very moment, the mule brayed, which caused them both to laugh. Then it brayed again. They laughed as if they'd been holding it in for a long time, then they were quiet together, listening to the sounds of the barn. The mule chewing. Cats chasing each other in the hayloft. Snow sliding off the roof.

She couldn't honestly say she was surprised when Pauline reached over and took her hand and squeezed it tight.

She could see that taking her hand was hard for Pauline. So she squeezed back.

HENRY WINCHESTER

Buck Leeper and his family had arrived and were settling in. He wanted to meet this fellow Mississippian with a great small-world story—Buck had grown up an hour from the town he and Tim called home.

'Henry Winchester, Buck, Tim's brother. It's good to meet you.' Big man, big hand, good face. 'I hear you're from Booneville.'

'One hour flat from Holly Springs, if you don't stop for boiled peanuts and sweet tea.'

'I've made the trip countless times, and enjoyed that roadside menu pretty often. I have a first cousin in Booneville. Roy Williams, they call him Sunshine or Sunny. About my age.'

'Sunny Williams! Sunny worked on a couple of my first jobs as project manager. He was great at livin' up to his name—very upbeat guy, always popular with th' crew. Played harmonica as good as James Cotton. Sunny still livin'?'

'Still livin', still making music. Fourteen grandkids, one teaching at Harvard, one teaching at Yale.'

'Could be a problem at their big game in November.'

They had a bit of a laugh. 'Higher education has its issues. Want to walk to the barn to see the mule that came home last night? There's a horse coming in a little while, it'll get busy out there.'

Buck zipped his jacket. 'I like mules. Stubborn like most of us.'

Beautiful day. Sharp, clean air. He noted the sound of their boots in the melting snow, crows calling from the ridge of the barn roof.

'Ever miss your home state, Buck?'

'I don't. I made some big mistakes down there. Father Tim may have told you.'

'I don't believe he spoke of mistakes.'

'I killed my kid brother,' said Buck.

'No, no. He didn't say anything like that, not at all.'

'He wouldn't. He'd say it wasn't intentional.'

'I'm sorry.'

'He was just a little kid. A great kid, a wonderful boy. I deprived him of growing up and having a life, of having a Christmas.'

'However it happened, brother, I'm sure it was not intentional.'

'Worse. It was not payin' attention.'

Buck unlatched the side door and they let themselves in.

The light was falling in patches through a couple of windows. The smell of hay. The snuffling of an animal. They went to the mule's stall.

'It's good to have a barn to retreat to once in a while,' he said. He wanted to give Buck a topic to change the conversation if he needed that. Buck didn't say anything, he was rubbing the mule's ears.

'Pedro,' he told Buck, by way of introduction. 'He's been neglected for a while. A sore on his leg, a good bit of weight loss. Nothing, they say, that a good diet and clean straw can't fix. Harley's taking Pedro under his wing.'

Cats. A lot of cats.

'I lost a nephew some years ago,' he told Buck. 'I was especially close to him. James. Named for the king who had the Bible translated into English. He died in my arms in the road in front of my sister's house, hit by a car. They never caught th' driver because they didn't look. His death made no difference at all to the authorities.

'I grieved little Jim like a child of my own. For a long time, I couldn't find a reason to go on except for my mother, I didn't want to leave her without whatever help I could render.'

'I'm sorry,' said Buck. 'A couple of times I thought about takin' my own life, but I took to alcohol instead. I thought that would be an easy way out. It was easy, all right, and another big mistake, one that wiped out years of my life. The only thing I got right was my work. I was the best hardhat in th' field, Henry, if I do say so. But I fooled myself into thinkin' that was enough.

'I finally got sober, then broke bad and started drinkin' again. It looked like Pauline and I couldn't make it, so I left Mitford and headed to Mississippi. I was a couple hundred miles out when I knew I was a goner if I didn't do something quick. Problem was, I didn't know what to do. I realized there was only one person in my life who would know—Father Tim. I wheeled out of there and drove back to Mitford and knocked on Tim's door and prayed this short prayer that don't sound like much but it changed everything for me. I still have some depression, you know what I mean, but it's different.'

'Love,' said Henry. 'Love.'

'That's it,' said Buck. He stroked Pedro's head. 'Welcome back, buddy. I hear you've got somebody who'll look after you around here.'

'Not everybody knows how to love a mule.'

'I was God's mule,' said Buck.

They walked back toward the house.

'Henry, I'd like to apologize. I've done most of th' talkin'. Christmas does it to me, thinkin' how Davey's not here to enjoy it. Maybe there'll be time today to hear your story. You were a porter on the *City of New Orleans*.'

'The good old days, the bad old days. Like most things in life, Buck, some of both.'

Buck took out his wallet.

'I'd like to give you something. I had these little cards printed and keep a few handy. Pass it to somebody who needs it. It's th' prayer I prayed when I drove back to Mitford lookin' for a way out. You might say this prayer helped me find th' way in.'

He read Buck's card aloud.

'Father, I've done many wrong and hurtful things. I come to you with an open heart asking your forgiveness. I hereby confess your son Jesus Christ as my personal savior. Help me to live in a way that pleases you. As I cannot do such a thing by myself, I turn my entire life over to you. Amen.

'Yes. That'll do it, brother. I'll pass it on when the Holy Spirit gives me the cue.'

'It's not exactly word for word what Father Tim led me to pray, but it was the best I could remember, and I meant every word. Still do.'

'I wanted to tell you that Tim says you're one of his favorite people.'

Buck laughed. It was the kind of laugh that comes out of a big man.

'He's got a few of those. It's an honor to be included.'

JACK

They always rattled the cowbell when somethin' big was happenin'. For Blake and Amanda gettin' in love, his dad told him to rattle it for ten seconds. He had to keep an eye on his dad, who gave a thumbs-up when he was supposed to rattle it.

He'd been nervous because he had to wait 'til Blake got down on one knee and as soon as Amanda said yes, he could rattle it. But all she did was laugh. And then Blake laughed and everybody laughed. 'That's a yes,' said his dad, and he rattled it then. It was confusin' that laughin' was the same as yes.

Mr. Hershell would be bringin' Daniel at two o'clock, which was three whole hours yet. He was so excited he'd thrown up this morning while trying to brush his teeth. They could not use the cowbell for Daniel because it could scare him.

One thumb up!

He rattled the cowbell as hard and fast as he could, as Uncle Sammy and Carolina and Taylor hurried to get to the kitchen fireplace, where somethin' big would happen. They were all holdin' hands because they were in love.

SAMMY

He was surprised that he could do this in front of everybody. But Carolina held his hand and he could see the look in her eyes and he looked down at Taylor and he could do this.

It was a big crowd with a lot of different people, a few he'd never met. Dooley was calling the people from Mississippi Uncle Henry and Aunt Lucille, the people from Jersey were Uncle Walter and Aunt Katherine. He'd never had aunts and uncles, he never even thought about it 'til now. The fact that he was an uncle was also something he didn't think about until he came home to the mountains and then wham, he was Uncle Sammy to all these kids.

'So a few years ago,' he said, 'I was in th' bakery around th' corner from my place, just havin' a coffee and mindin' my own business. And this really pretty woman came in with her son. She was in scrubs. Whoa, I thought. A nurse. She could tell me about this mole on my back that was worryin' me, I had a friend who died from a mole.

'So people are hogging all th' booths and tables with their laptops like they live there an' own the place, which I will never understand in this lifetime, but there was room at my table, so I got up and said, "Want to sit over here? Coffee's on me."'

'That's a good pickup line,' said Kenny. '"Coffee's on me." Has a nice ring.'

'It was totally good because Carolina and Taylor came and sat at my table and it was napoleons and dark roast all th' way.'

'Tell about the cookies,' said Taylor.

'Right. Why don't you tell about th' cookies?'

'So there were these chocolate chip cookies that we all thought were the best we ever tasted because they had a secret ingredient and Mom guessed it. So my mom said, Taylor and I can make these same cookies in a heartbeat. And so Dad came over th' next day and we made him the cookies with the secret ingredient and he said they were way better than the ones in the coffee shop.'

Sammy grinned. 'We've pretty much been together ever since.'

Laughter. Cowbell. Clapping. It was great to have people to tell your good stuff to.

CAROLINA

Her mouth was so dry. She didn't usually speak in front of people. Sometimes the families of babies in the NICU unit would be a dozen people or more, and she would say a few words. She had cried with them and rejoiced with them, but this was Sammy's family and they would all be wondering if she was up to the job of loving Sammy and keeping him in line. She loved him with all her heart, but it was not her job to keep him in line. He was learning to keep himself in line because she expected that of him, and he was doing a great job.

'Thanks for having me, everybody, and merry Christmas! Sammy and I both work and Taylor is in school and works hard at his studies so everyone stays busy. We decided the best way to live together is split our household chores fifty-fifty, with Taylor doing his share, too. So Sammy said we should split today's announcement fifty-fifty, with Taylor doing his share.'

She gulped air. Everybody was smiling at them; they looked so happy. She gathered some of that into herself and stood straighter and spoke with projection, like she'd learned from her high school debate team.

'It's an honor to be here. I was born in North Carolina and named for this beautiful state, and this is the first time I've been back since I was two years old. You all are so lucky to have this big family, and Taylor and I are so blessed to be welcomed into it. Sammy and Taylor and I just got four or five aunts and uncles in the space of about ten minutes. Like it's sweet to Olivia to say Uncle Henry and Aunt Lucille and Uncle Walter and Aunt Katherine. So thank you for that.

'I am a NICU nurse, and the thing I love most is when the babies make it. So many babies, you feel sure they can't make it, but I've learned not to grieve their loss ahead of God's plan for them, because sometimes they make it in such a beautiful, strong, and miraculous way that you could just shout it from the rooftops. I know families sometimes feel like they can't make it, either, but then they work on it and they spring back and things can be better than ever.

'Now it's Sammy's turn to do his part. But Taylor first.'

Taylor looked out to the crowd as if he could see everyone. He was smiling big. 'When th' horse comes, can I please ride, too?'

SAMMY

He was pumped about the aunts and uncles thing. Everybody in the room was becoming family to him an' Carolina an' Taylor. He saw his mother sitting off to the side. He tried not to look that way, but he looked by mistake and saw that she was nodding and smiling. Cynthia was sitting next to her and holding her hand. He had never seen anyone holding his mother's hand.

'So what we're sayin' this morning is that Carolina and Taylor and I are gettin' married.'

Cowbell. Clapping, hooting. Whistles.

'We'll be gettin' married here. At th' farm.'

Cowbell. More clapping.

'We'll pick a date in May or June when everybody can come. We'll need a preacher.'

Father Tim stood, saluted. 'Package deal,' he said.

'Thank you, Father. Taylor will be our ring bearer like you were, Jack, at your mom and dad's wedding.'

'I'm seven goin' on eight,' said Jack. 'I can help, too.'

'Thanks, buddy. We'll need all th' help we can get. April or May. We'll let y'all know.'

'So, Sam. What happened with th' mole?'

'He took off his shirt in the bakery,' said Taylor, 'and Mom looked at it and said he didn't need to worry.'

Clapping, laughter.

'He took off his shirt in front of everybody?'

'It was embarrassing,' said Taylor.

Cowbell, laughter, cowbell. You could get hooked on this.

HARLEY

They was dressin' to go to th' big house for Christmas dinner. Miss Pringle was supposed to come out with Father Tim an' Cynthia but had woke up with somethin' caught from a pupil. He did not have to polish his shoes, after all.

'I jis' thought of somethin',' said Willie.

'What's that?'

'We ain't got no furniture to put in th' new house.' He was downright shocked. He hadn' thought about that. Their setup seemed like it was him an' Willie's furniture but it was Dooley an' Lace's.

'They could be wantin' us to leave it for Sammy an' them,' said Willie.

He couldn' think of nothin' to say. He'd never thought about how people got furniture. When he lived in that trailer at the Creek, it was furnished. A bed, a table, a chair, a hotplate, an' a refrigerator that wouldn' work.

'Like Henry Thoreau,' Lace said, back in th' day. 'A man who lived by a pond in a one-room house he built himself. He had a bed, a chair, and a table. And was famous.'

He was a little put out that he had exactly th' same stuff but wadn' famous.

When he rented from Miss Pringle in th' basement of th' rectory, he had a double bed, a full kitchen, a full bath, and could set on th' back stoop in a wood armchair with a fancy cushion. He didn' know how a hardworkin' man could come home at night an' set on th' floor. A man had to have hisself a couch.

'There's your Habitat an' your Goodwill,' said Willie. 'But I've never set foot in neither one.'

It hadn' never crossed his mind that all they had to start housekeepin' with was his alarm clock, his thirty-two-inch TV, an' Willie's radio that mostly got static.

'That's the way it works,' said Lace. 'When you get your first house, you don't have anything to put in it. It just comes to you somehow. This is perfectly normal.'

'Me an' Honey went four or five years with nothin' in th' livin' room but a ironin' board,' said Mink.

Ever' cent of his money was tied up in th' house. Couches an' whatall would have to drop out of th' sky.

PUNY

She was readin' a paperback romance because she could not sleep.

She had just been diagnosed with premature menopause, which explained havin' insane night sweats—hair plastered to her head, T-shirt soakin' wet. The only good news to this is she would not have to have her tubes tied.

'You will not sleep again for th' rest of your life,' said Tammy Leigh. 'As soon as you get done with menopause, which takes forever, then you're old and you can't sleep because you're old. I hate to tell you this.' Tammy always said 'I hate to tell you this' when tellin' her somethin' awful. Tammy was the least favorite of her husband's aunts.

She was readin' in th' kitchen, where she'd inhaled every bite of her Hershey from Mamaw an' hid the ten dollars from th' kids. They considered all those tens floatin' around as low-hangin' fruit. Tommy had gone to everybody lookin' pitiful an' askin' people for their tens to help him buy a ten-speed. Then he found a ten layin' on th' floor an' announced had anybody lost a ten and somebody had. She was proud as anything to see him hand it over. It was like, Oh, look, I'm not a total failure as a parent.

She heard the bell toll at Lord's Chapel. Thank th' Lord she did not have to lift a finger tomorrow, which was historic. They had leftovers from Mamaw's an' she had hid back four of Marcie's yeast rolls for herself so Joe Joe would not find them even if he tore th' house apart. Everybody was crazy about Marcie's yeast rolls, they were her signature go-to for get-togethers. When Marcie died, it was in her will for the recipe to go to her oldest daughter.

She had done two trial runs to make Marcie's yeast rolls to surprise Joe Joe an' th' kids.

'Too cakey,' Joe Joe said on th' first trial run. 'Too dry, Mama,' Sissy said on th' second and last go-round. 'But they're delicious anyway.' She loved her kids, she really did.

Anyway, let Marcie have th' fame an' glory for her yeast rolls while she, Puny Guthrie, would continue to bake a cake of cornbread that nobody in the entire huge Cunnin'ham family could hold a candle to. Tammy's cornbread—overbaked. Marcie's—too sweet, cornbread is not dessert! Charlene's—embarrassing. Winona's—you cannot tell it from Food Lion's.

They had arrived at th' threshold of another Christmas an' nobody sick, thank th' Lord. Sassy was crazy about her piano, which was a vintage Kohler an' Campbell. It looked good in their livin' room, though she had to move th' ironin' board to fit it in th' corner. Sassy had sat down an' played somethin' truly amazing, an' she could see what Miss Pringle was talkin' about. All th' Guthrie kids now wanted to take piano lessons, if you can believe that, even Tommy, who was a tight end.

She had so much to be thankful for, she hated to complain, but Joe Joe had given her a toaster oven. He said he gave it to her because th' kids would love it as the old one could not bake pizza with a crispy crust. She should make him sleep on the sofa for all eternity, but she knew a police chief needed his rest so he could fight crime if ever there was any.

Th' fact that he was th' cutest man in Mitford had gone to his head ages ago, which did not give him an excuse for doin' dumb things. With all her heart an' soul she had wanted a pretty bracelet. An' no, she hadn't exactly told him she wanted a pretty bracelet because she thought he should know he had never given her one.

It was obvious that her two entire arms had been bare for years. Sometimes she would lay an arm out on the table after dinner and let him look at how barren it was. He had to have known she wanted a bracelet, an' with a free piano in the house he could certainly afford it. She would like to go upstairs and open his top drawer an' snatch back that battery-operated nose hair trimmer. He did not deserve such a thoughtful gift in a faux leather box with red silk linin' for thirty-nine dollars plus shippin'.

She fanned herself with the book. This romance was hotter than the ones she'd been readin' from th' church library. This one she definitely would not leave out where the kids could find it.

ESTHER AND RAY

Esther and Ray Cunningham slept like two spoons in a drawer. That's the way it had always been with them.

The fact that Ray's snore competed with the din of a chain saw no longer mattered—Esther's hearing had taken a dive in the last couple of months.

The fact that Esther's snore could wipe out the deafening roar of an espresso extraction no longer mattered—Ray had received a secret gift from Marcie. Why it had never occurred to him to buy ear plugs was totally beyond his understanding.

They had dreamed hard for decades and wanted a break from the whole folly of dreaming. They had each other and that was enough. Who would go first they didn't know or want to know, and however the Lord arranged it would be okay. They were going to the same place and would see each other again.

The girls would be fine without their old parents to boss around. Instead, they could boss their husbands exclusively, which would be a win-win for everybody but the husbands. That said, they loved their girls, they really did.

Father Tim had stopped by a couple of days ago for a few laughs and a prayer and was mighty grateful for his Hershey and a ten. He brought them a gift card from Sweet Stuff, which is exactly what they needed for their diabetes. Even people with diabetes forget that other people have it, too.

After the first of the year, they would finally get their last will and testament in order, which was past due to say the least. They entertained themselves by guessing what the girls would do with Mamaw and Papaw's Estate, which the girls privately called the MPE.

Tammy Leigh would buy out the sisters and have her heart's desire—an Airbnb rental in the house of her late parents.

As a back-to-the-studs person, Tammy Leigh would send everything in the house they'd lived in for sixty years to wherever the scatter rugs had gone.

There would be potpourri and battery candles out the kazoo, and canopied four-posters dripping with fake wisteria. Tammy Leigh's husband would close in the porch and make it a room with gas logs where guests watched Netflix on their iPads.

Winona would develop her plans when the money was safe in her hands and not a minute sooner; she had never been an optimist.

Marcie, bless her heart, would be sensible. Her share would go into a fund to help send her grans to college.

Charlene was another deal entirely. She would use her cut for a full-body makeover in a foreign country.

And Mona? She would buy a two-bedroom at the beach and be th' only Cunnin'ham daughter to ever move away from family. 'It had to happen,' she said to Ray. 'Just look how families scatter to the four winds these days. Why do you think that is?'

'Job opportunities.'

'It's prob'ly way more complicated than that.'

'You think about it, Cupcake, an' when you get it figured out, let me know.'

As they slept, the generous remains of the fruitcake from the family recipe continued its patient soak in a cup of Wild Turkey.

TIM

Henry and Lucille had gone up to roost, as Lucille put it, with a jug of hot tea and a cell phone overflowing with today's photo gallery. Roughly half of Holly Springs would receive pictures of white folks they'd never laid eyes on but were now considered family by Henry and Lucille Winchester.

'Happiness is this,' he said. 'Just this. Nothing more, nothing less.'

He and Cynthia were piled up with the dogs, a small fire on the grate, and their own jug of tea. This was the Christmas he always wanted, though he hadn't realized it 'til now.

'I have an idea,' she said. 'Let's help the kids with Geezer Cottage; they never ask us for anything. Besides, I'd like to get in on the beautiful history they're making out there. Their excitement is contagious.'

'Free labor can do a lot, but can't do it all. They had just enough funds to get the roof on and the doors hung and the windows in.'

'They're trusting God,' she said. 'And I think God is trusting us to pitch in.'

'Good thinking, Kav'na. When it comes to sharing in Meadowgate's history, we can't let them hog all the blessings.'

'There was another present for you,' she said. 'Somewhere. I just realized . . . '

'I don't need another present. Another present is the last thing I need.'

And there she went, crawling under the tree like a kid and emerging with a few spruce needles in her hair.

'I found it!' She handed him a gift, wrapped with her favorite paper and ribbon. 'It's your tweed cap, no need to open it now. And I found this, too. What is it? There's no gift tag.'

The green paper!

The book!

The letter!

'Good Lord!' he said. 'It's . . . '

'It's what?'

'It's . . . '

'What?'

He drew in his breath. 'It's your present!'

She peered at it. 'It looks like it's been around the block.'

He snatched it from her. 'I never finished wrapping it. Back in ten.'

Of all things. Under the tree! Of all things! He was knocked off his feet, disbelieving.

He stopped by the hall closet and grabbed the green paper, the tape, and a roll of ribbon, and hustled all of it to the Mausoleum of Old Bishops, where, heart pounding, he tore off the wrapping and took the envelope from the book.

Someone had been at the envelope. Who had tampered with it?

The flap was completely unstuck. He removed the folded letter; it looked fine but smelled different. Not of fresh stationery and India ink as any decent handwritten letter should, but of talcum, perhaps, or hand lotion. The porous fibers of paper were especially prone to picking up odors. He sniffed it like a German shepherd for the TSA.

He felt oddly betrayed. His letter had somehow been traipsing around with other people. What other people? He was rattled by this runaway letter arriving home in disarray. He darted down the hall to the study and took a fresh envelope from the desk drawer and grabbed the pen. 'Don't mind me,' he said to Cynthia.

He hurried to the Mausoleum and put everything on the coffee table, which, thank heaven, was the last time he'd ever use the mid-Victorian artifact, and sat down to wield the pen. While the proletarian ballpoint made a good argument for itself, there was nothing like a Montblanc.

My Beloved, he wrote on the envelope.

Blast! He meant to write a simple *Beloved*, as he'd done originally, but c'est la vie, My Beloved would have to do, and he flash-wrapped the whole thing and tied the best bow he could manage and sprinted down the hall.

What if it wasn't all he thought it to be when he wrote it? He'd zoomed though it a minute ago and it seemed to be pretty rock-and-roll, but now was not the time to wonder.

He sat beside her on the sofa and caught his breath. She had her eyes closed, serene as anything, while he had broken a mild sweat. Next year, for sure, a cardigan with pockets.

'So,' she said without opening her eyes.

'It's your letter.' He had the odd impulse to laugh and cry at the same time.

'Would you read it to me? I'd love hearing it in your voice. Not your pulpit voice, honey, just your lovely at-home voice.'

He was seventeen, just as she'd hoped, and nervous as a cat.

'Are you ready?' She smiled, not opening her eyes.

Was he ready? He untied the ribbon he'd just tied, unsealed what he'd just sealed, unwrapped what he'd just wrapped, removed the envelope from the book and took out the letter and yes, he was ready. He was ready!

Deep breath. Hold it. Let it out. He was grinning, couldn't help it.

'Dear Bookend . . . '

In the clearing, the snow-capped roof was a white square beneath a leaden sky, the new shingles no longer visible.

Where the heap of debris was once piled on withered grass, the soil was loamy and black. Through a crevice in the pile, the sun had shone for years, and a *Galanthus nivalis* had pushed through the loam and opened its shy blossom.

Taking advantage of the gloom, a hoot owl came out to hunt. It sat on the branch of a white pine, speculating, then took wing. The branch released a shower of powder.

The red fox nosed about the remains of a woodpile, having found mice there during the tearing-apart of the cottage. The coyote hung back. Recently moved into the neighborhood in the fall, she didn't seek the aggravation of the fox. She had already cleaned mice, voles, rabbits, and squirrels off this place, and apple cores bearing the scent of humans.

There was also an endless store of provisions at the creek: minnows wintering at the bottom of the silty bed, frogs, toads, all you could eat, it was a healthy creek that she would occasionally be forced to share with the fox. She left her predatory rival to his disappointing patrol and vanished into the brush.

The snow had descended as if to a marker where the sun would hit hardest in the growing season. Now melting and redolent with nitrogen and sulfur, the 'poor man's fertilizer' was busy nourishing the site of Geezer Garden for spring planting.

A mouse skittered across the yard.

The owl was swift.

Everywhere there was the promise of enough for everyone.

ACKNOWLEDGMENTS

My unbounded thanks to:

Ivan Held, thoughtful friend, counselor, and esteemed publisher.

My editor, Christine Pepe, for speaking truth and leading me out of the woods. We had our challenges!

Ashley Di Dio, my editor on the home front and a fount of organizational skills and cheerful courtesies.

Brennin Cummings, my marketer, and my publicist, Katie McKee—great to be together again, Katie.

Charlie Unsworth, for being a sort-of model for Jack and the smartest boy I ever met, and Maggie, who made our meeting possible.

My dear and generous friend, Renee Grisham, and to Curtis Powell, Tiger, and Nicholas Easter, for showing me that horses are loving and lovable. And thanks to the faithful Scout for standing by.

Jerry Torchia, brilliant friend from ad days gone by, and finder of the Turkey Club's vintage joke.

Daniel Martin of the Governor Morehead School for the Blind.

Jerry Lee Bach, the local roofing guru whose ancestor was—gasp—Johann Sebastian Bach.

Lynn Vogel Flessas, for her research on Father Tim's Christmas gifts, both given and received, over the series.

Mary Jo Tate, Mitford scholar and book club admin, who was the occasional concordance as I wrangled dozens of characters all over again.

Dawn Buchanan and Marguerite Reuger, Central VA APA League Operators, for your genius at creating competitive pool games for *Somewhere Safe with Somebody Good* and *To Be Where You Are*. I'll never forget your impressive in-person pool-shooting demo. I thought I understood nothing and yet the whole complex game flowed out naturally when I sat down to write it. Thanks for introducing me to Nathan Childress, the twenty-two-year-old pool savant, who proves that Sammy could live at Meadowgate and still make a living shooting pool.

Warren Gruber, who does so much as preparator for the Mitford Museum, thanks for helping rehab the fictional Geezer Cottage.

Andy Payne, for his F-250 input while fixing my bathtub drain.

Betsy Watson, for cheerleading.

Mark Transou, for banking savvy for Geezer Construction.

Reverend Bruce McMillan, for wisdom of the collar.

Arlette de Barros, who remembers the German occupation of France and the German general who occupied her grandmother's house.

Kim Harrell, secretary, Area 18 Office of Virginia State Troopers.

Melanie Berliet, for the Christmas jokes Grace tells the residents of Hope House.

Dale Hamby, for real estate counsel.

Geoff Haas, my computer tech who came when the glitches occurred, which was way too often.

Lou Jordan and her daughter, Grace, who know about the fine cuisine of Mississippi boiled peanuts and sweet tea.

Independent bookstores everywhere—in the early days, you put Mitford on the map and hand-sold it like crazy. Let's do it again! Thanks for believing in the story I came to the planet to tell.

Boundless thanks also to:

Our managing editor, Maija Baldauf; our production editor, Claire

Sullivan; our main interior designer, Katy Riegel; our copyeditor, Courtney Vincento; and Christy Wagner and Ted Gilley, our proofreaders.

Bruce Randolph Murray, 1947–2025
Michele Acosta McCreary, 1957–2024
Daniel P. Jordan, 1938–2024
Jerry Richardson, 1936–2023
Barry Dean Setzer, 1942–2022

AFTERWORD

Dear Reader,

When Cynthia asks Father Tim what he really wants for Christmas, he doesn't know.

It can be hard to know what we really want, what might give us true fulfillment. Tim decided to take the question seriously, to dig deep and find out. The answer surprised him.

What he really wants is to satisfy the simple human craving for more of the natural world, for innocence comingled with the warmth and vitality of his beloved.

Cynthia is his greatest treasure, and in the letter he writes in answer to her question, he bares his soul. Thus, while the letter itself is a gift, the bared heart of the writer is the greater gift.

While we're at it, let's take a look at what the author wants this Christmas. I want you to know that I appreciate you more than you imagine. I write from my heart for you, with the wish to give you something of the laughter and consolation we're all looking for. Though many (one hopes) may read this book, I'm always writing to just one person: you.

I see the relationship between writer and reader as a dance. Usually, I'm leading, but sometimes you're leading—because you're imagining nuances and emotions and scenery that never occurred to me. You're reading Mitford in your own way and for your own reasons.

You'll notice that I rarely write about what people are wearing or even how they look. Growing up with radio gave me the freedom to use my imagination, and I try to pass that freedom—and its satisfactions—along to you. By collaborating with me to visualize the story, Mitford becomes a small town of your own, born in part from your own unique imagination.

Some of you may know that I write with strong regard for my childhood culture and my mongrel DNA.

You, I, all of us come equipped with quirky stories, accents, and dialects. Mine chiefly derive from the sweetly crazy Irish with their theatrical exaggerations and the sober, pragmatic Scots with their do-or-die pronouncements.

For good measure, I include my protestant French Huguenot ancestors, who in the eighteenth century emigrated from northern France to my childhood home ground of Cajah's Mountain, North Carolina.

In western North Carolina, many of us harbor DNA from our Cherokee brothers and sisters. I'm not known to have Cherokee blood, but I was influenced in mystical ways by how they carved out their culture where I spent my early years. My grandmother collected and doctored our family with wild herbs on which the Cherokee relied. In my grandparents' woods and fields, I found arrowheads, sharpening stones, and earth mounds that I believed to be burial sites.

Though a sheltered country kid, I had a powerful sense of the indigenous people from whom our government stole every scrap we could get our hands on, including food from their family cook fires. And look at what's been given back for our thievery and deceit—music, poetry, dance, architecture; there's no end to what the voice of the early Americas speaks into the common good.

I owe gratitude, also, to another culture by which I was deeply affected—the brothers and sisters who lived and worked among us as stolen goods, with their inflections from the islands, the savannahs, the dusty African villages, and who, at great peril, became some of the world's finest storytellers through every arena of the arts, including education and homiletics. I knew them in childhood as helpers to my grandmother, shoeshine 'boys' in my grandfather's barbershop, and later as poets, fiction writers, painters, and friends.

My favorite way to tell a story is through voice. The voice of a character must get off the page and do its challenging task of animation. The voice must be authentic or the character can't fully show up. Because my work is set among ordinary people living ordinary lives in a mountain village, there's still much of the immigrant voice they grew up with. The more worldly we become in our adoptive cultures, the less we allow our native way of speaking to help define us. The voices that give me the most joy are found in the Harleys and Willies, the Coots and Punys.

The novels of Ernest J. Gaines (*A Lesson Before Dying, The Autobiography of Miss Jane Pittman*) are redolent with people talking, talking, talking. In the respectful voicing of his people, Gaines drives us under the skin of his characters with an empathy rarely available in narratives of the South.

Seeing vernacular speech on the page can be daunting for a reader—all those apostrophes! But I promise this—if you follow the apostrophes and the dashes and all the other road signs that come with dialect on the page, you will go in under the skin of the characters. You will live in the pages of the book.

I once (twice?) said I was done with Mitford. And that was completely true at the time I said it. Since *Bathed in Prayer* was released in 2018, years passed during which I didn't write. I founded the Mitford Museum in Hudson, North Carolina, in my former grade-school building, and later, the Mitford Discovery Center. I call the museum and Discovery Center 'my books without covers.' We are a nonprofit seeking to advance the common good through literacy, creativity, and community—three primary attributes of Mitford and of a healthy society.

During the challenging time of bringing the museum to life, I lost my only child and beloved daughter, Candace Freeland. Pancreatic cancer. Stage four. It was a loss that nearly finished me. I saw no reason whatever to live. Though taking my own life was never considered, I found life to be completely without meaning. Without savor. Pointless, really.

Candace was a multitude. She was Sunshine and Laughter, my best friend, first reader, faithful cheerleader, and greatest treasure. I learned that death takes more from us than an individual; it takes a small village contained in a single soul, and we grieve not one but many. Five months after her passing, my handsome, fun-loving, innovative brother, Barry Setzer, died. Cancer. Incurable.

More than two years after these losses, I was able to sit again at the keyboard and begin work on a book very different from anything in my writing career. Though I was making piles of notes, I was putting off the writing sessions; I just wasn't finding the passion.

Then I came across an unfinished short story set in Mitford, begun in 2008. I had fooled with it a couple of times, but couldn't get it moving. I thought, what the heck, I'll spend a few minutes and see what happens. Honestly, I didn't expect much. But holy smoke. The experience was like mounting a horse not fully tamed; I got up to speed really fast and hung on. What you're holding in your hand is the result.

The characters are essentially the same, but the author is different. In *My Beloved*, I opened up like I hadn't done since Candace's diagnosis. Opening up can be scary, but I didn't run—I surrendered.

As I worked into the story of a runaway letter, I was laughing, hard. And crying, hard. And I knew I was home.

Soli Deo gloria!

Jan
2025

Jen Fariello Photography

Jan Karon is the #1 *New York Times* bestselling author of fifteen novels in the Mitford series, featuring Episcopal priest Father Tim Kavanagh. She has authored twelve other books, including *Jan Karon's Mitford Cookbook and Kitchen Reader*, and several titles for children. The Mitford series was inspired by Jan's life in western North Carolina, where The Mitford Museum and Discovery Center now advances the Mitford ethos through literacy, creativity, and community.

VISIT JAN KARON ONLINE

MitfordBooks.com
TheMitfordMuseum.org
JanKaron